THE AUNT EDWINA SERIES - BOOK 2

Aunt Edwina's
Wonderful Legacy

A family history novel

Lynne Christensen

 FriesenPress

One Printers Way
Altona, MB R0G 0B0
Canada

www.friesenpress.com

Copyright © 2022 by Northleo Writing Inc.
First Edition — 2022

All Rights Reserved. No part of this book may be reproduced, uploaded, shared or transmitted by any means, electronic, photocopying, recording, hard copy, soft copy or otherwise, without written permission from the copyright holder and publisher except for brief quotations used for book reviews or as applicable law deems acceptable.

DISCLAIMER
This is a work of fiction. It is written in the form of a fun, charming, and fictitious genealogical adventure. Names, characters, places, organizations, businesses, and incidents are either products of the author's imagination or are used fictitiously. Any resemblance to actual events, locales, businesses, organizations, or persons, living or dead, is entirely coincidental.

For help with your own genealogy and family history research, please seek guidance from a trained expert at a genealogy organization and/or family history organization. Guidance and many helpful websites, articles, and blog postings are available either for free or via payment from a variety of sources. Note that the research strategies and advice in this work of fiction may not suit every person or family's goals.

ISBN
978-1-03-914519-1 (Hardcover)
978-1-03-914518-4 (Paperback)
978-1-03-914520-7 (eBook)

1. FIC016000 FICTION, HUMOROUS
2. FIC051000 FICTION, CULTURAL HERITAGE
3. FIC045000 FICTION, FAMILY LIFE

Distributed to the trade by The Ingram Book Company

Dedication:

To Uncle Hugh: Christmas isn't the same without you.

List of Characters (People)

Agatha Bremridge: Widow of vicar at decommissioned church in Limeknobble near Oxford.

Algernon 'Algy' Holgarth: Heir and proprietor of Holgarth Hall in Plumsden, Kent. Has penchant for tweed suits and formal estate living of yesteryear. Manages plant nursery and petting zoo at Holgarth Hall. Lance Holgarth's elder brother.

Aunt Lisette: Lives in care home in Carlingheath. Nephew is Rich Burrell.

Barney Dazzle: Beefy welder who secures the time capsule at Greymore Hall.

Bernard 'Bertie' Preswick, Fourteenth Duke of Conroy: Julie Fincher's aristocratic art patron. Incredibly wealthy Owner and President of Scotford Castle estate near Oakhurst, Kent, and country house in Brambleford, near Medchester, Kent. Reliable friend of all family history adventurers who need help getting out of incredibly outrageous scrapes.

Chris Undermead: Julie Fincher's so-called husband. Penniless stockbroker who foolishly sells when he ought to hold.

Constable Bud Snowdrop: Police constable trying to make his mark but forever blotting his copybook.

Dan Zerruly: Owner and Chief Executive Officer of Zerruston's Fine Confectionery.

Deirdre Lamerin: Harried mother to Rex and his sibling. Wife and solopreneur event planner.

Doctor Grierly: Local vet who is ultimately bemused by his clients' antics.

Donald Jerome Fincher: Julie Fincher's widowed father. Retired furniture shop manager.

Elridge Bacon: Ozzie Boggs's lanky cousin who works without a hairnet if bribed.

Elsie Rose: Archivist at Club 18th in London.

Ewan Kilburn: Owner/operator of Kilburn's Outstanding Antiques in Plumsden, Kent. Kind, handsome Scotsman who serves as treasurer of the Plumsden Family History Society. Uncle to one piano-playing nephew and one highland-dancing niece.

Finn Severs: Bertie Preswick's ex-security service chauffeur trained in evasive driving techniques, bodyguard protection, and rescuing his employer's friends.

Francine (Junior) Philmond: Widowed daughter of Francine Winloame. Lives in Carlingheath.

Frederick 'Fred' Aloysius St. John Todling: Pixleton, Devon-based, intellectual property solicitor who moonlights as a bookshop minder. Verbose with legalese and opinions. Owns potbellied pig named Barnaby plus another boisterous pet.

Gertrude 'Gertie' Porringer aka 'The Apricot Powerhouse': Boisterous female priest and slightly older cousin to Julie Fincher. Always available for a detailed pedigree chart review and exuberant karaoke.

Great-Aunt Winifred: Ozzie Boggs's relative who ages herself up in hopes of a party.

Harvey Hartmore aka 'Old Two Two': Good friend of the Major and valued member of the Twenty-Second Cheshire Regiment. Lives in London and restores old military vehicles.

Jacques Lesabrioux: Stoic senior bellman at Fizzleywick Hotel in Carlingheath, Kent, in need of a career change. Penchant for getting food service just right.

Jarvis Marlon: Goes by 'Marlon'. Underbutler at Club 18th in London with stoic eyebrows, overly tried patience, and razor-sharp knowledge of club rules.

Julie Fincher: Twenty-something bohemian-style painter who married for family duty then quickly abandoned the wrong path. Daughter of Donald Jerome Fincher. Favorite of Lady Edwina Greymore. Lives in converted barn on Scotford Castle estate near Oakhurst, Kent.

Kirby Danforth: Owner of The Rebel's Head pub in South Dorset who is desperate to prove that his establishment served a seventeenth century royal rebel before his competitor did.

Lancelot 'Lance' Holgarth: Younger brother to Algy Holgarth. Failed spicy samosa kiosk owner. Now lives at Algy's beck and call for hound walking, vegetable rescuing, luggage heaving, and general gopher duties. Resides at Holgarth Hall in Plumsden, Kent.

Major Barry Whitcombe: Retired military man who uses his pork chop sideburns, vast people network, and army expertise to reunite families with their history. Hobby is buying vintage uniforms then rehoming them with proper regimental museums. Based in Medchester, Kent.

Mark Cuthbert: Goes by 'Cuthbert'. Head butler at Club 18th in London. Pleasant and kind overseer of the private place where the movers and shakers come to relax.

Maude Livingstone: President of Plumsden Family History Society. Rattles around in vast Petmond Grange estate near Plumsden, Kent. Member of Lady Edwina Greymore's exclusive, upper-crust Sherry Club.

Mitchell Tumborne: Receptionist at Zerruston's Fine Confectionery. Huge fan of Gertie's singing abilities.

Oswald 'Ozzie' Boggs: Stocky, balding man with family secret. Notorious tightwad who lives on the cheap. Sanctioned when caught eating in the archives.

Pamela Fulham: Stylish woman who owns a string of pubs with zany names. Possesses heirloom box of treasures begging to be researched. Has a celebrity in the house.

Rex Lamerin: Teenager who loves loud music and has holes in his socks.

Richmond 'Rich' Burrell: Saddler by trade whose connection with his Aunt Lisette in Carlingheath proves invaluable.

Tad Cutling: Fred Todling's receptionist who is studying ballet.

Wesley Zottles: Dan Zerruly's one-stop-shop genealogist and solicitor who roots out falsehoods underpinning any sketchy family tree.

List of Characters (Furry Friends)

Answer: White, long-haired Persian cat with a burgeoning acting career.

Barnaby: Potbellied pig often on the lam. Owned by Fred Todling.

Gilligan: Caramel-blond-coated Afghan hound who herds lettuce and rabbits. Owned by Algy Holgarth.

Holophusicon 'Holly': Galumphing English Sheepdog.

Norris: Blue-grey-coated Afghan hound puppy. Registered name is 'Northern Thunder of the Gables'. Owned by Algy Holgarth.

List of Characters (Ancestors, Infamous and Portraits)

Arnold Higgenton: Nineteenth century businessman who sold feedstuffs and hosted lodgers.

Doctor Toffmerle: Beloved church benefactor.

Douglas Wormston: Co-founder of Club 18th in London. Co-founder of Zerruston's Fine Confectionery.

Francine Winloame: Proprietor of Francine's Matrimonial Bureau in London. She married up and gave back more to her community.

Franklyn Carmine: Navy man with a hidden talent.

Isabel Palmer: Pamela Fulham's maternal grandmother.

John Zerruly: Co-founder of Club 18th in London. Co-founder of Zerruston's Fine Confectionery.

Lady Edwina Greymore: Helped raise Julie Fincher after Julie's mother died. Was family matriarch and aristocratic owner of Greymore Hall estate near Oakhurst, Kent. Community philanthropist connected to all the right people. Left a rich legacy to help anyone interested in researching their family history.

Major Donoughan: Gift bearer of silver sphinx to Richard Palmer.

Richard Palmer: Pamela Fulham's great-grandfather.

Sylvie Palmer: Pamela Fulham's great-grandmother.

Theophilus Greenbough: Architect and member of The Royal Society. Drew up seventeenth century plans for Kirby Danforth's The Rebel's Head pub.

County of Kent – Aunt Edwina's Version

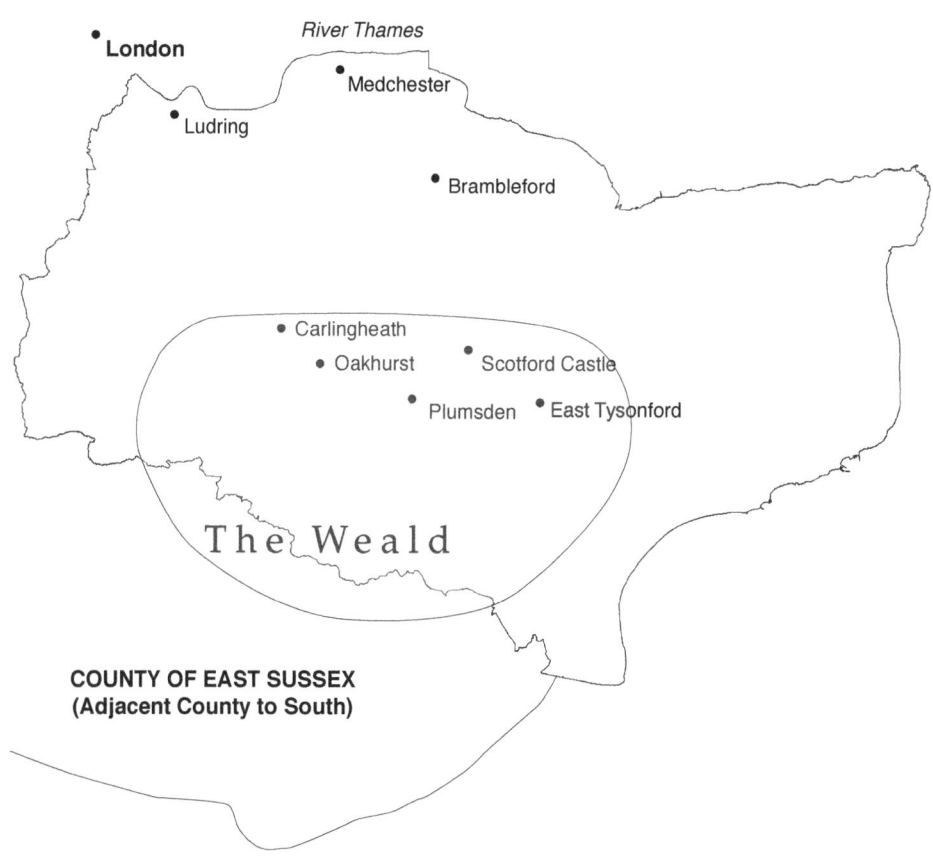

United Kingdom – Aunt Edwina's Version

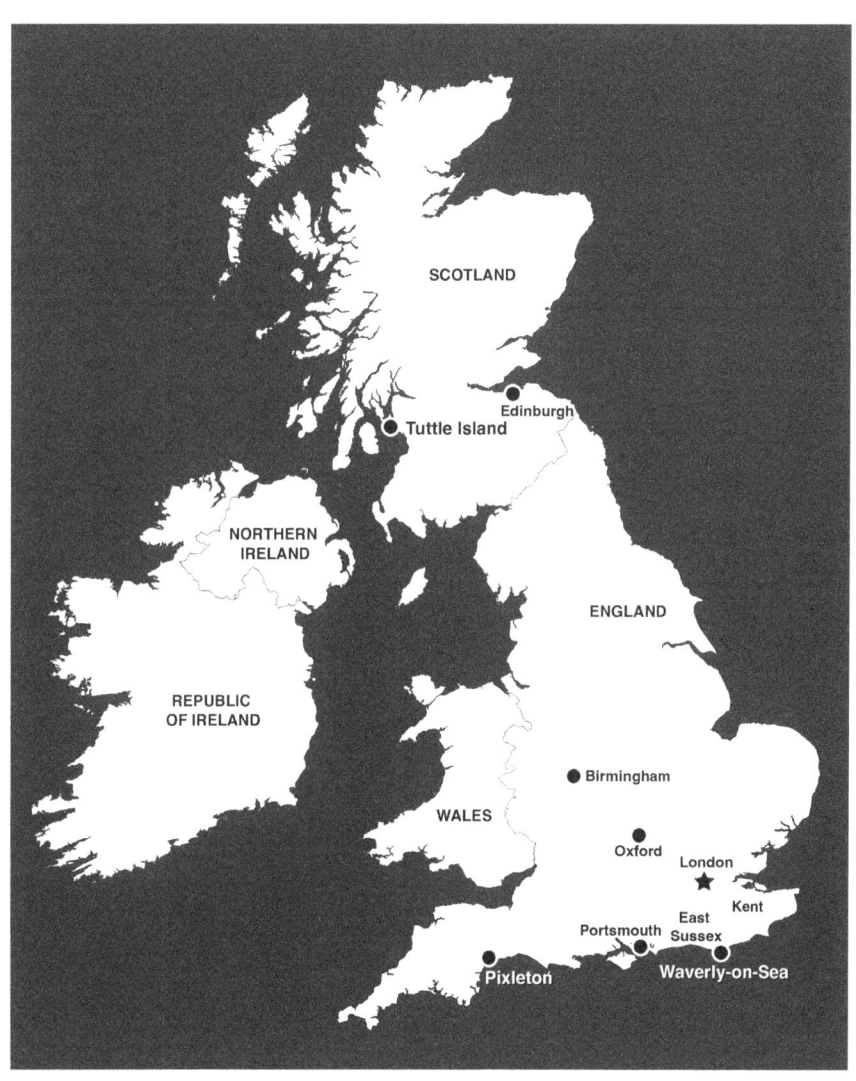

Chapter 1

Greymore Hall, Oakhurst, Kent. Late May. 6:31 a.m.

There are two kinds of people in this world: those who flatten their cardboard boxes for the recycler and those who don't. All of us here at the Greymore Genealogy Research Site (GGRS) were in the former category. We also assumed that my art patron, Bernard 'Bertie' Preswick, the present and fourteenth Duke of Conroy, would run his Scotford Castle estate that way too, but of course he wouldn't be doing the flattening. His people would.

The recycling truck was due at GGRS for its first visit today. I recalled inking my name in a careful line on the ever-so-serious waste disposal contract: *Julie Fincher*. Truth be told, I had done this so many times, on so many contracts over the past few weeks, that my signature was getting messier by the hour. Still, seeing all that cardboard flattened out in the bin gave me a good feeling. It meant that we had unpacked all our supplies and furniture and were ready for business.

"Julie, are you coming?" my father asked in a soft voice.

I turned to face my beloved dad. He was the parent I'd tried to make happy by marrying a man who turned out to be no good. Thankfully my cousin Gertie, a former priest, wasn't holding a license at the time she performed the ceremony, so I'd escaped that ball and chain. Thankfully too because Chris ended up being devious, broke, and with another woman. It was over, and I'd made my peace with it.

My dad and I were outside, standing behind the enormous Greymore Hall building where all the waste bins were kept. I'd arranged for regular pickup of compost and recyclables to encourage staff in the offices and café to keep the site tidy and environmentally friendly. This morning, my father and I were going for a walk to take a closer look at his new garden view.

"Yes, sorry. I just have a lot on my mind right now." I refocused and we started to walk out back towards the fields.

Dad was an early bird, and I accommodated that fact as much as I could. Lately, it felt like I was only getting about five hours' sleep a night simply because there was so much to do with the GGRS grand opening and two new tenants moving onsite. I didn't mind; this high workload was only for the short-term, and the long-term benefits would be simply marvelous.

The smells of damp honeysuckle and roses with the dew were simply gorgeous. One of my late Aunt Edwina's favorite plants was a huge rambler rose close to the house. It had grown over the tall brick garden wall, creeping its way down another thirty feet on either end. She'd grown it from a cutting twenty years ago and it had never stopped. The gardeners pruned it back a couple of times each year, but it kept expanding. Each year, everyone on the estate was treated to a wonderful show of creamy white flowers with pale yellow centers. The flowers were prolific, weighing down the boughs so much that one would think they must snap under the weight. The bees and songbirds loved it, as the plant provided both nectar and hiding places. It may be a simple thing, but to be witness to something so strong that occurred every year with little work was truly amazing to see.

We continued walking along the path that led to the back fields, on the way to Aunt Edwina and her first love Elliot's resting place near the hollow tree. We were going to such a special place, and it was made even more special not too long ago. Kind and wise aristocrat Aunt Edwina was recently buried here, and the special interment ceremony was something I would never forget.

"I always got a grand kick out of the fact that my mother never let you call her 'grandmother', only 'aunt'," Dad said.

"She didn't want to feel old. I remember her telling me something when I was eight. She put both her hands on my shoulders, looked me deep in the eyes, and said, 'Julie Fincher, never let this world age you.' That's always stuck with me."

"She was right on the money about that one," Dad said. "Lady Edwina Greymore always was, about everything."

"Aunt Edwina left some gigantic shoes to fill," I said as we walked through the meadow grass. A couple of doe-eyed Jersey cows mooed as we passed by.

"Yes, but try to see it more as a passing of the torch as opposed to a huge mountain to climb," Dad said. "She wouldn't want you to feel overwhelmed."

"You think she would approve of what I've done with Greymore Hall?" It was an important question, one I wished I'd asked Aunt Edwina directly when she was alive. Then again, I had no idea I was to be her largest legatee, so it would have been impossible. She'd left the bulk of her estate to me to protect its heritage and share it with the community. GGRS and a charitable trust with a museum onsite were my dutiful and creative answers. Greymore Hall was soon to be the place where our community members could research their detailed family history, as well as come to visit the first-floor museum filled with antiques and masterpieces from yesteryear.

"Of course she would, dear."

We walked some more and reached the top of the hill surrounded by lilac trees overlooking the vast estate below us. The hollow oak was nearby, and Elliot's stone marker, the one Aunt Edwina had so carefully arranged for her first love, now had a companion. Aunt Edwina rested here, up high atop her favorite hill, beside the love of her life. There was, of course, a memorial stone in the family plot at the Oakhurst Village church, but those closest to Aunt Edwina knew she was truly laid to rest up here on the hill as she wanted.

My father inhaled the fresh country air. "I'll never tire of this view, Julie," he said.

"It's inspiring."

His mouth trembled a little. "I miss my mother. She was an amazing person."

I stood beside him and looked out at the view. "I know, Dad. Me too."

As a tear ran down his cheek, I put an arm around him for comfort. Death was never easy. But the best way to pay tribute to a dear family member was to ensure that they had a strong legacy. Repeat their name when friends and family gather. Write a short story or a biography of their life. Include them on one's family tree with a photo and some funny stories or jokes they liked to tell. Keep their memory alive by repeating what they accomplished in their life and sharing their written or photographic work. Show the younger generations heirloom scrapbooks so they have a connection to past generations and feel grounded as they move forward with their own lives.

I laid a bouquet of cream, mauve, and pink roses on top of Aunt Edwina's memorial stone. It was a bittersweet feeling because I knew she would be pleased I was visiting her, yet she was silent. I missed her guidance. I missed her kind eyes and smile. I missed her mischievous references to decades-past music concerts and what she used to get up to in her twenties here on the estate. Of course, many of the secrets she and Elliot shared would always stay that way, hidden from the rest of the world and kept only between them. I knew she felt fortunate to have found the one strong love that eclipsed everything else in her life. She'd done her duty and married, had children, but for a moment of her existence, no matter how brief, she had felt Elliot's arms around her and knew how much devotion he showered upon her. It was so sad knowing that he had died in the war, the future they'd planned together never fulfilled.

The sun was brilliant today, almost as if Aunt Edwina cast a warm smile upon us to signal her gratitude. A gorgeous butterfly flew into our field of vision. It was a wonderful mixture of orange, white, and black, yielding quite a tigerish, tropical feel. Butterflies were notoriously busy in the air, beating their wings to stay aloft until they found the nearest, choicest bloom on their nectar quest. That's why it startled me when it landed on my shoulder. Dad slowly pointed at it, and I nodded back, noting that I had seen it. At that very moment, I posed three silent questions to

Aunt Edwina: *Am I doing the right things? Have I made you proud? Is this my destiny?*

I counted three seconds: one ... two ... three. The butterfly still sat there, sunning itself, opening and closing its wings as if there were no predators for miles. I wasn't sure if butterflies had dust on their wings like moths did, so I was scared to touch it. On the fourth precious second, the butterfly flew away of its own accord, heading high up into the oak tree and beyond. To me, it was signal enough that I had completed the initial outreach and future building activities that my dear Aunt Edwina wanted me to do. I felt settled, and for lack of a better term, also felt 'family-fied'.

"We'd better get back," Dad said. "We've got a busy week ahead of us."

I slid my hand in his, and we turned to stare at Edwina's and Elliot's memorial stones one more time. They were together at last. Despite my sorrow, I knew Aunt Edwina would want me to move on and do positive things with my life. I now had a solid group of friends, colleagues, and family members who would see me through with hope, comfort, and steadfastness.

Chapter 2

Back Terrace. 1:00 p.m.

It was a lovely day for a picnic. The golden sun shone down like a warm hug and a happy smile, enveloping us all. The group of us here at GGRS had arranged ourselves at various picnic tables at the back of Greymore Hall, a manor house that never failed to impress. Everybody enjoyed the plethora of miniature goats, Aunt Edwina's favorites. The estate was also home to various other livestock that enjoyed pastoral meadow views and white-washed, clean barns bedded with fresh, bright straw. If our training today was interrupted by the occasional bleating of a sheep or the antics of a goat kid, nobody would mind. It was one of the charms of Greymore Hall. It was one of the reasons why the group of feisty seniors who created their own walking club for fitness and camaraderie came back to this lovely estate week after week.

Each attendee was given a free packed lunch, all organized inside recyclable clamshell containers. It was fancier food, but at a picnic table and without the silver service. I asked the chef to keep it lower-key because the information shared was far more important than a five-star meal. I think I called it right. Maude

Livingstone, our new research site manager, checked off people's names as they claimed a seat at a picnic table.

Today, Greymore was hosting a beginner's class on family history sources. Maude wanted to make sure all of her staff and the regulars had places, along with those who simply needed the training, even though they denied they did. There was always something quite hilarious about a person who walked into a family history office claiming to have already 'done' their entire genealogy. They would claim that there simply was nothing more to be found because their half-hearted attempt had resulted in a brick wall that existed since, well, yesterday. Had they used correct research methodology, this bright spark might've been able to go back farther than their great-grandparents.

Even more hilarious was when they loudly proclaimed they'd been working like this for the past thirty years and were now self-professed experts in genealogy research. The inevitable happened next: a family tree would appear, on screen or unfurled across a long table, resplendent with gaps, unproven ancestry, and questionable linkages. I could see and hear Maude's response in my head. Her silver hair would gently move from left to right as she shook her head in dismay at the fallacy of it all. Maude would know it was risky assuming one's ancestor Mary Jones married that particular Samuel Thomas in 1795 when there were in fact six Samuel Thomases in that little village at the time. I would expect her to quietly cluck her tongue under her breath, likely thinking, *Here we go again. None are so blind as those who will not see.*

Maude was a real treasure. She was moving into Greymore Hall to live in one of the newly renovated suites I had prepared up on the top floor. My father was taking the other suite at the end of the hall, and I would continue living in the converted barn at Bertie's Scotford Castle estate. Maude and my father had become wonderful, platonic friends, united over their love of family history and quiet country living. Maude also served as the president of the Plumsden Family History Society and would manage the visitor work here at the research site. After selling her own manor house where she rattled around all by herself, Maude very much looked forward to her new commute, counted in footsteps rather than miles driven. She was precise, educated, and an expert in genealogy methodology. Proving things multiple ways was embedded in the very fiber of her being, and one always knew that if she was in charge of a research project it would be done both properly and on time.

 I sat at the picnic table with Gertie Porringer on my right. She was my jolly cousin who was defrocked for her unwitting part in a viral karaoke video. To my left was Ewan Kilburn, owner of Kilburn's Outstanding Antiques in Plumsden and my handsome—and single—friend. Together the three of us had lots of adventures together in the realm of family history, and I was sure there were many more to come.

 As we waited, kitchen staff distributed the packaged lunches. I saw Major Barry Whitcombe, retired military expert, come in along with a gaggle of research site staff. We ooed and aahhed over the elegant lunch revealed inside the clamshell packaging. Everyone was faced with an assortment of three different sandwiches—egg salad, roast beef and cheese, and cucumber—perfectly cut fresh vegetables with a cherry tomato on top, a small heap of grapes plus a decadent chocolate chip cookie for dessert.

For those of the vegetarian, vegan, or allergic persuasions, special clamshell contents were available. Here at GGRS we welcomed everyone and ensured that all disabilities and allergies were accommodated without the person struggling to feel comfortable and safe.

Staff watched guests, checking they weren't missing anybody who needed an extra glass of water, cup of tea, or second helpings. I truly felt blessed and honored to work with such a wonderful group of people. I finished my sandwich, vegetables, and fruit, then closed my clamshell to leave the cookie for a few minutes later, once the rest of my food had started to digest.

Today's lecture would be led by Maude. She was an efficient woman, and as soon as she saw all sixteen of us settled, she began:

"There are a variety of places one can get information to research family history. I always encourage researchers to begin with family sources, that is, information you may have at home or with various relatives. Start with the oldest relatives first because they likely have the most information both at hand and in their memories. Look at the old documents, ask them to share the family bible, and express interest in their slide collections from the 1970s. All of this will draw you further back into the past as well as spark discussion of other stories they hadn't even thought of sharing with you."

Attendees gave various nods and murmurs of appreciation. I even saw one volunteer trainee lean over to the person in front of her and whisper, "See, I told you. You should go and talk to Uncle Les about his time in Ireland."

"I'm glad to see we have such thoughtful team members," I whispered to Ewan. "Everybody's paying attention so they can really help people coming here to do research."

"I don't think anyone here would dare ignore Maude," he said. "And if they did, I'm sure she'd figure out a way to quietly lock the access doors to their personal family history until compliance was achieved." He gave me a teasing wink.

"She would never be spiteful, and you know that," I shot back at the friendly Scot with sandy hair and lovely blue-grey eyes that crinkled up at the corners.

"Children, children," Gertie said. "Teacher's going to send you a detention slip."

Ewan and I went silent.

Maude continued. "Other information sources include civil registration documents, the census, including both transcription index and actual enumerator notebook records, church parish registers for christenings, marriages, and burials, followed by will probates after death. If you look at all of these different sources and go through them in a logical, orderly fashion, then you will no doubt assemble the best family history records possible."

Gertie put up her hand. "Excuse me, Maude? I have a question."

"Yes?" Maude looked over at Gertie warmly. It was obvious that Maude was delighted that her audience was so engaged.

Gertie cleared her throat. "What about land records? Aren't they a valuable source of information as well?" People around her nodded, likely because they had the same thought.

"Ah. This is where a lot of people doing English research go wrong," Maude explained. "There are very few useful land records for the United Kingdom; land records of various kinds are much more suitable for North American research."

"But there's lots of detailed English manorial records that go back centuries," Gertie protested. "Why not look for ancestors there?"

"Yes, those that survive are helpful in ascertaining the heir to a rented farm or smallholding. But they are not indexed and can be hard to read, so are not one of the first sources for the average family historian. In the United Kingdom and much of Europe, the big land owners have been here for a millennium, but in North America the surveyors generally got there before the mass of landless immigrants. So, there are very detailed homestead and other records which are much more useful to the family historian."

She stopped the crowd in its tracks as they processed that in depth comment. Of course, it made perfect sense; we'd just never thought about it from a research perspective. It was all about putting proper context around the documents one was seeking. For example, when trying to understand why records were missing from a parish church in 1940, the smart thing to do would be to check World War Two records to see if it was bombed during the war. Unfortunately, many records were lost during the Blitz.

This was an excellent training session. Lunch was delicious, especially in this friendly outdoor ambiance. I was about to enjoy my cookie when I encountered a problem. I was sitting quietly, in between Gertie and Ewan, trying to reopen my clamshell lunch package. My mouth was already watering at the idea of that delectable chocolate chip cookie, all moist and gooey, waiting for me. The issue arose when the clamshell jammed like a rusted drawbridge. I had no idea how it got so stuck. I delicately wrestled with the clamshell for what seemed like ages as time ticked away. After about thirty seconds, I exerted a bit more force, and that's when the squeaking began. It was well and truly jammed. None of my attempts to open it quietly succeeded; it now squawked like two brightly colored birthday balloons rubbing themselves together, just without the static making hair stand on end.

I now had the non-compliant clamshell under the picnic table, wrestling to open it. I was in a delicate quandary: so eager to reach my cookie yet so embarrassed that I was making so much noise. Ewan looked under the table and saw my dilemma. He gestured for me to hand it over for him to have a go. As I did, of course it unexpectedly sprang open and my prized cookie shot out like a rocket. It catapulted through the air and landed in Gertie's lap.

Just.

Like.

That.

Taking everything in stride like she always did, Gertie picked up the cookie, nonchalant, then toasted me with it. "Cheers," she said with a grin as she sank her teeth into it.

Good egg Ewan shared half his cookie with me, gallantly hiding the smile trying to appear on his face. All along I'd been mortified at the thought of interrupting Maude's excellent training session. Hopefully my 'cookiegate' didn't spell impending, unabashed disaster.

Chapter 3

Later That Afternoon.

An eighty-pound English Sheepdog bounded through the covered entrance of Greymore Hall. The Major happened to be at the front, rearranging a couple of potted palms with the help of two delivery men. He was therefore in the exact right spot at the right time. The dog was having a grand old time clowning around, bounding in and around moving boxes, clipped topiaries, and a stunning assortment of colorful begonias.

"I say, that dog needs to be on a lead. Who owns it?" the Major asked tersely as the goofy dog nearly bowled him over, galumphing around another circuit of the drive. The English Sheepdog appeared to come out of nowhere and belong to no one. This was the unexpectedness facing my father and I as we came outside the front doors in a quest to ascertain additional bedding-plant needs.

I crouched down and patted my thigh. "Come here, come here," I said, making eye contact with the dog. "That's it," I said excitedly as the dog loped over. It ran like a bear, and with all that white and grey fur flying about, I was sure it looked about twice the size it actually was underneath. As a child, I remembered a couple who owned one of these dogs but because they lived in Boston with all of its summer humidity, they opted to keep their dog clipped. It looked like a different animal after a trip to the groomers. Today's vagabond, on the other hand, was here in all of its English Sheepdog long-haired glory. I could tell it was loved as I ran my hands through the happy canine's tangle-free coat. There must've been hours every week put into keeping this coat as smooth and brilliantly clean as it was.

I looked down at its paws, however, and shook my head. "Whoever does own you isn't going to be pleased." The dog's paws were covered in grass stains and plant soil, likely from the piles we had out back where Greymore gardeners were putting in the final touches on the new bedding-plant displays. I reached for the dog's collar and saw a brass tag attached that said 'Holly'.

"Holly?" I said to the dog's face. I was rewarded with an eager bark followed by an enthusiastic tongue swipe across my cheek.

Dad handed me his clean handkerchief without a word.

The Major handed me a piece of rope from the delivered plants to tie the dog up.

"I'm not sure what Aunt Edwina would say about an English Sheepdog racing through the new genealogy research site," I mused, reading the reverse of the brass tag. I groaned. There in clearly etched letters were two more words: 'Fred Todling'. The bumbling, verbose solicitor's phone number was underneath.

Some rapid-fire footwork was heard, growing louder by the millisecond. It wasn't usual for family historians to run a four-minute mile, so I looked up to see who on earth it could possibly be. I saw Constable Bud Snowdrop, the policeman who helped us when Gertie's vehicle was stolen while we were busy solving

Aunt Edwina's treasure hunt. Constable Snowdrop's hometown of Ludring was miles away from Greymore Hall. I was quite surprised to see this particular law-enforcement man approach us in what appeared to be a rather hot pursuit.

"Constable Snowdrop, are you interested in genealogy?" I called out to him. "Are you in search of a rapid family tree?" I teased.

The policeman grabbed onto one of the solid front pillars of the building and bent over in half, breathing heavily. He gasped for a few more breaths of air and reached for his travel pack of tissues to wipe his brow. He'd soaked through the sweatband of his hat and went through a thick wad of tissues in the 15-tissue convenience pack almost as quickly as he whipped it out of his pocket. He then straightened up and leaned back against the pillar, quickly checking that it would support his pudginess.

The lawman looked at me with eager eyes that appeared from under a shock of black hair. "I do like a good family tree once in a while, but today I'm in pursuit of a rogue animal."

Gertie came up beside me, mug of tea in her hands, and frowned. "It's not that potbellied pig again, is it?"

Shades of the past. She was still terrified of Barnaby, Fred's potbellied pig, after the docile pet surprised the three of us inside Ewan's holiday cottage earlier that year.

The Major brought over Holly, who was now obediently walking beside him. "Is this the animal in question?" The Major was such a prim and proper man. I was sure he was thinking, *You're in uniform, man! Pull it together!* There was no room in the Major's world for a law-enforcement officer to gasp, sweat, or act uncertain. It just didn't come with the territory.

Constable Snowdrop realized he was in the presence of someone who'd commanded troops. "Yes, sir, I believe that is the culprit." He emitted a high-pitched, nervous giggle.

The Major softened. He patted Holly's head and gave her a kind smile. "I'm certain she had a good reason for absconding. Perhaps an intriguing distraction. She's quite friendly."

Trouble never came in singles. That was a philosophy I tended to live by ever since entering the art world, hanging out with aristocrats, and making the luckily fixable mistake of being in a romantic relationship with my devious ex, Chris Undermead.

More drama. Double trouble now arrived in the shape of Fred Todling, a panicked look on his face.

The difference was he drove up instead of running up on foot.

The second Fred got out of the car he made a beeline for Constable Snowdrop. Fred had a confused expression on his face. "I called for help because there was a break-in at my new personal abode here in Oakhurst," he said.

"And I did my duty by following the motion I saw inside your home." Constable Snowdrop had now recovered and glared back at Fred.

It was a standoff I hadn't expected in front of the new genealogy research site. With all the moving and guests this week, this was the last thing I needed to witness. "Fred, I take it Holly is your dog?" I asked.

Fred nodded. "Yes, Holophusicon is my purebred English Sheepdog. A gift from my uncle for taking care of his bookshop in Devon whilst the former was in Spain for his holiday."

"Holo-what?" Gertie spluttered. She had a hard time swallowing her last gulp of tea without spitting it out. Luckily, she managed and didn't embarrass herself.

"Holophusicon. It's Holly's pedigreed name," Fred said. "The word's a mashup of Greek language meaning the whole of nature." Fred took the dog's leash from the Major and bent down to give his dog a hug.

"I'd say that's in straight competition with Algy and Lance Holgarth's Afghan hound puppy Norris." Gertie laughed. "'Northern Thunder of the Gables' is his registered name. Luckily they only call him Norris."

"A wise move," Fred said. It was then that we noticed he wasn't dressed in a fancy lawyerly suit and tie this time. No, right now he was clad in a shiny, royal-blue leisure suit, the kind with drawstring pants, slightly flared bottoms, and a zip-up jacket with elasticized sleeves. On his front right chest was a logo that read 'Miss Sympsonne's Ballet School'.

"Constable Snowdrop," I said, looking at the man who still didn't quite know what to do with himself. "I'm sure Fred appreciates you tracking down his lost pet. Holly is part of his family, and you've done the community of Oakhurst a very decent and good service today." I was sincerely hoping that the flattery would soothe Constable Snowdrop and make him feel like he had a win. He was, of course, the policeman who was trying to make his mark yet forever blotting his copybook. I thought back to a past incident when he authorized the power washing away of valuable street art, mistakenly calling it 'graffiti'.

A calm platitude might just do the trick here and let us get on with the real business at hand.

Predictably, it appeared to work.

Constable Snowdrop puffed up like a preening peacock and stuck out his chest in the most self-aggrandizing manner possible. "Well, miss, we are here to serve."

I cast a sideways glance over at the Major, who stifled a grin.

"Have you been transferred to Oakhurst?" I asked the policeman.

Constable Snowdrop nodded. "Yes, I was told my talents are better used here."

In other words, his superiors had figured out Constable Snowdrop's ineptitude was best squirreled away in a smaller town where he wouldn't be able to make as many mistakes with real criminals. The only crime that Oakhurst was famous for was a theft of three loaves of bread from the grocery a few years ago. It turned out that the thief was a down-on-his-luck carpenter, and the owner had refused to press charges. Showing the true spirit of Oakhurst, the community rallied together to ensure the carpenter and his family had decent food and accommodation until he could get back on his feet.

Oakhurst wasn't exactly Crime Central. It was a classic, quaint, tidy, and safe little village that everyone read about in their favorite English novels. Time slowed as one drove through the village and appreciated yesteryear's timber-framed cottages, narrow roads, and the old horse-watering trough at the side of the village green. Here, heritage was appreciated, as were hummingbirds, handmade lace, and a warm hello to one's neighbor. In Oakhurst, people checked on the elderly and the infirm, bringing them scones, hot soup, and companionship. Aunt Edwina always taught me that a strong community was made up of many warm hearts, and I intended to continue her legacy.

I just wasn't sure how Constable Snowdrop was going to fit in. Luckily, the policeman's radio crackled, and he was called away to some more suspicious activity, this time at the newsagent shop in Oakhurst's village center. Not that it was much of a center; basically, it was just a small newsagent, a tiny bank branch, the grocery, and the coffee shop. The rest of the winding streets were lined with lovely cottages boasting mauve wisteria, well-tended rose gardens, and a plethora of colorful flowers underneath dappled shade from artfully grown trees in the surrounds. This peaceful environs meant that any so-called action in the village was sure to catch the constable's attention.

That left us with the English Sheepdog and Fred in his ballet-company leisure suit. I tilted my head sideways. "Fred, I have to ask. Why are you wearing a leisure suit from a ballet company?"

Fred chuckled. He did that when he was either nervous or trying to explain something that he thought would come out as condescending due to his vast knowledge of the law. "My dear Julie, I am now the team manager for Ballet Oakhurst."

"Team manager? Whatever's gotten into you? Ballet's not football," the Major said.

Fred harrumphed. "Rightly so. However, the seventeen young ladies and young men who belong to the club are in need of sponsorship, and I suggested we turn it into a team sport to raise awareness. Just like golf or football, they, too, have a goal: to be the best that they can be in all parts, senses, and exclamations of the phrase. To achieve said goal, they need the proper attire and coaching. That, in a crisp, piquant, nutshell, is what my esteemed law practice is sponsoring." He rocked back on his heels and stuffed his hands into either pocket of the shiny jacket.

"Ah, here he is," he said with great satisfaction.

We all looked out at the narrow country lane fronting the estate and saw a young man cycling up on a bike loaded down with a well-worn leather saddle bag. He was lithe, someone who managed to gracefully ride his bicycle down to where we were standing at Greymore Hall's entrance. He applied the brakes a few feet away from us, dismounted, set the kickstand, and nodded a hello to our small group. He retrieved two envelopes from his saddle bag and headed over towards Fred.

"Thank you, Tad," Fred said, taking the overnight courier package and gold-embossed envelope from the cyclist.

And with that, Tad politely nodded again and was off, presumably heading for his next delivery location.

I looked at Fred. "Normally couriers drive small vehicles these days. I'm surprised to see one on a bicycle."

"Oh, Tad's not a courier. I've recently hired him for my office. He's just delivering some urgent mail I was expecting," Fred explained.

Things were getting more curious.

"Oh, I see. He's your new legal assistant?" Two-wheeled legal correspondence delivery seemed to be stretching the job description just a smidgeon over the customarily accepted boundary.

"Yes. He's also one of the principal dancers of the ballet company and is looking to earn some extra cash. He is very elegant with everything he does, and that translates superlatively into precise legal correspondence and file preparation."

Fred bowed his head and tore open the fancy envelope first. As he did, he exclaimed little mutterings of amazement, incredulousness, and self-satisfaction. I caught a glimpse of the return address and clearly saw my art patron Bertie's Scotford Castle gold-embossed logo. My guess was that it was an invitation to the Duke of Conroy's summer solstice party. I hadn't the heart to tell Fred that the rest of us got our invites over a month ago. Fred was either unfortunately forgotten until the last minute or in line for an invite when someone else dropped out. As a friend, I would never burst his bubble.

"An invitation from the duke. Well, I never. A dress code, a fancy event," Fred said. "It's amazing what proper networking can do for a man."

Ewan, Gertie, and I exchanged a secret glance.

Fred then turned his attention to the courier package and gently tore off the sealing strip. He removed a letter with another fancy logo at the top and emitted a warm grin. Then he clammed up, realizing he had an audience that he didn't want for the second letter.

None of us asked what the letter was because we assumed it was private legal business.

We were treated to Fred's surreptitious glance, one that said, "I have some legal business to attend to on the double."

Somebody had to say something to break this bizarre silence after the odd courier delivery by a ballet dancer who happened to moonlight at this lawyer's office.

"Say, Fred, is the ballet a registered charity?" the Major asked.

"You should install a donation box, just like the church does," Gertie suggested. "Just make sure it's secured. Because we all know that Constable Snowdrop can't be all places at once."

We all had a bit of a laugh at that one.

Fred took Holly and left.

"He doesn't exactly inspire confidence, does he?" my father added, coming closer. He'd been distracted by a rather loudly colored pot of geraniums.

"Who? Fred or Constable Snowdrop?" I asked.

"Take your pick. Both of them are a bit like water taffy without the pull." My father then gave me a serious glance. "Julie, please don't get sucked into another good cause. With Maude and I moving into our new suites, as well as the opening of the new research site here, your plate is more than full. In fact, you're filling up two plates right now."

I put an arm around him. "Don't worry, Dad. I'm going to leave Fred in charge of his ballet world. I have a job here to do for Aunt Edwina. That takes first priority."

I looked up at the oversized, fancy oil portrait of Aunt Edwina on the wall in the front hallway. Greymore had many portraits of Aunt Edwina in various rooms. I sighed. Perhaps she'd sent me that confidence-boosting, tropical-like butterfly a tad too soon.

Gertie, dear cousin Gertie, must've read my mind. She came over with a bright smile on her face. "Never you mind. This week is going to be a smashing success, you'll see. We just won't let it be any other way!"

***

Front Path. Greymore Hall. Two Hours Later.

"Stop!" Gertie hissed. "Don't move!"

I stopped dead in my tracks. "What's wrong?" I didn't like the looks of her wielding a trowel at me with a frown on her face.

She was crouched down in a bed of tall leafy stems topped with red-petal wonders that showed a dash of serious yellow inside.

She pointed. "There. Look."

"I don't see anything," I whispered back, seeing only the montbretias.

"Listen. Can you hear its wings beating?"

I bent over a teensy bit more. At first, all I heard was a robin singing a cheery melody to his missus, full of the joys of life. Listening some more, keeping ever so still and quiet, I finally heard the rhythm. It was like half a pack of playing cards shuffling into the other half at five times the speed, like a steady, fast drum. I knew at once what it had to be. I saw a flash of gorgeous, shiny, raspberry and silver feathers underneath a coat of emerald green: a hummingbird. It showed off great skill and dexterity as it darted in and out of the flowers' nectar reserves. Such a tiny bird, such an incredible creature. The beating of its wings permeated my ears, all-consuming. Gertie and I remained like statues until the small creature had completed its rounds and dashed off like a miniature plane zooming through the air. It was all so quick yet so elegant; we were frozen in place, thinking over what we had just witnessed.

"A stellar performance," we heard behind us.

We both looked to see Ewan standing there, his mobile phone in hand, held like a prize for the victor of a sporting tournament.

"You got a picture?" I asked.

"Better than that. Video. I just happened to be in the right place at the right time," he said.

"Lovely. We can use that in a future promotional video for the research site," I said.

"We need to let the world know that GGRS is open for visits soon," Gertie said.

"I'll ask Maude to put it on the research site's public relations folder in the cloud for you," he said. Ewan went inside to find her.

"Well, that's about as much damage as I can do in this patch," Gertie said, standing back and admiring her bucket full of weeds and the now-pristine flower bed.

"I really appreciate your help. With the opening so close and one gardener off ill, we need all hands on deck."

"Greetings, esteemed colleagues," return visitor Fred said, peering over his half-oval reading glasses as he approached. He was carrying a leather briefcase and now wore a freshly pressed pinstriped suit. He was back sans Holly. Fred was now in fully confident solicitor mode and appeared to be enjoying every minute.

He cleared his throat. "It appears that you've had a visit from the gentleman in the velvet jacket."

"The what?" Gertie and I both replied.

"The Moldy Warp," Fred said in all seriousness, looking closer at the damp piles of earth around the edge of the lawn where it met the paving stones. He stood up and cricked his back straight. Then he gave us a serious look. "A mole." He shifted weight to the other foot and looked at Gertie. "Oh, and you're back in."

Gertie dropped her trowel. She looked him, astonished. "No."

Fred nodded. "Yes, you're back in." He set his briefcase down on a wooden bench installed only yesterday. Luckily it wasn't yet clad in any unwanted white splatter gifts from birds flying overhead. Fred undid both brass latches on his briefcase, pausing for dramatic effect before lifting the top. "I needed to go back to my office and make a call to ensure that this wasn't some cruel prank, but it is correct. Everything is as it seems." He pulled out an official-looking envelope and handed it to her. "Read for yourself."

"As in, the big 'never thought it could happen' back in?" Gertie's eyes went wide with astonishment.

"Correct. It was a rather tidy piece of legal pleading, I must say. Plus the fact that my uncle, the devoted, dedicated, and steadfast bishop, took our serious legal correspondence plus a grassroots petition, backed up by a groundswell of community support from multiple counties of this Fair Isle, to the uppermost ranks of the church."

Phew. It always amazed me how many adjectives Fred could cram into a sentence. There must be a gameshow for that significant of a talent.

Earlier this year, Fred had helped us write a plea letter to the church asking it to reconsider Gertie's harsh punishment. It was long, convoluted, and hard to read, let alone recite … yet it appeared to have worked.

"You mean?" she spluttered, picking up her secateurs and then pausing.

"Yes, our letter reached those with the ability to obtain the loftiest and highest direction." Fred nodded and I saw the cowlick of hair on his head. It was like a giant had pressed his thumb right down on his scalp, leaving a permanent print impression.

Fred's words were good enough for Gertie. She gave me a big hug, not caring who or what she smudged with garden soil in the process. I had to dodge the secateurs in her hand. "Julie! I've got my ministering job back! Oh, thank you, Fred!"

She went over to give him a hug as well and he backed away, tugging on the lapels of his fancy suit.

"Ahem, might I ask you to holster your secateurs before continuing said gleeful embrace as they're rather close to a delicate part of my anatomy–"

"I'm terribly sorry," she said, putting the secateurs back into the loop on her toolbelt. Nothing could quell her excitement. "Julie, this is tremendous," she said, giving me another hug. She did a mini dance in her dark-green wellies.

"Just don't start singing. Please," I teased.

"Congratulations," Fred said.

"I think this calls for a celebration," I said. "Let's go inside for a cuppa."

***

It was like I had sounded the dinner gong. No sooner did I mention putting the kettle on, when all my family history friends showed up at the front door. Ewan, the Major, and Bertie were just back from a walking tour of the grounds, seeing how the gardens would be open to the public and any potential rabble kept orderly by a path and low fence.

Back inside, we all clustered in the lunchroom.

"I say, that is jolly good news," the Major said to Gertie. "I never thought you deserved to lose your frock."

"I'm just so glad to be back," she replied, narrowing her eyes. "You three men look like you're colluding on something."

Ewan grinned. "I was just trying to convince the Major to let me take a look at an old British army tank his friend is restoring. It's apparently from 1943."

Suddenly I was the center of attention. I tried to break away, but Bertie locked the door.

The Major's eyes got excited. "It's a rare cruiser tank, I believe less than three hundred ever built, and covered in rust now. Still, by the time he's finished with it, it will be museum-worthy."

"I think I understand why I'm being cornered. You want to bring in a full-sized tank and park it here at Greymore, don't you?" I asked.

The men looked a little sheepish. Ewan tried to salvage the conversation first. "I realize it's rather large–"

"Rather large? Calling it 'large' is like saying I'm going out to do some hill climbing and then seeing the sign for Mount Everest."

"Well–" the Major started.

"Look, I appreciate your enthusiasm, but we cannot park an army tank inside Greymore Hall."

"Actually, we were thinking an outdoor display with a World War Two family history exhibition. You know how people love looking at old machinery. It's part of our country's heritage," Ewan said.

"You mean, you didn't get enough of this when you were a little boy and now you're trying to relive your childhood on a second go around," I said. "Am I right?"

More sheepish looks and even more rapid nodding of male heads.

"Bring it up at the next GGRS board of trustees meeting and we can consider it. Right now we're going to celebrate Gertie's massive achievement."

"Hear, hear," Fred said, already into a new packet of chocolate biscuits. When he realized he'd started without us, he hurriedly wiped the crumbs off his mouth. "Exactly as I suspected. I can now confirm this is a fresh packet of biscuits."

"Considering I just bought them this morning, I would hope so," Gertie said.

"Raise your hand if you're in for tea." I looked around the room and saw every single person with their hand up. The kettle was well on its way to boiling, sitting on the counter behind us. "I'm taking this opportunity to check that we're ready for my father and Maude to move into their respective suites. The new research site opens in a few days, and we need to run through that as well."

Luring helpers in with tea and biscuits always worked.

The trick was not letting them know my ruse.

Ewan volunteered to pour the tea, and Gertie hustled up to me, her re-employment letter clutched in her hand. "Look at what it says here! I am to perform ministering that keeps youth engaged."

"You like working with teenagers. That's great!" I told her.

"But I don't want to be a stranger here, and I still want to work on my pedigree chart," Gertie said, a bit torn.

"Of course." I gave her another congratulatory hug. "You just need to balance your work and your hobby."

Gertie sighed. "It's never easy. I get so stuck on one line of my family tree. Figuring out one new ancestor who leads me back another generation is so exciting. And then before I realize, it's ten o'clock and time for bed because I have to be up early for work in the morning, when I really want to plow through the family tree for the rest of the night."

"Do I hear the world's smallest violin playing just for you?" Ewan asked with a grin.

"That's about the long and short of it," Gertie said. "Doesn't matter. I'm just happy to get back to where I want to be."

"Are you going to do something about your hair?" I asked her. "It's still bright red and quite frizzy." During our recent treasure hunt adventure, I had actually found her unusual coiffure rather helpful when seeking her out in a busy crowd. But now that the church had welcomed her back, it might be wise for her to tone it down just a smidge.

"I'm thinking a sensible auburn color," she said with great seriousness.

***

My father came into the computer room, a little tired from preparing for his move but altogether pleased that things were moving in the right direction. He found me arranging some topography reference books onto shelves at the research site. He put both hands on the nearby long counter and gave me a caring look. "Thank you for arranging a suite for me here at Greymore. It will be a lot more comfortable than that big old house."

"A big house for one can get overwhelming at times. Here you have lovely gardens to enjoy, plus the ever-present chaos offers constant and free entertainment." I emitted a grin.

Dad looked around the crew of eight tradespeople putting finishing touches on their handiwork. "Are you sure you're ready for all this?"

I nodded. "The final construction walk-through is first thing tomorrow morning. The staff orientation sessions are all done, courtesy of Maude and the Plumsden Family History Society. And I'm three weeks away from finishing my beginner's family history course."

Dad gave me a pert nod of the head. "A word of advice? Let the experts help the guests with their research."

"I know. I still have a lot to learn. Gertie's volunteering two nights a week. She's super up to speed on the latest genealogical research techniques, including the current websites."

"Bingo. It's critical for all staff to know the basics so they don't lead others astray. One doesn't want to climb the branches of someone else's family tree," my father said. "Good girl. Your mother would be proud."

"I hope my father's proud of me too," I said.

"Indeed, my dear, I am."

"Good. I've read three family history reference guides and signed up for an intensive level-two genealogical research methodology course after this beginner's-level one, so I can learn even more. All the current staff have passed their levels one and two, so the public is safe."

I watched him head into the lunchroom as I went to the front information desk and signed for delivery of two tall silk plants for the coat rack area.

Gertie breezed inside, with about ninety-five percent of the clingy gardening soil removed. I guess she thought it was safe to come in from the garden without a full shower because we still had plastic covering all the carpets and hardwood. "Bertie just arrived. He said that Polly is en route?" She looked a bit quizzical.

"Polly? We don't have anyone working here called Polly," I said.

"Polly, as in parrot needing a cracker?" Ewan asked, depositing some invoices on a nearby in-tray.

Our favorite aristocrat breezed in with a grin on his face. "I brought two baskets of treats from my estate's farm shop. And by the way, throughout history 'Polly' is short for 'Mary Ann'. Happens to be the name of my shop manager in charge of supplying the new Greymore café." He deposited a wicker basket filled with gourmet crackers, spreads, tinned meat, chocolates, and candies, all from Scotford Castle. The second basket contained perfect fresh fruit. This was, after all, the Kentish Weald.

"If that were me trying to figure out that name game, I'd need a GPS to find her," I said.

Bertie got a quizzical look on his face and then he replied, "Oh, you mean a sat nav? In the family history world, GPS means genealogical proof standard."

"What are you, Bertie, the family history fact machine?" Gertie teased.

"No, just spent rather a lot of my youth with my father in record offices and with the heraldry set at his gentleman's club. He was quite a fanatic."

"Oh," Gertie and I both replied. There was nothing we could say or do that would compete with that type of upbringing. Bertie just lived in a different stratosphere.

"What I can add from my training is that I know one should get a standard set of facts about every ancestor before it is considered completely proven. Those facts are an ancestor's full name, as well as birth, marriage, and death dates, including the relevant places," I said.

"That's it, well done," Gertie said.

"I have a genealogy research joke," Ewan said.

We all groaned and fortified ourselves with tea in the lunchroom.

"It's a good one, I promise," he said. "I was once doing some research and thought I had found a 'vixen'. I didn't know whether they meant fox or smart-looking lady, so I had to look it up. Remember how they used Latin on documents from earlier centuries?" he asked.

"A few centuries ago they also burnt women at the stake for witchcraft and beheaded a king. Trying times, to say the least," Gertie shot back.

"Understatement of the century." Ewan grinned. "But I must say I had a little laugh when I found out that my 'vixen' was actually 'vix', which meant 'vixit' or 'he lived', so I wasn't looking for a person or an animal at all. It was just the date reference."

"I don't get it," I said. "Where's the joke?"

"Well, it was just a muddling of names. I thought you might find it amusing." Ewan looked a little bit forlorn.

I patted his shoulder like he was a child having trouble with his arithmetic lesson. "In case you didn't know, jokes normally have a punchline. Don't quit your day job."

"She's got you there, Ewan," Bertie said, slinging an arm around him. "Here, try some of my new mango chutney. It's delicious." He held up a new jar in a tempting offer.

I left them haggling over crackers and chutney. Back at my locker, I retrieved my study notes and then walked over to Bertie in the lunchroom. "Seeing as you appear to be the bearer of genealogical trivia, I have a question that's been troubling me."

"Yes?"

"I found a person on a census who has an occupation as a 'BB Fingersmith'. For the life of me I can't figure out what that means. Is he involved in jewelry manufacturing, perhaps?"

Bertie looked at Gertie and the two experienced researchers shook their heads. I was issued a plaintive look.

Gertie was the one who put me out of my misery first. "Julie, it's nothing to do with jewelry. Your 'BB Fingersmith' stands for 'Baseborn Petty Thief'."

"In other words, the individual you are researching lived on the lower edges of society and pilfered things," Bertie said, swallowing hard on a piece of brie cheese over water cracker.

"We don't know his circumstance without more information, though," I said. "How do we know that he wasn't born in the workhouse, a pseudo-prison for poor people? Perhaps he was caught stealing a loaf of bread to feed his family. There are many examples of yesteryear where if you got into debt you were thrown into debtor's prison. It was actually against the law to be bankrupt."

"I wish they'd tell that to the banks and their overzealous lending officers today," Bertie said. "The nation wouldn't have so many people in financial trouble if they weren't permitted to over-mortgage themselves and use their homes like automated banking machines."

"Hear, hear," my father added. "When I courted Julie's mother, we saved for three years for our furniture and a down payment on our first house. I took nothing from my parents. Today's generation wants everything yesterday."

"And you had to walk uphill to work, both ways, right, Dad?" I replied.

He waved away my grin. "There has to be a balance, Julie. Too much, too fast, and one gets into trouble." Dad was well-settled into his book, one from the fully stocked library, courtesy of Aunt Edwina's will. My father had a particular interest in submarines and for days now was stuck into a very interesting one on World War Two concerning the decoding of the enigma machine.

Ewan and Fred were still helping themselves to food. "We'd better enjoy some of that before those two eat it all," I said to everyone else.

"I'm by appointment only now," we heard Ewan say as we plunked ourselves on the stools right beside the Scotford Castle estate baskets.

More word confusion. Bertie's mouth dropped. "You can't be serious?"

Ewan appeared taken aback as well. "Very. It suits me just fine."

"How on earth did you pull that one off? By Appointment to a Royal for all their antiques purchases? That's quite a coup," Bertie said, astonished.

Ewan laughed out loud. "Not by Appointment to *Royalty*, for goodness sakes. No, I meant my shop is open by appointment only. You see, I've caught the family history research bug as well, and by putting my store online and allowing in-store visits by appointment only, it permits me to spend more time on my family history. I've already found a highwayman for my pedigree chart, and he alone is absolutely fascinating."

We all had a good laugh over the misnomer. Ewan passed me a jar of olives along with a little fork to select a few to put on my plate. Our fingers met as I reached for the jar, which led to our eyes meeting. There was a moment where everything in the room went silent and I was just caught inside his gaze. The feeling was mutual. Where it would end up, no one knew, but I did know that it was going to have to go slowly.

Number one: I had two seniors moving into Greymore Hall.

Number two: GGRS was opening soon with an anticipated crowd of one hundred and twenty-three people in attendance.

Number three: Bertie's summer solstice party was a no-miss event, and I was the designated driver for the whole lot of us leaving from Greymore Hall in the research site's van.

There was no way I was going to mar Aunt Edwina's legacy by getting distracted with stars and hearts in my eyes. Ewan would just have to wait.

Chapter 4

Grand Front Hall, Scotford Castle, Oakhurst, Kent. June 20, 10:39 p.m.

Bertie opened Scotford Castle every June to celebrate the longest day of the year. It was always a twelve-hour marathon event. Guests started arriving at 10:00 p.m. to party all through the night, waiting for the glorious sunrise. It was one of the few times a year when a conservative aristocrat could really let loose; downstairs the stiff-upper-lip crowd was moving to the music, most like robotic flamingos walking over hot coals. The event wasn't tied to any particular organized form of worship; the party was a chance to appreciate nature and a clean environment, all in the company of good friends. All cultures and ethnicities were welcome.

Local school children had created a mural depicting an overview of ancient sun worship with a Viking horse pulling a sun chariot, Druids watching the sunrise at Stonehenge, the Egyptian sun god Ra, as well as a vibrant Native American sun dance. This year it was also serving as the annual fundraiser for the local stream preservation society. The ballroom was exactly twenty-three steps down to where a plethora of finger food, sparkling water, and wines awaited consumption. It was large, but capacity topped out at 175; that's why invitations were so coveted. Ornate, gilded candelabras were placed every few feet, casting a warm glow throughout the room. In the center was the most enormous flower arrangement, a cornucopia of lively hot reds, oranges, and yellows, all picked at their peak of perfection. The massive stone vase was eight feet wide and literally bursting forth with glorious, fresh, golden sunflowers, apricot roses, ochre gerbera daisies, marmalade dahlias, red chrysanthemums, fiery snapdragons, and lemon delphiniums. They were a perfect centerpiece for our celebration of Mother Nature on her longest day of the year.

"Problem at twelve o'clock sharp," I whispered in a frantic voice to Gertie and Ewan, looking at who just walked inside behind us in the line of guests.

Frederick Aloysius St. John Todling, aka Fred Todling, showed up to the Duke of Conroy's elegant summer solstice party wearing a toga and a tidy crown of leaves over his mop of brown hair. This costume was perfect for a fancy-dress party. The problem? Fred hadn't properly read the invitation. How the verbose legal eagle, part-time bookshop minder, and potbellied pig owner mistook the summer solstice party for a Greek toga party was one of life's great mysteries. Right under his nose, on the gold-embossed invitation, were the date, time, venue, and two distinct words: 'Cocktail Attire'. I distinctly remembered Fred receiving his invitation and mumbling 'dress code' and 'fancy event'—ah, he'd merged and rearranged the words 'fancy' and 'dress', resulting in 'fancy dress', resulting in the toga costume. Oh dear.

Had Fred traveled with the rest of us in the electric van, his faux pas would have been caught in time. Instead, we had a rather public dilemma on our collective hands.

Overhead, a domed glass ceiling was ringed with original Old Masters paintings depicting the third Duke of Conroy as Julius Caesar, his wife the Duchess as a golden-haired beauty. Both were painted in elegantly draped white and gold clothes. Guests were treated to a wonderful string quartet fronted by a singer with such a sweet voice surely she could convince the moon to hold back the tides. There was an ethereal representation of the sixth Duke of Conroy as a great warrior in Greek attire and his wife as Diana, the goddess of the hunt. Perhaps these paintings had subconsciously led now-solicitor Fred astray during a school group tour in his youth. No one could be certain.

Attendees were initially welcomed by two liveried footmen at the front doors and then walked across a massive expanse of gleaming travertine tiles laid out in a black-and-white checkerboard pattern. As their eyes adjusted to the interior light, they noted four different hunting scenes painted by Stubbs hanging under soft lights housed in discreet brass fixtures. Fred was about to be illuminated by a couple of wall sconces that framed the doorway into the domed center of the castle, a rather unique modification done in the late nineteenth century by a rather ambitious aristocrat.

I glanced down and saw the ballroom floor was antique, real hardwood polished to an infinite shine. Knowing social history, I really felt for the knees of the servants who'd scrubbed it over the centuries. Bedsheet-clad Fred's entrance was about to be spectacular. It would be even more spectacular than this castle's four turrets, centuries-old Flemish wall tapestries, and collections of swords lining the walls in gravity-defying herringbone patterns. All the guests were announced by Bertie's ex-security service chauffeur, Finn Severs, as they approached the top of stairs.

"What am I to do?" Fred mouthed at me as his grand reveal neared the end of its tense countdown.

At first I hadn't recognized the man in the bedsheet. I thought he was part of a skit that Bertie was hosting for the benefit of his guests. Ewan and I hung back, out of the guest line, as did Gertie and my father, quietly waiting for Fred to catch up to our group.

There were now only three couples ahead of Fred.

The solicitor had likely changed clothes in a hurry at the office. Looking closer, I saw a faded pattern of cartoon hummingbirds and bumblebees on the sheet; somehow I don't think Julius Caesar would have approved.

"Mr. and Mrs. Murdoch Hawthorne of Oakhurst," Severs announced.

My anxiety grew tenfold as I saw Fred grit his teeth and quietly inch his way forward. It was like he was in fluid quicksand, being tugged along by an invisible rope from which he couldn't let go. There was a long line of people behind him plus an absolutely cavernous space down those steps, filled with the who's who of the entire local area. It was a catastrophe in the making, something that would be an absolutely horrific introduction to the community for the newest professional brave enough to hang out his shingle on the streets of Plumsden.

Unfortunately, ancient castle builders tended to construct ballrooms without modern conveniences. These rooms were literally one big rectangle with a few small alcoves plus a couple of doors leading outside to the corridor. Fred had gotten himself into a very sticky situation, and his friends were gauging how to rescue him as best we could.

The Major escorted Maude up close to us. We were still all standing out of the line and off to the side. The Major asked, "I say, do my eyes deceive me, or has Fred gotten the wrong end of the stick?"

I caught the Major's eye. "We need to implement 'Operation Toga-Clad-Man Removal'. On the double."

"Right you are," the Major said with mock salute. He stood up tall and made his announcement in a clipped tone. "All those from the GGRS, prepare for an emergency drill. Formation, please!"

My father looked completely befuddled but soon caught on. Gertie had a big grin on her face and rapidly cajoled everyone else into the Major's plan. Quickly, before anyone else knew what was going on, we pulled bedsheet-clad Fred out of line and had him surrounded. Luckily we moved fast; Fred was down to a lone couple in front of him before he was announced, both very much in public and to his exceptional embarrassment.

A total of ten of us from the GGRS formed a tight rectangle around a mightily surprised Fred. Much like a posse of multicolored foam pool noodles on the vertical, we sidestepped in miniature towards the opposite side of the room. Halfway there, we broke through the line of guests, intersecting the lineup from the side at a right angle. We were a group of potted plants perambulating across a stage, the kind that theater scene designers pull on ropes from the wings to have silently glide across the polished floor into darkness. The only sounds we made were the occasional scrapings of shoe leather against checkerboard tile. No one in the ballroom below saw Fred because he was completely concealed inside our rectangle.

I leaned over to Severs, who wore a bemused look on his face. "Right guest, wrong costume," I said.

Severs nodded, realizing what we were trying to do. It wouldn't do if one of the Duke of Conroy's guests was embarrassed in front of everybody else. That wouldn't do at all. Severs leaned down to his lapel, while holding his earpiece with his right hand. Leave it to Bertie to employ a chauffeur who could play security-conscious butler as needed. With the rich and famous inside, security had to be tight, and Bertie was only thinking of everybody's safety. It was sad, really, that one had to think of these things, but it was an unfortunate reality of today's world. Long gone were the days where a royal or aristocrat could ride his white steed through throngs of admirers so close they could pat his horse and touch his boot as the man rode past.

I heard what Severs said: "Eleven guests are moving to the east alcove exit. Accommodate as needed. Repeat, accommodate as needed."

Out of the corner of my eye I saw the doors discreetly unlatch. As soon as our moving rectangle got close, the doors were swung wide open. We all rushed through like a herd of elephants. The doors quickly shut behind us and nobody in the ballroom was any wiser. Our little human rectangle broke up and we all turned to face Fred.

Jolly Gertie, the one I could always count on for blunt commentary, was the quick wit who spoke first. "I was actually looking forward to your show, Fred. What were you planning? A

Caesar versus Spartacus showdown?" After that she couldn't hold back her laughter.

Fred looked at all of our faces, one by one, and then started to chuckle. "I must say, that was a rather close shave, and I sincerely appreciate the thoughtfulness of all of my elegant and dear friends who have prevented the most agony-filled, excruciatingly painful, and downright shockingly embarrassing experience of said solicitor. I would have damaged my family name for future generations had I been allowed to stride downstairs clutching the banister, leaping headfirst into a sea of sequins, jewels, satin, and patent leather wearing nothing but my humble bedsheet."

There were no cartoon hummingbirds or bumblebees on the sheets of the painting subjects ringing the dome.

The imagery racing through my mind was quite something at this moment. I envisioned small, angelic cherubs floating on air, clustered around Fred as he tried to stay aloft.

Ewan gave Fred an incredulous look. "You seriously made that out of your own bedsheets?"

Fred nodded. "Indeed I did. I'm quite handy with a needle and thread when I need to be, but I did experience one small tear somewhere in the folds of the garment on the way here and–"

"No!" the Major yelped, leaping into the fray and standing directly behind Fred, batting his hands away from the fabric. "Save the adjustment for your retreat. There are ladies present!"

The Major eyed up the damage and stayed close behind Fred for the rest of our conversation. We were most grateful.

Ewan leaned over to the Major. "Thanks for taking one for the team."

We heard the curved side door creak open. In walked elegant Bertie, presumably to see what we were all up to ensconced in our little hideaway. "I heard that there was a bit of an incident?"

Fred decided to grovel. "Sir, please let me extend my absolute and most humble apologies for any distress my attire may cause you or your most illustrious, anciently fabled surroundings and abode. My good friends here have quickly, rapidly, and most expeditiously supplanted me away from the viewing abilities of your other guests, many of whom I note are the, shall we say, upper crust of those working and residing in this lovely Kentish Weald."

Bertie sized up the man who stood before him pleading his case with excessive words and, unfortunately, a rather skimpy toga. Contrary to what Fred had just told us, the solicitor's sewing skills did leave much to be desired.

"No harm done," Bertie said, giving Fred a friendly slap on the back.

Wrong move.

The bedsheet slipped down further.

I didn't know Fred waxed his chest. It was plainly obvious by the wax strip he'd forgotten to remove.

I also didn't know that Fred had a tattoo of Barnaby on his right shoulder.

Actually, I doubted anybody did.

But now there it was, in all its farmer tan, I-love-meals-with-dumplings-and-gravy-stomached glory.

The Major starfished in front of Fred, one limb short. "Will you cover up, man!" He glared at Fred.

"I think we'll set you up with my Scottish grand-uncle's outfit," Bertie said. "He left it here the last time he was in for a formal event. I've had it cleaned but he just hasn't picked it up yet."

"I would be most grateful, sir," Fred said, needing about five more hands to clutch the saggy sheet in all the right places.

Ewan, the Major, my father, and Bertie quickly escorted Fred off to another room down the hall where he could change into the clothes that Bertie had on offer.

Gertie looked at me and grinned. "That was a bit of a close fall. I mean call."

Maude giggled. "Oh my word! What fun! You ladies have shown me the best time already."

"We're thrilled you're here," I replied.

Gertie chimed in. "Great friends, a world chock full of family history, an event at a fancy castle plus a benevolent aristocratic host. What's not to like?"

"Exactly right, my dear," Maude said.

"I was a little bit worried when Fred's bedsheet started to slip down. I mean, don't get me wrong, I like Fred and everything but–" Gertie said.

"A little bit too much information?" I replied.

We all nodded.

"I don't understand how he got it so incredibly wrong. How do you go from a suit to a bedsheet when it's written right in front of you on the invitation?" Gertie asked.

I gave Gertie a knowing look. "Two words, Fred. Todling."

"All right, all right. Fred was probably distracted. Goodness knows where I would be with all that legalese to stare at every day," Gertie said.

"Agreed."

"I suppose we can go into the party and wait for the men to catch up? I need a snack, and those mini shrimp cocktails look really good." Gertie was raring to go. If she were a racehorse, she'd be chomping at the bit.

"Fine with me. Maude?"

The three of us linked arms and then headed back into the guest arrival line. We were duly announced and started to walk down the stairs. There were a hundred and fifty people in attendance and the room was abuzz with the latest happenings in Oakhurst, Plumsden, and surrounding areas. One simply could not live in an English village and avoid local gossip. What one did with it, however, would determine one's reputation discerned by both the aristocracy and the hoi polloi. One thing was true: when it came to ancestral research, reputation and way of life created good research leads. The juiciest family trees were the ones that contained highwaymen, dodgy tradesman, light-fingered servants, and petty thieves. Miscreants created more paper trails for researchers; unless your five-times great-uncle won the county prize for best cabbage, criminals, the very poor, or the exceedingly rich stood the best chance of being discovered by their descendants. Add in some assorted vocal-cord-defying first names such as 'Balthazar' or 'Tryphena' and one had the makings of a rather entertaining evening presentation at GGRS.

We'd made it down three stairs when we turned right around and came back up again to meet up with Fred once more. He was back, now wearing clothes. To be specific, Fred was clad in Bertie's grand-uncle's formal kilt, complete with sporran and muted tam o'shanter. Ewan, the Major, Bertie, and my father trailed behind.

Fred was now an out-of-place Scot, an imposter. And knew it. Flush-faced Fred cleared his throat. "When this is over, my first order of business is to scrabble through the embers of this illustrious event and retrieve any shred of my dignity that remains."

Bertie was right behind Fred. "It's all we had on site that fit."

"Never mind," Maude said. "Fred, you were rescued. It wouldn't do to have the newest solicitor in town make his first foray into society wearing nothing more than a bedsheet plus a ring of laurel leaves on his head."

"Are you moving your business to Oakhurst?" Ewan asked.

"No, to Plumsden. And actually, it's the shopfront right next to yours," Fred said with a wide grin.

"Oh, right. That place has been on the downward path for a couple of years. One of the partners died and the other one retired."

Fred straightened up, as much as the waistband on his kilt permitted. "Exactly. It's time for a new brand of law in town. I mean, not in the New World, arid western plains, swashbuckling weapon carrying type of way. I meant in the application of the minutia of intellectual property law. And I am also branching out into real estate, broadening the horizons, so to speak."

"How interesting," Gertie said as she sidled up to Ewan. "You've got a new neighbor. Think of all the cozy business lunches you could have together, the office supply orders you could team up on to save by purchasing in bulk …"

Ewan looked somewhat pained, likely wondering how he would get through life with the tap of legal verbal effervescence running all day.

"I say, won't that be fun!" Fred chortled. "I was in finalizing the paperwork a couple of days ago with the land agent, and you know we discovered a false wall? Don't know what's behind it yet, but we'll find out when we remove it during renovations."

"It's likely in need of some paint," I said.

"Oh, no! Not just paint. A full gutting. Rapid top-to-bottom refurbishment for the modern era. Contactless payment, automated greeting, easy-to-clean vinyl reception seats."

"Easy to clean?" I asked.

"With a disinfecting wipe." Fred was quite pleased with himself. "I just have to remember to dry them off; there's nothing worse than standing up and realizing the furniture or the loo seat's left you with a wet bottom!"

"You really plan on cleaning the chairs after each use?" Ewan asked.

Fred nodded. "Have to. One of my clients, a lady of most noble and regal bearing with an incredibly fine lineal family heritage, is rather fussy. I also have a client who must bring her Persian cat to our appointments, so I must be mindful of others with allergies."

"Your client brings her cat to an intellectual property discussion?" Ewan asked.

"Indeed," Fred said with a gleam in his eye. "Since the cat earned over half a million pounds last year in personal appearance fees, I think it's well worth the accommodation."

"You represent a cat who acts?" I asked, still amazed we were having this conversation.

Fred nodded. "I take any type of client, human or animal, so long as invoice settlement is promptly achieved."

❋❋❋

Next Morning. 4:43 a.m.

A hush fell over the crowd. There were murmurs as the domed roof three floors overhead retracted to show the open sky. Bertie had a surprise waiting for us down below. As the newly risen sun hit the floor below, words secretly painted on the floor were now revealed. They read 'Happy Solstice from Scotford Castle' alongside a logo of the castle, the one Bertie had on his estate's letterhead. Invisible ink, lemon juice, who knew what his special-effects experts had used; all that mattered was that the sunlight revealed an amazing surprise. Everybody clapped and Bertie looked rather chuffed standing in amongst the crowd, reveling in their appreciation.

He raised a glass and gave an announcement. "Now that we've had the grand reveal, I invite you outside for a light breakfast to close our summer solstice party. Thank you, everyone, for attending, and see you next year!"

We all trooped outside where a series of open-sided tents awaited. Inside were dozens of catered breakfast dishes awaiting the duke's guests. It was a genteel, high class, yummy, and above all else, friendly event. Everyone had their fill. As the party tapered off, people made promises to see each other later in the week to trade stories and bragging rights on how long they were able to stay up the next day before collapsing into bed.

The best thing about Scotford Castle was that it had a moat, and it was downright impossible to ignore the grandeur. One hearkened back to a past era when armor-clad knights on horseback rattled across the drawbridge to meet a noblewoman or their king. All fourteen Dukes of Conroys had preserved Scotford Castle as a pristine reminder of the past. Its four-foot-thick stone walls came from the late-Elizabethan period, giving the entire structure a commanding air of elegance. Bertie, Ewan, and I leaned over the stone-bridge wall, watching the stragglers depart. Everyone had tidily parked in the designated gravel lot off to the side near the tourist's entrance. The only vehicles left were Fred's moped and the GGRS's handicap-accessible van. In about half an hour I was due to shepherd all these very jolly family history friends back to their respective homes. It would be quite the trolley tour. I'd already decided anyone too merry to climb the three steps up into the van could be dollied onto the van's electric ramp and then strapped in for the journey home.

Bertie looked at Ewan and I. "Moats, at least I've found, have a mystical allure. It's guaranteed every single tourist will stop on the drawbridge, grip the handrail, and peer down into the deep water."

"We've all done it," I said.

"Most comment on the water lilies floating on the surface and wonder what marine life lives below," Ewan said.

Bertie smiled. "There isn't any marine life because it's all freshwater. The best they would do is find some gargantuan goldfish I released when I was a little boy." He waved off some guests entering a taxi that just drew up in the parking lot. "I've been known to tell school children here on tours that a cousin of the Loch Ness monster lives in the moat."

"Bertie, you probably scared them half to death," I said.

"Mmm." Bertie nodded, pointing out a frog swimming through the moat. "Their teachers are getting a bit fed up with their students wading into the moat in hopes of capturing Nessie Version Two. I'm sure they wanted to bring it home and convince their parents that it followed them there, slimy scales, catfish whiskers, fins, and all."

Ah, the inner workings of a fancy historical estate. Scotford Castle was about much more than legends and stuffy history. Family historians reminded people that there was also fun associated with living in a structure that was hundreds of years old. The floors weren't one hundred percent even, and sometimes pictures had to be hung off level to compensate for an ancient building settling, but it was well worth it to belong to this place. I wouldn't trade my rented converted barn on the estate for anything. I loved it here and had no plans to move out.

According to the latest planning department survey, Scotford Castle estate comprised 478 acres of land. From two different rooms, the castle had a commanding view on a rise overlooking a 360-degree view of High Weald fruit, vegetable, hops, and hay production. Bertie's tenants raised sheep, cattle, a variety of fancy poultry, and one of them was even trying water buffalo. Bertie was gung-ho for just about anything, and the local agricultural association was pleased with his devotion to environmentally friendly and organic farming practices.

Bertie turned to look at us. "It's going to be a busy week."

"I know. What with Dad and Maude moving in, the new research site grand opening …"

"And now I've got a new business neighbor," Ewan groaned.

"Never underestimate the power of a good solicitor nearby," Bertie warned. "Besides, it doesn't sound like the show-business cat's complaining."

Ewan nearly chucked Bertie over the wall into the moat below us.

Chapter 5

GGRS's new onsite café was open on a two-week trial period. For the first two weeks of operations, all of its beverages and treats would be given away for free as staff figured out the new machines and tried out recipes. It wasn't expected to be smooth sailing nor perfect snacking until all the kinks were worked out.

The café was meant to keep researchers on site for longer periods, encouraging them to do as much family tree investigating as possible. It was also there to accommodate those who needed to eat periodically throughout the day for medical reasons as well as those who needed a larger social space to interact with others while discussing strategy over tea and a scone. Or a latte and a bun. Or an iced tea and a chocolate croissant. The goal was to accommodate everybody's tastes with a wide-variety menu. All café and kitchen staff were trained in health and safety regulations as well as undergoing customer service and food-preparation training. I was especially thrilled that we could use so much that was produced right here in Greymore's gardens and also from Bertie's Scotford Castle estate. Keeping it local, organic, and fresh made it a real pleasure to offer to any visitor.

I had to say, my expectations were somewhat dashed as I stared down at my soggy Victoria sponge cake and lukewarm tea. The sponge cake was supposed to be a golden yellow, light-as-air concoction, two layers sandwiched with seedless raspberry jam and then covered with powdered sugar. Unfortunately, it appeared that this particular confection was undercooked, resulting in a pudding-like consistency throughout most of my triangular portion. Somebody had microwaved it, which had made the jam run into a thin, syrupy liquid that stained the Greymore Hall logo on my white plate. The tea, although the right flavor from the assortment I was offered, was only lukewarm and served without milk. I wasn't one to complain, but I knew guests would, and it had to be remedied. *Growing pains, new café pains, that's all they were. Right?* I sold myself on it.

My father was already busy tucking into his croissant and coffee. His beverage was piping hot and looked perfect. "I believe I out-ordered you this time, daughter," he said with a grin. He wiped some of the flaky pastry crumbs off his mouth with a paper napkin.

In keeping with Aunt Edwina's high standards, I'd made sure that our napkins weren't the thin, disintegrating kind that one got with cheap hotdogs at the seaside. Never would I purchase the ones that were so flimsy they fragmented with the slightest bit of moisture and always stuck to ice cream cones. No, these were triple-ply and able to wipe up almost every spill put in their path. Of course, all paper went into the easy-to-use compostable bin near the 'return trays here' signage. I'd purchased compost, recycling, and waste bins with open tops plus scent-allergy-friendly, odor-control technology, as opposed to bins with closed flapped lids nobody wanted to touch. I knew people were willing to recycle and compost as long as it was made easy for them.

This included not having to touch slimy or greasy waste-bin lids. Common sense.

I gave a pained smile back to my father. "I believe you're right. Yours looks great. Mine, well, it leaves a lot to be desired." I mashed around the pudding-like cake a bit more with my fork and ultimately decided to abandon ship, pushing the dessert aside to a spare spot on the table. I took my tray over to the counter and asked for a top up on the tea. This time I chose a raisin scone. Surely they couldn't mess up a scone? As long as it wasn't burnt on the outside, then I should be on safe territory. It was kind of like a travel-safe breakfast: savvy road warriors knew it was pretty hard to mess up an omelet or porridge.

I was right.

"Miss Fincher, whatever on earth is that?" I heard to my right in a clipped French accent as soon as I'd sat down with my replenished tray.

I turned to see Jacques Lesabrioux, the pert bellman from the Fizzleywick Hotel, where my short-lived marriage took place earlier that year. Jacques was the stalwart who never complained. He'd helped Gertie and I escape the wedding craziness as we began our treasure hunt after Aunt Edwina's unexpected death.

Jacques was peering over at my Victoria sponge, shaking his head. "I believe a graveyard is the best place for that dessert," he said with all seriousness. He nodded over at my father, who also recognized him.

"It's nice to see you, Jacques. At first I didn't recognize you out of uniform," I said.

"I recently helped Ms. Livingstone with some estate duties as she sold her Petmond Grange estate. I'm here today to assist with the arrangement of her living quarters."

"How nice of you. I'm sure you'll make everything quite proper and organized for her." I was a little bit curious as to why Maude hadn't mentioned Jacques coming to help. Not that it was a problem, I was just surprised to see him, that's all.

Our eyes focused on the squelchy Victoria sponge cake.

I prodded it with my used fork. "It does look quite sad, doesn't it?"

"You certainly cannot serve that to visitors. I have some French pastry training and could speak with your staff, if you wish," he offered, his eyes nearly begging me to let him go and try and sort out the pudding cake.

"I appreciate the gesture, but I don't know about more cooks in the kitchen. I think my chef might get a bit upset."

Jacques shook his head. "Impossible. This is far below the standard of Greymore Hall. It must be corrected. Allow me to do this for you."

With all his years of experience, I was positive that Jacques knew his way around every different department, including the kitchen. "Be my guest. We are in our trial weeks, after all, and feedback is supposed to be quite welcome in the kitchen."

In a flash, Jacques whisked himself and my delinquent dessert off through the double doors leading to the kitchen. He was back a few minutes later with a smile on his face. He was a pert, unobtrusive man, yet firm in his needs to make the guest ultimately satisfied. "Miss Fincher, I have resolved your problem. It appears that kitchen staff are working without a chef; he walked off the job and has no intention of coming back."

"What?" My stomach did a flip flop. Twice.

Jacques spread his hands as if in apology. "He was in the running for a sous chef job at a London restaurant and apparently it was just announced that he was their successful candidate. He left his notice with Ms. Porringer last night."

"Oh dear." I put my head in my hands, feeling totally overwhelmed. "I think I've taken on too much. Gertie and I have been so busy. It's hard to connect and share all the details. And now I've got both move-ins and the site opening this week …"

"Perhaps I might make a suggestion, from one Parisian-trained artist to another?" Jacques asked. There was clearly something good in the offing here.

Jacques had gotten me out of every other scrape I'd put his way in the past. "I am all ears, Jacques," I said. "Please sit down." Great anticipation coursed through my mind.

"Allow me to supervise your staff for one week and get things organized. After that, we can discuss the future."

It was a very bold suggestion that he made to me. My father got up under the guise of having to return his tray, leaving Jacques and I alone to talk.

"But the Fizzleywick Hotel? What about your work there?" I asked.

Jacques shook his head. "My final day was Thursday last week. I just did not see the hotel fitting into my future. Here at Greymore Hall, I can see that I could make a bigger difference to receptive minds. And we already know that we work well together. Do you still have the miniature stuffed goat on your keychain?"

I smiled as I pulled the keychain out of my purse and showed Jacques the raggedy, old, stuffed toy goat that clung to my keychain. We'd talked about it the very moment I had arrived at the hotel for my ill-fated wedding, and Jacques had been kind enough not to mock me. It was precious to me because Aunt Edwina kept miniature goats. He'd showed Lady Edwina Greymore and her family every bit of respect that she deserved at her fine old age of ninety-two.

"What was the Fizzleywick Hotel missing, Jacques?"

He thought on it for a moment. "Character, heritage, and people like you."

Our eyes met for the briefest of moments. Budget wasn't a problem because we'd already put in a generous salary line for a future senior manager of the café and guest services for the entire estate. As for me, I was more interested in helping researchers with their family history, finding myself more and more engrossed in the latest online genealogy training course. It was just becoming such a fascinating hobby for me that I knew I'd be much better placed in the family history world than I would be with soggy Victoria sponge cakes. The answer to my conundrum was right in front of me, eager to help. Best of all, Jacques was somebody I knew I could trust with my life. There was no other hospitality industry professional I would want beside me when confronted with a man dressed as a tomato, a philandering husband, or an unexpected passing of a beloved family member onsite. Jacques had already proven himself through all of these incidents back at the Fizzleywick Hotel. He was discreet, competent, and kind.

Perfect.

I looked up and gave him a big smile. "I think Aunt Edwina sent you to me in my time of crisis." I leaned over and whispered the proposed salary in his ear. I knew it was a fair compensation package because we'd already commissioned a proper salary analysis from a human resources firm.

"Very good, Miss Fincher."

"Call me Julie, please. And you're hired. You can start immediately, assuming you can balance your duties with Maude's moving needs for the time being."

Jacques reached out and shook my hand. It was a solid and cool—not clammy—handshake, the kind that inspires confidence from the person giving it. "Delighted. I am absolutely, positively delighted."

"Welcome to Greymore Hall and all of its quirks," I replied, giving him a wide smile. "I know that with your background and training you can handle it all. From my family history training, I realize we need to be prepared for anyone and anything walking through our doors."

Including dealing with a police constable chasing an English Sheepdog galumphing around the parking lot.

We needed to get used to it. Family history brought out skeletons from the closet, mysterious records hidden away in walls, and some of the most heartfelt reunions ever imagined. I was already super eager to be a part of this fascinating new world. I knew that this was my new purpose in life. All I had to do now was trust my team and help make it happen.

Chapter 6

Greymore Hall. Next Day.

"Good morning, good morning!" Algernon 'Algy' Holgarth's strong, aristocratic voice boomed through Greymore's front hall. He was a pleasant-looking man, a Plumsden aristocrat with a penchant for tweed and yesteryear. He strode down the hardwood floor looking confident and purposeful.

I went over to greet him, walking under the twelve family portraits that hung in gilded frames. Aunt Edwina always insisted they be revered, simply because they reminded the current generation of the heartache, hard work, and military battles ancestors fought to provide for their heirs. "Algy, how are things with the bed-and-breakfast business at Holgarth Hall?"

"Guests number thirty and thirty-one departed this morning. I'm quite pleased at my new little revenue generator." If Algy were a cat, he'd be preening his whiskers right now.

"Glad to hear it's working out for you. And your vegetables?"

"Rather a lingering sore spot between myself and my darling brother at present. I still haven't figured out what happened to my lettuce crop this year, although I do suspect Lance is somehow involved. I will, of course, get to the bottom of it eventually."

Lettucegate was one of the more hilarious events we'd experienced when Gertie and I had stayed at Holgarth Hall for a few nights during Aunt Edwina's recent treasure hunt. Algy's younger brother Lance had managed to hide the fact that the petting-zoo rabbits had escaped to eat his brother's prize-winning lettuces. Lance had managed to blame it on a mysterious and altogether phantom slug infestation, therefore escaping all blame. For now.

"I see." I made sure to say nothing that would give Lance away. He was the longer-suffering one of the pair and deserved no further browbeating from his elder brother. I smiled. "Thank you again for your generous donation to the research site. Our grand opening isn't until later this week. Is there something else you needed from us?"

"No, no. I'm just here to help Maude install her marquetry side table. I borrowed it for a talk I was giving about fine eighteenth century furniture to a local grammar school class. Now I'm returning it, safe and sound. In person is always the best thank you, from my perspective."

"Oh, you have it here today?"

"Yes, outside in the SUV."

"Is it heavy?" I asked.

"Good gracious, no. It's a one-man job ... well, a one-person job, to be more politically correct. To be extra careful, I would like another set of hands on it, just because we're going up in the elevator."

I gestured at Ewan and roped him in to help Algy right then and there.

"How's Lance and your Afghan hounds?" I asked.

"Doing fine, doing fine. I look forward to attending the grand opening here. You've done some excellent work for the community, Julie. Edwina always said you had hidden talents."

A compliment from one of the local aristocrats was always welcome. Modernization and development of new facilities always became a bit of a craw in their throats if you messed with history. Converting Aunt Edwina's beloved Greymore Hall into a public facility was a process akin to dancing on jagged eggshells in bare feet. It had to be done with extremely refined taste and elegance, yet also serve a functional purpose for the researchers and visitors who were going to be on site. Algy and Lance had managed to achieve that with Holgarth Hall. Their estate now provided upscale nursery plants and entertainment for children without making any of it cheap and tacky, like a garish seaside attraction. As Algy loved to say, they either had to commercialize or sell the Old Masters paintings on the walls.

The two men were back in a flash with Maude's half-oval side table, one that would fit perfectly under an intricate hallway mirror. It was covered in bubble wrap, but even with that plastic, poppable disguise, one could see the delicate maple and elm leaves beautifully set with inlaid wood on the top polished surface. They started to walk it, ever so carefully, down the hallway towards the elevator.

I looked up at the portrait of Aunt Edwina again and smiled. She would be happy to see the activity in Greymore Hall. She would be relieved to know that her son Donald Jerome, my father, wasn't going to be lonely in his big old house anymore. Ever since he retired from the furniture store, he needed something more in his life, and Greymore was going to provide a plethora of new friends and activities. Thankfully, his health was good apart from a little bit of sciatica nerve issues. I really, truly hoped he had many enjoyable golden years of freedom.

The next visitor to arrive was Bertie, this time laden down with five jars of the brand-new mango chutney he was flogging from Scotford Castle. It was rather amusing to see an aristocrat so tied up with his estate farm shop's retail sales. Surely his 'people' could do that, but it was obvious he derived an insane amount of pleasure from it.

"Tell you what," I told Bertie, giving him a firm look in the eye. "You tell me what Fred's English Sheepdog name really means and I'll take all five jars."

"You mean Holophusicon? Simple. It means a collection of various stuffed animals and artifacts, the whole of nature."

Interesting. And Fred hadn't sold me a false line. "So why on earth would Fred name his dog that excessively verbose name?"

Bertie caught my eye and we both laughed.

***

Law Offices of Fred Todling Esq., Plumsden, Kent. One Hour Later.

Fred was true to his word. His law office did indeed have easy-to-clean chairs. The waiting area had five magazines arranged in a neat fan on top of the coffee table, two of which splashed his famous white Persian cat client on the cover. On the wall was a group photo of Miss Sympsonne's Ballet School's company; Fred was in the picture off to the right, proudly wearing his logo leisure suit. Another photo showed Fred with Barnaby the potbellied pig, looking so content in his pen that it appeared he was smiling.

The entire space was modern, with pot lights, low-pile carpet, elegant orchid plant décor, wood accents, and granite counters. It was just the feeling a lawyer wanted to exude: modern and calm but not ostentatious. I recognized the receptionist; he was one of the young men in the ballet school photo … and the bicycle courier. From the fine print I remembered his name was Tad Cutling.

I approached the desk. "Hi, I'm Julie Fincher. I'm here to see Fred about the GGRS paperwork?"

I was issued a welcoming smile and a pert nod of the head. The young man couldn't have been more than nineteen; likely he was working part time to pay for his dance endeavors. Kudos to him for pursuing his artistic passion. I didn't see anyone else in the office. Surely Fred's legal empire wasn't big enough for him to expand into having multiple employees on payroll just yet.

"Please have a seat and Mr. Todling will be with you shortly," Tad said.

I sat for about two seconds.

Then the side office door sprang open and Fred made his pudgy presence known. "Please, please, do come in. I have something quite unusually historical that I've just discovered."

Let's hope it wasn't a costume from a toga party past.

Thankfully, I had nothing to worry about in that regard. As I came into Fred's office, he gestured for me to come over to the wall beside his sprawling, shiny desk. There was an odd yet neatly finished three-inch-square cubbyhole in his wall, recessed into the drywall.

"Go ahead and open it," he encouraged me.

I reached in and pulled on the small round handle attached to the cubbyhole's tiny door, much like a knob on a dresser drawer. When I pulled it open, I was shocked to have a clear view right into Ewan's antiques shop. Specifically, I had a bird's eye view of Ewan's collection of pewter tankards and in the background, the sloped-ceiling area where Ewan did his paperwork and ate lunch. I turned to Fred in amazement. "What is this?" I whispered.

"Have no idea. It appears that the prior tenant had a habit of peering in on his neighbors."

"More like spying, I would think," I said. "This is quite rude. I mean, imagine what they could have witnessed?"

"I know. Completely violates privacy laws." Fred looked quite horrified at what he'd found. "I wanted to show it to you so it didn't come as a huge surprise."

The other shoe dropped. I looked at Fred in amazement. "You mean you haven't told Ewan yet?"

Fred winced. "I only found it two days ago, and I was hoping the builders could provide me with some sort of historical explanation as to its existence. But all they came up with was that the prior tenant was nosy and perhaps not quite all there. So now I am stuck with a rather horrific dilemma. Admit to the neighbor that there is a secret door between us and act disturbed, or perhaps we could embrace this new link between our businesses and, well, I'm really not sure."

"As a solicitor, Fred, your clients demand confidentiality. How would you like it if I came in here looking for confidential legal advice and I knew that the antiques store owner next door was listening in? Surely you can't have that."

Fred looked at me, aghast. "You don't think that Ewan would do something like that? I thought that man definitely had higher moral standards than to be a looky-loo with large ear holes."

"Fred, I certainly wasn't implying that Ewan–"

"We'll just have to go next door right now and fix this immediately."

I didn't get any chance to respond and felt rather like the goldfish gaping inside its bowl as Fred gathered up a notepad and pen then headed to the front of his office.

"Wait!" I called out at him. "I think you missed something. Fred! Come back!"

By now, I was sure that Tad out front was wondering what we were up to in Fred's office. Surely confirming the GGRS board of trustees roster wouldn't result in all this drama. Rumor had it we were a pretty tame group. Knowledgeable, fun, but not the black leather and loud music crowd. Well, come to think of it, Gertie did like her black leather jacket over her floral dresses, but that was a story for another day. I refocused.

Fred was back at my side. "Yes, what have I missed? Do you perhaps have a solution to this rather awkward and illegal perusal of the neighborhood?" His eyes peered at me as if I was a genie escaped from its bottle.

"Look," I told him. "See here? Those are burn marks from centuries ago on the framing."

"You mean there was a fire here?"

"Just a little one. Centuries ago they believed that burning a little of the building was like inoculating it against a larger blaze. These burn marks are the sign of superstition from past generations. They have been written up in Family History Society magazines or journals. They give a wonderful insight into the past."

"Well, I never," Fred said. "Perhaps my office could be profiled in the upcoming Plumsden Family History Society magazine."

"You should ask Maude about a cover story. This burn mark, along with your sponsorship of the local ballet school, well, that could make for very good copy." I sold my suggestion with great fervor.

"I see, I see." The marketing wheels inside Fred's head were turning more rapidly than he could process. He sat down at his puckered brown leather sofa. "Perhaps I was a little too hasty in thinking that Ewan has a door somewhere on his wall that he keeps open on his side to spy on me. I would hate to be shown a fool in front of such an outstanding purveyor of all things olden and of the antiquarian variety."

I sighed. "I'm sure Ewan will understand. Let's just finish up this Greymore paperwork and then go visit him next door."

"But what if he's upset? What if he thinks I've been eavesdropping on him since I moved in? Because I assure you I have not. A man's place of business is his sanctuary, his quiet place, his–"

"When did you move in?"

"Two days ago. The builders worked around the cubbyhole due to possible historical significance."

"You've had the local blue plaque society out, then?" I asked, referring to the commission that determined if a building was to be put on the register of protected historical places.

Fred looked as though he'd swallowed a wriggly eel. "I hadn't thought of that."

"You may have a listed building here, that is, one about to be in the running."

"A sleeper historical wonder?" Fred's eyes opened quite wide. "A cubby spyhole could really have that much historical significance?"

Chapter 7

Next Door. Kilburn's Outstanding Antiques. Later.

Fred and I stood in front of Ewan, both of us a bit overeager.

Ewan, rightly so, looked at our odd, fake-calm expressions with a healthy dose of skepticism. He was, after all, a man I'd put through a few more-than-odd family history adventures in the not-so-distant past. What saved Ewan was his easygoing nature. Plus the fact that I'd noticed a surreptitious thief at a recent antiques fair and saved Ewan's business from undergoing a significant loss from the light-fingered criminal shoplifting valuable stock.

"Oh, the hole in the wall?" Ewan asked, quite nonchalantly. "A long previous tenant, a pottery seller, heard rumors, but nothing was ever substantiated."

"So you've never seen it?" I asked him.

Ewan shook his head. "Never. I would've told you guys if I had."

"I'm afraid I have found one on my side, and I feel assertively uncomfortable about it. My builders worked around it because they thought it might have historical significance." Fred spoke in a very agitated and formal tone.

"Whereabouts is this door?" Ewan asked, his interest now piqued.

"It's behind your pewter tankard collection over on the far wall," I said, pointing out the right place.

We all trooped over, and Ewan took the tankards off the shelf, one by one. It was a very clever design because against the creamy white wall background, it was extremely difficult to see the hairline outline of the cubbyhole door.

Ewan peered closely and put his hands against the wall in an attempt to trace the door. He scrabbled with his fingernails to try and open it, but to no avail. It could only be opened from one side as it was a firm fit. "I wasn't sure if I should believe the rumors or not when I first heard them. It just kind of fell by the wayside as I got so busy with my business. I didn't have time to go looking."

Fred cleared his throat. "Ahem. This leads me to my next important announcement. I wish to let you know I have never, never, ever spied on the goings and comings, business dealings, or antiquarian investigations inside your shop."

Ewan tried to hide a smile. "That's fine, Fred. You only took possession forty-eight hours ago, and quite honestly there isn't much in here to eavesdrop on. Unless you're some stealth competitive antiques dealer that I don't know about, you're really not going to find too much exciting to listen in on anyways. I do appreciate your honesty, though."

Fred coughed. He did that when he was nervous. "I thought perhaps I could purchase a couple of these pewter tankards as a gesture of goodwill? Shall we say an outreach of goodness towards my new neighbor?"

"Well, I'm never going to say no to a sale, but don't feel obligated." Ewan looked at me and shrugged. Fred really was too much sometimes. Actually, most times.

"I'll take the one engraved with the wheat sheaf and that one with the farmer's fields on it. Reminds me of how Barnaby likes to visit his donkey friend."

The escapades of Barnaby were now widely known throughout Oakhurst as well as Plumsden. The friendly pet was a legend in his own time.

"No problem, Fred," Ewan said, taking down the two pewter mugs and bringing them to his till for ringing up. "Are there any other items I can interest you in today? I just brought in some really nice hat pins as well as a couple of Art Deco dining room chairs."

"Alas, my wallet has been rather parsed by the recent renovations at your next-door neighbor's legal offices. Perhaps once I have built my client base into a bit of a larger entity, I shall return and revisit that exceedingly generous offer of yours."

"No problem, Fred. Thank you for your custom," Ewan replied. He and I exchanged a small, somewhat cheeky grin. Fred was definitely a man who knew what he liked, and he also had to be handled in a certain manner. At least his heart was in the right place.

"Er, what shall we do about the secret door?" Fred asked. "That's the main reason I came here today."

"I think you need the historical commission to take a look at it," I said.

Ewan got a look of panic in his eyes. "I cannot believe I completely forgot to show you." He scurried to his back alcove, the one with the sloped ceiling, and returned after a moment or two of banging file-cabinet drawers. He emerged holding a red binder full of hopefully acid-free, plastic page protectors. He handed the binder over to us. "This came from underneath the floorboards. The builders I had in a while back found it, and I never quite got around to finishing sorting it out. I knew it had historical value, but I didn't want to give the local archives a disorganized shoebox full of messy, dusty old paperwork. I got as far as organizing this binder and then, well, life happened."

"I think you'd find that the local archives is more than used to receiving shoeboxes filled with dusty old paperwork. What is it?" I asked. Fred loomed over my shoulders.

"It's varied. There's some correspondence, old invoices, bills for whiskey deliveries, the prices of local goods. A real mishmash. I should have dealt with it sooner, but I've just been too busy. You know how it is with a small business trying to make a go of it in today's world. You have to be a computer expert, a brilliant marketer, accurate bookkeeper, have excellent products and services, plus manage your team. At least in my case the team is only one, so that's a few less people I need to worry about."

"You're still busted," I said to Ewan. "Those historical records belong in an archive and you know it."

He sighed. "Guilty as charged. I did ask the landlord and he told me he wasn't interested. So, the records sat."

"Well, as long as we have access, let's take a look through the binder," I said, curious. "To me, there's nothing more exciting than finding old lost records that relate to one's own life and then seeing how the jigsaw pieces fit together."

"Do you think the eavesdropping door will be explained?" Fred asked.

"There's a good chance it will. The history of the building often reveals the history of its occupants. In my genealogy course, I learned the preliminaries about estate records, census records, manorial records, and even old newspaper clippings that can provide priceless information about who used to occupy a building as well as any scandals that occurred within it."

Fred cleared his throat. "Well, I certainly hope there were no scandals in this building. I'm running a very above-board law practice using the absolute strictest of professional standards."

Ewan shook his head. "Fred, I can tell you that when I originally looked at these records, the latest date I saw on them was about 1892. So I think any scent of a scandal has long faded from Plumsden residents' memory. In fact, any scandal that arises out of this paperwork would likely make your law practice famous rather than infamous."

That was good enough for Fred. He cracked his knuckles and then sat down beside me in the alcove. "Right. Let's get to work."

***

Two Hours Later.

"Imagine stuffing all these records under the floorboards. What on earth were the prior occupants thinking?" Fred asked, astonished.

"Just be glad the records are here. Lots of records are found in odd places. I once went into a builder's office and saw that they had put three eighteenth century land title deeds in frames, behind glass, and hung them on the wall," I said.

"The originals?" Ewan asked.

"The very same. What a travesty," I said. "They should be in an archives."

"What a shame," Ewan said.

Fred got a bit antsy. "Anyone should know not to put original antique paperwork on the wall as mere art."

Ewan nodded. "Totally agree. Which is why that binder safely sat in the back of the cabinet since I moved in a few years ago. I will say, though, that I had an antique lampshade in this store made out of old land title deeds. I've also seen a framed apprentice tanner's indenture in a house clearance. That one I did snap up right away and donate to the local archives."

"Good on you," I said, giving him a smile.

"What did you two find in the binder?" Ewan asked.

"Something exceedingly interesting from three gentlemen named Jas, Fras, and Chas," Fred said.

I shook my head. My new genealogy research course had taught me this one. "Jas is short for James. Fras is short for Francis. Chas is short for Charles."

"My goodness, you're a fountain of knowledge," Fred said, obviously impressed.

"So what did this merry band of three have to do with our building?" Ewan asked.

"It appears that they were three brothers who owned this building back in 1799. One of them lived here and the other two were business partners in an onsite pottery."

"I wonder if that's related to the potter who used to occupy this space a couple of tenants before me?" Ewan mused.

"I wouldn't be surprised if it was," I said. "Trades tend to be passed down from father to son, and industries have stuck in certain English villages for centuries. There are villages all over that are known for leatherworking, silver working, wool, glassware, and more. The list is endless. It's a great way to find your ancestors if you know they were in a specific trade or industry. A lot of them are listed in guild records that you can access for information."

"I just planted a quarter acre of broccoli in my back garden," Fred suddenly announced.

"And what, exactly, does that have to do with the price of eggs?" Ewan asked.

It was definitely a rather out-of-order comment that Fred just made.

He coughed. "Permit me to explain. When you were talking about trades and industries, I happen to know that my family were largely greengrocers going back many generations. I think that's why I have such a green thumb."

"Why so much broccoli?" Ewan asked. "It's a very gassy vegetable."

"Not if you cook it properly. My digestion has rather improved since I've been eating a lot of it. It improves colon health immeasurably. And I make a most delectable broccoli jam."

Ewan and I simultaneously cringed at the thought.

Ewan was the one brave enough to speak first. "What on earth do you use broccoli jam for?"

Fred harrumphed. "On rye toast, of course. It's also good in ham sandwiches. I also make a sweetened version with kiwi fruit and sometimes blueberries to put on slices of date loaf."

"That must be a rather acquired taste," I said. "I can't see the GGRS's café carrying that anytime soon."

"I thought I might ask Bertie for his advice on setting up a retail line of goods," Fred said. He'd obviously thought this through and was serious.

How could a man with that much broccoli not be serious about it?

"I think you should speak with Algy. He's the one winning prizes for his produce, when he actually manages to grow them the full-size," I said. Inside I was laughing at Lettucegate again but there was no way I was going to blow Lance's well-kept secret.

"Ah, the indomitable aristocrat from Holgarth Hall. I was actually planning on calling on him to see if he had any legal work he could gently guide my way. The broccoli jam might be a good conversation starter. I'm chuffed that you gave me the idea," Fred said. "Thank you."

"Oh, I'm sure it will start a conversation with Algy, all right," Ewan said. "So what about the rest of the paperwork in the red binder?"

I continued. "It's about their suppliers, there's some households bills, a few legal disputes, and handwriting I had a hard time understanding. Overall, I need to take it back to Greymore so we can go through it properly with trained experts. I'd hate to lead you astray because I only have basic training in genealogy research at this point."

"Perhaps after the grand opening?" Ewan asked.

"It's a date," I replied, not thinking.

The word 'date' just slipped out.

And there it was again. Awkwardness. It was something we'd faced during Aunt Edwina's treasure hunt, something we had both ignored at the time. Now that the GGRS was officially well underway, all the renovations done and ready to welcome visitors, it seemed that this simmering and pleasantly burgeoning attraction between Ewan and I was rising to the surface again.

Ewan decided to bridge the gap yet again, acting as the kind, chivalrous man he was. "How about a quick snack before you go?" he asked, rummaging in his small kitchen.

Fred shook his head. "Alas, I have solicitor business to attend to with a star cat."

"Oh my goodness! The move-ins. The grand opening. I still have a ton to do! I need to go, I'm so sorry." I gathered up my purse plus the red binder and raced out the door, leaving Ewan alone. He looked ever so forlorn, standing there with a tin of my favorite chocolate biscuits in his hand.

Chapter 8

Greymore Front Hall. Two Days Later. 2:00 p.m.

Large white tents were temporarily installed on Greymore's front and back lawns, one for food and one for our time-capsule ceremony. Each tent accommodated one hundred and fifty chairs. There was no way we could put all of those people inside at the same time, simply because we'd taken over the ballroom for the research site's equipment and specialty rooms. Instead, we'd hired two outdoor tents in case it rained. However, we were graced with a perfect day and bright sunshine. Thanks to Mr. Murphy, our tents weren't really needed, but I knew if they weren't in place it would have rained canines and kitties.

A shiny red ribbon was looped onto an easel, ready to be strung across the double-door entrance. Vases of cream, mauve, and pale-pink roses were everywhere, honoring Aunt Edwina's memory. I stood inside the grand front hall and looked up at her portrait, misty-eyed. "I hope we do you proud," I whispered.

"You will. We all will," Gertie said in a jolly voice behind me. She threaded her arm through mine. "Everything looks just smashing. And the catering? My goodness."

"You really think so?" With so much pressure on the team, I was just waiting for something to go wrong. Because it had to.

"Everything will go fine, just you wait and see," Gertie reassured me. "Look who's coming to give us support."

I followed her line of sight and saw Ewan confidently striding up the building's steps, carrying a bouquet of pale-pink roses. He stepped across the threshold to enter the hall and handed the flowers to me. "Best of luck on your grand opening, Julie." His eyes held mine for more than a brief moment, making it obvious that the attraction between us was still strong. Not yet acted upon, but still strong. Perhaps one day it would come to more than rushed hellos and goodbyes. I had to admit I felt super awkward after rushing away the last time I saw him.

Today, however, I had to be much more focused on ensuring the new handicap-accessible front entrance ramp was in perfect working order. I was bracing for a gaggle of aristocrats, dignitaries, and guests who were all descending on Greymore for its official opening.

"I'm looking for a saggy bottom knocker," I heard to my left, farther down the hall, nearer the back. A stranger had arrived, yet oddly entered through the back door we'd left open for the catering team.

"Pardon me?" I said, standing back to accommodate the newcomer announcing his need in a booming voice. He was a stocky man, about five foot, seven inches tall, and balding. He had a round, jowly face and wore a tidy navy golf shirt plus tan poly-cotton trousers with a razor-sharp crease. Overall, the impression he gave was one of permeating righteousness.

Both Gertie and I gave furtive looks around the immediate area, automatically checking if impressionable young ears were present.

"Oswald Boggs. But everyone calls me Ozzie." He extended a smooth, well-manicured hand to each of us. "A saggy bottom knocker, my ancestor's trade. I understand that you research them here." The man's eyes darted between Gertie and I. It looked like he was wondering if he was in the right place.

"Well, sir, you're a little bit too early. You see, our grand opening is today. We're not officially open for research until tomorrow morning." I looked Ozzie up and down, wondering how on earth he'd gotten both his days and entrance doors mixed up. All of our press was very well organized, and the date had been consistent on every single publication, social media, and radio announcement.

"So it's a private party, then?" he said. It sounded like he had accused us of throwing down the gauntlet, testing to see if we truly were friendly to the public or simply a closed shop for upper-class hoity-toities.

"You're very welcome to stay, have some refreshments, and take the inside facility tour. We just aren't rolling up our sleeves and getting into proper research work until tomorrow." I gave him what I hoped was a competent, settled smile.

"Well, I might just do that," he said.

One could take his last statement as a challenge or an acquiescence. Either way, Ozzie Boggs was a new researcher whom we needed to accommodate. He drifted away to look at a family history poster in a frame on the wall.

Another guest arrived through the front doors. Monitoring both front and back entrances was starting to make me feel like a silver sphere battered about in a pinball machine. I smiled to greet Algy. He was full of the joys of life plus what appeared to be genuine enthusiasm for his pending performance alongside Bertie for the customary aristocratic grand-opening speech duties.

"He'll be back," Algy said. "One can always tell by the fervor in their eyes."

"He was pretty serious, wasn't he? Although his request caught me off guard," I admitted.

Algy laughed. "The look on your face said it all. You thought he was using blue language."

"A sagger maker's bottom knocker is actually someone who works in the pottery craft making containers, the ones they use for firing in the kiln," Ewan added. "I know that because the prior tenant in my shop left a couple of old pamphlets behind. They retailed a lot of products from Derbyshire and Staffordshire."

"Stick with it. Perhaps you've just met your first polyglot," Bertie added, joining our conversation at an opportune moment.

We all had blank looks on our faces.

"Someone who speaks multiple languages," Bertie explained.

"You had a far different education than I did, Bertie," Ewan said. "I've never heard that word."

"Ah, the good old days in Professor Fenshaw's advanced linguistics class. He used to drum his fingers on the table to the rhythm of iambic pentameter." Bertie got a wistful expression across his fine features.

"Regardless, we're here to help everyone, no matter how esoteric their genealogy research request," I said.

It was in our formal organization mission statement crafted by the board of trustees, staff, and volunteers: 'To help all family history researchers with accurate, timely, and knowledgeable guidance using educated and modern research techniques.'

It had first said 'investigative techniques' at the end, but several of us had argued against it. My main point was that the GGRS shouldn't sound at all like some sort of law-enforcement organization. That point had won out, and now the mission statement was engraved on a brass plaque on the wall just beyond the research site's front doors, inside the main Greymore Hall building. It was a daily constant reminder to everyone inside that there was a purpose here never to be forgotten. No matter how difficult, no matter how strange, we were there to help people. That was what Aunt Edwina would have wanted, and it reflected how she lived her life. Everyone was proud to continue her goodness.

What the GGRS offered was absolutely hands down the best resource center our budget and space would allow. We had fifteen computer stations in a quiet room that was jokingly called our 'no chat room'. We also had a soundproofed breakroom with comfortable recliners and sofas that we called the 'chat room'. This was where people could assemble to discuss various research woes and hopefully get ideas from other people who had traveled a similar road.

Our toilets were amazingly self-cleaning, like the ones Gertie and I had seen on the continent a few years back. The stalls were all floor-to-ceiling and offered complete privacy. Each toilet had a plastic cover on the seat that changed on a continuous loop after every usage. The bowl got a spray of disinfectant after every flush. The flush mechanism was industrial strength, so strong there was no chance of a clog. A sink stood within each stall, along with soap and free toiletry supplies. All these features were important to a public facility expecting high usage. We employed two full-time janitorial staff for the facility, and they were tasked with keeping up with daily and longer-term cleaning plans.

We'd installed a robust intercom system to cover every different type of announcement, ranging from opening and closing-time reminders to emergency alerts. Due to the size of the space—the research site took up 9,926 square feet—we needed an announcement system that could permeate the entire facility. We had an activity board on the wall that was replicated online; it was filled with all sorts of notices about upcoming lectures, conferences, field trips, online webinars, researchers' no-longer-needed birth, marriage, and death certificates, and even car boot sales. Family historians were noted for sharing their finds with others and trying to reunite lost certificates and photos with their rightful owners. I had even done it not too long ago when I reunited some photos I found at an antiques fair with family members through a military memorabilia dealer in London. This type of gesture was second nature to us. We cared. The internet made it all that much easier because orphaned items could be posted for free in the hopes of matching them up with the right people.

There were two tall bookshelves for reference materials as well as individual consult rooms for talking one on one with an experienced member of staff. We had ergonomic chairs for researchers, and the chairs had adjustable backs, heights, and arms. There were no gaps in the backs of the chairs, so researchers' lumbar support pillows wouldn't fall through the open back. All of the chairs were on sets of five casters for added mobility and stability.

Nonglare task lighting was at every computer and desk carrell. During the design phase, I banned fluorescent lights anywhere through the building because of their cold, blue light and harshness on the eyes. Libraries were always supposed to be warm, inviting places, and that's what the GGRS would deliver.

Maude came over, her eyes shining with joy. "Oh, Julie, isn't this the most marvelous day? All the space, organized collections, modern computers. What an absolute delight."

I smiled back. "And you now have a very short commute to your office."

"Forty-two steps from my fourth-floor suite to the research site's front doors. Marvelous."

"Wonderful."

"We've sublet half the Plumsden Family History Society's office space to the local tombstone-rubbing association. We'll keep the rest for a presence in town, but the bulk of the research will now be conducted here and we're ever so grateful," she said.

"I'm glad you're happy." I noticed a guest was waiting patiently to speak with Maude, so I let them be and continued my own tour of the facility.

Our reception center was the half-oval-shaped, centralized oak information desk that served as a one-stop traffic-directing function. It had three computers for staff members, with ample space in between each one. Inconspicuously off to its right were ample coat and boot racks along with clear door lockers for stashing belongings. One could also lock up one's coat on a wire cord if desired. We had big, friendly posters on the walls for newbie researchers; they explained the first steps to take regarding looking at a certificate or census, or even taking a field trip to an ancestral home. Our favorite poster so far was the one that had a brick wall being blasted through, with all the bricks going flying as the words 'proper, accurate research' busted their way through the hole.

Even though they were old technology now, left over from the 1980s, we still had one microfiche and one microfilm machine for any donated collections. Although many of the family history societies only produced online magazines now to save on expenses, we'd acquired a donor's collection of printed magazines going back twenty years from five different county societies. These half-page-sized, saddle-stitched booklets were all added to additional shelving lining the far wall. Each magazine holder was labeled with the issues contained inside. Down a long aisle we had a high counter for people to spread out charts and maps plus review them while standing. We kept our map collections in the drawers underneath the counters, thus maximizing space and efficiency. A frosted wall etched with the GGRS logo separated these long counters from quiet-area computer workstations. Behind the counters we had a newsletter creation room for staff, including dedicated workspaces and two computers for writing and graphic design. It was purposely separate from the reception area to ensure yet another quiet place for concentration.

Further down the rows we had a cabinet for film and fiche donations. Everything here was wheelchair-friendly, right down to the adjustable-height desks, making it easier for anyone with a disability or sore joints. The lunchroom had comfortable chairs with tables, a full-size refrigerator plus coffee, tea, and microwaves.

I noticed the Major was absolutely fascinated by the new coffee machine, and he'd rapidly become the expert operator.

He'd already taken up the station, standing there during the grand opening, now busy doling out fancy lattes and cappuccinos to whoever was interested. In the private staff room, we had a computer desk for paperwork; this was a sanctuary where team members could retreat for a private setting. We valued our team members beyond anything else. Their safety, health, comfort, and continuing education were super important to everyone associated with the research site and serving on the board of trustees.

At the opposite end, with a separate entrance to the main hall, was a meeting room that sat fifty people, classroom-style. Temperature controls, whiteboards, easels, and beverage stations were all conveniently located, and the room was soundproofed. I'd attended far too many hotel conferences where a flimsy airwall did nothing to prevent the next-door meeting from invading mine. That wasn't going to be an issue here. The pièce de résistance was our new theater room, which had a big, twenty-foot-square flat screen and thirty comfortable recliners with footrests, cupholders—the theater and lunchroom were the only two places food was allowed—and motorized self-risers for those with mobility issues. The projector had a dedicated laptop, and it was perfect for showing family history movies, training webinars, and anything else that required a large viewing area for a group.

"Excuse me, please?" Jacques was at my side. "The catering is ready. The temporary and experienced staff we contracted for the event worked out perfectly, and we've just completed a final safety check on the tent out front."

"No more pudding cake?" I replied.

"Certainly not. All is in order." Jacques looked quite pleased with himself.

1:55 p.m.

Dignitaries on site? Check.

Staff ready at their stations? Check.

Speechmakers had speeches in hand, or in pocket, and were near the microphone? Triple check.

We were ready and headed for the tent at the back of the building. I stood behind the microphone and leaned over to it. "Ladies and Gentlemen, we're about to get started. Could you please take your seats?"

All the food was served outside. Food inside a research site's open shelves and collections area just wasn't allowed. Crumbs attracted pests and dirt; sticky fingers left marks and damage. And don't even get me started on those who lick their fingers to turn pages; the next person doesn't want to touch the prior reader's saliva on the page. Gross. We had plenty of rubber fingertip sleeves on hand to prevent this type of problem.

Generous and continuous food service out back. Formal ceremony, complete with time capsule, out front. All was in order.

I leaned over the microphone for a second time. "Ladies and Gentlemen, I'd like to introduce the Duke of Conroy, Bernard Preswick, Owner and President of Scotford Castle estate." I shook his hand as guests applauded.

Bertie said all the right things. How Aunt Edwina would be proud, how the repurposed Greymore Hall was a wonderful addition to the community, how people could reconnect with their past and learn about their roots as well as how future generations would benefit from such a caring, community-minded gesture. I'm sure he was called upon to give a hundred speeches like this every year, but this one sounded exceptionally heartfelt.

I was grateful for Bertie's kind friendship, art patronage, and support of the new research site. In fact, I was grateful for all the dignitaries who showed up. They came both out of respect for Aunt Edwina as well as recognition for how important this new research site was going to be. Algy had kindly started off the donation drive with a £25,000 check he'd presented at Aunt Edwina's wake. Hopefully it was the start of many more checks flowing into our coffers. Running the site wasn't going to be cheap. Thanks to Aunt Edwina's will, I had plenty of capital to keep it running for ten years. Still, it was better to save capital and exist on the interest. Community buy-in was also better if people donated towards the research site's operating costs. The nice thing was that it appealed to everybody because researching family history was always intriguing. The only sketchy questions ever raised were the ethical ones about a mysterious skeleton found in somebody's closet. It was hard for volunteers to share these hidden secrets with guests. To tell or not to tell their client was also at the heart of every professional genealogy researcher's decision-making process. The fairest thing to do was disclose, albeit gently, because that's what the client was paying them to do.

The two-week training period for the café, along with last-minute help from Jacques and his culinary connections, allowed us to self-cater. The café had outdone itself for this event. After the pudding cake incident, I was relieved to see that the food looked fantastic. All ingredients were listed on tiny tent cards to alert guests to potential allergens, a holdover from Jacques's hospitality industry training. Tables were laden with miniature sandwiches of eight different varieties, including vegetarian. We had five different kinds of dessert squares, plus an assortment of fancy-decorated sugar cookies. On offer was a full selection of hot and cold beverages, minus anything alcoholic.

When the speeches were over and Bertie finally cut the fancy red ribbon, a large cheer went up amongst the crowd. I looked out at the guests from Oakhurst, Plumsden, and those who'd come from even further away, including a couple from Glasgow, Scotland. This was a community. I couldn't ask for more. Today we'd thrown the doors open on the entire facility so the public could see our new offices, equipment, and resources. All staff and volunteers were on deck to provide tours and answer any questions. So far, so good.

"Did we put on a good show?" Bertie asked me as the crowd dispersed into polite mingling mode.

"Brilliant, thanks for being here," I said. "Now I hope our trained staff's answers will impress newbies and experienced researchers alike."

"It's important not to take research advice from those not specifically trained in genealogy standards."

I nodded. "I heard the horror stories in my genealogy training class. One student took a pretty dangerous runback on a family tree for six generations without having proved he was actually related to the one closest to his own birthdate."

"The horror!"

We exchanged a grin.

Everyone was so eager to start researching in our brand-new digs. The first research site newsletter was already well underway, with a partly designed document showing on a monitor in the newsletter-creation room. The place was abuzz with people, and the Major was counting the number of attendees using a tiny silver clicker in his hand.

Gertie came over to me in the middle of all this with a forced smile. "Guess what, Cousin? The toilets are running out of soap. I've been trying to fix it but unfortunately got foam everywhere, so I think I'm going to have to pass that one off for some help."

"Oh dear. Was there no one around to assist?" I asked her.

"Both janitorial staff were busy working on a jammed plastic toilet seat cover across the hall. I honestly thought I could fix it myself, so I just dove right in, but–"

"But?"

Her face fell. I'd seen that look before. Not good.

I followed her down the hall. I hesitated when I saw the foam emerging from underneath the restroom's door. It was like a bubblegum-pink mass of confusion, a monster slowly escaping its confines. I bent down and noticed that it was doubling in size as soon as it escaped the crack between the door and the sill. This wasn't a job for the faint of heart. When I pushed on the door to open it, there was so much soapy foam behind the door that it actually prevented me from doing a full hinge swing.

"Oh, Gertie. This isn't good." The soap was rising up to our ankles.

"Well, we can look on the bright side. It's nearly finished the entire container," she said apologetically.

"How on earth did this even get started?" I asked. "This is supposed to be the modern facility where everything is kept in order through good engineering."

"My fault. I tried to refill it with the wrong-size dispenser, apparently. Then water got mixed into it and I tried to rinse it away, but that only made it worse. The drain clogged, overflowed three sinks, got onto the floor, and now we're left with a sea of foam."

It was like trying to walk through a vat of soapy cotton candy, except that this kind didn't smell sweet. Instead, it reminded me of antiseptic geraniums.

"I think the only thing we can do is shut this room down and call maintenance. At least the drain's in the middle of the floor so if we sweep the foam back inside it should clear away on its own once the bubbles subside." I picked up the squeegee mop that lay against the wall, already wet on its bottom black rubber strip.

"I can give you a hand," I heard behind me. I turned to see Ewan's friendly face. He had an extra mop in hand.

"Send sponges, please. It's a torrent of foam!" I joked. "Gosh, if you could help, it would be very much appreciated. I have a c'meeting to prepare for in the morning."

"A c'meeting?" Gertie and Ewan both looked quite puzzled and had every right to be.

I explained. "Sorry. I've just been so stressed with this grand opening, trying to keep everything organized. I meant 'committee meeting'. I must have merged the two words together out of stress. Sorry for any confusion."

"No problem. I can fix this. I'm a pretty handy guy when I need to be." Ewan surveyed the mess in front of him. "It looks like a midnight rave party in here, minus the disco lights."

I saw Jacques hustle by and quickly asked him to find a janitorial team member to help.

"At least the bank of stalls on the other side of the hall are still in working order. They are in working order, correct? With soap?" I asked.

Gertie rapidly nodded. "Of course. I'll just put an out-of-order sign on this one and then stand here and direct people to the other toilets."

"And such is the glamorous life of research site staff," Ewan observed. "Not that this isn't a noble thing to work on, just not exactly how I expected to be spending my day."

"Hand me that mop. I think if we just guide the foam towards the drain and then maybe pour some water over top of it, we can fix this ourselves," I said.

Ewan rolled up his trouser cuffs. In my heels, I gingerly stepped around the worst of the foam, knowing that my nylons would be ruined and I would smell like foam hand soap for the rest of the evening. No trouble at all. I was raised to get involved, and that was exactly what I wanted to do. Maybe I'd even get to my c'meeting tomorrow on time.

Chapter 9

Half an hour later we'd corralled it. All thirty-nine thousand liters of the gloopy, flyaway, pink foam soap. Slightly disheveled and slightly worse for wear, Ewan and I returned to the research site main-floor space and were quickly taken aside by Bertie and Algy.

"We must get the time capsule buried soon," Bertie whispered. "There's a busload of elderly guests who are leaving in a couple of hours."

"Oh, early bedtime, right?" Algy said with a kind, understanding smile.

"Bedtime? No, they're going ballroom dancing," Bertie said.

We all laughed.

"I love that," I said. "Just don't tell Gertie, because there might be a microphone onsite."

"The Major has the time capsule container ready, welder on standby. All we need now is a run-through of the contents …" Algy said.

There was a specific list of items we'd determined at the last board of trustees meeting. "It's important we announce each one to the crowd as it's filled." I looked to Algy. "You're the person on tap for this speaking engagement."

"Of course, just give me a cue," Algy said.

We all headed back outside, this time to the front of Greymore Hall and under another tent hosting a microphone, lectern, and long table draped with a white cloth in front of audience chairs. On top were all the items going into the time capsule, shaped like a hollow, oblong vitamin made of stainless steel. A brass plaque on one half read 'Time Capsule: GGRS'. A beefy-looking welder stood off to the side; his logo shirt read 'Barney Dazzle's Welding Services'. I was sure Barney would do a dazzling job sealing up our capsule, making it impervious to insects, vermin, and moisture for the next hundred years.

I approached the microphone. "Ladies and Gentlemen, we're now going to have our time capsule ceremony. It gives me great pleasure to introduce Sir Algernon Holgarth of Holgarth Hall, one of Aunt Edwina's dear friends."

After the customary polite smattering of applause, Algy took over speaking duties:

> "Welcome again, everyone. It is my honor to lead this treasure trove of deposits that future generations will enjoy long after we are gone. Think back to the various news articles that you have read over your lifetime, paper format or on the internet. Remember how you felt, filled with wonder, when they unsealed that precious time capsule removed from a building's cornerstone or dug up from a grammar school yard. Most of these were buried fifty or a hundred years ago. That's a lot of decades of change, growth, and technological progress. A hundred years ago it would've been hard for people

to imagine we could land on the moon, talk to our relatives overseas by a telephone for a few pence, and send messages through thin air using computers. Even more unbelievable were the eradication of polio, advanced medical diagnoses and treatments as well as infrastructure and transportation grids never seen before. Today, we want to capture all of those in our time capsule. We want future generations to understand where we came from and also what we hope to offer the future. A time capsule isn't something simply to amuse children. It's more than a packet of bubblegum and a few coins tossed into a container buried a few feet underground. I humbly suggest that the time capsule we are preparing today is one of the most important ones this country will ever see. Why? Because it involves multiple family historians who know how to parse the truth and the important bits of information from our history into something understandable and readable in the future. As you think back upon the other time capsule stories you've read or perhaps even witnessed, never underestimate the power of the past. Remember that as you take part in this very important ceremony here today."

A hush fell over the crowd as guests contemplated Algy's deep words. I actually got a little teary-eyed hearing him speak, knowing how passionate everyone here was about history and genealogy research. My heart swelled with pride as I looked out at the objects all the community members had donated for the time capsule. I wasn't the only one who thought that this was a very important activity.

Algy continued:

> "I now ask that you turn to page three of your programs and read along with me as Julie holds up each object we are placing into the time capsule. I will call out the item, and she will place it inside. When we're all finished and done, Barney will seal up the time capsule and it shall be buried in the center of the circular drive at the front entrance to Greymore Hall. And for those of you who don't think you can wait a hundred years for it to be opened, Greymore Hall has a wonderful security team on site, so don't get any sneaky advance-unearthing ideas."

The crowd laughed and Algy put away his formal speech.

I picked up the first item and held it aloft. I looked over at Algy and nodded.

He began his announcements. "One Plumsden Family History Society magazine, current quarterly edition."

This was followed by two books, one on the history of Oakhurst and Plumsden plus another on the history of manor houses in the area, including Greymore Hall, Scotford Castle, Petmond Grange, and Holgarth Hall. One modern cellular phone with charger. Two newspapers, one local and one national. A jump drive containing multiple how-to guides from the Family History Society as well as examples of social media sites. One verbose legal analysis of intellectual property law from Fred Todling, Esquire. Pictures of the GGRS's interior. One electronic photo frame with photos from the area. One celebrity magazine and one magazine showing great farms of the area. One antique silver spoon from the eighteenth century, courtesy of Ewan. A soap wrapper. Fifty-, twenty-, ten-, and five-pound banknotes plus one- and two-pound coins. The menu from today's grand opening along with a picture of Jacques's ancestor who, decades ago, was a cook at Windsor Castle. A supermarket receipt. A bill for streaming television and movie services. One list compiled by local schoolchildren predicting what would become reality in fifty years and in a hundred years. A second list compiled by local senior citizens predicting what would become reality in fifty years and in a hundred years. The list of the top-ten most important scientific developments in the last twenty-five years. A guidebook to all the crafts still undertaken in England. A piece of fine lace handmade by a local artisan. A staff and volunteer photo from the GGRS.

That completed what I had on the table. It was now bare. I looked over at Barney and nodded. He approached, flipping down his welding mask and gesturing for everybody to step away as he fired up his blowtorch. In a moment, our history would be sealed for the next hundred years. It was a bittersweet feeling because the history we had created up until today was essentially going to be halted inside that time capsule. Anything we did after the capsule was sealed would have to go into a future ceremony. I looked around at the supportive group of people here today. Many were dear friends, and yet some were visitors whom I had yet to meet. One thing was definite: I knew that we were off to a flying start, and we all had many positive dreams for the days ahead.

Chapter 10

Greymore Hall. Fourth-floor Suites. Next Day.

The newly renovated apartment suites at Greymore Hall were gorgeous, one with masculine décor and the other feminine. My father had his deep, forest-green walls in his suite's wood-paneled library. Maude had her pale-rose-pink chintz sofas and water-color painting studio in her suite. Dad liked strong, bold colors such as rich ruby reds and deep blues. Maude was into the pastel tones and floral design. The suites were designed with seniors in mind, yet I told the designer not to make them look like an old folks' home or hospital. Comfortable senior living was all about efficiency and convenience for people who might move a little slower and have less-quick reaction times. It did not, however, mean that one had to live in a sterile, medical-like institution expecting to smell disinfectant and seeing ancient, mint-green-painted walls at every turn. There was a way of aging gracefully and aging in place; my goal was to provide it for my beloved father and dear friend Maude.

The appliances I specified were all fingerprint-resistant stainless steel. Each kitchen had an ample island. Grab rails were in the showers, plus anti-slip flooring. Horizontal curved handles rather than circular knobs were on all the doors to help arthritic hands. Televisions and stereo systems were linked so they could all be controlled by the same central system in each unit as needed. Each room had its own temperature control via flatscreen thermostat. It was so technologically advanced that one could even pipe music into a certain room of the suite with two presses of one's finger. Homebuilding had come a long way in the last twenty-five years, and I continued to be impressed by all of these technological advances that helped one live more efficiently and in greater comfort.

"How is Jacques doing?" I asked Maude as we stood inside her elegant front hallway. She was only partially unpacked but was making good progress.

"Jacques is simply wonderful. I had a butler at Petmond Grange and was quite stressed about losing him. Having Jacques around makes me feel even more at home here at Greymore. I don't need a lady's maid, but I do like a house kept in good order."

"I'm so glad. Jacques is a great addition to our team."

"And your father seems to be settling in quite well. I know he enjoys his views of the garden. It's lovely having that rose and topiary garden underneath our bay windows that run along the back of the building. The garden is so organized and well laid out with the raked pea gravel."

"I'm glad you like it. The gardeners like stenciling a different wildlife animal into the center circle of gravel each morning." I noted that today's animal was a badger.

Maude smiled, ever so kind. "Such a delight for a pensioner. Thank you so much for this opportunity." She leaned forward and gave me a quick hug.

"You will let me know if you notice anything wrong with my father?" I asked in all seriousness. "I do keep a close eye, but I'd love to know he's got more than just me looking out for him."

"Of course. And it will stay between you and I." She put a finger to her lips.

"Thank you."

She took my hands in hers. "And now, let's go and do some research here at our new site. I'm very excited." Her eyes twinkled and she had a spring in her step. It was wonderful to bring such joy to people's lives.

***

Ten Minutes Later.

"I don't know if I like being called a Perspicacious Perambulating Priest," Gertie lamented over leftover caramel squares in the lunchroom.

"I can think of much worse things to be called," I said.

"Oh, Fred's alright. Just a bit over the top sometimes," she said. "He did mention he's dropping by later with some legal papers. He just wanted to get them notarized first."

"Perfect. Thanks for letting me know." I looked around the site. I saw eager faces from staff and volunteers due to work the first shift. Everything was in order, everything was unpacked, and the lunchroom was fully stocked. The posters on the wall were bright and enticing for any newbie. They encouraged everyone to do their research slowly and correctly as opposed to zooming up the branches of the family tree in hopes of getting back to the fifteenth century overnight. Those who understood genealogy research, the ones who really had done their homework and learned the proper methodologies, understood that this was a lifelong passion and hobby. Some turned genealogy research into a business of their own once they gained expert-level knowledge. Regardless, all the smart ones knew that it took time to get it right. They also knew that the stumbling blocks and the wonderful discoveries made along the way could not be duplicated by any other pastime.

The Major was our first guest on site. He strode through the etched glass doors with an effervescent smile on his face. He had a colleague with him, someone dressed in casual business wear, yet a man who also had the air of military authority about him. I got the feeling that those who had served in the forces for more than a few years had an incredibly strong network of people all over the country, in various disciplines. The Major actually was the person who put me in touch with the military memorabilia company in London when I was reuniting my antiques-fair photo find with its proper family. It was during this activity that I learned about the Major's extensive network.

The Major stood right in front of me now. He guided his friend beside him and introduced him with a wide grin. "Julie Fincher please meet 'Old Two Two', a valued member of the famed Twenty-Second Cheshire Regiment. He lives in London now and restores old military vehicles."

"How interesting. You must have a pretty large garage if you're working on troop transport vehicles and tanks."

We shook hands.

"Harvey Hartmore. Currently I have five vehicles inside a garage that I share with my son's autobody repair shop."

"Well, that's handy. Welcome to GGRS. How can we help you today?"

"I'm hoping to find a link to my ancestor who fought in the Boer War. Now, I've got some regimental information, but I'd like to know more about his wife because that's the line I'm following at present."

"You need to speak with Maude. It sounds like you're already well underway, but she can get you started with our computers and online research programs," I said.

"That will be lovely. Thank you."

The Major and Harvey went off, happy as honeybees in a blooming patch of yellow saxifrage.

"And Major?"

"Is there something else?" the military man said in an efficient, courteous tone as he turned to look at me.

"You still need permission from the board of trustees to park those army vehicles on site."

I was rewarded with a salute and mischievous grin. The men were up to something ... of that I was certain.

The next person to breeze in was none other than Ozzie Boggs, purveyor of the 'saggy bottom knocker', as he liked to call it.

"Mr. Boggs, welcome back," I said.

He looked like a man who wasn't taking any no's for answers today.

He grunted. "Morning."

I thought I saw an unexpected gap inside his mouth. But I wasn't sure, so I acted like there was nothing unusual. "One of our staff is ready to help you with the pottery-maker research you're after," I said, guiding him to a computer carrell.

"Good. Thanks." He tried to speak without moving his lips, almost like a ventriloquist.

Then I saw the unmistakable dark, cavernous gap again. I wasn't imagining things. Ozzie Boggs was now missing his two front teeth.

He noticed that I noticed. The ruse was up. He spoke with some difficulty, owing to the vast amounts of air that were now entering his mouth with every breath. "Er, I forgot my dental bridge. Didn't want to waste the petrol going back for it."

Any answer would require all the tact of an international diplomat.

I'm not aware of any regulation that requires GGRS visitors to wear a full set of teeth. Or dentures, for that matter.

Ozzie harrumphed.

"One of our staff team members would be quite happy to help you," I said.

"And this is all free, correct?" Ozzie shot me a beady-eyed look.

"Yes, use of this facility is free, but any specific resource ordering, such as certificates from record offices and archives, that is something that you would have to pay for."

Ozzie looked incredibly shocked. "You mean to tell me, with all that surrounds you, this great manor house, I still have to pay to find my ancestors?"

"We are run on donations, including a capital investment from my aunt's legacy. This isn't a government-funded institution."

"I would've expected more."

"I'm very sorry we don't stack up to your expectations, Ozzie," I said. This man was beginning to test my patience.

"I'll just leave it with you to give me a quote, and then I'll decide whether or not I want to continue," he said. There it was again, that focused stare, goading me to defy him. I had a hard time deciding what to look at, his angry round face or the gap in his teeth.

I shook my head. "You'll find that certificate prices vary, depending on the particular archives or government record office. We don't have a list because sometimes they change from year to year, and there are thousands of places you can order things from throughout the world."

"That's fine. I'm sure your experts can figure out where I need to get my certificates. Just tally it all up and then call me with the quote. We can go from there." He picked up a pencil and piece of notepaper lying on the information desk counter. He scribbled down his telephone number and email address. Then he handed it to me with a nod. "There you go. Just don't telephone me after eight o'clock. I like to watch the snooker from America."

I was rather taken aback. "I'm sorry, Ozzie, but I don't think you understand. We're not a research-on-demand, paid service. We provide the facility and staff to advise, but each guest does the actual research themselves."

"You mean you won't do it all for me? I was never very good in libraries."

"No, I'm afraid that's not how it works. If you want one-stop shopping, then perhaps you need to find a professional researcher. They usually charge by the hour, and you would have to sit down with them and explain your entire history in detail so they know where to start."

"Well, I'm only really interested in one line, and I heard that you people here could be trusted. I'm very disappointed that you're fobbing me off."

I was at a loss. This was most unexpected, because everyone else we had spoken to so far was thrilled just to have the facility to use. Other researchers certainly didn't expect someone to spend weeks and weeks doing someone else's genealogy research for free. I thought back to an earlier conversation where I was told 'we don't *need* all types, we just *have* all types'. This was how I got to move forward again with Ozzie Boggs.

"That's how it is here. You're welcome to stay, and a member of staff will help you get started, but we're not going to do it for you. You need to put in the sweat equity yourself."

"Kind of like learning the piano?" he asked with a grin on his face.

The attitude was starting to shift, finally. A few sentences prior I had run into an iceberg named Mr. Ozzie Boggs, an unyielding structure that tore my steel hull open foot by foot with its impertinence.

"Exactly," I said with a smile. "You can't expect to play well and explain the instrument to others if you're not willing to put in the rehearsal time. Why don't we set you up in the theater, where I can play the Introduction to Genealogy Research video?"

"I'd be starting at the very bottom, because I know nothing about this. All I have is a few names and scant rumors," Ozzie said, a furtive look on his face.

"A very popular response, and you're in good company. Please follow me."

Maude and Gertie silently clapped at me, of course well out of Ozzie's line of sight. I had just shown them how to maintain my cool while getting to the end goal without permanently ruffling any feathers. The reasons I was able to do that were simple. Number one, I had already survived a cheating ex-husband. Number two, I learned from a wonderful woman named Lady Edwina Greymore, one of the most diplomatic, elegant, and well-spoken people on the planet.

Yes, bring on more Ozzie Boggs personas, because I was ready to handle whatever came through those GGRS front doors.

Ozzie and I walked towards the theater. He darted looks at the computer carrells, bookshelves, posters about new software programs as well as the various breakrooms. "I grew up in pretty humble surroundings. In my village, a pedigree chart meant horses or dogs."

I smiled. "Well, here a pedigree chart means starting with yourself and working back through your parents, your grandparents, your great-grandparents etc., listing all of their births, marriages, and deaths as properly proven by your research. Assumptions and single sources for dates aren't good for correct genealogy research."

He harrumphed again. I hoped that there wasn't another volcano waiting to erupt. But I was pleasantly surprised when he slowed down to take a closer look at a poster showing an actual pedigree chart. He stopped right in front of it and put his fingers to the heavyweight paper. "I go back five generations on one line, but I'm stuck on my father's line."

"May I ask why the interest in getting your chart figured out, and that line especially?" I asked him as we walked down the sloped walkway inside the theater.

"It's my Great-Aunt Winifred's one hundredth birthday this year and I want to get greetings from the palace sent to her home in Hampshire. She's lived there all her life."

"Well, there's a number of sources we can get you started on, including internet research and the Hampshire archives. Sometimes archives will have pretty good resources posted online."

"Don't I have to look at Iggy?"

"I'm sorry?" This was a term I'd never heard before. "Are you perhaps referring to a long-lost relative, one who caught your interest in a family record?"

"No. Iggy. You know, the database of records." He was adamant.

"Oh, the International Genealogical Index. It's generally referred to as the 'I.G.I.' and used to be available on microfiche. That's old technology now and it's been replaced by online databases."

"I see," he said.

"Are you able to use a computer?" I asked.

"Of course. My great-aunt and I have a video chat most days at one o'clock after she's finished her smoked-kipper sandwich." He stood up straight, almost defiant.

The mental image of Ozzie Boggs sans front teeth, clickety-clacketing away at a laptop keyboard and chatting onscreen with his elderly aunt brought a wonderful smile to my face. It just went to prove that you could never judge a book by its cover.

I gave Ozzie a quick nod. "Excellent. We'll be able to get a lot done this afternoon. Why don't you sit and watch this twenty-minute introductory film and then come over to computer carrell number four. I'll make sure everything is set up for you and a staff member is ready to assist."

He reached out a tentative hand and shook mine again. "I'm sorry if I came in a bit too strong. I'm a little nervous about what I'll find going back in time with my family, and forgetting my teeth, well–"

"Say no more of it. Enjoy the film."

I pressed the 'play' button for the introductory film from the audio-visual database menu and came back out of the theater room, hearing the opening music start behind me. I headed over to the information desk to make sure we had a staff member hovering near carrell number four. Slightly difficult guests needed a bit more handholding than others.

I saw about eleven other visitors in the research site as I exited the theater room. There were murmured conversations happening all over the place, as well as some excited glances as people pointed to something fantastic that just popped up on their computer screen.

Gertie was explaining something to Harvey as the Major stood nearby. "ALS is short for 'alias' or 'aka'. You may actually have a criminal in your family tree."

Harvey looked quite upset. "I was worried about that."

The Major leaned over, concerned.

Gertie continued. "You know, we may think he has committed bigamy, however, if they just forgot the aka on the registration, then perhaps not. Transcribers make mistakes; that's why you need a couple of other sources to confirm before you leap to any definite or nefarious conclusions."

Everyone appeared to take this in with a great deal of serious thought.

Gertie nodded. "You should count yourself lucky if you have a criminal in your background. Because criminals, the very wealthy, and the very impoverished are the easiest ancestors to find."

"Because of all the paperwork that was kept on them?" Harvey asked.

"Exactly. And see here? It looks like this couple had five daughters. Go on the line of the youngest daughter, because she was normally tasked with staying home to look after aging parents. She would be the one who likely heard the discussions of family histories. These she could pass down to her descendants, as well as stories and paperwork found in the household."

"My sister has the family bible, and there are also a couple of files with some letters from our grandmother talking about her own grandparents," Harvey said.

"Treat those like gold. Or platinum," Gertie advised. "But just be careful. Again, prove it a few other ways because memories have the ability to change over time; events can be forgotten or enhanced depending upon the social situation."

The Major chortled. "In my family, we had an aunt saying that there was a fancy heirloom diamond-and-pearl necklace passed down from generation to generation. We finally tracked it down with a distant cousin. As it turned out, the necklace is made of paste and was part of a crown jewels replica museum exhibit back in the nineteenth century."

We all had a good, quiet smile together. It was apparent that correct research techniques were being used. People were also speaking in hushed voices, which kept noise to a minimum; this was important so as to not disturb others.

As I approached the front information desk, I walked into yet another genealogical crisis unfolding. I saw a well-dressed woman in her late thirties breeze in through the etched glass doors. She was one of those artsy types, the kind who wore gigantic paisley scarves, had a redhead tousled pixie cut plus used makeup in beiges and burnt oranges. She smiled through elegantly whitened teeth. She strode right up to the information counter as if she was on a specific mission. The staff member behind the desk greeted her pleasantly and listened. It took no more than a few sentences out of the woman's mouth before the staff member's face fell and she turned around, looking at me for rescue.

I intervened as quickly as I could.

Chapter 11

―

"Hello, I'm Julie Fincher, the founder of the research site. Can I help you?"

Our newest and windswept visitor replied with alacrity. "Yes, my name is Pamela Fulham. I understand you do genealogy research here?" Her ochre-painted nails drummed the countertop. She also carried an expensive, chain-strap designer leather bag that perfectly matched her coat.

"Yes, we do provide research facilities here. You're welcome to use them if you'd like to come in and sit down?"

"Oh no, I would just like you to print out my family tree. I've got a taxi running outside and was just hoping you could quickly do that for me."

Ah. The blissful ignorance of those not in the know about anything genealogical.

Apparently, obtaining one's complete, proven family tree was as easy as pressing the cappuccino button on our lunchroom coffee machine.

I was the lucky one tasked with informing our visitor that this was not the case.

I gave Pamela my best, least-tedious smile. "I'm afraid that's not quite how things work. Even going back on one line of the family tree can take months, if not years."

Pamela's face fell. A lot further down than I expected, like her jaw was going to hit her paisley scarf and sit there for a couple of weeks on holiday. "You mean, you don't just have them all stored in some central database?"

"We have databases of census records and parish registers and much more, but it's not all automatically assembled into family trees for every living person." As soon as I said this, I realized how fantastical it sounded. There wouldn't be a need for any Family History Society or even the GGRS if what Pamela assumed to be true actually existed.

Millions of people would need to find a new addictive, all-consuming hobby.

It would be utter chaos.

"So, I'd actually have to come in and do all this myself?" She sounded absolutely incredulous.

"Yes, that's how it's generally done, unless there is someone else keener in your family who wishes to take on the task. Or you could hire a professional." I was still making up my mind as to whether Pamela was just a nitpicky, lazy woman or if she genuinely didn't understand. I decided to give her the benefit of the doubt, like Aunt Edwina would want, and treat her with kindness and courtesy.

"Oh dear, this isn't what I expected at all. And my taxi's running ..."

I tried again. "Well, you're welcome to stay and start your research. You can always send your taxi away, and we'd be happy to call you a new one in a few hours if that would help?"

"It's just, it's just ..." And then completely out of the blue, Pamela broke down in tears.

I reacted swiftly and held out a hand. "Please follow me. We have a private breakroom that's not in use at the moment." I mouthed at the information desk staff to pay her taxi driver and send him away. At this point, it didn't matter to me; I would just treat it as an extraordinary researcher assistance operational expense.

Once we were ensconced in the private room, I offered Pamela a cup of tea and sat down in a comfortable chair opposite her, door closed. "We're very happy to help you get started. I know it can seem overwhelming but there's no reason to be stressed about it. Some people actually consider family history to be an intriguing hobby. They make lots of new friends and–"

"No. It's not that at all. You and your staff team here have been more than wonderful. It's just, well, my mother recently died and I'm clearing up her estate. I thought I could get a family tree together for the funeral in her memory. I know she was always interested but never had time to actually get one done. The funeral is in a few days, and I'm just at a loss without her. I'm going to miss her so much." Pamela cried some more, and I handed her the tissue box. When she composed herself, she took a few sips of tea and then looked at me, alarm in her eyes. "My taxi!"

"Never mind. We already paid the fare and sent him away. We'll get you another one when you're ready to go."

She dug in her purse for the taxi fare and handed £40 to me. "Here. It's more than enough, and please keep the change as a small donation. I cannot begin to thank you for your kindness. I literally thought this was a five-minute stop and I would be doing something so good for my mother and her memory. Now I suppose it's just another thing to add to my lengthy to-do list."

"Does she have a large estate to clear up? Because I can relate to that. My Aunt Edwina recently passed, and it was quite the undertaking to get all of her wishes and inheritances distributed." I did a brief reminiscence. Bertie had a connection to a quality building firm that owed him massive favors due to all the work he'd thrown their way over the years for Scotford Castle's constant conservation and upgrades work. As such, fifty tradespeople had descended upon Greymore Hall the minute the plans were approved by the local council, chaired by none other than, yes, Bertie and his group of community-minded friends, including Algy Holgarth and Maude Livingstone. Construction was completed in record time. We'd used local materials whenever possible to reduce our carbon footprint and also to support community businesses. This tactic sped up construction considerably, and the GGRS was built and opened in rapid fashion.

"This research site is what you created with your inheritance?" Pamela asked.

"Yes, indeed it is. It was a lifelong passion Aunt Edwina had. She really enjoyed doing genealogy research and also combined it with family history."

"I always thought they were the same thing."

"No. Family history involves more of the social history, crafts, and village happenings in one's past. We both found it fascinating, as do the GGRS staff and volunteers."

"It sounds like a very happy group here," Pamela said.

"It is. We're pretty proud of what we've accomplished already."

"So what do I do now?" Pamela looked at me through red eyes and a puffy face. She was a professional-type woman, likely some sort of administrator or accountant in an office somewhere. She dressed and spoke well, but the death of her mother had just taken all the stuffing out of her.

I wanted to help. I really did. "I would suggest starting with your living elderly relatives. Interview all of them and see what information they can tell you about your family. Also, gather together any family history documents you may have in your possession or that were in your mother's possession. Your relatives may have some items as well."

"I'm sure they do," she said.

"Ask them questions, make gentle requests for the documents, or copies of them if they don't wish to part with the originals. It is quite likely that somebody, somewhere, is already working on a branch of your family tree. Remember that online resources from reputable, safe organizations are great places to share research. Just make sure to check out their terms of service and privacy policies. And be aware that a family tree made on assumptions doesn't have a very strong set of roots."

By now, Pamela had put herself back together, courtesy of tea and a few swipes at her face with a tissue while she looked into a compact mirror. "What type of questions do I ask my relatives?"

"Get them to talk with you, particularly in person, about names, dates, and places. Ask them about family stories you've heard. If someone can prove to you, for example, that your great-grand-uncle was from Scotland, it saves you from searching in the wrong country."

"I suppose a photo album is helpful to get them to speak with me about their memories."

I nodded. "Chocolates and scones also work really well too."

As if on cue, Gertie came in, deposited two cups of tea and a package of cookies. She then beat a hasty retreat.

We laughed.

"It's good to see you smile again, Pamela. I'm very sorry for your recent loss."

"Thank you," she said, dabbing at her eyes with a tissue. "My mother and I were very close." She picked up one of the basic research pamphlets that I'd ensured were placed on every table throughout the entire research site. This particular one read 'Don't Believe Everything They Tell You' on the front. She flipped through it, and I saw her concentrate as she learned about relatives changing names of siblings, altering the number of siblings, fixing the occupations of their real parents to sound better than they were, concealing adoptions, forgetting black sheep, and much more.

"It appears to be quite a labyrinth drawing out a solid family tree," she observed.

"That's right, and it's truly part of the fun. I've lost count of the number of times I've read that a researcher had no idea his cousin immigrated to America to become a wealthy merchant. Or, better yet, their fourth great-grandfather was discovered to be a devious highwayman who was simultaneously married to three different women."

"No!"

"Yes." I grinned. "Things are much different even a mere century in the past. It's not like we had any control over what our ancestors did. All we can do is find out the truth, and if you don't agree with something in their life, try to improve it for the next generation."

"It looks like I have some serious homework to do," Pamela said.

"Remember, it can sound rather brutal timewise, but all these research tactics are definitely a means to an end."

"And once I've spoken with both my elderly relatives? It's a fairly small family, and I only have one uncle and one aunt left. All my grandparents have passed away and I'm an only child."

"Then we get into the birth, marriage, and death civil registrations, census records, parish registers, and probate. All for another day."

Pamela stood up and brushed off a couple of the biscuit crumbs from her skirt. Somehow through our talk we'd gotten into the packet of shortbread cookies Gertie had silently deposited on the table beside us as I was trying to console Pamela.

We were all working together seamlessly, staff and volunteers. And that's how I wanted it to be. If someone was in trouble, then we should dive in and help. If someone was having a bad day, we should try and cheer them up. Because what I'd found through my initial foray into family history, and all that I learned over the years from my beloved aunt, was that learning about the past made the present and the future less scary. It gave people a sense of connection, not only to their specific ancestral past, but also to their present group of family and friends. If you understood the history of an area, then you understood more about the people who lived there today. That was such a warm, comforting feeling, one that I never wanted to let go.

"Thank you so much for your kindness. I think I'll go home now," Pamela said.

"I'll have someone at the information desk call a taxi for you. Whereabouts are you headed?"

"Oh, I just live in Plumsden. It's a house a few streets away from the grammar school. Right on the border of urban and rural living."

"Lovely. Plumsden is a very nice area. Many of us here have friends from that area. Ewan, you saw him out front helping the man wearing the green shirt?"

"Yes, I remember seeing him."

"He owns and operates Kilburn's Outstanding Antiques in Plumsden. Couple of doors away from the Family History Society."

"Wait. Is his shop next door to the law office?"

"Why, yes, it is," I said.

"Well, I never. My lawyer is right beside him. I have a beautiful Persian cat, you see, she's in commercials and films. Fred Todling handles all her business contracts and makes sure no one steals her likeness."

"How on earth do you steal a cat's likeness?" I asked. This was perplexing.

"Here, I'll show you," Pamela said, bringing out her mobile phone. She scrolled through a few screens and then brought up a picture of a gorgeous white Persian cat. It was immediately apparent why she wanted to protect everything about this curious feline. For although the cat was snowy white and had amassed a long, perfectly groomed coat, there was one thing quite exceptional about this pet. In the middle of its forehead, unlike anything I'd ever seen before, was a distinctive black question mark, right down to the separation between the tail of the curl and the period underneath.

"My goodness. What an unusual marking," I said.

"That's what the breeder said. They told me it was a genetic defect and they couldn't use her in shows. I got her at a discount when she was just a kitten. As she grew, the mark only became more distinctive. Now she earns five figures every time she's on television."

"What's her name?"

Pamela smiled and then she laughed. "My cat's name is Answer."

Chapter 12

Next Day. 8:00 a.m.

"I need to wear more comfortable shoes," Gertie moaned to me as we did our rounds of the large research site ten minutes before opening to the public.

"How long can you stay?" I asked.

"Another fourteen days. My new youth ministering job starts Monday fortnight. In the meantime, I'm supposed to create a new video warning church youth I'm back on their trail."

"Meaning?"

"Meaning, I need to record something short and sweet to post online. So far I've just posted tamer things like Bertie's grand-opening speech and a video of Lance feeding the rabbits at Holgarth's petting zoo."

"Really, Gertie. More videos?"

"Yup. Got to keep the youth engaged," she said. "Don't worry. No more unplanned karaoke, though."

"Thank goodness for that."

I went over to unlock the door and there stood my worst nightmare.

My ex.

Chris Undermead. Recently apprehended in remote Scotland for pilfering lobster traps where he thought Aunt Edwina's treasure was hidden. He sported a fading red mark across his nose, no doubt from wrangling a lobster without sufficient dexterity or skill.

My father stood right beside Chris, seething. "Found this recalcitrant standing here like a bump on a log a few minutes ago."

Chris looked as though he wished a hole would open up in the floor and swallow his entire body.

"Good morning," I said in a halting voice. I looked straight at Chris, using my very best strong, steely gaze, or at least that's what I hoped to project.

Dad had a few more choice words for my philandering ex. "Need any stolen crustaceans or broken commitments? The perfect candidate's standing right beside me." Dad pushed past us and disappeared inside the research site, muttering something about needing to sit down because his sciatica was bothering him.

Good one, Dad.

"Um, hello, Julie," Chris said.

"Chris." There was nothing else I wanted to say to this dishonest man. Thank goodness Gertie wasn't licensed when she married us; my annulment was preceded by an invalid ceremony, so that scrape was gratefully avoided.

I didn't know how to conquer being so mortified. The last time I'd spoken with Chris, it sounded like it was going to be the last time he was ever in my life. I was to send his belongings to his parents' house, and then he would start again without me after he had cleared up his Scottish legal woes.

Unfortunately, that appeared to have happened much earlier than expected.

"I just wanted to pay back what I owed you, all the two-pound coins that were in Gertie's suitcase I stole with her van." He looked at me with pleading, puppy dog eyes, the kind that he got when he was being a leech.

"Couldn't you just mail me a check or do an e-transfer?" I asked Chris. After all he put me through, the last thing I wanted to do was have another conversation with this man.

He shook his head. "Judge's community service order. She mandated an in-person apology."

"I see."

Just then, Ewan strode into the main entrance and saw my dilemma. He came right over and put himself squarely between us. "Is there a problem here?"

"No problem. I'm just here to give Julie back her money. Well, rather Gertie's money." Chris looked nervous and placid.

"Julie, do you need help?" Ewan asked.

"I ... I ..." I started, flailing for words.

Ewan immediately seized control of the situation. I'd never seen him appear so strong or tall. "Chris, Julie doesn't have the time or the stomach to deal with you. Give me your money. I'll make sure she gets it. Is that alright, Julie?" Ewan gave me a firm look.

I swooned a little inside. If the men were pasta, Chris would be soggy overcooked and Ewan firm al dente.

"Fine by me. Thank you." I turned on my heel and strode back inside the research site, trying to keep it together. I had way better things to do with my time than deal with the one person who had toyed with my heart and then stomped on it, crushing it into tiny little pieces. It was only through kind friends and family that I'd recovered from the wedding disaster. I was determined that Chris would not ever dig up those horrible, buried memories.

Five minutes later Ewan was back, certified check in hand. "He dropped off £802 and I made him promise never to contact you again."

"You are my hero. Thank you."

Ewan looked serious then chuffed with himself. "How you ever got hooked up with him in the first place, Julie ... One of the world's greatest mysteries."

"I'm all for turning over a new leaf, but with Chris Undermead, boy, I need to turn over an entire log." I laughed.

Our eyes held and there was a moment. There had been several moments like this ever since I met Ewan. He was a kind man, and I could feel the attraction between us was just as strong as when we first discussed postcards and antiques. I suppose what kept things in slow-motion was the incredible heartbreak Chris had put me through. I just wasn't ready to jump into anything else at present. I didn't think it would be fair on my mind or heart to ask for anything more at this particular time. Right now I was perfectly content with friends, family, and a successful grand opening. I was glad that my father and Maude were well settled in their new suites. I was ecstatic that the research site was open to the public and starting to prove its mettle as a family history powerhouse.

"I hope I didn't overstep any boundaries. That guy just needs to leave you alone," Ewan said.

"I was glad you were there. Chris kind of had me speechless. You know when you see an ex and you really are done with them and don't have anything left to say? It's pretty hard to come up with anything that rolls off the tongue. Of course, I can think of zillions of fabulous comeback lines an hour later."

"If it helps, you could unleash them on me, just to get it out of your system," he offered.

I smiled. Ewan really was a good person.

"I'm here for you, if and when you need me." Ewan looked deep into my eyes and then closed the door behind him. We stood alone in the newsletter-creation office and there was no one else around. "I meant what I said, Julie. Just save me a place for when you're ready for something more."

"I'm worried you won't wait that long," I said, spreading my hands wide in frustration. "You see, I'm just not ready for a new relationship."

"Julie, I live in Plumsden, not exactly the grandest metropolis of the world. My life consists of running my antiques shop and volunteering here at the research site. Oh, I also eat, sleep, and go cycling for exercise." He gave me a kind smile again. "In other words, where am I going to go?"

I shook my head. "I don't know. You seem to have friends from all over."

"You've been to a couple of antiques fairs with me already. Most of the women there are late fifties and up, plus happily married. Or happily divorced and staying that way."

I was silent, contemplating the handsome, kind man in front of me, wondering why I was dallying. Overcautious, perhaps. Scared to mess it up again.

"Right now, all I ask is that I'm first in line when you're ready. Being friends is fine with me for now."

"But for how long?" It was a question I'd asked myself multiple times over the last few weeks. It wasn't like Ewan was exceedingly wealthy or came with a grand aristocratic title. However, he was kind, strong, soft-hearted, smart, and definitely one of the good guys. No other woman had snapped him up yet. I wondered why.

"Why aren't you with somebody already? You seem pretty normal to me," I said.

"Normal. I suppose that's a compliment coming from someone who's just dealt with Ozzie Boggs," he teased.

"Yes, I know the missing teeth and free-genealogy-research-expectations story has made the rounds. Where on earth Ozzie got that impression from, I don't know."

Both of us chuckled over that one.

I looked at Ewan, a bit tentative. "I like you, Ewan. But where do we go from here? You know how I hate awkward."

"There is nothing awkward about being friends. The more you think about this, the more awkward it's going to be. So just let life unfold," he counseled.

"Sometimes I wish I was born two hundred years ago when life was far simpler," I said. "Long courting walks, a suitor formally asking a father for a woman's hand ... so romantic."

"No question of swiping left or right, what an online profile looks like, or how embarrassing your latest post was on social media. Whatever happened to the innocent days that Edwina and Elliot had, walking outside near their favorite hollow oak tree and lilac forest?"

"Those days are long gone, my friend." I gave him a happy smile. "Now let's get back to work."

***

"You mean I need to kill them all off?" Ozzie Boggs looked quite shocked at the mere suggestion. Were we standing in a modern police detachment, I would worry. Instead, I was at Ozzie's computer carrell, listening to Gertie instructing him how to do his genealogy properly.

Gertie was far from finished with him yet. "Of course you do. If you can't prove that your ancestor died, you're missing something about their past. Perhaps one went to America, one married again, one died of something odd. If they disappeared from the record, you need to explain why. Consider the child who died at a very young age and therefore couldn't have married twenty years later. If you run across two people with the same name, then you'll understand which one isn't your ancestor."

"Perhaps the parents gave the next child the same name as the deceased one?" Ozzie said in a hopeful voice.

"That's right. It's a strong possibility and it happened quite often. Logic and common sense go a long way."

Gertie's pupil moved his cursor around on the computer screen, dutifully taking all of this in. She had Ozzie well in hand now and gave me the thumbs-up sign.

"So how do I get back on the ancestral line I'm after?" Ozzie asked.

"You get the certificates and work your way through the records. Just keep these dates in mind. In England, there are no death records prior to 1837, just burial records. So before 1837, one has christenings, marriages, and burials, aka CMB. From July 1, 1837, after an Act of Parliament, the government recorded births, marriages, and deaths, aka BMD. There are online indexes of these BMDs, and you purchase the certificates containing the details from the General Register Office."

"Some of those church registers are pretty messed about, aren't they?"

Gertie nodded. "I once read about a vicar using his old seventeenth century registers as fire-starter strips because he thought no one would ever want records that were centuries old."

Ozzie clucked his tongue, easy today because he had his teeth back in, then he shook his head. "It's a travesty. I need to get back to the seventeenth century. It's important on this particular line."

By now, I was curious about all this furtive activity. Ozzie started shuffling through the folder of paperwork he'd obviously brought from home. All of a sudden, a single page with a colorful heraldic crest slipped out. It floated out behind him, like a misbehaving feather cruising on the wind, and landed at my feet.

I picked it up, intensely curious. "Do you have royalty or aristocracy in your ancestry?"

"Here, give me that, please," was Ozzie's gruff reply as he held out a hand for his paper. He didn't answer my question.

I looked at Gertie and shrugged. Time to move on.

Maude came up to me, a couple of opened postal parcels in her hand. "We just received two new books for the Family History Society to review. One's a really good one on beginner research, going through the basics of civil registration, census records, parish registers, and probate. The other one showcases railway history. I'll get two of our trustees to review one each and then we can publish the write-up in the next quarterly magazine."

"That's a great idea. Members love reading about new genealogy and family history books."

"One of the authors is doing a free book giveaway contest. That would be a great repost on our social media channels."

"I agree." We'd hired a part-time student to handle our social-media work. We knew it was very important to get the news and messages out to the public, and students were the most in-the-know about what was popular and what was not. I was certainly not, however, ready to let Gertie loose with our passwords. She definitely had a large following; however, I didn't think the GGRS wanted to be known for viral karaoke videos. Perhaps there was some other type of video that we could develop to entice the younger generation into family history. We were always looking for new recruits.

I heard a scuffle at the side of the room. Specifically, it emanated from the fourth computer carrell. I saw Ozzie Boggs frown, push his chair back from the counter, and throw his hands up in the air. There was no denying he was a gesticulating researcher, someone who made the highs and lows as obvious as an actor on stage.

I hurried over. "Ozzie, whatever is the matter?"

He turned to me and looked exasperated. "I've just found my great-aunt's marriage, but not in the parish she said it was in."

"Well, family history research can present you with all sorts of surprises."

"But that's not all of it. The marriage record shows her as only twenty-one years old."

"Marriage record or marriage index done by a transcriber?" I asked. "Careful, because perhaps the transcriber only wrote twenty-one, whereas the marriage certificate said over twenty-one."

He harumphed. "It's the actual marriage certificate."

"Alright, just checking."

He continued. "She told me she was married when she was twenty-nine. If I find her birth certificate and it confirms this date is correct, then she's not turning a hundred this year. She's only turning ninety-two."

I rocked back on my heels ever so slightly. Ozzie had just uncovered one of those lovely gems that gave one massive pause for thought.

It didn't look like he knew what to do next.

"I suppose that kiboshes your hundredth birthday party plans for Great-Aunt Winifred?" I said it in the kindest tone I could muster.

"I can't believe this is true. We were so looking forward to celebrating."

"She may have had good reason for disguising her age and then just forgot over time. Over the years, men and women have both aged themselves up on purpose to either qualify for military service, ensure the vicar would let them marry, enable them to get out of the household because they were of legal age and more. The reasons go on and on."

"I'm just appalled," he said.

I shrugged. "Perhaps look at it this way. At least you have eight years to get more research done and prepare for the party."

He cocked his eyebrow at me and sighed. "I suppose that's looking at the positive side of things."

"You see that poster over there, the one about busting through brick walls? At least you have found the information as opposed to being told that all the records were burnt up in a fire when the building was bombed in the Blitz."

"Small mercies, small mercies ..." He gave me a weary look, and somehow I knew there was more to his research quest than Ozzie Boggs was letting on to anybody here at the GGRS.

Chapter 13

One Week Later.

"You've done it already?" I asked Pamela as she stood in front of me, carrying a slightly battered wooden box that looked suspiciously like something to house fancy, silver-hallmarked cutlery.

She nodded, a bit more rapidly than expected, given her intense enthusiasm. "I only have two elderly relatives, and they were both able to meet with me last week after I came here for the first time. So, I've now got two separate three-hour interviews with each of them in a digital file. My husband is getting them transcribed as we speak. I also took notes as we went and learned some absolutely amazing things about my family history."

"And the box?"

"That is the best part of it all. Is there an office where I can show you what my uncle gave me?"

"Sure, let's go into our chat room." I caught her eye. "That's our insider joke."

"I know, you had me in there before."

"Oh, that's right. I'm sorry, the past week has been such a blur. We've seen over two hundred visitors come through our doors in the last few days, so it's been nonstop. All good, mind you. That's what we wanted."

I did take a bit of quiet pleasure in how well the research site was perceived by the community. The fact that we'd had so many visitors in our first few opening days told me that we were on the right track. And keep in mind, those were only the researchers. The research site's numbers didn't account for the tour groups that only came through to see the lovely furnishings and gardens of Greymore Hall itself. My overall goal was to make the entire facility, including the research site, self-sufficient. I didn't want to have to keep dipping into my capital to fund it. Capital was a nest egg there only for emergencies, and my banker agreed. If we could generate enough revenue each year to maintain ourselves and pay our staff, then we had it made in the shade. To that end, I'd installed a donation box near the site's entrance, a high-traffic area.

Maude and Ewan looked at Pamela and I expectantly. Any time a secret or unexpected closed box was brought in, it piqued the curiosity of all of those around it.

I gestured towards the others. "Pamela, do you mind if these two join us? I'd like to prevent my door from caving in due to them leaning on it to eavesdrop."

Everybody laughed.

The hungry stares from Maude and Ewan were back.

"Of course, be my guest," Pamela said. "It is quite exciting."

There were relieved looks from my colleagues.

"I think we better go into the meeting room. Much more table space," Maude suggested.

"Good idea."

We all trooped down past the tidy shelves, posters, computer carrells, and cabinets. Once we were all inside the meeting room, Pamela gently laid her box down on the table and opened the lid. We all peered inside and saw that the box contained a jumble of assorted family relics and heirlooms. It was a wonderful mixture of fascinating trinkets, yellowed documents, official-looking papers, and much more.

"I can tell that this is quite a treasure trove for your family," Ewan said. "Who gave it to you?"

"My uncle, actually. My mother's younger brother. He said it was about time that I had it and knew the truth. Then he told me that's what my mother said to tell me after she was gone. And that's all he knew."

"Your mother told him nothing else?" I asked, dumbfounded.

"I don't even know what family generation these items match. Apparently, it was passed down from one woman on my mother's line, but I don't know how far back it goes. I've never done any of this type of research before."

Maude took charge. She stood up straight, squared her shoulders, and spoke. "Right. Let's take everything out of the box and lay it out on the table. We can catalogue everything and then hopefully things will start to make sense."

"I volunteer to get on the whiteboard," Ewan offered. He picked up a black dry-erase marker and uncapped it, standing poised next to the vast new and shiny writing surface.

Pamela reached inside for the first item and then looked up at us. "I feel like I'm drawing the numbers for the lottery," she said with excitement.

"It may be just that for your family tree research," Maude said. "I met a researcher years ago who had a sailor's chest that contained the secret to finding out where a precious family painting was stored. Turns out the painting was worth over £500,000 and saved the descendent from near bankruptcy."

"Amazing," Pamela murmured. "Well, I'm sure there's nothing like that in here. It just appears to be a bunch of family memorabilia. I did a quick sort through and didn't find any enormous diamonds or gold nuggets. There is one pretty ring, though."

"Often times, family memories are worth far more than expensive baubles. The letters my Aunt Edwina left me are priceless to me," I said.

Pamela looked at all of us, a sheepish grin on her face. "I do want to apologize for being so clueless when I came in last week. I really had no idea what I was doing. I'm sure all of you had a good laugh after I left."

I shook my head. "That's not what this research site is about. Family history can get overwhelming if you don't know where to start. We're here to help and to understand."

Pamela smiled, grateful. "I certainly appreciate what you've done for me already. And now look at where it's led ... to this wonderful treasure box." Pamela dipped her hand inside the box and took out the first object. Followed by another. And another still ...

When she was done removing items, Ewan had a list on the whiteboard that read like this:
- Black bowtie
- Pair of new silk stockings from America
- Luggage receipt signed with porter's name, Ned Smythe

- Photo of five army men in barracks, standing in front of the canteen
- Small unknown tool, well-used
- Ostrich feather dyed pink
- Letter from a man named Richard to a woman named Sylvie, telling her his love for her and how they must separate if he's ever discovered
- Picture of a handsome man and pretty woman labeled on the back in brown fountain-pen ink: *Richard and Sylvie*
- Boarding house visitor book page, blank
- Silver sphinx ornament engraved *From a grateful company, Major Donoughan*
- Military medals
- Ticket stub to a Cairo cabaret
- Ring with a ruby and sapphire inscribed with 'I will return to you' on the inner band
- Receipt from Francine's Matrimonial Bureau: 'Tasteful Matchmaking for the Discreet' printed in fancy script at the top. Proprietor Francine Winloame.

We all sat contemplating the items Ewan had listed on the whiteboard. It was a rough assemblage of lives past, a bygone era that was starting to unfold before our eyes.

Ewan left his scribe's post and went over to pick up the cabaret ticket stub, bowtie, and stockings. He arranged them in a delicate pile and then looked at us. "Sounds like a fun evening out. All that's left to do now is look for a birth certificate about nine months later."

I happened to be sitting the closest and elbowed him in the ribs.

"Oooph," Ewan replied with surprise. "Perhaps I deserved that."

Pamela laughed. "I wouldn't be surprised, looking at this collection. There was obviously quite a romance here between a military man and a dancer. Put them in the middle of a war and I'm sure sparks flew."

✳✳✳

One Hour Later.

"Do you mind if I go back to the theater room and watch the beginners' video over again?" Ozzie asked. "With all these results, I'm just wondering if I'm doing something wrong?"

"How about we set you up with the beginner followed by the intermediate film?" I said. "You do have to learn to trust yourself after a while, and just accept the fact that those darned ancestors don't always turn out the way you'd hoped."

He spluttered. "But ... but I now have four generations of thieves in my family! I found a highwayman, followed by a petty thief, followed by a jailed vandal and a lottery ticket forger! My family cannot be ne'er-do-wells. They simply just cannot."

"Sometimes we're dealt a different hand of cards from what we expect, Ozzie. It's nothing to be ashamed of, it's simply your history," I counseled.

"Thank goodness a man can choose his friends," he said in a dejected voice.

"Come on, I'll set you up in the theater room."

Once Ozzie was safely ensconced in his leather chair, a glass of soda and ice in his hand, I returned to the main room. Maude and Ewan stood there, watching, looking expectant for any reaction on my face. "Ozzie doesn't believe it. He's doubting his research because the records don't match what his family told him."

"I assure you, our staff have spent hours with him making sure that he's following all the right protocols," Maude said.

Ewan chimed in. "And he was wearing his reading glasses the whole time. I checked."

"He needs time to process the fact that his ancestors were criminals. Perhaps his parents told him that he came from a long line of wealthy merchants. Put yourself in his shoes and you can understand what kind of a shock it is."

"At least he didn't find out he has secret siblings," Maude said. "Back in Plumsden, we had one researcher in the society's reading room who discovered she had three half-brothers all living within fifteen miles of her home."

"Well, that's not so bad," Ewan said. "Maybe they'll all get on like a house on fire."

Maude winced. "Not when there is a significant inheritance involved and the courts were just about to confirm her as the sole heir."

"Oh dear," Ewan and I both said at the same time.

"She had to sell her convertible and Italian villa to pay them out."

"You mean–" Ewan started.

"She went shopping before her bank account was topped up."

"Ouch."

※※※

Two Hours Later.

I opened the theater door and was unexpectedly faced with a boisterous documentary film about the history of the tank. Deafening booms and explosions. Flames were launched and boulders blown apart. Creaking metal tracks sliced through thick, sticky mud in warfare. The Major, Ewan, and Harvey all sat right up close to the screen, three abreast and glued to their seats. When the tank tossed out its latest ammunition and blew up a straw bale target a quarter of a mile away, all three men cheered and exchanged high-fives.

"Gentlemen, what would Aunt Edwina say?" I called out during a lull in the intense cacophony.

"This is genealogy research. My uncle drove one of these!" Harvey yelled back as the action picked up again.

"I suggest you get busy on your red binder research, Ewan," I said.

Ewan looked chagrined at first. Then he brightened. "But I did go through the red binder. That's how we got onto this film. It was referred to in the floorboard records." He said it to me with all innocence on his face.

"From the eighteenth century?" I said. Now my hands were on my hips.

"They weren't all records from the eighteenth century," the Major added, injecting a note of serious legitimacy to the story.

"Why do I not believe any of you three?" It was quite hilarious. The men, one in his thirties, the other two in their late fifties, sat tightly packed together, looking like seven-year-olds with freshly scrubbed faces and completely innocent looks. At this point I'd have bet they all wore clean underpants to boot.

"Stay and watch with us," Ewan suggested.

"Um, no thanks. I have important work to do with some census records," I said.

"But we're just getting to the best part," Harvey said. He pointed at the screen, and we all watched twenty tanks climb a tall hill and come down over the other side.

"Sorry, boys, you're on your own with this one."

As I left the theater, amidst this incredibly loud film, I saw Ozzie Boggs fast asleep in the back row.

Back outside, I told Maude and Gertie. "I think Ozzie's genealogied out for today," I said to them.

Maude smiled. "Let him be. There's still two hours to go until closing time."

Chapter 14

Next Day.

Maude's gasp was audible to all those nearby. It was quickly followed by her rapid crossing of the carpet then leaning over Ozzie Boggs's computer carrell.

I swiftly gestured to Gertie. "This ought to be good!"

We were like two squirrels perching on a log as we watched Maude unleash her diplomatic diatribe at our unusual guest.

"Sir, you absolutely cannot eat here in the computer room. We have a lunchroom for that. No food. No drinks. Not even a stick of chewing gum is permitted. It is a policy implemented by the board of trustees and is on the researcher code of conduct you signed to gain facility access when you first arrived."

Maude wasn't kidding when she said that this was her pet peeve at any library, archives, or research facility.

Ozzie looked up, quite shocked at her tone. This was Maude, president of the Plumsden Family History Society and all-around good egg who loved helping researchers. But bring a stick of carrot or a crumb of cookie into your workspace at her research facility and you had an instant problem.

"I'm sorry. I got so caught up in my research I completely forgot. I'll put my sandwich away." Ozzie was like a little boy caught putting a frog on his teacher's desk.

Gertie and I giggled, loudly enough to attract the attention of other researchers. When the disapproving look was sent our way, we pretended to be deeply interested in a long screed of poor law legalese that Maude had left on the information desk. Truth be told, it was the remains from helping another researcher earlier in the day.

Maude stormed back over to us, checking that Ozzie was indeed moving his fishy food items into the lunchroom. "Can you believe it? They all sign the code of conduct when they arrive. Why do we even bother? The rules are there to be observed, not to be broken."

"We agree," Gertie said. "You did the right thing."

"Do people not understand how pests are attracted to precious archival paper and photographs even by a single breadcrumb?"

Gertie and I nodded, in complete agreement.

"There's a reason why the code of conduct exists. It's so we can maintain the facilities in proper order for everyone," I said.

"After all the time I spent with that man," Maude said, still upset with what she'd had to mediate. "I need a cup of tea."

"Um, one thing?" Gertie said with a tentative voice. "Remember tea is made in the same room where Ozzie is currently eating his lunch."

"Oh, I couldn't handle smelling a smoked-mackerel sandwich right now. I'm going up to my suite for a fifteen-minute break."

I went over to hold the door for Maude. She exited, heading for the elevator that would take her to the fourth floor. As she left, Jacques entered.

"Ladies, how are you?" he asked in his French accent.

"It's been an interesting day, Jacques," I replied. "How are things at the back of the house?"

"I am very pleased with our two new chefs. All our front-line staff are now quite competent in the café."

"No doubt due to your good instruction and management," Gertie complimented him.

Jacques gave her a smile. He wasn't one to preen after receiving praise. "I am just providing what I promised to deliver." He turned to me with an expectant look. "You wished to see me, Julie?"

"Oh, right. Yes, there are two motions from the board of trustees meeting that I have to show you." I wrestled through some papers at the information desk and brought out the meeting minutes binder. "Here we are," I said, flipping to the correct pages.

Jacques took the binder from me and whipped out reading glasses that he perched on the end of his nose. He read carefully:

> *Motion #1: To allow a yet-to-be-named fifty-five-plus walking group formal use of the trails at Greymore Hall for exercise between the hours of 6:00 a.m. and 9:00 a.m., seven days a week.*
> *Motion passed with unanimous consent.*
>
> *Motion #2: To permit the Military Geniuses Club to exhibit a World War Two restored tank in the north*

field of Greymore Hall in conjunction with a related exhibition in the main floor museum complex.
Motion passed with unanimous consent.

I had already spoken with the Major about no tank parts being cleaned in the research site kitchen sink. Any oil runoff was to be collected by a special absorbent pad placed underneath the machine to catch any stray drips. The Major had assured me this was no problem and that they would not let their commander-in-chief (me) down.

Jacques looked back at me. "I see."

"No comment?" I said, awaiting a diplomatic barrage of concern from the proper little man.

"Julie, I am in complete agreement with the walking group using the trails. However, a tank in the north field?"

"I know, I know. I just thought because Aunt Edwina's Elliot flew an airplane, also a big machine in World War Two, and because we are exhibiting war memorabilia here in a special exhibit at Greymore ... Well, saying yes just made sense."

"I would highly recommend we check our liability insurance plus that of the military club."

"They assure me everything will be fine. They've got an expert restorer who's worked on it. They plan to drive it in, park it for the exhibit, and then drive it away when the exhibition is finished."

"Just like that? So easy?" Jacques sounded quite incredulous.

"I'll check the insurance. I promise."

Jacques then stood there, showing me a rather curious look on his face.

"Was there something else, Jacques?" I asked.

"Well, there is one other thing. More of a bit of information I thought you might wish to know."

"Yes?"

"Chris Undermead is now the manager of the former Fizzleywick Hotel in Carlingheath. The new owners have renamed it, and also downgraded it to a three-star facility."

Gertie and I exchanged a quick look. The Fizzleywick Hotel held bad memories for me. It was where Aunt Edwina passed away and also where my tainted wedding vows took place.

Gertie was the one brave enough to speak first. "That sounds exactly like the right place for him."

Jacques issued a small smile. "I was hoping that would be how you felt."

***

I caught Ozzie staring at a poster that said 'Free Wi-Fi On Site'. He turned to me.

"Can I use your network to download some emails on my phone?" he asked.

"Well, it's really only supposed to be for genealogy research."

"How about we just leave it as our little secret?" He gave me a surreptitious smile.

"Mis-ter Boggs! We're not here to facilitate other non-family history business or vast downloads of unrelated information."

"Oh, I just need some information for my accountant, that's all. It is all related, because I had to pay for some photocopying at a record office and those are a part of the expense summary he's sending me."

I was reminded yet again by my sixth sense telling me that there was likely much more to Mr. Boggs than met the eye.

"Let me show you something," he said. We went over to his favorite computer carrell, number four, and he opened yet another one of his manila file folders. "This is my birth certificate, my parents' birth, marriage, and death certificates, as well as those for both sets of my grandparents."

I was stunned that he had this much information. "Why didn't you show all of this to us before?"

"I wanted to see if you lot knew what you were doing here first."

"Whatever do you mean?"

"I can't risk this getting spread around. And I don't want to get misled." And that was as far as he would go with it.

I chalked it up to him being an odd man, and there was no reason for me to pry further. I was just happy that at the present moment he wasn't eating at his carrell or falling asleep in the theater room.

Ozzie flipped through some other curled bits of paper in the file. "Unfortunately, this one is on ancient thermal fax paper and all the type on it has faded away."

"The way around that is to photocopy it," I said.

"Of course, before it fades," he said, emitting a small grin. "Oh, and one more thing. I do have this photo of my distant uncle." He hauled out a picture of a scruffy-looking man, likely in the early 1900s, sitting on a bicycle and smoking a pipe. The man looked like a vagabond with a tattered flat cap and torn clothes. He had a mischievous look on his face and for some reason was carrying a canvas bag full of metal pots and pans.

"What is he doing?" I asked.

"Collecting old pots and pans. He'd go around and ask all the housewives during the day if they had any old metal to get rid of. He collected them up, doing them a favor, and then sold them on for scrap. They called him 'Gregory the Gatherer.'"

"So you've got another sketchy ancestor?" I couldn't resist. After all, Ozzie had taken such incredible offense to finding out that he had criminals in his ancestral past. Perhaps it was a bit forward of me, but after his antics in our research site, I considered us beyond mere pleasantries.

Once again, Ozzie looked a bit dejected. "At least he tried to make an honest living."

I smiled. "Think of it this way. If you think your family is descended from royalty, then all you'll prove is that your family's actually gone downhill."

He thought on it for a minute and nodded. "There might be something in that."

I heard somebody turn on the intercom. The initial static as they began to talk was unmistakable:

> *"Would the owner of a dark-grey pickup truck please attend to their vehicle in the parking area? Repeat, would the owner of a dark-grey pickup truck please attend to their vehicle. Thank you."*

How perfectly British. Perfunctory and polite. There were about fifteen other people in the research site, but my money was on one in particular. I looked at Ozzie and he was already heading out the door. All of us rushed over to the window to see what was going on outside. There in the parking lot was Ozzie's pickup truck, its open bed completely filled with black plastic trash bags. Seven noisy crows hopped about on top of the bags, tearing open the plastic. One crow held a rather greasy-looking piece of tin foil in its beak. Another one was holding up a crumpled, shiny bag from a packet of crisps.

"Whatever on earth is he doing bringing all that rubbish here?" I asked no one in particular.

"Watch and learn. He knows what day of the week it is," Gertie said.

"Day of the week? What does that have to do with anything?" I was completely kerflummoxed.

Then I saw Ozzie get in his truck and drive over to meet the larger, lime-green vehicle that just entered the site. Our rubbish pickup service had arrived and sure enough, Ozzie followed in his pickup, smooth-talked the driver, then tossed his own plastic bags into the open back receptacle of the larger truck.

"Doesn't he have bin pickup at his home?" Gertie asked.

Ewan shook his head. "He lives in a rural area. I saw his address on one of the family record sheets he was working on. I doubt they have regular pickup service. He likely has to drive his rubbish to a dump and pay a tipping fee."

"Yet another free service the GGRS is providing to Ozzie Boggs."

Ewan laughed. "You have to give him points for creativity."

I bristled. "I'd like to give him points for something else. Imagine driving your trash to a research facility, inviting a pack of crows–"

"Murder. It's actually called a murder of crows," Gertie corrected.

"Whatever." Then it hit me. "You know, if we hadn't called Ozzie out to the parking lot, I wonder if he was going to say anything about using our waste-removal service. I mean, how long has this been going on for?"

"Likely as long as he's been coming here. The driver's his pub buddy," Ewan explained.

"That's just dandy."

For the first time since we opened, I was starting to wonder if we could ban certain people from the premises like pubs did with rowdies.

Chapter 15

Pamela sat with Maude and I in the breakroom to chat. "You need to have a goal, pick the ancestral line you want to follow," Maude advised.

"That's easy. I want to go back on Sylvie's line. She's my mother's ancestor, and looking at all the things we just found in this box, I'm keen to know how it's all connected. Also, who was this man named Richard?"

I sat and listened, because I knew Maude had been at this for thirty years compared to my scant few months of basic training. I had bootcamp; however, Maude had all the badges and stripes. It was good for me to hear Maude help another guest develop their research plan.

Maude continued. "You must keep going on the birth, marriage, and death certificates. Once you are back before 1911, then we'll go to the decennial censuses, 1911, 1901, 1891 etc."

"And is that all online?" Pamela asked.

"Yes. There are just a few things you need to remember. Before 1841, the census only recorded the number of people in households. And that was for the first four census enumerations. In 1841, the census started to record people's names, followed by 1851, when the census really becomes useful for research. This is because it contains each recorded person's exact age, relationship to the head of household, and parish of birth. There was also a census-like register of inhabitants taken in 1939, at the beginning of World War Two, and that can be helpful too. It was done to set up the ration-book program."

Pamela adjusted the turquoise paisley scarf around her neck. It was definitely her calling card. "I ran across a term the other day. 'Nuncupative will'. What does that mean?"

"That one I know," I added. I felt very good at having learned something in my class that I could share. "A nuncupative will is an oral will, usually given on a person's deathbed."

"Last-minute change of heart?" Pamela asked.

"Something like that. Usually they realize they are dying and haven't already made a will. Maybe someone's been especially good to them in their time of need or illness. Maybe they suddenly realized that there's a family member they'd forgotten."

Maude shook her head. "Unfortunately, it could also mean that somebody was taking advantage of a vulnerable person. So, one always has to look at these things with a grain of salt. The best wills are ones that list all the heirs with full names, how the heirs are related to the deceased, plus a complete list of household goods called an inventory."

"I'm just fascinated to know what all those things in my box mean," Pamela said. "I think perhaps Sylvie was a famous dancer and Richard met her overseas. Why else would there be a silver sphinx and a cabaret ticket in the box?"

"Just don't let it mislead you until you have it proven," Maude advised.

Pamela held up a new genealogy research book, actually the same one Maude was having reviewed in an upcoming quarterly Family History Society magazine. "I just purchased this and it's already been extremely useful. I used the tip sheets you gave me the first time I was in as a guide for how to interview my relatives. It made sure I asked all the right questions."

"Excellent, dear," Maude said.

"I'm going to start getting all those birth, marriage, and death certificates. I should be ready for the census research soon. I'm guessing Sylvie's mystery occurred in the 1940s."

"And be realistic too. Expect to hit some brick walls, because we all do," I added.

Pamela smiled. She pointed to the poster of the brick wall and how proper genealogy methods bust through it. "I'm counting on this research site to help me with any unexpected ones."

Maude and I smiled. "We'll do our best," we promised.

Pamela dug into her purse. "I do want to give you a token of my thanks. My husband and I own a string of pubs. The closest one's in Carlingheath. We'd like to give you some gift certificates as recognition for your kindness."

"That's certainly not necessary-" I started.

"Nonsense. Letting a complete stranger in, treating her with kindness, and then when she breaks down in tears you sit her in a private room, offering her tea, biscuits, and a gentle shoulder. You then also paid her taxi fare assuming you wouldn't be repaid. That's the definition of a good person to me." She handed over three £50 gift certificates, each marked with the name of the pub, 'The Jolly Scallop'. "Julie, one of these is for you to use. I insist."

"Well, thank you, that's very kind. Interesting name," I said.

Pamela smiled. "It's an insider joke. We have all these outrageous sea-creature names for our pubs. 'The Grinning Lobster', 'The Laughing Clam', 'The Octopus Reach'. We always have a ball coming up with the next one as we expand the business."

Maude and I both grinned back.

"It's important to enjoy life," Maude said. "Can't be all work and no play."

"I'd like Maude to have one and then also one for that kind antiques dealer man who was in here the other day. He was the one who called me a taxi home," Pamela said.

"Oh, that's Ewan. I'll make sure he gets his."

"Now, if I could just get settled at a computer then I'll start prowling online for those certificates," Pamela said.

"Number five is free; all the others were prebooked," Maude explained.

I silently hoped that Ozzie in carrell number four had left his smelly smoked-mackerel sandwiches in the fridge today.

※※※

Next Day. 6:00 a.m.

There was something incredibly special about Greymore Hall and its grounds so early in the morning. Everything was pristine, covered in the mist of dew. The birds were singing their little hearts out and there was a buzz of tiny insects in the air. The walking trail was absolutely perfect for this group of people sporting an average age of sixty-seven. I joined them because my father was interested, plus I wanted to see how he did with his sciatica. There was a small loop of one mile and a large loop of five miles. Today we were going to loop around the smaller one twice and see how everybody took to it. Comfortable track suits and athletic shoes were the order of the day.

"Now this is the pastoral type of activity I want to enjoy in my dotage," my father said, a smile on his face. I could tell he was happy, enjoying the peace and quiet. I saw the miniature goats still hanging around inside their warm shelter, likely sensing the early morning damp in the air.

We were about halfway into our walk when Algy and his beautiful Afghan hound Gilligan joined us. It was as if we were a royal court on parade, except that kings and queens of yesteryear didn't wear shiny nylon athleisurewear nor sparkling white sneakers. Regardless, the outdoor ambience was still the same as what they would've set eyes upon centuries ago. Greymore wasn't a place so much as it was a way of living. The genteel customs, the politeness, the friendliness towards everybody; those were the values and spirit in which Aunt Edwina lived. And everyone tried to keep those sentiments alive.

I looked up at the sky, a common affliction for everyone who lives in England. A few drops of rain fell on my face, and I thought we'd best hurry to finish this loop of the trail before the heavens opened. It appeared that I wasn't fast enough because the rain came down in a staccato, changing from a gentle few raindrops to showery cold. An army of umbrellas went up and then suddenly the mass of rainbow-colored shelter stopped. Huddled. Twisted sixty degrees.

"Good gracious!" Algy exclaimed in his toffee-nosed accent. "Whatever on earth is that?" Gilligan nuzzled into his tweed trousers, the brave hound uncharacteristically uncertain.

A couple of seventy-year-olds extended their arms out from underneath their umbrellas to point at something rather odd lumbering across the south field, aiming directly at our walking group.

Before us, in the driving rain, was one monstrous, camouflage-painted, closed-hatch 1940s World War Two tank.

A couple of the members of our walking group screamed. People scattered. Walking turned into skipping, somewhat hobbled loping, and even outright running. In the middle of all this rain, I was glad I had insisted on anti-slip gravel for the walkway loop, as it gave athletic shoes something to grip.

"He's not supposed to be here. Wrong field," I said to my father. I went over to the tank, waving my hands up in the air. With a clang and a shudder, the tank stopped, and the top hatch opened. Out popped Harvey's head, the Major's at his side. "Good morning, Julie. It's a shame about the rain."

I was beside myself. "Gentlemen, you're in the wrong field! This is for my goats and walkers. You're tearing up the turf."

The two military enthusiasts looked around them and gasped when they saw what the metal tank tracks had done to the delicate meadow grass. There were prominent marks, four to six inches deep in the softer areas.

"The north field has much coarser undergrowth and tougher ground-cover plants," I said.

"Oh dear," the Major said.

"We appear to have misinterpreted some vital logistics. Most unusual," Harvey said.

I surveyed the damage. Getting the tank out of the meadow in this rain would likely tear up more turf. "Gentlemen, I suggest you park it here and we'll figure out what to do with it once the rain stops." I remained safely ensconced underneath my umbrella.

The Major raised his umbrella over Harvey and himself. It looked most odd, two pale-pink heads popping out of the tank hatch underneath now-torrential rain. Mind you, they soon had that problem solved with a blue-and-white striped golf umbrella.

It didn't solve the problem of the battle tank in my field—the wrong field.

Only me. It could only happen to me.

Chapter 16

Two hours later, an enormous bouquet of flowers from the florist in Plumsden arrived. The bouquet was a rainbow of every color imaginable. The card read: *With our deepest apologies. From Three Sad Men inside a Tank.*

There were multiple definitions of the word 'sad'. 'Incompetent' seemed the best fit at this particular moment.

A drawing of a doghouse was on the bottom of the card. The card also contained a deposit receipt from a local sod farm, accompanied by a scheduled work order promising to repair the damage as soon as the weather permitted.

After the tank documentary film and the machinery's miscalculated journey, I had to give the men kudos for enthusiasm for history. Military history was a large part of many families' ancestry, and it certainly merited preservation to educate future generations. I only wished it hadn't been at the expense of Greymore's miniature goats' meadow turf.

We placated our nervous walkers with copious amounts of free tea, coffee, and cinnamon buns. Greymore's main hall had turned into an early morning steam room, lightly scented with sweaty socks and diluted perm solution. Jacques was a stalwart, dispensing towels and calming words to everyone. I'd never forget his last words as we finally saw the last of the walkers depart.

"Julie, I would not recommend a military equipment display again," Jacques said from underneath his quivering moustache, from which several drops of rainwater dripped down onto his chin.

"I'm going for miniature dollhouses next. A nice, calm, indoor activity," I said.

"A wise choice made by the lady of the house," he replied.

We exchanged a grin.

"The walkers have come up with a new name for their group," he said.

"I expect it's something like the 'Genealogy Gallopers' or 'Edwina's Exercisers'?"

"Alas, no. The new name the group wishes to be known by is the 'Terrified Trotters'," he said.

"No."

"Yes. Pardon me, I must get back to planning my lunch menu." Jacques turned on his heel and was gone before I even had a moment to compose myself.

Ewan replaced Jacques in my line of view. "One very sheepish military enthusiast reporting for duty, Miss Fincher."

I smirked. "You know, I'd hoped that my seniors' walking group would go by something like the 'Topaz Trainers'. Instead they're now calling themselves the 'Terrified Trotters', thanks to you three."

"That's why I'm here. I was hoping I could buy you lunch to start making amends." He gave me a cute little-boy grin.

"Lunch? You just tore up my back field and want to buy me lunch? How will that conversation go over appetizers? Gee, how's the weather? Does it look like a good day for laying new sod?"

"I'm afraid there's nothing I can say. Good comeback, by the way, though," he said.

"I've had hours to think of appropriate comebacks. It's pretty hard not to when you've got fifteen upset seniors racing around your miniature goat herd, neither group knowing which is more frightened. Thank goodness I don't have fainting goats." I gave Ewan my sternest look.

"Lunch?"

"To accomplish what?" I crossed my arms over my chest.

"To refuel? I thought we'd go and try out The Jolly Scallop, Pamela's pub in Carlingheath. I did a bit of research online and it sounds like quite a good place."

"You do realize you'd have a hostile companion with you for at least part of the journey?"

"Never fear," Ewan replied, patting his chest, "I've got my chain mail on."

I smirked again. "It's not exactly buying somebody lunch when you're using a gift certificate."

"Well, then how about this," he said, opening his wallet and fanning out a few £20 notes. "Keep my gift certificate, and I will pay for lunch with my own money. It's what I intended to do anyways because the gift certificate, as you may recall, is still sitting locked up in the petty cash box for the research site."

"Oh."

He held his arm out for mine. "Lunch."

Lynne Christensen

✳✳✳

The Jolly Scallop Pub. One Hour Later.

The pub was decorated in a seafarer's theme. Shiplap-paneled walls were resplendent with old life preservers, yellow sou'westers, taxidermized fish, nets, trawler cables, and even a few planks from the hulls of old fishing boats. Luckily, they'd been preserved and cleaned properly so it didn't smell like rotting tuna inside the pub. Shiny, varnished wooden tabletops with cozy, starfish-embroidered booths made for a total seating capacity of about sixty people. Hit pop music was on low in the background, enough to provide a bit of liveliness yet not even close to drowning out pleasant conversation. One thing I hated was going into a restaurant and then having to yell to be heard by one's fellow diner. It just wasn't on.

"How does this rendezvous not constitute us being on a date?" I asked him.

Ewan shrugged. "We've eaten lunch together tons of times at the research site and while visiting antiques fairs. This isn't any different."

"Fine."

"Don't sound so excited," he teased.

"I'll ignore that last comment." I perused the menu. It was one of my favorite kinds: tons of salads with heaps of protein as well as a lot of healthy, lean hot dishes. I was toying between the chef's salad with egg, chicken, cheese plus a load of greens and vegetables or the lamb pot pie. Tough decision.

"What looks good to you?" I asked Ewan.

"I'm having a steak."

"You'll need to build up your strength for laying all that sod," I shot back.

"And the hits just keep on coming," he retorted. He patted his chest again. "So far, the armor's working."

"You need your two co-conspirators here to help defend you. It's not really fair, me sitting here taking it all out on you. You're slightly under-gunned."

"I can hold my own, thank you very much," he retorted.

I shook my head. "You're forgetting one thing. I outsmarted my ex. Don't even think for one minute that you could take me on over this turf incident and win."

"I think I need a solicitor," Ewan joked. His smile turned into a look of disbelief as he saw none other than Fred Todling amble over. Fred had a wide grin on his face, as if he'd just found friends in a sea of antipathy.

"My day's fortunes have instantly changed, now that I see two of my most illustrious friends." Fred stood beside our table. He seemed to first wonder if he was interrupting, then wonder if he could join us.

I scooted over in my bench seat. "Fred, have you eaten already?"

He sat down before answering. "No, I just had coffee with a client."

"Oh, Pamela? I noticed that a photo of her cat Answer is on all the menus." I pointed out the feline on the menu I was perusing.

"No, not Pamela Fulham. A different client. Pamela's just been rather generous with her meeting space."

"What about your new office?" Ewan asked.

"The spy door. I find it rather troubling," Fred admitted.

"So you're meeting clients in a pub nineteen miles away?" I asked.

"That appears to be the case. I have the builders in to plaster up the hole."

"But what about the historic commission? You can't do that without their approval," Ewan said.

Fred sighed. It was a grandiose sigh. He laced his fingers over his ample chest and breathed out again. "My fellow neighbor in progressive commercial enterprise, I hesitate to tell you, but I must divulge the absolute, sterling truth. This spyhole is not from the seventeenth, eighteenth nor nineteenth centuries. The historic commission has actually been out to rule on it. I'm rather embarrassed to tell you but the hole was created in the 1970s, given the tiny scrap of paper found coiled up inside the doorknob."

"Was it a secret code?" Ewan said, opening his eyes in false amazement. It was obvious he was actually far more interested in the dried chewing gum stuck to the sole of Fred's shoe.

"I'm afraid not," Fred said. "It read 'Andy installed this door to talk with Scott, 1974'."

I laughed. "So the great historical mystery was really no exciting mystery at all."

Fred clutched his throat. "My dear colleague, there were indeed three brothers who owned the building centuries ago, all sons of a lord and lady. Once their parents died, one brother prospered, one got injured, and one served the others."

"Really?" Ewan asked.

"I found a bit more after doing a simple internet search. There was an article published in a national family history magazine about forty years ago. The prosperous brother was into banking but got run over by a loose carriage horse. This injured banker brother succumbed to his injuries at the age of twenty-three. The brother who served the others was actually found to have set the carriage horse free and was convicted of manslaughter the next year."

"And that's good enough for the historical commission not to be interested?" I asked.

"Following the demise of the brothers, it became a greengrocer's store that secretly supported key suffragettes. I am pleased to announce that the building qualifies for a blue plaque noting its historic importance. In the meantime, I've been granted permission for us to plaster up the hole in the wall so Ewan and I do not become Andy and Scott repeated."

"Such a shame," Ewan said.

I issued a warning glance over at Ewan.

"So who were Andy and Scott?" Ewan asked.

"Ah, these two young gentlemen, and I use the term loosely, were a pair of ratty delinquents who were part of a building crew renovating buildings back in the 1970s. They were known to the police and have quite long criminal records." Fred explained it smugly, as if he were implying that he had an 'in' with law enforcement. I knew it would make him feel good if we played along.

"And you figured all this out on the internet? Well done," Ewan said.

By now Fred had his glasses on and was looking at his menu. "Are we doing appetizers?"

Ewan gave me a look of exasperation and I just smiled sweetly. Butter would not have melted in my mouth. It was one thing to get taken out for lunch, but having verbose Fred join us ratcheted Ewan's guilty apology meal up to an entirely new level.

Chapter 17

Greymore Hall. The Gardens. Next Day.

The hummingbirds at Greymore Hall liked a particular group of montbretias in a certain corner of the garden. I'd encouraged them by frequently watering the plants using the estate's eco-friendly irrigation system that drew from rainwater collection barrels. Lots of water translated into lots of nectar; the sugary sweet concoction was exactly the energy source that humming-birds needed. I was always amazed at how rapidly they beat their wings to stay aloft. When two males got together in the same territory, they often had dogfights in the air. It was hard for one's eyes to keep up with them because they moved so fast.

I came down to see how the montbretias flowers were doing and noticed Ewan was standing off to the side with some lumber, a pot of nails, and a hammer.

"Are you building something?" I asked him.

He nodded. "Yes, and it's a surprise. I'm hoping to improve upon my lunchtime apology."

"Actually, I rather enjoyed lunch. The fact that you had to sit and listen to Fred for an entire hour made me feel somewhat placated."

"You just wait. This one's going to make up for it and then some."

"I await my knight in shining armor with bated breath. Also, considering the miniature goats have taken up residence all over your tank, I think we've come out the winners."

"What?" Ewan looked over at the field, and much to his chagrin saw six tiny goats, in a range of black, grey, brown, and white coat patterns, all contentedly asleep on top of the tank. It was actually quite pastoral, and I supposed the sun had warmed the tank's metal exterior just enough to make it a cozy, yet not too hot, place to sleep.

"Score one for Aunt Edwina, zero for you three," I said with an evil grin. "That's payback for you."

"Yet another epic fail," Ewan said, playfully smashing his palm against his forehead.

I headed back out into the fields, needing an escape from the busy hours of the past few days. Even though we'd just had our grand opening, I felt like I'd already been here for a lifetime. And that was good, because it meant there was a lot of positive research happening. I knew, however, that it was important to take breaks for oneself once in a while and get the opportunity to relax.

Today I was taking a relaxing walk of my own. I made it to the top of the hill and looked at Aunt Edwina's and Elliot's memorial stones. Every time I came up here, I felt comforted and confident. Both these stones were reminders of two strong people who had lived life on their best terms, with great love for each other.

I crouched down beside Aunt Edwina's stone. "Aunt Edwina, I know you can hear me. And I know you had a great love in your life. But how did you know Elliot was the one?"

Help me know how to proceed with Ewan.

Silence was my contemplative friend.

"Is it wrong to ask you for a sign?" My words got lost on the gentle breeze blowing up amongst the bushes and trees. I looked over the wonderful landscape below me, the huge expanse of the Greymore estate. This view always calmed me and made me refocus on what was really important. It was nice to have someone to care for, but not if it meant sacrificing freedom and comfort.

I turned to go home and nearly ran into a metallic shiny-green-and-raspberry coated hummingbird hovering right beside my nose. Its beating wings made me smile. The chance of that happening up here, where all the lilacs had been on their last legs for days already, was slim. There were no nearby clusters of nectar-laden flowers.

The hummingbird was out of place.

It was a sign that Aunt Edwina was listening.

Some people would call me crazy, but I called it being in tune with the past.

A branch snapped underfoot off to my right, and I looked to see Ewan striding up the path to meet me.

He smiled. "Thought you might like some company."

Was Aunt Edwina's spirit here? Was Ewan her sign to me?

"How much did you hear?" I asked, nervous.

He looked quizzical. "Just 'oh' when you were startled by the hummingbird." He smiled again. "Come back with me so I can show you my surprise. I've just finished building you a hummingbird blind. You can watch them up close now without fear of startling them."

He held out his hand this time, not just his arm, and I knew Aunt Edwina would want me to accept.

So I did.

※※※

GGRS. Thirty Minutes Later.

"Kirby Danforth here says his pub in Dorset served King Charles the Second's first illegitimate son, the Duke of Monmouth, during his rebellion against King James in the seventeenth century." Gertie shared this tidbit with me as the slightly panic-stricken man stood beside her.

"That's fascinating," I said, wondering what the visitor's ultimate request of us would be. He'd obviously heard of the GGRS and made the trek here hoping we could help.

Gertie continued. "Kirby's problem is that his competitor told him to prove it, else stop advertising it."

The man, a short, stumpy character with a freshly shaven face and meaty hands, decided to add his two cents' worth. "You see, they make the same claim. But they're wrong."

"And how do you know they're wrong?" I asked.

"Because I have proof," he said. He reached inside a hard-sided briefcase and hauled out a tattered banner. He unfolded it, all four feet by five feet of it, and I read 'Fear Nothing But'. The rest of the material was missing. The banner was of hand-stitched material and had an aristocratic look to it. But was it a royal standard? It was hard to tell and would be guesswork without the experts.

"Fear nothing but what?" Gertie asked.

"Ozzie Boggs's smoked-mackerel sandwiches," I joked.

Gertie laughed in that brutally honest, stomach-jiggling manner of hers.

Kirby realized it was an insider joke.

"Sorry, we had a guest in here who brought a rather pungent sandwich to the facility," I hastily explained.

"Awful smell, if you ask me. Any kind of fish sandwich should be relegated to outdoor dining only," Kirby said.

"Totally agree on that front," Gertie said. "We nearly had to fumigate the place."

"Where did you find this?" I asked him.

"In a dried-out leather bag, drawstring all crumbled away, in the attic of our pub. We found it twelve years ago but just haven't done anything with it."

"Why is that always the case? People find such cool stuff but then just squirrel it away."

"Mainly because we just don't know where to start," Kirby said. "I knew it was important, but it's not like something the wife and I could take to a jumble sale. As long as our pub was running well, we were happy leaving it as an interesting relic. Something to show friends and family when they came for a visit."

I shook my head. "It should definitely be sent to a textile museum and not only authenticated but also preserved. I know they have acid-free boxes and tissue paper, along with display cases that resist ultraviolet light. It's important to take care of these precious things." I gave Kirby a serious look, hoping he was taking all of this in with an eye toward actually doing something about it.

"I know, I have been feeling guilty about it recently. We just had a clear out—"

"You didn't sell anything related to this, I hope," Gertie said. Her tone was disapproving.

"No, just some old cardboard recycling and a few bits of damaged pressboard furniture. That's when we came across this again."

"You said your nearest competitor's giving you grief?" I asked.

Kirby leaned over the information desk. "Yes. He says unless I can prove it, he's going to say the same thing about his pub, thus eroding an advantage we have in the marketplace. You see, we're both on the same side of town, and people tend to come to our pub because of the Monmouth connection."

"And what is your competitor's claim to fame with Monmouth?" Gertie asked.

"Nothing. All he's got is rumors and a creative marketing department." Kirby looked quite disgusted. "I'm the one who's the real deal."

"Do you really think this flag is one of Monmouth's battle standards?" I asked.

"I'm hoping you can help me find a record that refers to it, or somewhere I can start looking for some relevant information."

"Well, we do have a good selection of English history and topography books on the shelves. The other place I'd suggest starting is either the Victoria and Albert Museum or going online to The National Archives and see if they have any records. Keep in mind, you're going back many hundreds of years," Gertie advised.

"Yes, back to a time of rebellion, royalists, roundheads, and religious conversions," Kirby said.

"Unfortunately, some of the records were destroyed or burnt out of overzealousness, but you may just get lucky," Gertie said.

"What is 'The National Archives'?" Kirby asked.

"The National Archives, also known as 'TNA', is one of the most wonderful places on this planet," Gertie said. "It's an absolutely fabulous repository of millions of records including ancestors and social history, as well as certain military, political, and royal records. You can visit and see records that are hundreds of years old, pour over parchments that were written by a scribe in the actual century you're researching."

My mouth hung open. I'd read about The National Archives in my beginner's genealogy class but hadn't visited there yet. It was definitely on my to-do list. "Where is it located?"

"Just a short walk from the Kew Gardens underground station. When you arrive, just follow the crowd of canvas-bag-toting, sensible-shoe-wearing people. They'll all be heading to the same place. You'll pass several bed-and-breakfast signs on the way in."

"Sounds fascinating," Kirby said.

"What's the name of your pub?" I asked.

Kirby straightened. "The Rebel's Head. Built in the early seventeenth century and apparently named not too long after Monmouth was executed."

Ewan ambled over. "I can take Kirby to the correct bookshelf, if you'd like," he offered.

"Very kind, thank you," Kirby said.

"Oh, and I nearly forgot. We also have this," Kirby said, bringing out a folded sheaf of papers.

Gertie carefully unfolded them and saw we were looking at old building plans authored by one 'Theophilus Greenbough', architect and member of The Royal Society. "I take it these are plans for your pub?"

Kirby nodded. "And not a stick of framing has been changed since then. It's built like a tank."

I buried my head in my hands.

"Did I say something wrong?" Kirby asked.

"No, not at all. She's just had her fill of military vehicles this week." Ewan pointed out the window at the tank in the south field, the deep tracks an obvious mar on the landscape.

Five Minutes Later.

Ozzie Boggs was now a fixture at the research site. He arrived every morning at opening time and stayed until it closed. We all assumed he was retired because he didn't seem to have any other pressing demands on his time. Today he'd brought in a box of six scones to the lunchroom. A nice gesture, except for the fact that he had a donation saucer right beside the box that read: 'Scones £1.50'.

"Who wants to wager that he's making a few pence on every scone he sells?" Maude asked me.

"He wouldn't," I responded. "Surely not."

Maude smiled and lifted up the supermarket bakery box. Underneath was the red markdown price tag: 'Raisin Scones: £4.50'. They were also one day past their expiry date.

"I thought mine felt a little hard when I picked it up," I said, looking at my forlorn coins lying by themselves in the saucer. "I had to microwave it to soften it up."

"At least you know he hasn't fiddled with them. I broke the seal on the box this morning, but I had no idea he'd be setting up a bakery stand in our lunchroom. We mustn't let this upset café staff."

Ewan popped his head inside the door. "Maude, a word, please?"

She left me with my sorry-looking scone crumbs and then came back ten minutes later. "Seems as though Kirby's architectural plans are pretty helpful. Right now Ewan is trying to convince him to dig up the ancient privy out back."

It appeared I now had bigger things to worry over than Ozzie's pseudo-bakery stand in our lunchroom.

"He's doing what?" I was out of my seat in an instant. "We can't teach people to dig up toilets here. That's completely unsanitary."

I put my plate in the dishwasher and hustled out to meet at the information desk with Kirby and Ewan before Maude could protest. "Ewan, what exactly are we doing here?"

"It's the privy. There are a lot of important historical finds located after digging through old night soil. When Kirby told me he'd located a privy on the original seventeenth century architectural plans, I thought he might be sitting on a gold mine."

"I already know what people have been sitting on over that privy for hundreds of years, thank you very much," I retorted.

Ewan looked amused. "Have you heard of composting?"

"Yes, but I still don't want to touch it."

"What would you rather he do, lob over a grenade and explode it instead of using a trowel?"

"No ..."

"Well, then." Ewan looked at Kirby. "I recommend you dig it up. Using all safety precautions, of course."

"Safety and hygiene being of critical importance," I reminded. "Hire a professional to do the job, one who carries the proper liability insurance."

Ozzie gestured at me for help, so I beetled over to carrell number four.

"Look at what I've been able to put together," Ozzie said, so proud of himself.

I saw a blank computer screen.

"Where?" I asked.

"Right here," he said, handing me a stack of used, mismatched beer mats. Squares and circles.

"I'm sorry, I don't understand."

Ozzie explained. "I was at the pub yesterday, meeting with my solicitor. After we were done, I wrote out all the information I had on these." He flipped them over and I saw a jigsaw puzzle of names and lines.

"You mean, this is how you've documented your family tree?" I was stunned.

"My solicitor's a bit long-winded. Ran out of paper talking to him. So, I used the next thing handy. I like how they fit in my pocket, may start a new trend."

I envisioned a global shortage of beer mats if Ozzie persisted with this line of genealogical organization methodology.

I proceeded to watch Ozzie lay out his upside-down beer mats. One in particular caught my eye, a mat where the advertiser had printed its offering on both sides. "The Jolly Scallop? Who is your solicitor?"

"Fred Todling. Newly qualified chap but he's much cheaper than the London toffs I used to have."

Useful information to know.

I now had a mental image of Ozzie Boggs sitting with Fred Todling over a pint. Ozzie's penny pinching would likely compete with Fred's verbosity. If Fred charged by the ten-minute increment, as was typical of most solicitors, I doubted Ozzie would approve any charges for excessive synonym usage.

"I see. You know, we do have proper pedigree charts you can use for working copies, and you can enter the details online."

"Of course. These are just my portable drafts." Ozzie looked quite smug. "Thought I was rather creative."

"I see."

He ignored my clipped remark. "There is one thing I don't understand."

"Yes?"

"This name. Last name 'Jupp'. I can't find it on the census, but I have proved this ancestor exists on the birth, marriage, and death certificates."

"You may have a mispronounced name."

"How's that?"

"There was a lot of illiteracy in prior centuries, even in the early twentieth century. Sometimes the clerk couldn't understand a heavy accent, or the person being recorded didn't know how their own name was spelled. Perhaps they were literate but had bad handwriting or the clerk was hard of hearing. In this case, try saying the word in a different way."

"You mean with an accent or a lisp?"

I nodded.

Ozzie reached into his mouth. "Luckily the dentist just gave me a temporary replacement."

"Mis-ter Boggs! No saliva in the computer carrell. Absolutely not!" I glared at him.

He looked a bit hurt. "But you said–"

"Mis-ter Boggs! Think about it in your head. Jupe, Lupe, Supp, Tupp ..."

He wiped his hands on a clean handkerchief and leaned back in his chair, closing his eyes to get deep in thought.

I left him alone but knew the image of him reaching into his mouth to remove a saliva-laden temporary denture would be forever engrained in my mind.

Chapter 18

Later That Day.

Pamela came in for another research session, eager to continue looking for answers about the contents of her heirloom box. I found her near the information desk, engaged in a detailed conversation with Ozzie; he told her a story of hard luck with a lot of 'ag labs' in his background.

"Ag lab'? As in a dog?" she asked.

He shook his head. "No, I was reading an online self-help guide. 'Ag lab' stands for 'agricultural laborer'. I'm afraid it's looking like I come from a line of pretty lowly people. Criminals and laborers."

"Well, we cannot change the past," she said with a sigh. "I'm just hoping to get some answers to my Egyptian question." She showed him the list of items in the heirloom box, and Ozzie's eyebrows went up with amazement.

"Sounds like you have a real mystery on your hands," Ozzie said.

"It's a cracking one. I have a good feeling about this."

Bertie breezed in, lugging a cardboard box with contents that clanked. "Julie, I have more of that mango chutney you ordered for the café. Where should I take it?"

It was a question asked by one of the most aristocratic and wealthy people in the county. Here he was, standing right in front of my information desk with a box of condiments, looking ever so much the delivery man for a large firm. I suppose one could consider Scotford Castle estate a large firm; it employed a significant number of people and was well-known throughout the world. Bertie hosted a lot of tour groups; they appreciated his handicap-accessible facilities as well as the clean restrooms, baby-changing facilities, and extensive gift shop. Certainly, he pandered to the tourist trade, but owners of large estates had to these days in order to survive. My mind always went back to Algy when he first told us that they commercialized Holgarth Hall in order to protect his Old Masters paintings from going to the auction block. In some ways it was sad, yet in others I was glad that this financial necessity existed, because it made these grand homes available for viewing by more than just the rich elite. We'd come a long way over the centuries, and it was a fine balance between preserving and financing the maintenance of these grand estates.

I turned my attention back to the Duke of Conroy, who stood in front of me with his mango chutney. "They need to go in the back with the kitchen staff. I'll take them to Jacques if you want."

Bertie drew himself up to his full height. "I wouldn't dream of it. I'll take it back myself; you're quite busy enough here," he said. His eyes roamed the room, and I could see he was doing a mental count.

"Loads of people since we opened, and most of them have been here for serious research, not just to gawk," I said.

"Perhaps they came for the free beverages and snacks?" Bertie teased, as he set the box down for a moment. "Mind you, that's one thing I insist upon for my staff: free tea and coffee, always the good brands. None of this watery, discount-store stuff for my employees. What I put on my own table is what I provide for Scotford Castle's staff and volunteers."

I sighed. "I wish more people thought like you. Staff should never be an afterthought."

"Indeed. Loyalty is earned." He gave me a smile. "I'll let you get back to it. Oh, one more thing?"

"Yes?"

"I hear you're going after the fishing fleet. Let me know if you do, because I have some interest in that as well."

"The fishing fleet?"

"I heard about Pamela's heirloom box from Ewan when he delivered a couple of eighteenth century chairs to Scotford Castle yesterday."

And with that, the aristocrat was off, leaving me to ponder what the heck he meant. I sat down at one of the information desk computers and did an internet search for 'fishing fleet'. Beyond the obvious arctic char and giant squid, I found that 'fishing fleet' was a colloquial term used for women going over to India during the heydays of the British Empire. Because the ratio of men to women was so overwhelmingly on the male side, willing and eligible women were actually encouraged to sail to India to become instant brides. Hence the name 'fishing fleet' because of how their particular vessels were filled with women unabashedly trawling for a husband.

There was even a term for making the best of the journey. Women were advised to be 'POSH' or 'Port Out, Starboard Home', advice for being on the correct side of the ship to avoid the intense sun.

Was Pamela's ancestor Sylvie part of the fishing fleet, and did she somehow end up in Egypt?

Hardly likely if she was there for wifely duties in India.

No. The cabaret ticket, silk stockings, sphinx, and photo all said there was a bigger story just waiting to be revealed.

I heard somebody clear his throat in front of me. I looked up and saw the Major standing there at attention. "Ahem," he started.

"Hello, Major."

"Julie, about the tank. I hope that we can move forward from this horrifically invasive incident."

"Aunt Edwina would not be amused," I said.

"No, I don't believe she would be."

It was now a staring contest between us. I hated being in one with such a revered man, but the Major's renegade tank episode had significantly marred my back field. I decided to take the higher road, one decidedly tank-less.

"Well, I'm sure the sod farm can put it all back together again." It was hard getting the sentence out, but I'd achieved it. I gave him a perfunctory smile.

"They have given me their assurances. Not that that means much to you, another assurance coming from someone like me but–"

"Major, mistakes happen. Let's try and move beyond this."

He breathed an outward sigh of relief. Even he, the stoic military man, couldn't hide his dismay at this large mistake. He switched gears. "Has Pamela arrived? I'd like to get a look at those medals in her heirloom box and see if I can figure out the military connection."

"Computer carrell number five. Right beside Ozzie."

"The man with the beer mats?"

"The very same." Apparently interesting family history hijinks spread like wildfire. They definitely spread faster than any jam, marmalade, or chutney I'd ever seen.

***

It didn't take the Major long to figure out where the medals came from. "These are from Cairo Branch in the 1940s. Do you have any military service records?"

"No," Pamela said. "I wouldn't even know where to begin."

I smiled because I now felt much more in the know. "Perhaps TNA keeps declassified military records?"

"They have some, there is also a good chance a regimental museum would have some information as well. I'll ask that you ladies work with the computer because I'm a bit fumble fingered on keyboards. In the meantime, I'll find the right regimental museum and ask some questions," the Major said.

Pamela and I both nodded at his suggestion.

"Oh, and Major?" I called out after him as he began to stride away.

He turned on a shiny shoe and looked at me. "Yes, Julie?"

"Where's Harvey?"

"At this precise moment he's inside the tank in your north field. He's triple checking the braking system to make sure that there are no other incidents at Greymore."

I took a deep breath and exhaled. "Good. The Terrified Trotters will be glad to hear it."

***

Lunchroom. Next Day. 8:30 a.m.

"How did you get the information so fast?" Pamela asked the Major over tea. The research site had just opened, and everyone was getting back into the daily groove.

The Major sat even straighter in his chair. The crease on his trousers was razor sharp. "I happen to know a field marshal and a lieutenant general, both retired, of course, who sit on the national board of trustees for the regimental history association. They put out some feelers and within a few hours I had the exact information I needed."

"So, family history research is all about knowing the right people and having the right connections?" she asked.

He shook his head. "Not so much. Family history research, which includes genealogy, military, and social history, is greatly aided by research sites such as this one. If you go in with an open mind and an attitude that you're willing to learn, the networks will appear. It's not a question of being born the right way or having a silver spoon in your mouth."

Pamela nodded in agreement. "It's so true. I was treated with such courtesy and respect when I came in the other week, a complete mess," she admitted. "It can be quite overwhelming when you start. But it's people like you, Ewan, Julie, Gertie, Maude, and fellow researchers who've been of tremendous help."

"But you do need to spend the seat time doing research on your own," Maude said, pouring herself a cup of tea. "We can't possibly find the time to do it all for every researcher."

"And doing the research is most of the fun," Pamela said. "I actually get flutters when I'm scrolling through online records, hoping that my relative pops up one day. It's like I'm honing in more and more specific, drilling down to the actual record that I need. When I finally find it, I'm sure I'll shout out with glee and then subsequently get kicked out of your marvelous facility for being too noisy."

"Well, if it's only a short shout of glee, then perhaps you'll just get a minor reprimand and be asked to adjourn to the lunchroom for a few moments," Maude said diplomatically.

The Major rubbed his hands together. "Let's take a look at those online records from TNA. Perhaps we shall find what we need."

Chapter 19

An hour later the Major and Pamela still didn't have anything to show for their efforts. Their online search had turned up nothing for the medals nor Richard's specific officer or soldier service record.

"It appears we're down to two possibilities," the Major said with great authority.

"The records were destroyed?" Pamela asked, wincing.

"That's one possibility. Although the British Empire was overwhelmingly organized with its paperwork, there could have been a conflict, or somebody at that particular office in Cairo who didn't do his job properly. It could have been as simple as dropping cigarette ash by accident into a filing cabinet and the whole thing catching alight. Everybody smoked back in those days."

"And the other possibility?"

"He was part of Special Operations or a secret unit that's still not declassified," the Major said in a firm voice.

"After all this time? Surely it's long enough ago?" By now I'd joined the conversation, curious to know more.

The Major nodded. "It can happen. There are some official secrets that will never be released. I'm privy to one of them and shall take it to my grave. It's what I signed up for when I joined the forces."

"But I don't understand," Pamela said. "There are no discharge papers. It's like he joined the forces and then there's nothing about him. There's no death certificate, nothing at all."

"What my course taught me is if you can't work backwards, then start sideways or forwards. Perhaps that will help. We have the matrimonial bureau, right?" I asked.

Pamela rummaged in her box and pulled it out. "Yes."

"So why don't we start there, and perhaps that record will have more information about Richard, which will in turn lead us to more information about his time in Cairo."

The Major nodded. "I think you may be onto something there, Julie."

"Can we find the matrimonial bureau online?" Pamela asked. "That would make it really easy."

"We can give it a try," I said. I went on to the TNA website, something I'd just started to use. It contained loads of easy-to-use help guides for researchers, real treasures to help us hone in on the right record category and then the specific item we were searching for. It turned out TNA had over three feet of records for 'Francine's Matrimonial Bureau'. Unfortunately, the records were not yet digitized.

"Do I hear field trip?" I asked. "You should order these records in advance to maximize our research time. Don't want to waste time putting in record requests while you're onsite and could be reading documents instead."

"Oh, I couldn't possibly ask you to accompany me there." Pamela paused. "Could I?"

Maude and I exchanged a glance. "Well, we haven't actually discussed that," Maude said. "We're not supposed to allocate too much time to one particular person's search; however, we could use it as a staff training exercise that happens to refer to your particular search interest."

"Maude, that's rather creative." I looked at her with a new-found appreciation.

"Like one of my favorite people used to say, there's no sense in getting old if you don't get crafty." She gave me a perfunctory, mischievous smile.

※※※

GGRS Electric Van. Tuesday Morning. 6:30 a.m.

A happy party of eager family history researchers assembled in the van early Tuesday morning. Gertie, Maude, Ewan, the Major, Pamela, Ozzie and I were all on the trip. Harvey offered to drive the van and deal with parking during the day as part of his 'meadow turf mea culpa'.

Everyone wore dark clothes, owing to the dust expected to emerge from archive files and boxes, some of which likely had not been opened for years. Apparently, the only people brave enough to wear white were the chefs in the café.

It was all very exciting. This was our first big trip in the new van. The vehicle smelled new. It signified that this was a new era at Greymore and we were taking the full opportunity in stride. I looked around the interior. Gertie and Maude's heads were bowed together over a notebook, and they were deep in discussion about some intricacy of advanced genealogy research. Ewan was speaking with the Major and showing something on his phone, no doubt the latest antique find he'd brought into his shop. Ozzie drummed his fingers on the armrest, looking at his collection of beer mats laid out on the tray table ahead of him. Pamela sat next to me, looking out the window at the glorious countryside.

Everybody was doing their normal thing, and this was good.

"I can't believe we're actually going to TNA. It's my first time," I said to Pamela.

Gertie overheard me and I was rewarded with her kind smile. "You won't believe it. Millions of records. A café serving hot meals, a snack bar, a bookshop, displays, multiple floors of incredible resources. Wonderful staff. They even do online talks and children's classes," she said.

"I can't wait."

"We've done the smart thing, because everyone's ordered their records in advance," Maude said. "It's definitely important to have a research plan before arriving onsite, otherwise you waste half the day looking up things in the online database that you could just have easily done at home."

Gertie nodded. "Exactly. When I stride through those doors, I'm on a mission and I'm organized. I also arrange my schedule to go on weekdays and usually the late opening days. This makes for the best use of time."

"Sounds like a ginormous facility," I said.

"There are millions of documents in their collection. But everyone is there to help and more than happy to answer questions. It's just the same as with any smaller family history facility; don't expect staff to do all the work for you," Maude said.

***

TNA at Kew, London.

Harvey dropped us as close as he could to the front entrance. In front of us stood an imposing multi-sided concrete building attached to a glass-fronted atrium. The later-1970s construction evoked a feeling of flowing geometrical design. As we walked up the pavement, we passed by a small pond and saw ducks, geese, and a heron enjoying themselves in the water. The birds were obviously used to people because they didn't flutter away as we stopped to take pictures. We headed up to the main entrance and went through the glass doors. We then headed to the left for the locker room.

"Now, don't make the silly mistake I did once," Maude said. "When they say no pens or glue, that includes lip balm. I once had to put a single stick of lip balm all by itself in a locker near the safe room because they wouldn't allow me to keep it in my pocket. It looked very lonely behind the clear plastic door, all by itself."

"I'm glad they're serious about protecting all their one-of-a-kind, ancient records," Ewan said.

"Yes, of course. But what's a safe room?" I asked.

By now we were inside the locker room, which contained a huge array of approximately two-foot tall, clear-plastic-fronted lockers. You used one for the day and kept the key with you. All your approved belongings went into a clear plastic bag so the security guard could easily check that you weren't bringing any banned materials upon entry nor stealing any documents when you left.

Maude explained. "The safe room is where they keep the incredibly precious documents. It has an even higher level of security. I once examined a royal letter in there and felt quite nervous, cameras everywhere."

I found this fascinating. "How old was the letter?"

"It was early eighteenth century, and I was literally shaking. I asked the staff to put it back in its folder when I was done because I didn't want to chance a mistake," Maude said.

Ewan chimed in. "Well, it goes back to the age-old question again, doesn't it? Do you squirrel away precious archives, antiques, and fanciful jewels in rich people's houses so hardly anyone looks at them, or do you let them be accessible to the wider population, thus educating more people?"

The Major had been pretty quiet throughout this entire discussion. "What do you think?" I asked him.

He cleared his throat. "I like the idea of history being available to more people. So long as the safe room is watched and people are vetted, then I think it's all right."

"Alright, everybody, choose a locker and no lip balm in your pockets," I instructed. A middle-aged man a few lockers down looked at me as if I was a bit bonkers. I shrugged, and then we exchanged a grin.

We were like a line of recruits stripping off coats, bags, thermoses, and anything else we brought along with us. The only things that went into our onsite clear plastic bags were pencils, blank sheets of paper, records-request printouts, cellular phones set to silent, and wallets. Maude had instructed everybody to wear layers because large coats weren't allowed in the reading rooms.

"How's this?" I asked Maude, holding up my clear plastic bag to the light.

"You're nearly there." She dipped her hand inside my bag and pulled out a yellow highlighter and twenty sheets of loose paper. "The highlighter is considered a pen, something that can easily wreck archival documents, so that's not allowed. Also, just take your notebook instead of all this loose paper; it makes the security guards' lives easier. They have to flip through each page as you enter and exit the facility."

"It sounds like we're going through airport security," the Major said. "I couldn't even imagine stealing an archival document. That's just not cricket."

"Oh, the antiques world has seen its cases of it over the years," said Ewan. "Some nefarious researchers without scruples have tried to walk out with valuable archival documents to sell on the open market. Sad but true."

"Sad indeed," Gertie said. "Right. Everybody ready?"

Our group emphatically chorused back, "Yes!"

"Eyes forward, the stairs are on the right as you come out of the locker room. No detours to the café or snack room; we'll rendezvous back here on the main floor for lunch at noon to avoid the one o'clock rush," Maude said.

"I say, that's not British," the Major said. His feathers looked a little ruffled. All this over switching the lunchtime by an hour.

"Loosen up, Major," Ozzie said. "You'll get your vittles sooner rather than later."

"I'm so excited that I may skip lunch," Pamela gushed.

"If we don't hurry up, I'm banning lunch," Gertie injected. "Let's hoof it upstairs, troops."

I gave the Major a stern glance. "We're trying to maximize our time here. When you get busy in the stacks and the boxes of archives, you'll be lucky to remember to take lunch, let alone worry about what time you're taking it."

"Right."

***

We were like a loosely connected centipede heading out of the locker room, one by one, focused on our mission. Pamela, Maude, Gertie and I had tasked ourselves with going through the collection of Francine's Matrimonial Bureau records. Considering they came in four full boxes, we decided an all-hands-on approach was wisest. The Major and Ewan were doing more research on the Cairo detachment of the army where Richard was posted. Ozzie had his own business to take care of and wasn't exactly forthcoming about his plans; back at Greymore, once we'd shown him how to use the online catalogue, he'd brushed off any further assistance. All he'd said was, "Make sure I'm booked on the van." As the GGRS van offered the most direct route to reach TNA, Ozzie's request was a no-brainer, considering the magnitude of planning logistics around a capital city such as London.

Ozzie had a plan, alright, but he was busted before we even got to the staircase. Out in the main hall, where there were ample comfortable chairs and the bookshop was nearby, Maude put up her hand and stopped the entire group. Ewan ran into the Major, who ran into Gertie, who then stopped the centipede from disintegrating even further. We were effectively reduced to human bumper cars.

Maude grew about three inches in height. "Ozzie, we went over the requirements for what you are allowed to bring into the archives. Look at what's in your bag," she said in a disapproving tone.

Multiple sets of eyes laser-focused on the clear plastic bag Ozzie had in his hand. Inside was a gooey caramel chocolate bar, a bottle of fizzy grape soda, plus three fountain pens clustered around his laptop.

"I thought if I was careful it would be fine," Ozzie pleaded.

"And why do you consider yourself above the rules?"

I stepped up to support Maude. "Ozzie, the chocolate and the sugary soda can either damage documents or attract pests. All three fountain pens can damage documents."

"What about my laptop and charger?"

"Laptops are fine."

"Fine." Ozzie turned on his heel and went back to the locker room to unload his stash. He was back in a minute, all of us perturbed he'd delayed our start time. It was important to get to the archives early and start on time. Every minute counted when one took a trip to this humongous facility.

"Ozzie should shell out for our lunch after that escapade," Gertie muttered.

"No, thanks. He'd only spring for three-day-expired sandwiches," I said with a grin.

We finally made it up the stairs. At security in front of the reading room entrance, a very competent guard checked all our bags. He then directed us over to the photo card reader's ticket desk. Gertie and Maude had been here before, so they already had their credit-card-sized photo identification produced by TNA.

The rest of us had to provide two types of identification and sit for a photo so our reader cards could be made onsite.

"Why do they need this?" Pamela asked me as we sat next to each other and answered questions for the TNA staff person.

"It's so they can track where the records go, contact you if there's any issues, plus it's how they scan out documents on loan within the facility," I said.

"Oh, I see. That's pretty clever."

I nodded. "They've modernized archival research. I did a lot of reading about it in my beginner's genealogy course."

Pamela grinned. "I can't wait to look at those matrimonial bureau records. It's just like Christmas and New Year's rolled into one!" Her eyes were bright and eager.

"Just no shouts of glee if you do find something, please," I teased her. "We can cut you a bit of slack at the GGRS, but around here noise is definitely frowned upon."

"Are you saying the van would leave without me?" Pamela asked.

"You might have a very long trip home. And remember, because we live a bit out of the way, then you'd likely have to take the Tube quite a few stops, change at Victoria Station for a main-line train back out to Carlingheath, and then take a taxi to get home to Plumsden, unless the night train goes out that way. Because I know you wouldn't leave until TNA closed for the day." I grinned.

"I'll be quiet, I promise," Pamela said, slightly alarmed at the prospect of a milk run longer than the milkman's own.

"I never knew the threat of a difficult public transport journey home would be so effective," I said.

Once we all had our new reader cards in hand, we trooped over to the reading room and found Gertie and Maude already established at a big oak table surrounded by bookshelves, computers, and other research tables. There were two spare chairs around the table, and in the middle were four large bankers' boxes of paperwork.

Pamela touched me on the arm. "This is it!" she whispered.

"Yes. How marvelous!"

Ewan and the Major went over to the pickup counter to retrieve their requested order of military records from the British Forces in Cairo. The Major's contacts had told him they might have something on file here, and at any rate, since the group was going to TNA anyways, it was worth a shot. They'd found a couple of records online before our trip and wanted to give it a go. They took another table a few spots away from ours and opened some files protected inside acid-free folders.

"How soon do we have to return records before lunch?" Ewan whispered as he and the Major came over to ask.

"I'd say ten minutes. A few other researchers will be doing the same thing, and you want to make sure you're recorded as having given it back," Maude whispered back.

"Got it. By the way, where's Ozzie?" Ewan asked.

"I think he's gone to the library; it's on the same floor as this reading room," Maude said. "Something about wanting to research Calendars of State Papers."

"Ozzie thinks he's related to the Royal Family?" the Major asked. "Who wants to run a book on that?"

A slew of five-pound notes emerged from wallets all around the table and were gently slapped on the oak surface.

"How am I to make any money on this one?" the Major quietly protested. "Everyone's betting against him."

"I'm not," I whispered. "Put my fiver on Ozzie finding he's related to a royal."

"A brave woman. Yes, I shall gleefully take your money," the Major said.

"I have to be brave with you lot around, don't I?"

Everybody smiled. We would've laughed out loud but this was, of course, a place where noise was shunned.

Chapter 20

We refocused at the matrimonial bureau research table of four. A lot of what we were doing consisted of sifting through old files. Considering the tiny poofs of dust clouds that emerged when we opened the folders, it was likely that no one had looked into these files since they were first catalogued by the archives. Thank goodness someone had the sense to send the records to the archives for preservation. The dates ran up to 1951, when it appeared the business closed. Inside the boxes were Francine's old ledgers, newspaper articles showing happy marriage announcements, as well as individual files on each client who had registered for her services.

Francine herself was quite an open book. She'd taken the time to write a five-page, single-spaced, handwritten memoir that detailed her own background as well as her love for matchmaking. She was raised in the East End of London by a very poor family. She'd had a very inauspicious start in life, including picking up scraps of discarded cabbage leaves from underneath greengrocers' barrows and bringing them back to her mother for the midday watery stew pot. Any meat the family did come by was sure to be tough and full of gristle. By chance, and it was a very big chance indeed, she was noticed by a prosperous lady with a big heart who took Francine under her wing and vastly improved her circumstances. It turned out this lady had a soft spot for the poverty-stricken children of the East End and was patron of both the local orphanage and the Poor Relief Society in the 1920s.

Francine had her first set of new clothes at the age of eight and was then sent to a proper school to learn etiquette. She never quite lost her Cockney accent, but at least she knew of the finer things in life and what made a good marriage partner. Her patron made sure of that by blessing her own son's desire to marry Francine; his mother was one of the few upper class who believed that love, not social status, made a good marriage. And never once did Francine forget the fantastic opportunity she was given. Many of her peers had died before they reached the age of fourteen from diphtheria, measles, or malnutrition. Francine was a survivor, determined to make something of herself, and gave back by helping others. Her successful matchmaking service was her way of doing just that, and she also enjoyed great happiness in her life after such a gut-wrenching start.

"Look at this. Francine's doodled personal comments on some of these applicant files," Pamela whispered.

It was true. Each applicant was assigned a simple, typed index card. The card listed their full name, age, nationality, hair color, eye color, height, weight, hobbies, and occupation. Francine took the time to write often brutally honest comments about those looking for love: 'could do with a bath'; 'excessive cologne, enough to choke an elephant'; 'no hope due to rudeness'; 'needs a haircut to show off his lovely eyes'; 'runs in both stockings, not an upscale candidate'.

"Do you think she was being sarcastic?" Gertie asked. She showed us an index card that read 'Rather snobbish and snooty. Best match for woman who owns diamonds and a poodle'.

"Here's another one." Maude showed us a card that read, 'Hard-working girl who would be satisfied with a faithful man who works in an office or as a craftsperson'.

"You wouldn't get away with those comments today. Totally inappropriate," I said.

"The 1930s were not a time of political correctness. They were a time of fascism, poverty, and extremism. I think people were just looking for safety and security with somebody who cared for them. If we haven't walked a mile in their shoes, I don't think we can judge Francine or her clients too harshly." Maude pursed her lips in a firm line.

We all silently contemplated her statement.

Pamela nodded. "It's just so fascinating, looking back at the files containing your ancestors' life histories." She smiled and held up a file marked 'Sylvie Carmine'. Her hand was nearly trembling from excitement.

"Are you serious? You found it?" I gave her a huge smile and rolled my chair over closer.

"It was actually pretty easy. They're all done alphabetically by last name. In my box, I started at the letter 'A' out of curiosity, to get my mind acclimatized to the organizational system Francine used."

"And then you got distracted by about five other rabbit holes," Gertie said. "I do that a lot too. You're researching, say, the last name 'Green' but in the surname 'Brown' you find something neat about somebody's fancy dress shop and playing bridge with the local carriage tradesman, and it just goes from there."

"Thank goodness they make announcements near closing time. Otherwise I'd end up sleeping at this very table, falling over my archive box, reading until I dropped," Pamela admitted.

We all had a quiet snicker over that one.

"What does Sylvie's file say?" Gertie prodded.

Pamela laid the file in front of her and opened the cover. There was the index card in question, neatly typed with all of Sylvie's statistics:

Name: Sylvie Daphne Carmine
Age: 23
Nationality: British
Hair color: Brown
Eye color: Hazel
Height: 5'4"
Weight: 8st 11lbs (123 pounds)
Hobbies: reading, walking, gardening, wireless, cinema, rabbitry
Occupation: War Office – repatriation of deceased soldiers' personal belongings

There was a picture of Sylvie, looking ever so glamorous and just like a movie star. Her hair was done in a roll making a half-circle around the nape of her neck. She had wide, expressive eyes, soft ruby red lips—likely tinted by hand owing to the age of the photo—plus a hint of blush on her cheeks. There was a headshot as well as a full-length photo showing a slim, elegant woman. Francine's notes about Sylvie read:

Sylvie seeks a decent, honest man with a thirst for adventure and an incredibly committed relationship. She wants to be more than a housewife, yet appreciates the value of a well-kept home with a helpful partner. Her war work makes it hard for her to meet somebody, as she spends many hours in a warehouse packaging the war-deceaseds' effects. She feels great duty to her nation yet longs for more positivity and optimism in the future.

Pamela looked up from the file and sighed. "This is amazing, truly amazing. I feel a real connection with her. Imagine doing that during wartime. Every single package you handle during your workday involves a dead man."

"We can research more about what her days were like, if you wish," Maude offered. "How about I go to work on the computer and see what records they hold about women who repatriated soldiers' belongings?"

"I'd like that very much, thank you," Pamela said.

We dug through the files looking for Richard's paperwork. A few moments later we found it under 'Richard Palmer'.

Name: Richard Palmer
Age: 28
Nationality: British
Hair color: Brown
Eye color: Blue
Height: 6'
Weight: 12st 4lbs (172 pounds)
Hobbies: reading, wireless, cycling, hiking, cinema
Occupation: Officer of the British Army

"Nothing about Cairo, hey?" I asked.

"It appears not. Maybe Ewan and the Major are having more luck on that front," Gertie said.

"Is there anything else in the file?"

"There is this," Pamela said, gingerly opening a small notebook filled with pencil drawings. It depicted life in India on a grand estate as well as people in the streets. The artistry was amazing

"It appears to be someone's documentary of life while they were posted overseas," I said. "It was a common pastime amongst those shipped overseas for military duty."

"Richard was quite a talented artist," Pamela said.

"Are we sure it's his?" Maude asked.

Pamela turned to the very back of the book and saw Richard's name printed in clear letters. The date read 1940. She went back to the matrimonial bureau index card Francine prepared for Richard. It was dated 1938. She then checked Sylvie's card, and it was also dated 1938. Francine had marked on both index cards that she matched the pair in January 1939. Going down a little deeper inside Richard's file, there were some other odd, short pencil scratchings saying that the two had met for tea one rainy Wednesday afternoon. Following an absolutely charming courtship, Sylvie and Richard married the day before he was shipped overseas. Their futures were sealed to each other.

"So, the notebook and the matrimonial bureau papers both confirm that Richard was shipped overseas sometime in 1939 or 1940. His destination was India at that time, based on his notebook." Pamela went to the picture of the Cairo ticket stub on her phone; she was smart, not traipsing the original heirloom with her on the trip and risking it being damaged.

"We still need an army record to be totally certain, correct?" she asked Maude and Gertie.

They both smiled at her. "Now you're starting to think like a true genealogist," Maude said with praise in her voice.

We all started to flip through more pages. You never knew what you'd find in another file, even if it wasn't for the specific person you were researching. It was even possible that a prior researcher had misfiled the records; that's why it was important to do a thorough read. In this instance, looking back at old files for other people who used the same matrimonial bureau would easily give us insights into how the organization was run, the typical kind of client, any issues that were repeated, any social history flags. The list was endless.

Gertie looked at the rest of us, ready with a good idea. "Why don't we eat in shifts? Those who are the hungriest can go down at noon and then the rest of us will go at one o'clock. That way we don't have to box all this up and return it to the depository only to have to call it out again when we're back."

"Great idea," I said. "Shall we draw straws?"

"I want to stay until one o'clock. This is too thrilling," Pamela said.

"Julie, why don't you and Maude go at noon? Pamela and I will stay here and woman the fort until you're back," Gertie said.

This was teamwork at its finest. We'd all get refueled yet wouldn't waste precious time without our records. It was a group project today, and the plan made total sense.

We left all our personal research papers with Gertie and Pamela. No sense in bringing along all that extra paperwork. Maude and I went back through security, having our now-lighter plastic bags re-examined. I needed my wallet for lunch, and my phone, although set to vibrate, never left my side. The GGRS had wonderful, competent staff, but one was never quite sure when the next unexpected military vehicle would rumble over the goat meadow, resulting in an emergency call.

We went down the stairs and headed for the cafeteria. The clock read 11:55 a.m. and there was a smattering of people ahead of us in line. Today's hot lunch on the menu was roast chicken, potatoes, and vegetables. We helped ourselves to cold drinks from the cooler on the way down the counter. After paying for our food, we sat in the middle of the cafeteria, ready to enjoy our hot meal.

"I think we're really making progress today," I said.

Maude finished chewing, swallowed, and looked at me with wise eyes. "I agree. It's so nice to bring a new person to the archives and see them discover something truly remarkable. I love seeing people get an early win, as it really helps motivate first-timers to keep researching."

"I think we're unfortunately going to get dead-ended with Richard's army service details. I just have a feeling he was into something secretive, something beyond what would be just left in a historical record file."

"There's the Major and Ewan. Perhaps they found something." Maude gestured over towards the counter.

We saw the men waiting patiently and waved. At least down here in the eating area we could call out their names without violating noise-level protocol. Ewan raised his eyebrows, signaling he'd heard us. The men shunted their trays along the counter to get their meals, joining us a couple of minutes later.

"You meet the nicest people here in the archives cafeteria, don't you, Ewan?" the Major observed.

"Please join us. The food here is marvelous," I said.

"So, gentlemen, how did it go with the military records?" Maude asked, getting right down to business.

"Not an iota of data, absolutely nothing. Richard? The man's like a ghost." Ewan looked frustrated.

"So the elusive Richard continues his myth," I said. "Major, perhaps you were right. Richard has a secret he is hiding with him in his grave."

"Well, if that's what His Majesty's Service wanted back then, then I'm afraid there's nothing we can do. No amount of my military connections and network will breach that confidence," the Major said.

"So Richard was working on something that wasn't exactly legal?" I asked.

"It could be that; perhaps a secret unit that the government promised to disavow if they were ever found out. It could be espionage, it could be something else we haven't even thought of." The Major tucked into his hot meal then quietly put down his cutlery. "Is there any Worcestershire sauce?" he asked, rubbing his hands together.

"For roast chicken?" I asked.

He shook his head. "I like it on my potatoes and gravy."

"I can go and get you a packet if you'd like. I must have missed it on the counter when Maude and I went through the line."

"Never mind. This old man will get through lunch without his dearly loved precious sauce. So long as I've got my sticky toffee pudding for dessert, I'm a happy man."

"I saw those, and we missed it on the counter. What a shame," I said.

The men grinned at their dessert coup. That was, until we made them divide each of their puddings in half to share with Maude and I. We ate the rest of our lunch in near silence. Silence was a good thing, amidst the random, pleasant chatter of fellow researchers around us. Our early morning departure also had something to do with our lack of verbosity. Fred Todling would have felt distinctly out of place at this moment.

It was a cozy, comforting feeling, being here with friends, all working towards a common goal. None of us needed action-packed fireworks days in order to be fully contented. There was a lot to be said about the quiet of the library, the methodical turning of an historic tome's pages, and the excitement of opening a yet-to-be-read archival file. Everyone at the archives, at least the stalwarts, shared this view. Perhaps we were just a different segment of the population. I was certain that there were some people out there who felt that libraries and archives were too stoic and dull. But give me a stack of old archives over a fancy car chase or zombie alien movie any day. I didn't mind what anyone else thought. The archives were my safe, happy place, and I knew I'd be back many times in the future. I knew that the rest of the researchers felt like I did, with the exception of that one afternoon when three men decided to blast their tank documentary film at full volume in the theater room. I could only hope that it was an unusual aberration of their normal moderation and comportment.

Chapter 21

We did a seamless handoff to Gertie and Pamela at 12:59 p.m. Pamela still looked woebegone at having to tear herself away from the matrimonial bureau files. It was obvious she was really enjoying herself ensconced with these records.

Pamela's eyes looked a bit bleary, but she spoke in a bright whisper. "Julie, I've left you and Maude this file to read. It's Francine's personal diary record of how Sylvie and Richard met and married before he shipped out to India. Much more detailed than the other notes."

I took the couple of pages from her, amazed. "You are extraordinarily lucky to find this. This is most unusual for an archive file."

"Beginner's luck? Doesn't matter. I'm just thrilled at what we found here today." Pamela gathered up her wallet and phone, waiting for Gertie to get ready to go downstairs.

"Imagine finding this," I said to Maude. We silently read it together:

> *Sylvie, dear girl, worked for the Army unpacking deceased soldiers' personal effects and arranging delivery to their next of kin. Her care and attention were what caught Richard's eye at the very start. Sylvie is a*

lovely girl, caring and talented, someone who should be on stage. She sings as a hobby, courtesy of her family history of vaudeville acts. An uncle and second cousin were quite famous in the 1890s with a touring song and dance comedy show called the 'Hopscotch Pudding Men'. I am very proud that Richard and Sylvie were engaged and married, courtesy of this Matrimonial Bureau and before Richard shipped out overseas. They deserve every happiness. I received a postcard from her when they reunited in Cairo. Sylvie finally took the plunge and asked to be shipped to Egypt where she sang and danced in the cabaret after joining the Entertainments National Service Association. (I realize that the association's popular nickname was 'Every Night Something Awful', but I choose to disagree. I liked how it cheered people up). I have a photo of them on their wedding day on my desk, pride of place. The last time I heard from Sylvie was in 1944 when she came home, pregnant. Richard came home in 1945 but was killed in a tram accident the following year.

"How tragic," Maude whispered. "After all Sylvie and Richard went through, imagine losing the love of your life in a tram accident. They both survived an horrific war yet it all came down to a traffic accident ... It doesn't say anything about the baby's gender or where Richard was killed."

"Exactly. Don't ever make assumptions. Richard could have just been home for Christmas and then shipped out again," I whispered back.

"Perhaps, but wasn't everybody de-mobbed in 1946?" Maude asked.

I wasn't familiar with that term. "De-mobbed?"

"Sorry. Demobilized. After the war, they certainly had the cleanup to do in Europe, but a great percentage of the men were demobilized the next year."

"And if we think Richard was a spy, then it makes sense he came home. He wasn't somebody who was guarding borders in Germany, for example, between various allied forces. It sounds like he was focused on something else," I said.

"Besides, if the war was over, what was there left to spy on?" Maude asked. She turned the page over and saw there was nothing written on the back. We'd come to the end of the last file but there was a stray photo in the box, inside its own little envelope. This last thing in the back of the file box was a picture of Francine's office storefront. It had a 1930s-style sign, obviously hand-painted, with her firm's name and slogan plus a drawing of two entwined wedding bands. The address of her office in London was on the back of the photo. Guaranteed there wasn't a single person among us who didn't want to go and see what it looked like today.

"Heaven help us if they've turned it into public toilets," I said.

"Or a fish and chips shop," Maude added.

"Love deserves a better memory than that," I said.

We ruminated on this thought and then silently nodded in agreement.

***

Later That Day.

Ewan approached our research table with a slightly panicked look on his face. He placed a small scrap of paper underneath my nose, encouraging me to read it right away: *Ozzie's breaking library protocol. Can you come with me on the double?*

"I'll be right back," I whispered to the other ladies.

Ewan and I hustled from the reading room area to the library section of the floor. This was an area filled with computer carrells and long shelves full of old volumes from multiple centuries past. The reason Ewan had sought me out became rather obvious. There, in a rather bold manner and completely breaching protocol, was research site crowd-favorite Ozzie Boggs. He'd managed to spread himself out across not one but four reader spaces, a stack of nine fat reference volumes surrounding him like a child's enormous snow fort.

"I don't know what he's researching, but it looks pretty intense," Ewan said.

"Let's check this out and see if he needs help," I said.

Ewan and I walked over to Ozzie and waved a brief greeting. He looked up with a grin. "This is really helpful information. I've discovered Calendars of State Papers. Did you know you can find out what a king or queen did on a specific day of a specific year?"

"You'll see what they publicly wanted known they did on that day and year. I'm sure there was a lot that didn't make the record book," Ewan said, "or perhaps got embellished."

"Maybe so, but that doesn't matter here. I've made some tremendous advances today," Ozzie said, quite pleased with himself.

I leaned over to him. "Ozzie, you're not supposed to take out more than about two books at a time. Other researchers may need these volumes."

Ozzie sat up straight. He looked around and then seemed embarrassed. Yes, the man who thought nothing of bringing a smoked-mackerel sandwich into the records area was actually embarrassed. "I just got so caught up in my research. I've completely forgotten my tea breaks, lunch. And all this? What a mess. I've got the King Georges mixed in with the King Charleses. That won't do," he muttered.

"Give us the volumes you're finished with and point us in the right direction. We'll go and reshelve them for you," Ewan said.

I gave Ewan a look of relief.

"Thank you so much. I don't want to be kicked out of TNA the very first day I'm granted reader privileges."

***

Reshelving done, we went back to Ozzie, now working in a much tidier workspace. Luckily the library wasn't too crowded today, so his faux pas of spreading out across multiple workstations hadn't caused any major disruptions. Still, bad habits weren't wise to start, so I was glad we nipped this one in the bud. I looked over at Ozzie and he had a rather confused expression on his face.

"What's the matter?" I whispered to him.

He didn't need to reply because as I looked down at the ancient book laying in front of him, I could see his exact concern. It wasn't apparent if the tome was from the open library shelves or from a box he'd called up from records storage. As he turned the pages of this wonderfully illustrated book of heraldry, it was clear that multiple pages were stuck together and in the process of disintegrating. There was no way any archive could perform a check on all its holdings every single month; with millions and millions of pages within the records, it was an impossible task. So, archivists had to rely upon the good nature of researchers to call their attention to anything that needed restoration.

"Ozzie, I wouldn't go any further than that. This needs a professional on it right away. If you turn any more pages, there is a real risk that it will be permanently damaged."

I went over to the information desk and sought the pleasant-looking librarian at her computer station. She looked up, taking off her reading glasses and letting them hang down in front of her on their glitzy chain. "Yes, can I help you?"

"Hello, I'm working with our colleague, who is sitting over at that table. Number one, he apologizes for taking up too many books and workstations at once. We've corrected that problem."

"Well, we're not too busy today, so we didn't get ruffled about it. But he really should stick to one workstation."

"I know, and also try not to have the entire library on his desk at one time," I said.

"Indeed. Is there something else?" she asked.

"We appear to have a book that needs conservation. It's disintegrating, and it looks like some of the inks used are not holding up over time."

The librarian was instantly concerned. "Oh dear, that's most unusual for this part of the archives. I'll come over and take a look straight away."

She gestured to a colleague who was reshelving a stack of books. She then followed me over to Ozzie's desk. "Now, what have we here?" she asked him. She saw how the beautifully drawn heraldic crests of aristocrats through the centuries were in a severely damaged state. Although the colors were still vivid and the inks had maintained their richness, certain inks were causing the paper to just crumble away, leaving jagged edges within the heraldic crests sticking down on top of the ones behind them.

"I'm very glad you called us over. This is in need of a conservationist's immediate attention. I'm going to call somebody down for you."

Ten minutes later a conservationist, a petite woman with intense blue eyes and a curly bob haircut, came over to us. "Are you the researchers with the damaged book?"

We nodded. "I'm scared to touch it, it's in such a bad state," I said.

Ozzie was a little antsy and the conservationist noticed it right away. "What page were you hoping to view, sir?"

"It was in the seventeenth century," he explained, "the noble Pifflewhist family."

The conservationist flipped through extremely carefully, as her training had taught her to do. "Here's the page you're after. Would you like to take a picture using your phone, without flash, of course, and then I'll take this away for conservation?"

Ozzie did as he was told yet he still didn't explain what he was actually looking for in the bigger picture.

"What will you do with it?" Ewan asked.

The conservationist smiled. "I suspect that this ink contains an iron compound that's eating the paper away. We'll likely separate out each page and put it in a protective cover and possibly put a backing on each crest as well. We do our best, but sometimes a deterioration is so bad it's just fragments that we can save. It really is a shame when something like this happens. You should be very proud of yourself for bringing it to our attention. Thank you so much."

"We just want to preserve it for future researchers. The minute we saw what had happened, we knew it was best to call over an expert," I said.

The conservationist took the book in her careful hands. "You did the right thing. Thank you again."

"So the mystery continues, hey, Ozzie?" Ewan asked.

There was a chain of silence between the three of us.

Ozzie coughed. "Family history always is."

"Did you need any more help?" I asked, trying to figure out what he was researching without being overly obvious.

"I didn't come down with the last shower. I'm researching something private and don't want to talk about it. I'm not Pamela with a cozy family romance. Mine's a bit more confrontational, so I'd appreciate some space on this one." Ozzie spoke in a clipped tone.

Ewan and I were quite taken aback. All we had done was help the man, both here and back at the research site.

Ozzie knew it and sensed our surprise at his harsh words. "Look, I can't discuss it. I know you're curious but it's best to leave this to me. I don't want to drag you into my problems."

This from the man who came in missing front teeth, invited a crow-fest into our parking lot, and stank up our pristine research library with smoked-mackerel.

Oh yes. It was pretty ripe, indeed.

"Ozzie, we'd better pack up. It's time to go," I said.

***

GGRS Van. 7:23 p.m.

Harvey was at our designated spot right on time. He'd even brought along a cooler of fresh sandwiches and bottles of water. Oh, and chocolate. He seemed to have read our minds as to what we needed following a long day at the research desks. Everyone in our group wearily clambered onto the bus. Like creatures of habit, we all took the same seats we had on the drive in from Oakhurst. The bus was a comfort, everyone's heads plumb full of all the incredible archives we'd laid eyes on today. It'd truly been like entering a wonderland, somewhere completely unexpected, where a whole new world opened up as one viewed a file that brought the past to light.

"Everybody safely stowed?" Harvey called out as he started the engine. He was acting the part of the jolly tour bus driver, as if he'd done this gig many times before. He was wearing a cute train engineer's cap embroidered with 'I'm Retired: Be Envious' and had a big grin on his face. I suspected he was rather enjoying himself. It wasn't really a surprise, because when I'd asked if he had a license to drive a larger vehicle, he had produced his accreditation without hesitation. As it turned out, he was licensed to drive anything from a car up to a fifty-three-foot big rig hauling dangerous goods. It'd been part of his army training, and he had also done some side jobs after leaving the military upon retirement.

It just went to prove, never underestimate anyone with a lot of life experience.

"Did you get pictures of all the relevant documents?" I asked Pamela.

She nodded. "Every single page that was relevant to Richard and Sylvie is now on my phone and uploaded to the cloud as backup. For personal use only, of course." She patted the little device with great care. "Wonderful devices, these mobile phones."

"Imagine how romantic that cabaret was in the 1940s," I said to the group. "Late at night, candlelight, sparkly sequins, and the voice of an angel up on stage."

"All those men weary of war and looking for an escape. I'll bet there were quite a few of them after Sylvie," Maude said.

Pamela shook her head. "It's quite obvious that Sylvie only had eyes for Richard. Why else would she give up her life in England and travel halfway across the world to be with him?"

"True. Back then it was rather an exotic and scary place for a single woman," I said.

"Ah, but she wasn't single."

"I wonder if she told them," Pamela mused.

"Who?"

"The army."

"I don't see why she wouldn't. It's not like being married was a crime back then."

"I know, it's just a bit awkward with all those single men around. I'm sure there were regulations about fraternizing with the entertainers."

Ewan smiled. "Ladies, believe in the power of love. Richard was an officer, and I doubt he was roaming the streets late at night in search of seedy entertainment. The ticket stub's from an officer's club, much more of an upscale venue, and right on the British troops' base."

"Thank you, Ewan, for remembering the good in people," I said. I was growing to like this man more and more each day.

We all munched on sandwiches and started to run another bet on who would fall asleep first, Ozzie or the Major. They were sitting in opposite rows, both leaning dangerously towards the aisle. I finally took pity on them and had Ewan go over and encourage them each to take a window seat and lean against the wall of the bus instead of risking crashing headfirst onto the rubber matting.

Maude looked over at me. "So, is Ozzie royal?" she asked in a whisper.

I shrugged. "That still remains to be seen."

"What about the tidy pot of money the Major's collected?"

"I think he'll be playing bookie for a while longer. This is far from over."

Chapter 22

GGRS. 9:37 p.m.

"I have a few antiques shipping out tomorrow," Ewan announced as Harvey pulled the van up in the Greymore drive. "So I likely won't see you until the day after."

"That's fine. It's just going to be another busy day at the research site here anyways," I replied.

"Well, um, we should do this again sometime." Ewan looked a bit lost for something scintillating to say.

"With this crew?" I asked him with a smile.

We looked around the van's interior. Pamela's adrenaline had finally run out and she was asleep at her seat. Ozzie was snoring, as was the Major. Maude was consulting her research notes, ever the genealogy fact checker. Gertie had her earphones on, busy applying some kind of captions to a recent video. That scared me. Her social media posts usually went viral, and often unintentionally so.

"Their hearts are in the right place," Ewan said. "GGRS showed everyone a fabulous day today."

"I had great fun too. Thanks for coming along and helping out."

"One day I'll get busy and research my own family tree, but for now it's rewarding enough helping others discover their own unusual histories."

"As Aunt Edwina used to say, every single person alive is only two generations removed from some sort of petty scandal."

We laughed. Then Ewan got up and there was an awkwardness. He quickly bent down, twisted his frame to be near me and gave me a kiss on the cheek.

I felt my cheeks redden. "Thank you, Ewan. See you in a couple of days." I gave him a firm smile.

He nodded back. "See you soon."

Maude and I watched him leave. She was sitting in the row right ahead of me and swiveled around to meet my eyes. "He will wait, Julie, but not forever. Ewan's a good man."

"I know. It's just everything with Chris and that embarrassing sham of a marriage …"

Maude looked a bit huffy. "I didn't say you should marry the man tomorrow. Just put him out of his misery and let him take you out for dinner to see where it goes. You might actually enjoy yourself."

"I know."

"Besides," she said in a teasing voice, "I've got £10 riding on you and him having a first date before the quarter is out."

"Maude, honestly …" I was both exasperated and tickled pink.

***

GGRS. Next Morning. 9:00 a.m. Sharp.

"Julie Fincher, please," Constable Snowdrop said in his overly officious voice.

"Good morning, Constable. Is there a problem?" I heard Gertie ask.

"I would like to talk to Miss Fincher, please. Immediately, if you can see to it."

My goodness, talk about having ants in his pants.

"Good morning," I said. "How can I help you?" I looked at Constable Snowdrop, who was wearing his ever-present, too-tight uniform. This time he had a serious look at his face, one that was much more intense than when we'd last seen him chasing a galumphing English Sheepdog.

"Good morning." He gave me a firm stare.

"Good morning?" This was getting to be a standoff of trite greetings.

"Er, may I have a word?" he asked.

I showed him through into the private chat room inside the research site facility. We sat down and he brought out a shiny new tablet device. He scrolled through a few photos, then showed me the next one in all its glory. I was looking at two youths scrambling all over the exhibit tank, in the dark, in my back field.

"Oh dear," I said.

"Oh yes," he said. "These two youths then proceeded to go on a graffiti spree in the village of Oakhurst. And yes, I am positive it is not valuable street art that they are producing."

"You're sure about that?"

He brushed off the joke with a withering look. "I'm sure you do not want vandals on this site. What type of security do you have around this military machine parked in your field?"

"Whatever Harvey and the Major are providing."

He wrote down my answer like he was interviewing a key witness in a bank robbery. "I think you may be in a violation of a couple of local bylaws. Number one, inadequate protection of a military vehicle."

"It's an antique on display."

"Does it have a motor?"

"Well, my miniature goats certainly didn't haul it into the field," I said.

Constable Snowdrop checked that off in his notebook as well. "Secondly, do you have a permit for this exhibition?"

"Our charity is a properly registered one that displays antique items and ways of life. It's all in our charter and permitted by the local council."

"Have you registered the tank with the village constabulary?"

I couldn't believe this was happening. Surely, after all the good we were trying to do here at Greymore, we wouldn't be hamstrung by an overly bored police constable. "Look, if we made a mistake with the right permits, then I'm happy to go and get one today." Inside I was still tired from the big trip we had yesterday and was itching to get to the mountain of paperwork covering my desk. Tank permits were about the last thing I wanted to be working on now.

"I'm afraid I'll have to fine you first for noncompliance."

"Noncompliance how?" I demanded.

"Failure to comply with the permitting requirements. How long has the tank been parked there?"

"Since a few days ago."

"Hmm. Did you obtain a special parking permit from the council office?"

By now the pudgy policeman was getting on my nerves. "It's our land. We don't need a special parking permit," I said.

Constable Snowdrop consulted his tablet, scrolling through a detailed table of contents. "As I thought. Right here it says, Article Nine, Section Three, Subclause Twenty-Nine, Subpart B: 'Vehicles over regular cartage weight or for extraordinary purposes, such as movable circus vehicles, must obtain a special permit prior to arriving at the intended destination.'"

"But the tank's not a circus vehicle."

Constable Snowdrop took a quick look out the window at my torn-up meadow. "That's not what the village locals are saying about its arrival. Imagine army men getting the logistics incorrect. Tut tut on that misadventure. I am ordering you to obtain a permit post haste, as well as issuing you a fine."

I took the ticket from him. "£100! For parking on my own property? That's insane."

"I'm sorry, Miss Fincher. I do not make the rules, I just enforce them." He actually looked quite pleased at handing me the ticket. "I only fined you for a first offence. A second one will cost you £500."

I wanted to tear up the ticket right in front of him. "After all we have done to enhance family history in this community, you're giving me a parking ticket for a vehicle on my own property?"

"As I said, Miss Fincher, I do not make the rules, I just–"

"Enforce them. I heard."

"Well then, I'll be off. Wishing you a pleasant day."

I watched the policeman go as I quietly seethed under my breath.

Gertie approached me. "Why the long face, cousin?"

"This." I showed her the ticket.

"It matches the £40 fine I got for parking my car an inch over the line on a B road near Greymore the other day. I just got out to film a pheasant strutting through the fields. Gorgeous shimmery plumage, all coppery, carmine red, and deep forest green. Next thing I know, Constable Snowdrop leaps out of the bushes and tickets me."

"I can't believe it. The tank's on Greymore property. I would understand if we had active military exercises going on, but a museum exhibit? Surely it's none of his business."

Gertie grinned. "I take it you haven't heard about the new quota imposed on Constable Snowdrop?"

"Quota?"

"Yes, he's been tasked with bringing in an extra £5,000 through ticket revenue over the next six months. It appears that the local council mucky-mucks want to improve their bottom line."

"I'd like to give them a piece of my mind. Do they have any idea how much it costs to run a facility like this?"

"We'll just get the military association to pay for it, it's their machine. Aren't they the ones who are supposed to be taking care of the proper insurance and all that?"

"Yes, but Greymore is hosting the exhibition, and it's on our land, so technically we are responsible. That's why I double checked that the insurance is in place in case something goes awry. I guarantee that Greymore's insurance policy is not going to cover a parking ticket."

Gertie scoffed. "These days, it doesn't pay to claim against an insurance policy for legitimate losses unless it's an expensive catastrophe. Some insurance companies use any type of claim as an excuse to non-renew your policy the next time it's due."

"What a sorry state of affairs the world has become," I said.

"It's because they've had fraudulent claims in the past. They're just trying to protect their own bottom line."

I moaned. "Why does everything in the world have to be about money? Can't people just relax and enjoy friends and family plus ancestral research for a little bit, without getting all wound up about their wallets?"

Gertie looked at me and took each of my hands in hers. "Take a deep breath and go have a cup of tea. Take a walk around the building. You'll feel much better after that."

I took her advice. I breathed slowly, and the cup of tea helped. I was halfway around the building and feeling much calmer when I set eyes upon the best stress reliever of all. There, in Greymore's parking lot, was Constable Snowdrop desperately trying to start his police car. After hearing the engine fail to turn over about five times, I knew it was obviously not going to happen. I stopped at the hood of his car and gave him a winsome smile. "Car troubles?"

He looked awfully embarrassed. "Er, yes. I've just called for a tow. It should be here in an hour. Busy schedule today, it seems."

I looked down at how he was parked. We both saw it at the same time. He was three inches over the line separating the last parking stall from the fire hydrant. My fire hydrant, the one that

I paid to have installed for visitor safety when we had renovated Greymore Hall.

I crossed my arms and stood there, staring at him. "Do you have anything else to say?"

The man dithered. He really dithered. I could tell he'd already run up my £100 in his mind long ago as a good helping towards his £5,000 quota.

I took out my cell phone and called the Oakhurst Village Council office. "Yes, hello. I've got somebody who parked their car right in front of my fire hydrant. What is the fine for that?" I waited. I listened. I took a photo of Constable Snowdrop's stalled car, including license plates, blocking my fire hydrant. With glee, too, I might add.

Constable Snowdrop's face fell.

Busted.

Finally, a policeman in the exact place at the exact time when I needed him.

Seeing Constable Snowdrop illegally stranded in Greymore's parking lot made up for all the times I'd been ambushed by a dangerous maniac driver who'd either tailgated, cut me off, or woven in and out of traffic up ahead of my vehicle.

I smiled at him. "Care for some tea and a tour of the World War Two exhibition while you wait? They're sending over an officer from Plumsden right away. And, oh, ticket books are standard issue for every member of the police force, correct?"

Constable Snowdrop buried his face against the steering wheel.

Later.

Luckily, things got far more productive as the day progressed. The Major and Harvey promised to take care of the parking ticket, and within minutes I had a stack of five crisp £20 notes on my desk with profuse apologies from them for not having checked the permitting requirements before arriving on site with the tank.

Pamela was in working on obtaining birth, marriage, and death records from online sites. I leaned over her shoulder to watch as she worked. "Finding what you need?" I asked.

"I got a bit stuck on Sylvie's line, so I'm trying her brother Franklyn now. What I'm basically trying to do is have more sources to confirm Sylvie and Richard's marriage date and location. I also think that my new hobby here may rapidly expand onto other branches of my family tree. It's addictive!"

"Are you using the census or are you not there yet?" I asked.

"Maude said that the September 1939 register by the British government listed everyone in the population, with the plan of getting them an identification card and ration book. They are online, and we can look at records for those people who have already passed away."

"Well, that qualifies because you've already found both Sylvie's and Richard's death certificates, right?"

"I can do better than that. I've got their daughter Isabel's birth certificate from 1944. My mother always told me that her mum's name was Belle. They apparently had a falling out when my mother was in her mid-twenties, and they severed all ties. I never knew my grandmother and I always wondered why."

"You never tried looking for her?"

"All my mother would tell me was that my grandmother Belle, whom we now know is Isabel, had done something she didn't approve of. I didn't really question it until I was sitting here today looking at these records. I wondered what she didn't approve of and how bad it really was."

"Well, one thing we can at least put to rest is that Sylvie, your great-grandmother, wasn't part of the fishing fleet. I did some homework, and it was only operational between 1850 through 1890. That was at least fifty years too early for Sylvie."

"Plus, we already know that she was madly in love with and married to Richard, so there would be no need for her to come over on a ship like that."

"Did you happen to look up the Hopscotch Pudding Men vaudeville act? There's often online records of things like that," I suggested.

"I did find one non-digitized record on a county archives website near London, but the record's sealed until 2028. That made me wonder if it was a criminal front."

I shook my head. "A closed file doesn't necessarily mean that the company and its performers were into something nefarious. A lot of organizations just put a fifty or a hundred year hold on the records to protect the privacy of those who were still living. Sometimes you can get around it with a freedom of information request, but Maude said she doesn't like to rely on those unless it's absolutely necessary. There's usually another way through the door," I said.

"I see."

Maude's voice came over the intercom.

"Julie Fincher, phone call, line two. Julie Fincher, phone call, line two, please."

I left Pamela to her research and went to take the phone in the breakroom. "Julie Fincher speaking."

"Julie, it's Bertie," said the clipped, posh voice on the end of the phone. "Any idea why a visitor of yours is poking around my private club in London?"

"Pardon me?"

"It's this Ozzie Boggs character. Apparently he's made quite a few calls to the club's butler and is asking some rather insensitive questions, implying that I'd put him up to it." There was an elegant pause in Bertie's voice.

"Oh, he did, did he?" This was not good news. The last thing I wanted to do was upset Bertie. "Well, it's news to me, and Ozzie certainly didn't have any goading from us. Did you get any details of what he's looking for?"

I could hear the cash register of the estate shop in the background. Glass jars were rattling against each other, and then I heard Bertie walk outside the shop. Songbirds surrounded him now, and I could envision him walking out to his car.

"It's something about a seventeenth century duel and well-to-do ancestors."

The lightbulb was starting to get a little bit less dim. "Ozzie's been researching Calendars of State Papers along with heraldic crests. We caught him at it in TNA's library yesterday, but he wouldn't share any details."

"Julie, it is rather embarrassing. Would you mind having a word?"

"Of course." I thought on it. "You don't think Ozzie's some sort of secret viscount, do you, Bertie?" It would be quite the skullduggery achievement if it was true.

"Julie, the sordid affairs and secrets of renegade aristocrats usually get around the peerage pretty fast. They circulate faster than the invitations for my annual solstice parties, which are, as you well know, legendary."

"Alright, then. I do apologize for any embarrassment Ozzie's caused. Please understand this is all news to me."

"Thank you, and I'll leave it with you. Toodle-oo!" Bertie rang off as I heard him start the engine to one of his expensive SUVs. I always got a kick out of talking with him when he was about to go on one of his chutney delivery runs. I equated it to the lord of the manor mucking out his horses' stalls. The lord may indeed have staff for that job but just happened to enjoy doing it himself.

And with that, my art patron was gone. Speaking of art, I hadn't picked up a paintbrush in months. There was simply no time to indulge in painting while the Greymore renovations were taking place and I was training to become a qualified genealogist. My summer hiatus from teaching art classes was now turning into my skipping the fall and winter semesters, promising to re-evaluate everything closer to next year's spring semester. I guess I just hadn't expected dead people to take up so much of my time.

Chapter 23

Computer carrell number four was occupied. I strode over immediately and cleared my throat, loudly and on purpose. "Ozzie, have you been telephoning the Duke of Conroy's private club in London and asking impertinent questions?"

His look was far from innocent. "Well, yes. I'm doing some family history research."

Now I was nervous. "You cannot imply that the Duke of Conroy is approving your behavior. Nor should you be using the Greymore Genealogy Research Site's name. What exactly have you been researching?"

Ozzie sighed, then motioned me closer. "Very well, I'll tell you. I have a highfalutin' ancestor who stiffed my family out of our proper inheritance three hundred years ago. I'm going to prove what's mine is mine and I'm taking it back."

A clever approach but riddled with chance.

The main problem was that 300 years provided a lot of wiggle room. Documents were forged, disappeared, burned, altered, torn up, and discarded. The list was endless. Yet here was Ozzie Boggs, giving it the old college try. The very least he should do was consult his solicitor before he started harassing members of the aristocracy.

"Ozzie, the duke just phoned me and is quite upset that you're bothering the concierge of his private club."

"I'm just asking some simple questions about my family background." He gave me the innocent look an eight-year-old boy would give to his mother as she stared at his muddy, torn trousers and the half-eaten tea cake in his grubby hand.

"What kind of questions?"

"About their membership. About what went on hundreds of years ago. Where else can I get that information?"

"Have you tried the archives?" That was the obvious first place to look.

He sat up straighter in his chair. "Of course I've tried the archives. I tried London. I tried all the surrounding counties. I can't find a thing. The truth of the matter is, the club is still in existence and hasn't donated any of its old records."

"I hope it's keeping all of its old records in proper climate-controlled conditions. Paper is super sensitive to moisture and heat," I said.

"I wouldn't know. They're very cagey with answers, and I can't seem to get anything out of them."

"Private clubs are notoriously respectful of their members' privacy."

"Including those who were members in 1722?"

"No, really?" I was a bit stunned. "You've gotten that far back?"

It was as if he'd read my mind. "Yes, and I've proven it properly through all the right certificates, parish registers, land records, and census documents. I even found actual letters in my father's safety deposit box dating back centuries that prove this is the right line."

"What kind of inheritance are we talking here?"

"All I know is that there was a duel with someone royal involved and our family line was shafted out of a bunch of money. It's not proper." He was firm and definite on those items.

"Well, if you're related to the family, I don't see why the private club can't at least give you the names of your ancestors." This was starting to sound like an unnecessary cover-up to me.

"That's what I keep telling the concierge. All he does is brush me off like I'm some country yokel who has no business even using a telephone. I'm treated like someone who thinks an upscale meal is one requiring cutlery."

I pondered it. I didn't like how things were so restricted from an immediate descendent. "Two things. Number one, have you spoken with your solicitor about the Freedom of Information Act that came into force in 2005? Secondly, I can talk to Bertie and see what he can do from his end."

Ozzie held up his hands in self-defence. "I'm not trying to be difficult, I'm just trying to prove my point. At this juncture, it appears they're protecting the other side, and that's not fair. I'm the one who was shafted." He jabbed his index finger at his chest.

My heart went out to this man, an ordinary citizen, who just wanted to figure out a genealogy mystery. He shouldn't be barred from having basic information about his relatives. I made my decision to help him right then and there.

"I think we both have some follow-up to do, Ozzie."

***

Solicitor Fred Todling arrived at Greymore, briefcase in hand, a mere hour later. It was raining outside, and I could tell that he was concerned about his new shiny leather shoes. His footwear was obviously the recipient of some recent, careful polishing. Fred took a furtive glance around the GGRS to see if there were any potential raincoat or umbrella stealers lurking in the alcoves. Having decided that the coast was clear, Fred hung up his coat on the rack and put his umbrella in the stand. I'd insisted on making it easy for visitors to store their outerwear; England was known for its rainy climate, and the last thing we wanted was to introduce water droplets onto valuable items here in our library.

"And a very good day to you, Julie," Fred announced. "I must say, you are to be heartily congratulated for perpetuating such a wondrous group of family history researchers in our little, loyal community. What once was deemed impossible has now been brought to full fruition through the labors of your love and dedication. On behalf of the community and all of its surrounds, thank you for turning Greymore into such a stupendously glorious resource for so many heartfelt projects."

It always took me an extra second or two to process what Fred was saying, mainly because my brain had to wade through all the excess nouns and flowery adjectives. Thank goodness I wasn't paying to have this conversation with him; this was all on Ozzie's dime.

Ozzie, Fred, and I sat at one end of the large table in the meeting room.

I started. "Thank you for coming, Fred. We are unfortunately not in the Duke of Conroy's good books right now–"

"Perhaps you're not selling enough of his mango chutney?" Fred asked with a grin. "If your customers prefer something different, perhaps I can suggest some of my pickled broccoli garnishes. They go well with ham, salami, even chicken or egg sandwiches."

"Er, no, Fred, it has nothing to do with condiments." I gave Ozzie a lead-in.

Ozzie leaned back in his chair, and the ergonomic piece of furniture moved to accommodate his shift in body weight. "I'm afraid that I am the cause of this problem," he said.

Fred looked alarmed. "You've upset a valued and esteemed member of the peerage? We must correct this faux pas with immediacy! Posthaste!" The grin disappeared off the solicitor's face. He opened his leather-bound notebook. His fountain pen was rapidly uncapped, and he sat poised to make notes on how he could best rectify this apparently horrific situation.

Ozzie continued. "I need to learn about members of this fancy private club in London in order to prove my family's claim to a wrongly diverted inheritance."

Fred furrowed his brow. "I take it one of your family members belongs to this private club and is not releasing information to you? What is this person's name, please?"

"Douglas Wormston."

"And he resides where?" Fred continued, rapidly scribbling down this rather plummy-sounding name.

Ozzie looked confused. "Er, he's in London."

"And his specific address, please?"

It would be interesting to see how Ozzie would handle this one.

"Er, Swain's Lane in London, near the Archway Tube station."

"Right." Fred scribbled this down and then he looked up, pen poised in the air. A single drop of ink left the tip of his pen as he hovered it too close to the paper. The dark-blue ink spot grew. "Say, isn't that the address for–"

"Highgate Cemetery? Yes, of course it is. Man's been dead for nearly three hundred years," Ozzie said matter-of-factly. "Friends in high places got him moved to that particular cemetery when it opened in 1839."

"I'm afraid I don't understand. You're trying to find a three-hundred-year-old member of a private club to prove an inheritance from today?" You could almost see the wheels turning in Fred's head.

"Sort of. In 1851, this club ensured my inheritance went to a cousin instead of to me. That mistake has traveled through the course of time, and I'm the first one on my family tree to figure out what went wrong and when."

"Well, I do have some senior clients, but I think this one certainly qualifies as the oldest," Fred said.

The solicitor was serious, but I found his blatant understatement to be rather hilarious. I had to bite my lower lip to prevent myself from laughing.

Time for me to intervene. "Ozzie says he's been through all of the normally available records such as certificates, census, manorial records, and online research sites, but it's this private club that holds the real records. It's some kind of dispute between a royal and his ancestor. I'm guessing this royal unduly influenced the court back in the day."

"Thus relieving me of the inheritance I was due," Ozzie said.

"Well, Ozzie, you are yet again expanding my law practice," Fred said. "My first question is do you have a copy of the will?"

"Yes. I found a copy of it in my father's safety deposit box. That's how I know the name of the man that I'm after."

"Your distant ancestor who is now warming the ground at Highgate Cemetery?" Fred asked.

"Yes," Ozzie said.

"What are the chances of going back this far in time and figuring it out?" I asked Fred.

"It depends how serious it is and if we can convince a judge that we have an ironclad case. Some of our present-day laws were created in medieval times. For example, consider the rights conferred on the British people that originated with the Magna Carta issued in 1215."

"So you're saying there's a good chance I can right the wrong that was committed centuries ago?" Ozzie asked.

"I'd say there's more than a good chance, so long as you have the correct records in hand. The law doesn't work on hearsay and sketchy witnesses. For example, you cannot tell a judge that a man you know heard from someone two villages away that his cousin two generations back told him the will wasn't probated. That simply will not hold water, beit drawn from a well, distilled, sparkling, and–"

"But he has the will, and if we can get the records of what's at this private club in London, then I'd say he has a pretty good chance," I added. I hastily quieted myself because I was certainly not trained as a solicitor.

Fred gave me a kind look. "An excellent observation, Julie. I would be more than happy to extend the full breadth and scope of my legal training onto this case as soon as the documents are produced forthwith."

More bafflegab from the king of the thesaurus.

"So what are our next steps?" Ozzie asked.

"First I need to take a look at the will from your father's safety deposit box," Fred said.

"Oh, I have that here," Ozzie said in a bright voice. "Been carrying it around for a month or so now."

Fred and I both looked at Ozzie, mouths agape. "You mean you've been sitting on it for all this time and not telling anybody?" I asked.

"I wanted to make sure you lot knew what you were doing before I let my family secret loose."

Ozzie said it with a slight bit of disdain, as if we were peasants or minions whose only sure talent was opening a cardboard box. This from the man with loose false teeth, who used our state-of-the-art theater room for siesta time.

"I assure you, Ozzie, that we have no intent of spreading your possible good fortune amongst the rest of the visitors here at the GGRS. That's just not what we do here," I said.

"And if it does get out? What are you going to do?" Ozzie persisted.

"Then we'll put you into Greymore's witness protection program. You'll have to leave the world as you know it behind, move overseas to South America …" I looked at Ozzie to see if he was buying any of this tripe.

"Really?" he asked, eyes open wide.

"Ozzie, really–" Fred started.

"The truth?" I continued. "We'd probably ask the rest of the group to help. If only you'd let down your guard a little bit and realize that Greymore has a wonderful team of expert researchers here to assist. They'd find it a fascinating thing to work on with you. But until today, you chose to squirrel yourself away in computer carrell number four and work alone." I settled back in my chair, hands calmly folded over my lap.

There was now dead silence in the meeting room. At the present moment, there would be more noise at a mime show.

"I didn't think of it," Ozzie said. "I've always had a hard time making friends and trusting people."

Fred looked at me, and we knew our client and friend needed some reassurance.

Fred was the first to offer an olive branch. "Well, you're in good hands here now. I will also confirm with you that I am one hundred and ten percent dedicated to helping you with this illustrious possible inheritance that you may encounter on your walk down this path we called life. How about we get started?"

Chapter 24

Now that the ground rules were established, we moved on to more specifics.

"Could you tell me exactly what types of probing questions you asked the private club concierge?" Fred asked.

"About member records and the scandals from the nineteenth century," Ozzie explained. I noticed that his checkered shirt was rumpled and there was grease under his fingernails.

"Aha. Now I understand the club's concierge's reticence to communicate with you. I am familiar with the private club you refer to, 'Club 18th'. The name stands for the century in which it was founded," Fred said.

"That's rather odd," I said.

"When it was originally founded, it was called the 'Peregrine Bluebloods Club'. A few centuries later, there was a rather unfortunate outcry from well-heeled members about being associated with an endangered species. So, they subsequently decided to rename themselves sometime in the 1950s. Eighteenth century roots translated into 'Club 18th'."

"This is one of those fancy clubs with dark cherrywood paneling, overstuffed leather club chairs, and zebra pelts on the walls, isn't it?" I said with a bit of disdain.

Fred gave me a condescending look. "I'm afraid it is, Julie. But never fear, they admit more than just men today."

"I've done some reading on the gentlemen's clubs of the 1950s. They were quite sexist and elitist," I said. "Fifty men squirreled away in a building with unlimited cigars and whiskey is a recipe for all sorts of mischief."

"Or perhaps a jolly good time?" Fred suggested with a grin.

"If you had a nagging, battle-axe of a wife who consumed a bottle of vodka every day, you'd need a private place to run to, trust me," Ozzie said.

"And do you speak from experience, Mr. Boggs?" I asked in a sweet tone.

"More than I'd like to admit," Ozzie said.

I rolled my eyes. "Just tell me there's nothing too forward involved, though I'm sure Bertie wouldn't sanction a club with that behavior."

"I'm quite certain it's not that type of club," Fred said.

"Have you been?"

He nodded. "Trying for a fourth time to get membership."

"You were blackballed?" I asked.

He nodded again. "The last time Barnaby escaped, he ate half of my neighbor's rutabaga patch."

"And your neighbor is?"

"Club 18th's esteemed membership secretary," Fred said with great sorrow.

"Oh dear."

"I am running out of amends to make." Fred coughed in all politeness. "Now, we must get back on topic," he said with some serious urgency. "Ozzie, you said you had a copy of the will along with you?"

"1750. And yes, I put a copy of that right here in my file." Ozzie hauled out a ten-page photocopy of an ancient document. Thankfully it was clear and easy to read.

"Two things," I noted. "We need someone who is an expert in reading this old style of handwriting. Number two, how come your family has the will and not the family that actually received the inheritance?"

"And that's the real question," Ozzie said. "My cousins do hold the original will, but it was written prior to the one that I have in a safe deposit box at the bank, the copy of which you are looking at now. I've already had it transcribed by an expert and here's the transcription." He handed it over to me.

"Ozzie, you've really been holding out on us," I exclaimed. "We could have gotten started ages ago if you'd only disclosed that you had all this lot."

He shrugged. "Again, trust issues."

Fred interjected. "Well, as your solicitor I would advise you that the other will definitely needs to be reviewed to ascertain which is the legitimate one. Oftentimes the courts go on the historical record beyond what is written on the will, if there is a smudged date, for example."

"This is why there's a few witness statements in the file too," Ozzie said.

"Is there a royal connection?" Fred asked, his curiosity intensified. He rearranged the lapels of his blazer and straightened his tie. "A royal connection. Imagine the people that we would need to speak with on a purely legitimate, legalistic basis." Fred seemed quite lost in a reverie thinking of the future networking opportunities this presented.

"Yes, there is some type of a royal connection, but it all leads back to the records of the club," Ozzie said. "We need access to figure it out."

I looked at both men in the room. "Do I hear field trip?"

***

We restricted this particular London trip to a small insider group consisting of Gertie, Fred, Ozzie, and myself. Gertie was along for her advanced genealogy research expertise. Fred would provide the legal speak, Ozzie was the claimant, and I provided the link to their current member, the Duke of Conroy, my art patron, Bertie.

Jacques and Maude were in charge of Greymore while we were away. Ewan was busy at his shop in Plumsden shipping out antiques and Pamela was away at a hospitality conference specific to pub owners. In other words, I had the all-clear to go on another genealogy research adventure. I loved doing this, as did everyone else accompanying me to the Plumsden train station.

We decided to take public transport simply because it was a pretty straight in and out route to Club 18th via Victoria Station. Bertie was going to meet us at the club, and generously offered the use of his London townhome if we needed to stay another day to do research. He'd already arranged with the archivist to pull the exact ledger book that we were after for Ozzie's research. Once Fred and I had gotten the concierge, club archivist, and Bertie on a conference call, fully explaining the historical dilemma faced by our rather unpolished gentleman visitor, they all decided to help. Club 18th had a long-standing motto of 'Be kind to others and expect less in return'. Knowing that we might have cause for changing a 300-year line of succession in a private wealthy family, as well as the potential of a royal connection that might possibly get leaked to the press ... well, let's just say Fred and I both made it rather enticing for the group to participate in figuring out our little research mystery.

Gertie and I assumed that there was a dress code of business casual or higher, and we were both dressed appropriately in suits and nice low heels. Fred was in his standard navy three-piece suit and was completely appropriate. Ozzie, on the other hand, showed up in dark trousers, shiny cowboy boots with silver tips and heels plus a bolero tie over a denim shirt. All he was missing was the ten-gallon hat and silver belt buckle.

The front door to the club was a nondescript dark-brown surface. The entire surrounding wall was of matching appearance. Two humongous potted ferns stood watch on either side of the door, in muted brown pots. A wall-sconce lamp, emitting a warm orange glow, hung on the wall directly above each fern and cast a warm shadow. The ferns were so large that if I picked up a single one of their fronds and waved it in the air, surely people three blocks away would feel the breeze. There was a burnished wooden door knocker affixed to the center of the door, carved in the shape of a peregrine falcon. It was incredibly accurate for the club's history, right down to the bird's blue-painted beak.

Fred reached out and knocked a few times.

An intercom off to the side slightly crackled, making me jump. Not one of us had noticed it, because it was hidden behind one of the ferns. "Membership number, please?" a formal British accent requested.

"Solicitor Fred Todling and colleagues here to see the Duke of Conroy," was Fred's officious response.

There was a pause. "Please come back when you're dressed appropriately."

The intercom crackled off.

Everybody looked at everyone else, wondering what on earth the voice meant.

I talked everyone through it. "Gertie and I are in suits. Fred, you're wearing a business suit. Ozzie, I'm sorry, but that leaves you."

"They can't ban cowboy boots," he complained. "This is my best footwear."

Fred held up his phone, the club's website visible. His face crumpled slightly. "Perhaps not the boots, Ozzie, but they do require a jacket."

"Do you happen to have a spare one in your briefcase?" Ozzie asked.

"Alas, I do not," Fred said with incredible diplomacy.

Ozzie opened the plastic shopping bag that he'd jammed under his arm. "Well, I do have this jacket," he said, hauling out a very wrinkled, flimsy, nylon rain jacket that looked long enough to cover his lower waist. It was one that you pulled over your head and immediately felt like you were in a steam bath with no oxygen.

"Er, I don't think that's quite what they mean by a jacket. A sports jacket, a suit jacket, more formal attire?" Fred prompted.

"Oh. No, I don't have one of those," Ozzie said.

Gertie pointed across the street. "Would that do?"

I followed her line of sight and saw a men's clothing shop. "It's worth a go," I replied.

Twenty minutes later we were all back clustered around the club's unique front door, this time with Ozzie kitted out in an extremely sharp navy-blue, double-breasted yacht captain's blazer and crisp white dress shirt. It turned out that the shop across the street was where yachting club members purchased their tailored goods. Ozzie looked rather odd with cowboy boots and a yachting blazer. The only question a passerby might ask now was if he planned a cowboy hat or ship's captain's hat to complete his unique ensemble.

Ozzie was having a bit of fun with this, and he pushed ahead of the rest of us to use the peregrine door knocker.

The intercom crackled again. "Membership number, please?"

"Ahoy! Fred Todling and colleagues, please, guests of the Duke of Conroy."

There was another pause, thanks likely to the dual security cameras watching our every move.

The intercom crackled again. "One moment, please." The intercom shut off and four seconds later we heard three large door bolts unlock. The door swung open without a squeak. In front of us stood a tall, slender butler dressed in a formal uniform, right down to his pinstriped trousers and incredibly shiny patent-leather shoes. "My name is Marlon, the underbutler. Welcome to the club."

"Like the magician? Excellent," Ozzie said as he strutted in like he owned the place.

"Mar-LON, not Merlin," the underbutler corrected. I followed his eyes as he watched Ozzie's silver-tipped cowboy boots parade across the undoubtedly priceless oriental carpet.

The rest of us came in at a bit slower pace, taking in the new world we'd just entered. It felt like someone had whispered 'Open Sesame' and granted us access to Aladdin's secret cave.

All the magazine columnists had it right. We were in a dark-cherrywood-carved paneled hall, and the paneling covered the entire ceiling as well as all four walls. The warm orange light sconces continued on the inside of the club, leading a straight line towards a set of rather imposing-looking stairs. There was an elevator off to the right with burnished brass doors, obviously for those who were unable, unwilling, too busy, or too important to take the stairs. I caught a glimpse of Marlon's workstation to the left: he had nine security cameras all going at the same time, in full color. There was also an advanced computer station set up with three flat-screen monitors. The shelves were lined with work orders in three priority piles. A bowler hat and a light rain jacket were on a stand to the right, hanging on elegant, curved hooks. In the far, far distance I could hear the gentle clink of glasses and murmurs of laughter. Ah yes, the elite were in their hideaway.

The elevator dinged. The brass doors opened and out walked Bertie, resplendent in a dark-maroon smoking jacket with a black velvet collar. The name of the jacket itself was a large misnomer because Bertie wouldn't ever go near anything containing tobacco. Still, it was a moniker the establishment would certainly never try to change because it was a legendary part of British history and upper-class culture.

Bertie gave us a big grin. "You made it!"

I went over and let him kiss me on the cheek, as was the manner of all well-brought-up gentlemen. "We did. Thank you for facilitating our visit."

"Nonsense. We just had some early communication errors. You have to understand, Mr. Boggs–"

"Ozzie, please," Ozzie said, extending his hand and shaking Bertie's.

Bertie continued. "This club is where a lot of the movers and shakers of London and some from overseas like to come and relax after a busy day. We've unfortunately been the target of those dreadful gossip columnists who want to dish the dirt on anything remotely unsavory. We even had one of them coming undercover as a Scottish baron last year; he did untold amounts of damage to one rogue marquis hiding from his debtors up in the Lake District. So, when you phoned asking directly about a scandal, you simply rubbed the bristles on this hedgehog the wrong way."

Gertie and I smiled because we couldn't decide if stuffy Marlon realized it was just a figure of speech or if Bertie was actually referring to him as a small, spiny-coated creature.

"Sir, shall I call down for someone to assist your guests with any of their ... belongings?" Marlon asked, eyeing the plastic bag under Ozzie's arm, appearing to consider our friend as one of the great unwashed.

"I shall do it myself, Marlon. Thank you for your help. Now come on, troops, up the stairs and I'll introduce you to our archivist," Bertie said.

Five minutes later we were all ensconced in a private meeting room with overstuffed leather chairs on casters, a huge gleaming walnut table, black leather blotters at each place, and a cabinet behind us filled with expensive cut-crystal glasses. Menus were already at each place setting, precisely parallel to the nearest table edge. Equestrian prints covered nearly every wall, including the stairwell plus the common area we'd glimpsed on the way to this meeting room. Before settling in here, we'd passed a collection of non-politically-correct safari taxidermied big-game heads in the snooker room.

"I thought we'd have our tea and discuss things with our archivist. After the food is cleared away, we'll go into the archives room and Elsie can show us the records you are searching for." Bertie looked at us with the gregarious nature of a good and friendly host.

The club lived up to its reputation. It was a high tea unlike anything I had ever experienced. At the very centerpiece of the polished walnut table was an intricate sugar sculpture display of an underwater sea kingdom. An octopus was at the center, airbrushed into a grey blue, its eight curled tentacles complete with pink suction cups underneath. A variety of tropical clown fish, painted in bright orange-and-white stripes, were adhered to tall bits of colorful coral that gave it a truly authentic feel. This was a chef's artistry at its finest.

The requisite cucumber sandwiches were present, indeed measured to perfect proportions for each platter. We also had salmon and cress, ham and egg, cheese and pickle, roast beef with mustard, and tuna. Of course, the tuna at this establishment wouldn't smell; they'd undoubtedly figured out a way around that pesky problem too. Five different types of tea were on offer as were an assortment of cold beverages. There was a white linen tablecloth, bone china, silver cutlery and condiment jars. The sandwiches were followed by a raspberry almond tart, a feather-light apricot roll as well as a rainbow assortment of macarons. The room soon devolved into a focus on our delighted tastebuds sincerely enjoying the luxurious foods we were served.

Fred was still trying to take all of this in. He had been awfully quiet since our arrival, appearing overawed by the place that wouldn't admit him to membership. He knew that this was where the great prosecutors and defenders came to swim, play squash, read newspapers, and meet the important people, the ones us mere mortals usually only saw in magazines. Perhaps Fred wondered if he would ever get to this level of the law with his own little practice out in the country. Perhaps he was also going through a reckoning of his own, wondering if this really was something to aspire to or whether he was happy enough with his lot.

I knew I didn't miss the big-city career lure; I valued cozy homes, my dedicated, kind friends and family as well as the untold numbers of humorous incidents that rural life provided. Cucumber sandwiches could either have their crusts on or their crusts removed. Today they would be served with crusts cut off, and I was sure the chef used a ruler to measure out the width of each sandwich to match. It was all part of the service that club members bought with their annual dues package. It was definitely an interesting world to visit, one that had to be respected because this was where some of the big decisions of the world were made. However, I was far from willing to diminish the importance of Oakhurst village and the great manor houses that surrounded it.

I wasn't sure if Ozzie hoped to be connected to royalty or not; that was something we were going to find out soon enough. Most of us had money riding on the answer. But as I looked at the man in his yachting blazer and cowboy boots, I couldn't help but wonder if the very same thoughts were running through his mind.

Chapter 25

Archives Room. Club 18th, London. 2:17 p.m.

"I'm very glad you persisted. It's quite a thrill to meet a living descendant of one of the club's original two founders." Elsie Rose, the club's archivist, spoke from under a fringe of yardstick-straight chestnut hair that flowed effortlessly into a silky bob cut. She was of mid-height and wore stocky wedge heels, likely to look her male colleagues right in the eye. It effectively forced her point across with unyielding emphasis.

"I put aside a few of the record books from the pertinent time for us to look at. If there's anything else you need as we start reviewing, don't hesitate to ask. Bertie and Cuthbert told me it's all access granted."

"Cuthbert?" I asked.

"Oh, Mark Cuthbert, our head butler," Elsie responded.

As if on cue, another man in tails, pinstriped trousers, and shiny shoes popped his head around the corner. This one looked a lot more pleasant than the underbutler Marlon we met downstairs. He stood in front of us with a kind smile. "Please allow me to introduce myself. My name is Cuthbert, and if you require any extra services during your visit, please do not hesitate to let me know. You can contact me by pressing the brass button on the wall in any room of the house."

Ozzie dug his elbow into Fred's side. "Imagine calling this humongous club 'the house'."

Cuthbert heard. Of course he heard. He was the one in charge of taking care of all of these oddities in the social circle and was attuned to every little nook and cranny, surreptitious comment, or carpet fiber bent out of shape. "We call the club 'our house' so all of our members and their guests feel most welcome. Please consider me at your service." He left, closing the door behind him.

We stood inside a plain office with three desks filled with computers and modern-looking file folders. There were some filing cabinets, telephones, a shared printer, and a few tall windows that looked out onto the busy street below. This was the fifth floor, a complete oasis of calm. On the back wall hung a painting of fourteen men from 1722. I walked up to the painting and read the gilded plaque on the frame: 'Douglas Wormston and John Zerruly, Founders, with Club Members'. The founders each held a small golden mascot statue of the Peregrine Blue Club, and it looked like both statues' beaks were made out of expensive sapphires. All of us crowded around the picture, fascinated.

"Is that my ancestor?" Ozzie said with excitement, pointing at Douglas Wormston.

"If you can prove you are indeed related, then he most certainly is," Elsie said. "This room is where I hang my hat. I share an office with my assistant but she's away on holidays right now. This place is the true center of this club's history."

"I don't understand. Where are all the records?" Gertie asked.

"Our world revolves around a series of buttons and codes," Elsie explained. "Here, just watch." She went over to the painting and entered a code on the keypad next to it. The bookshelf beside it suddenly moved aside, opening up into a glass-walled room that contained rows and rows of archived record books. At the end of the room, we saw a vast table where one could sit and consult the documents.

After the murmurs of surprise had died down, Elsie explained some more. "The room is climate controlled for moisture, heat, air quality, everything like that. With these records going back hundreds of years, we can't be too careful."

"Is it expensive to maintain something like this?" I asked.

"Yes," she said. "But luckily I've got really dedicated bosses. I'm given the budget to do whatever I must to maintain these records in perfect condition."

"Don't you want to donate them to a government archives?" I asked.

"No, for us that doesn't make sense. We're still an active club, and our members refer to these records quite often."

Ozzie was interested in this comment. "Have you dealt with any other member disputes or family grudges?"

Elsie nodded. "Let's see, there was a dispute between two club members over who owned an elephant in Kenya. Something about a drunken poker game that happened on safari."

We all looked perplexed.

Fred was brave enough to push on that one a bit. "You're serious? The ownership of a gigantic mammal was determined by a hand of cards?"

"Well, it turned out to be more than just a single hand of cards. It was more like an entire evening that just got wilder and more of a blur as things progressed. But essentially, yes."

"What on earth would you do with a live elephant? Did they want to bring it back home?" I asked.

"By then we had two members very upset with each other. The butler at the time stepped in along with the club's executive committee and arranged for the animal to be maintained at a wildlife preserve in Kenya. The owner got recognition in the form of a plaque hung on the front gate. The elephant was happy, and the problem was resolved."

"Anything else?" Ozzie asked. "I'm just trying to understand how unusual my particular request really is."

"Well, we've of course suffered all the usual political-party disputes in the common room, complaints over the squash-court lines being too dull for regulation play, and in the 1850s we had a rather ugly dispute over a hansom cab company ownership. Both claimants were club members and ended up dividing the membership into two factions. We eventually got legal advice and told both parties to take their dispute to court. It was then that the archives really proved their worth because our club records proved that one man hadn't been at his bank at the time he claimed he was paying for his majority share of the company. In fact, our records showed him having high tea here with two members of the peerage at the time in question. The butler testified to that fact."

"Music to my ears, in terms of evidence," Fred said. "I assume the case was dismissed?"

Elsie grinned. "As soon as that lie was brought to light, the entire case started to unravel. The judge granted the motion to dismiss, and the original cab-company owner was able to recoup his legal fees from the other party. I just love it because it proves the power of historical records."

"Hence why your members are so keen on maintaining their records on site," Gertie said.

"Government archives are usually pretty good about giving you access, and also on a prompt basis," I said.

"Oh, I know, they're wonderful people and facilities," Elsie said. "The concern that a lot of our members have is with keeping convenient access to their family records that go back centuries. They frequently refer to these records, but usually for less drastic reasons, such as pure genealogy and history interests. Remember too, not every organization has the budget to build and maintain a facility like this. If we didn't have climate control, there is no way I would want these records on site."

We all stood in the climate control room and gawked; Elsie had closed the glass door behind us as soon as we entered. The machines monitoring the humidity had started politely whirring at a higher volume in our presence. Our breath clouds were changing the moisture levels inside and thus the machines worked harder to ensure the environment was kept on a super steady, even keel.

Elsie pointed to the table at the back. "I already put four record books out for you. Minute books from the club's inception along with a scrapbook that shows all the donated leaflets from the eighteenth through the nineteenth centuries."

"Leaflets? What are those from?" I asked.

"We have a long-standing tradition with any member in private business to donate a corporate brochure, leaflet, or report for our records. It's just a way of us maintaining the social and industrial history of our members."

"What a clever thing to do," Gertie said. "You had a wise archivist back in those days. Someone was really thinking ahead."

"My favorite is the leaflet for the stuffed toy firm that started operations in 1879. They had ten different teddy bears and twenty-one different exotic animals. The firm's quality and workmanship were exquisite."

"I'll bet one of those toys today goes for thousands at auction," I said.

"The rarest toy was the tiger model. One recent example went for £29,000 at auction," Elsie replied.

"I'd like to look through the scrapbook," Ozzie said.

"Of course." Elsie handed us pairs of new white cotton gloves. They were the kind that one could use for overnight beauty treatments or, in this case, archival work. "These prevent the oils from your hands getting onto our papers."

"There's a bit of a controversy about these right now, to use or not to use, correct?" I asked.

Elsie sighed. "Yes. Personally, I believe that the oils from one's hands actually help preserve leatherbound books by keeping the hide supple and conditioned. However, I don't like the idea of hand cream seeping onto pages that are perhaps more damp than ideal conditions. I always wear gloves just because it's my personal preference. I think that's what the archival industry has concluded. It's all about personal choice."

Gertie laughed. "Whoever thought we would be calling 'archiving' an industry?"

We all had a good laugh as we sat down at the table. Fred and Ozzie looked the most hilarious wearing the white gloves. They reminded us of cartoon characters in their bright-white gloves as they slowly thumbed through pages one by one.

The earliest records book revealed the club's first set of trustees, bylaws, and articles of incorporation, both dated 1722. The Peregrine Blue Club's founders, Douglas Wormston and John Zerruly, had set it up properly, implementing all the legal requirements. Their first twelve members were the elite of British society and included businessmen, politicians, and three members of the peerage. With all of those fancy people, beyond a doubt the club had royal connections right from the start.

"I think there was something very fishy going on," Ozzie said as he flipped forward in the record book. He was reading to find every reference to his ancestor. No doubt there were plenty of meeting minutes that referred to his ancestor's equal partnership in the club.

"Are you saying that your family was cheated out of this club's ownership?" Elsie asked.

It was an extremely logical question and one that wasn't yet answered. The will Ozzie had from his father's safety deposit box unfortunately wasn't one of those super detailed ones that made it really easy to track. It just said 'all related businesses I own that my heir is due'. His heir was defined on the will as one son: Joseph.

"Not exactly, but that's how this whole mess started," Ozzie said.

"You ought to have given us a bit more to go on, because unless we know what inheritance you've been cheated out of, we don't know how to apply the law," Fred advised.

Ozzie reached for the scrapbook of leaflets. "Hand me that, please," he said.

Gertie pushed the scrapbook over to him and Ozzie started turning pages until he reached 1749. He stopped and stabbed his finger at a leaflet that stood out from everything else. It read 'Zerruston's Fine Confectionery'. It was an incredibly gorgeous, hand-drawn, single-page flyer that depicted a store filled to the brim with chocolates, mints, and striped sweets, all in glass jars and boxes.

"No. You're claiming ownership of the Zerruston sweets company? They're absolutely massive," I said, stunned.

Ozzie merely nodded.

"But their revenues are in the hundreds of millions every year. There was just a report in the paper about England's top fifteen businesses and–" Gertie stopped herself.

Fred looked happy as a clam. He was probably thinking some notoriety for his law firm was on deck, likely a splendiferous way into club membership. He would be a mover and shaker. He would be famous. He ... tipped his chair too far back, fell out, and landed on the floor, smack on his bottom.

Fred quickly righted himself.

"Are you alright?" I asked, standing over him.

"Yes, yes, just bruised my solicitor's pride," Fred said, brushing off his suit.

"It's a famous company, indeed," Elsie said, taking us through the leaflet and pointing out products of interest. "Going back in time, we see the Georgians' fancy ices, including one made out of Parmesan. In the seventeenth century, the English adored their sweetmeats, something like our petits fours and candies."

"Similar to today's macarons?" Fred asked.

"Yes, quite similar," Elise said.

"Douglas Wormston, my ancestor who co-founded the confectionery company, had one surviving son, Joseph and no other children. Joseph died before his father did, and that meant the firm passed to Joseph's son Samuel. Samuel had a son, Samuel the Second, who then had a son Samuel the Third. Samuel the Third is the one who got shafted by some royal at this club," Ozzie said.

Ozzie then brought out a sheaf of transcribed wills. "I've got every single will here from everyone in my confectioner family. They all passed their money and goods down to their family heirs, shutting my branch out with each successive generation. It's been going for hundreds of years. Lucky for us the confectionery firm is still in business today and has just as good archives as this club does."

Gertie narrowed her eyes. "Why would they let you see their records if they knew you wanted to muscle in on the firm's ownership?"

Ozzie smiled. "They don't know yet. But I happen to know that all of the company's records, except for the last twenty years, were donated in bulk to their county archives office for preservation. Turns out they didn't see the value of them or the need to review them first."

Donating boxes of old paperwork without going through them first was akin to running down the shopping mecca called Oxford Street in a tattered, see-through nightie and bare feet.

It was too revealing.

It just wasn't done.

"Fools, complete and utter fools," Fred muttered.

Ozzie sat there like the canary who outlived the coal mine. "The records are available to the public. I suspect they have some manager over there at the confectionery firm who took a look at them and said, 'We don't need all this old stuff kicking about. Either bin the lot or donate it to the archives. I need the space.' Some quick-thinking peon probably saved them from the tip."

"Can you imagine throwing out centuries of history just because somebody doesn't see the relevance of it today? Oh, the horror," Gertie said.

Elsie winced. "It actually happens a lot in England. I got an emergency call once from a colleague asking me to meet her at a recycling yard. A quick-thinking recycling staff member noticed a laboratory getting rid of 251 years of experimental information."

"Were they not concerned about confidentiality?" I asked.

"The lab director certainly wasn't. It was all to do with nineteenth century experiments on mushrooms and fungi in a remote part of Yorkshire."

"So you jumped in your car and had a little treasure hunt of your own?" I asked Elsie.

Gertie smiled at me. She and I knew exactly what that entailed.

Elsie shuddered. "We rescued the documents and donated them to the local archives. It turns out one of the most illustrious residents they'd ever had in that tiny village played a big part in that research. Now social and agricultural history are both largely enhanced because of these documents being accessible to all," she said.

"Getting back to Ozzie's confectionery conundrum. You mentioned something about a royal involvement?" Fred asked.

Leave it to Fred to ask about the higher-up mucky-mucks.

"And now for my pièce de résistance," Elsie said in a dramatic tone.

I was beginning to see her as a rather unusual archivist; she liked drama a bit more than the others I'd met.

Elsie went over to a nearby shelf and pulled down a banker's box, then put it on the table. It was one of those light-brown boxes made with acid-free cardboard dutifully protecting whatever was inside. She removed the lid and took out something soft wrapped in archival-friendly packing paper. "Mind we're very careful here," she said. "What you're looking at is a fencing uniform from 1851."

We gazed down upon a tidy pile of linen and leather protective clothing, silk necktie and wide trousers, a mask, and an assortment of connected straps.

Fred looked confused. "I'm not sure I follow? What does this have to do with confectionery and Ozzie's claim?"

Ozzie nodded. "Elsie's definitely on the right track. There was a reference to a duel in the wills, and it looks like Elsie's about to prove my theory correct."

Chapter 26

Elsie continued. "I did take a detailed look through the records when Bertie told me what the research topic was. I found there was an initial dispute about ownership of the co-owned confectionery firm that was solved by none other than a duel right here at the club."

"Two grown men decided their company ownership using swords?" Gertie asked.

I smiled. "And they say that chivalry and knights in shining armor are dead. This is a harkening back to an old way of life."

"Samuel Wormston the Third fought Adam Zerruly in 1851. The referee for the duel was Her Majesty's gamekeeper. He was chosen as the most impartial and trustworthy individual. It's all written down here in the record," Elsie said.

Ah, the strong, mysterious network of concierges and butlers was alive and well even back then.

"Both Samuel the Third and Adam Zerruly used to cater royal children's birthday parties and fancy dinners. Their sugar sculptures were the talk of London and the Continent, earning them a royal warrant. They fought here, on the club's third-floor pistes. They're on the same level as the yoga studios."

"Yoga at this private club. That's a new one," Gertie said.

"We've modernized over the centuries, you know, trying to keep up," Elsie said with a lilt in her voice. "Allowing female members has made all the difference."

"I'll say. And what was the result of this duel?" Fred asked.

"Ozzie's ancestor won," Elise said. "Samuel the Third was the clear victor."

"HA!" Ozzie yelled, earning instant glares of disapproval from everyone in the glass room.

Elsie held up a finger to restrain his excitement. "Not so fast. Your ancestor won the club's duel, indeed, but that's where the records get cloudy. I have the accomplishment signed by Her Majesty's gamekeeper. However, I also found a personal letter from your dueling ancestor opponent's solicitor. It goes to great pains to explain that his client, your ancestor's brother-in-law Adam Zerruly, was the true and rightful heir to the confectionery company."

"A signed will and Her Majesty's gamekeeper's attestation trumps a lawyer's letter any day," Fred said.

"Indeed it does. However, the filing with the court states that as Samuel Wormston the Third had no legitimate issue, all rights went back up and then horizontally across on the family tree. It went to the nearest and only sibling, Samuel the Third's sister Margaret who was already wed to Adam Zerruly, a descendant of the original club co-owner John Zerruly and also a confectioner."

"What do you mean, no legitimate issue? Samuel the Third had a son, my direct ancestor," Ozzie said.

Elsie was fascinated to watch our conversation unfold before her eyes.

"If there is any shadow, cloud, shading, or inkling of a doubt whatsoever, it makes sense to gather up whatever records we can to stack the file," Fred said. "Judges adore decisions made with absolute, overwhelming certainty. Permit me to do a bit more research on old court cases to see what I can find."

"Why don't we let Fred do his research while I take you up to see where the fencing bouts are held?" Elsie suggested.

We all trooped after her and took the elevator to the proper floor. This was one of those wonderful old sporting places with a creaky wooden floor, dozens of bits of fencing gear hung on a wall on brass hooks, and trophy cases lining the other. There were two men fencing there at the moment; of course, this was all just for fun nowadays. Fencing, after all, was now a sport on the international stage.

Ozzie leaned over to me. "I think the Zerruly family shafted mine."

"I believe you. It's just a question of the courts holding the same perspective," I told him.

Gertie went over to look at the fencing gear, and as she turned to say something to me, her bracelet caught on the edge of a protective jacket, and it came tumbling off the wall. This caused a chain reaction of three fencing masks to come off their hooks and roll across the floor in a wobbly, oblong run for freedom. After a few tense seconds, she looked like she was at a jumble sale for marshmallow-colored costumes.

We hurriedly put things back on the wall, hoping we didn't look like fools. It was hard to tell what the members on the piste thought. We watched the men fence for a while, amazed at how upper-class the soft clinks of sword tips sounded as their foils clashed. There was a buzzer that went off every time the sword made a direct hit on the opponent. I was beginning to feel that this research for Ozzie was quite similar to a duel.

We met Fred back in the archives room half an hour later. His eyes were bright, and he emitted a great big smile. A few of the record books were open in a logical order around him. "Duelling was outlawed in England in 1819. Therefore, any impact on the firm was prima facie illegal."

"But if Samuel the Third died without heirs, then his sister and her husband Adam Zerruly would have inherited anyways," Gertie said.

Fred shook his head. "No, because apparently Samuel the Third left all his assets to charity, none to his family."

Thankfully this time Ozzie refrained from whooping and disturbing the entire floor. Archives, after all, were places of respect and quiet.

Chapter 27

One Hour and Nineteen Minutes Later.

"Is that the lot of it?" I asked, huddled around the photocopy machine in Elsie's office.

Gertie looked up from the glass scan bed and nodded. "Everything relevant to Ozzie's case, and it's pretty strong stuff, if you ask me."

"This is quite the family rift," Fred said.

Ozzie checked around the room, a guilty look on his face. "Everyone, thank you for today. You've given me more help and insight than I ever expected, probably than I ever deserved."

"That's all right," Gertie said in her jolly tone. "Fred's paid to behave. Julie and I are just really glad that the GGRS can be of assistance."

Fred was still trying to think up a good comeback. He seemed to decide to let it go.

Wise move.

"I'd like to think that my family dilemma will be easily resolved, considering we now have a good stack of historical reference material," Ozzie said.

Fred shook his head. "I never like to tell clients anything is sure until we have the judge's signature. Courts can be odd places."

"So, you think I have to worry?" Ozzie asked.

"I wouldn't say worry. You can be cautiously optimistic. Just don't run out and buy a gold-plated limousine and a large mansion with three swimming pools before you have cash in hand."

Gertie frowned. "As if half the people living in those mansions can really afford them. Talk to their banks and they're mortgaged to the hilt."

"True, true."

"Can I make a somewhat obvious suggestion?" Ozzie asked the group. He looked furtively around to make sure that it was only the Greymore home team in the room at the time.

We all nodded back, wondering what on earth he had up his sleeve this time. Hopefully it was no more false teeth or smoked-mackerel sandwiches.

"How about we all just nip down to the pub and get rid of these toffs for a while? They've been very courteous today, but I don't think I could eat another meal near that fragile, overdone sugar sculpture. I need a less formal place, somewhere with a dartboard and football instead."

"Fine, but we must say our thank yous to Bertie and Elsie before we go," I said.

"And to the butlers," Fred added.

"The butlers? I don't know if it's protocol to go around thanking the butlers," Gertie said.

"But they run the house," Ozzie said.

"I think you only thank them when you're in their immediate presence and they're doing something for you," Gertie said. "If they work for you, it's definitely more of an obligation, but I don't think guests are required to race around a building looking for the butler to thank." She looked to me for support.

"I need Aunt Edwina to answer that one. I didn't grow up with a butler, that was all her purvey," I said.

"We could telephone Jacques at Greymore," she suggested. "He would know."

"How about a handwritten thank-you note? We could send one to each of them, thanking them for their assistance. That's classy," Fred said.

"Tell you what, let's make tracks for the pub down the street and you can write them there and hand-deliver them back. I heard that's pretty impressive after any type of meeting," Gertie said.

"Do they have a mail slot at the club?" I asked.

"Yes, his name's Marlon," we heard behind us. Bertie entered the room, looking quite pleased at the tidy stack of photocopying we had assembled. "Find what you need in the archives?"

"Definitely. Thank you so much," Ozzie said.

"Should we expect to read about a changing of the guard at the confectionery company?" Bertie asked, a slight smile on his famous face.

Fred hurriedly jumped into this conversation. "I've instructed my esteemed client that he has a bit more work to do before we start getting ahead of ourselves."

"Likely a wise move. I must dash. I've got a dinner meeting a taxi ride away. The city arts council has summoned a fundraising meeting, and I'm on the committee," Bertie said.

I seized the opportunity. "No problem at all, Bertie. We were actually just packing up to leave."

I could tell Bertie felt guilty about not hosting us for another meal.

"We're taking a jaunt down to the pub at the end of the street," Gertie said.

"You should enjoy it, for at least two different reasons," Bertie said.

"How do you mean?" I asked.

Bertie smiled. "They make a mean lobster sandwich, and the name of the place is 'The Dueling Lords'."

***

GGRS. Next Morning.

Pamela was already waiting at the door when I came in to open up the research site. "How did it go in London?" she asked politely, although she seemed ready to bubble over with something exciting to share.

"Really well, thanks," I said.

"I do hope Ozzie found what he needed. I don't mean to pry, just hope that he was successful."

"Well, it's with him now, and I think he's still got some work to do. No one's family tree is ever really finished, is it?" I gave her a smile.

"How true. Do you have a moment? I am absolutely thrilled to show you what I discovered on my trip to the hospitality conference in Liverpool."

"Sure." I opened the doors and let her in, flicking on the lights and doing my initial cursory glance around to make sure nothing looked out of order. I always joked that this included any researchers who unexpectedly slept there overnight after getting caught up in their family history research. I refused to operate the research site like a casino and insisted upon large clocks on the walls so there was no excuse to ignore the time. I was also the dragon lady who'd promoted the intercom system, and it had already more than proven its worth. I smiled, thinking back to the crows pecking at Ozzie's plastic trash bags in the back of his truck.

I didn't get a chance to take off my coat before Pamela thrust a picture in front of me.

"I went online to a database of old London pictures and found the storefront for Francine's Matrimonial Bureau. It's all here and the building still exists! It's a bookshop now. I've already called the owner and he's very willing to show us around." Then her face fell. "That is, if I'm able to ask you to come on another field trip?"

I nodded. "Gertie and I had a long discussion about that on the train back yesterday evening. For those new to genealogy, we realize it can be quite daunting going to these large government research facilities alone. We decided that it would be a neat idea if we could go along and help solo researchers, be a supportive colleague to share a bit of guidance and expertise."

"It's wonderful. Oh, I'm so glad. My husband just isn't very interested, and it's nice to share my hobby with somebody."

Pamela reminded me of a woman who was successful in life yet perhaps was at a loose end after she'd made her mark in the corporate world. Once people reached their middle thirties or forties, many started to get involved in their family history research. Perhaps middle age was when it became important to reconnect with roots and to really understand the purpose one had on earth. A lot of that purpose came from what ancestors did and from their legacies they left to descendants.

I heard the courtesy rap of freshly scrubbed knuckles on my desk and looked up to see the Major.

"Good morning, ladies," he said.

"You look particularly dapper this morning, Major," I said, admiring his subtle, elegant tartan suit.

"Thank you. Now, I have quite the report for you both."

"May I take off my coat and get a cup of tea before we start?" I asked.

Pamela and the Major looked at each other and their faces fell, guilty. They were both like kids who'd raced home from school with a glowing report card and couldn't wait to tell Mum.

None of that changed the fact I'd had a long day yesterday and was still getting into gear for today.

"But of course," the Major said.

I was apparently allowed two minutes to make that happen. Both of them cornered me in the kitchen. The kettle took five minutes to boil. Everybody knew that. Microwaved tea just wasn't the same.

"This is the photo," Pamela said, thrusting it in front of me for the second time. No rest for the wicked. I looked at a nondescript picture of a three-story building on a busy London street. The cars gave away the 1930s timeframe when the photo was taken. Also, a couple of people on the street were dressed in that era's attire. I often longed for the days when men wore hats and women wouldn't be caught dead in pajamas outside the house. It just seemed like a more genteel, formal era. Perhaps I was born a generation or two late.

My attention was captured by the photograph. "How wonderful. And you say it actually still exists today as a bookshop?"

"Yes. They carried forward a bit of the old name and now call it 'Francine's Bookshop'."

"That's amazing," I said, studying the photo closer. "I think that might be Francine in the front window, you know." I traced the woman's outline with my index finger.

Pamela nodded. "I realize that. I enlarged it on my screen at home and I could just make her out."

Francine was a sturdy, brunette, decent-citizen sort. The picture showed her sitting at a desk wearing a high-collared blouse and a skirt in a darker color. I'd bet she was wearing dark oxford shoes with a bit of heel to them. Her clothes were of quality, no doubt expensive, yet not overly flashy.

I looked up at the Major. "And what do you have to report? I can tell it's something pretty significant. Have you already told Pamela, or is this news to both of us?"

"Ladies. What I have discovered is something that will keep your socks white for an entire year," he said in a grandiose baritone voice.

With great flair, the Major brought out four eight-inch by ten-inch photos of the medals we'd found in Pamela's heirloom box. "On first glance we assumed all of these medals were for Richard. It was only when I took the photos to a medals expert that the truth became much clearer."

I gasped. "You're kidding."

I looked at Pamela. She was heartily shocked and lost for words.

"Of the five medals, four of them definitely belonged to Richard for his service in the army as well as for specific assignments he performed in Cairo during World War Two. The fifth medal, this one here, was given to civilians who served the United Kingdom during World War Two."

"Meaning Sylvie did something incredibly daring while she was in Cairo?" I asked.

"Possibly. It could also have been nursing or homefront defense work as well. The most intriguing thing here is that this medal was given to civilians who really stepped up and did behind-the-scenes war work."

"Wow," Pamela said.

"The fact that I cannot find any records of Richard's wartime service leads me to believe he was involved in a secret mission, one that remains classified to this day," the Major said.

"Do you think Sylvie was in on it too? Leading enemy agents astray as she worked the cabarets of Cairo?" I asked.

"A tempting thought, but I haven't been able to confirm anything else about her yet. The records are either missing or sealed. There's nothing online at TNA, and no one in my network has any other sources to suggest."

"My course taught me that if you get stuck on an ancestor, then one of the best things to do is to go sideways," I said.

The Major nodded. "Precisely. We know Pamela's great-grandmother Sylvie had a brother named Franklyn who was in the navy. The last three letters of his first name are 'L-Y-N', so it's a bit unusual. I've found a rather interesting record at the National Maritime Museum, but it's not digitized."

The pleading look in Pamela's eyes was quite apparent.

"Tomorrow?" I suggested.

The kettle finally boiled. The Major and Pamela looked pleased as punch. Call them keeners, or call them pushy, but there was nothing that brought a bigger smile to my face these days than locating an elusive ancestor for a dedicated researcher.

Aunt Edwina, this should make you proud.

***

Two Hours Later.

Maude had the research site running like a well-oiled machine. I felt incredibly comfortable with her at the helm, employing her expertise to assist researchers from beginner to expert. It was just perfect for both of us, and the commute from her suite a few floors up was pretty awesome, indeed. There was a quiet hum of machines and low murmurs inside the research site today.

Now that Pamela and the Major had shown me their finds, we went back to whatever one could call ordinary business. All the computer carrells were taken up by researchers looking up certificates, census, or a myriad of other online records. A few people were scattered at various tables reading books from our library, while one person was using the microfiche reader for some extremely obscure reference that was still in dark-ages format. A husband and wife examined an old map of the County of Cheshire from 1850, trying to recreate the route that one of their ancestors had taken when moving his family from one end of the county to the other.

All was tickety boo.

That was, until Ewan walked in.

One of my favorite people sported a bright-white cast on his right arm. He had a sad look on his face. "Good morning, Julie."

"Whatever happened, Ewan?" I asked him. Casts meant bad accidents.

"I was playing rugby and fell on my arm the wrong way," he said.

"I didn't know there was a correct way to fall on one's arm," the Major said.

By now, there were six other people who had clustered around Ewan, all murmuring their sympathies.

"I didn't know you played rugby," I said.

"Neither did I. My sister volunteered me when their village team was short," Ewan replied.

"I think you should stick to shuttling your nephew around for his piano lessons."

"I agree."

"Do you need help with something?" Maude asked. She was fussing about Ewan in a caring way; there was no way kindness-personified Maude could ever be annoying.

Ewan shook his head. "I'm just here for some in-person sympathy. Can't really do much at the antiques shop with this bum arm. Had a friend drop me off because driving's out of the question right now as well."

"Oh dear. You're welcome to hop on a computer in the newsletter design room. We don't have anything going on in there today. At least you could look at your inventory or dictate a blog. Hunt-and-peck keyboard or you can use our snazzy new dictation software," I said.

His face relaxed into a friendly grin. "I knew you'd make me feel better. This injury was such a stupid thing to do. The last thing I need is to be laid up with a broken arm."

"Well, your friends will help you through it," the Major said, clapping Ewan on the back. He clapped a little too hard and it made Ewan cough.

"I'll go put the kettle on," Maude said.

"Are you going to be alright with your antiques shop?" I asked Ewan.

"I've got some muscle to move the heavy stuff out. But being right-handed makes it awfully hard to type and even manage oneself at various antiques fairs." He gave me a pleading gaze and a charming smile.

I narrowed my eyes. "Do I sense an invitation?"

"I'm going to be in this cast for six weeks, minimum. I was wondering if you could come and help me at an antiques fair in three weeks? It's one of my favorites, and if I miss out, my shop inventory will go far below where I like it to be."

"Sure, just let me check my incredibly busy social calendar," I said with a grin. "Wait a minute. I just remembered. I have no social life."

"Oh, I wouldn't say that," the Major said. "How about all these field trips you're taking with the fabulous people here? Those count."

"Of course they do. I was just teasing." I looked at Ewan. "Where is the antiques fair?"

"Yorkshire."

"Yorkshire? That's not exactly commutable from Oakhurst."

"No, it's not. I would spring for the hotel room, er, rooms, of course. Separate rooms, absolutely no pressure there at all." He looked up, babbling, realizing that his offer was now being keenly listened to by everyone able to eavesdrop.

"Would anybody like some date loaf?" Maude called out in a cheerful voice from the kitchen. "The café just baked some this morning and it looks lov-ell-ee!"

Saved by the date loaf.

Everybody slow-stampeded to the kitchen, leaving Ewan and I by ourselves.

"I meant what I said, Julie. No pressure, not at all." He looked so forlorn standing there, such a kind man, almost like a lost person in his bright-white cast. He was sidelined, unable to help with things that he normally jumped in with, like moving a box or heaving a printer from one table to the next. It was going to be hard for a man like him to be incapacitated for a while.

"I know. And you're a gentlemen for saying so." Our eyes met and the spark was there. Heck, it'd been there from the day we met. I remembered meeting Ewan on the pavement when Gertie and I were first looking for the Plumsden Family History Society office to get help with Aunt Edwina's treasure hunt clues.

Jacques entered, dressed in kitchen whites. Ewan faded into the background, seeking tea in the lunchroom and to chat with the Major.

"Good day," Jacques said in his efficient tone. "Julie, I have some information about one of Pamela's heirlooms."

"Right. Let me just page her."

A minute later Pamela and I were clustered around a table in the meeting room, looking at something on Jacques's phone.

"Remember when you emailed me a photo of that tool from your heirloom box because I thought it perhaps had something to do with kitchens?" he asked Pamela.

"Yes. You thought it might be some part of a bread mixer, I believe," she said.

"Well, I was completely wrong. It is actually a tool belonging to a saddler."

"Really?"

He nodded. "I sent the photo to the Saddler's Guild in London, and they tell me it's from the twentieth century, quite common."

"No one in my family is associated with that craftsman's trade, at least that I know of," she hastily added.

I shrugged. "That's a tough one. Unless you can find the direct historical reference, it could have been something picked up at a jumble sale and used for a tool around the house. For example, my father used a carpet-cutting hook to get crabgrass out of the cracks between the paving stones. Worked like a charm."

"Well, for what it's worth, I thought I'd better report what I'd found," Jacques said. "I'm sorry I wasn't able to be of more assistance."

"How's the cake baking going?" I asked, a gleam in my eyes.

"You sampled our date loaf this morning, I believe?" he asked.

"And it was very good. Much better than that pudding cake we tried right before the café opened."

He shook his head, almost violently. "That would never, ever be served on my watch. It was not up to Greymore nor Lady Edwina's standards."

We were now officially standing in the GGRS discussing cake batter. Jacques noticed and realized that he needed to get back to the café. Not that I didn't enjoy talking with Jacques; he always had interesting, intelligent observations to share. It was just that there were two other people politely hovering around the information desk and we needed to serve them. Both were seeking family history tidbits, not cake.

Ewan and I would have to wait.

Again.

Chapter 28

Royal Observatory, National Maritime Museum Grounds, Greenwich. Next Day.

The National Maritime Museum was a sprawling complex surrounded by a vast expanse of lawn. King Charles the Second had commissioned a now-famous observatory high up on the hill. It overlooked the site and was open to the public. Great polymaths, including Flamsteed, Halley, Newton, Boyle, Wren, and Hooke were part of this great scientific age, one that yielded umpteen discoveries in mathematics, astronomy, and physics. It most certainly helped that the king was a rabid devourer of all things scientific, and wholeheartedly threw his support behind the construction of this magnificent building. Beside the Maritime Museum were the living quarters used by the king and queen in the seventeenth century. In the museum, one waded through centuries of exhibits dealing with maritime life, including shipping, military, and fishing worlds.

The onsite archives research center was a quiet refuge from the delighted cries of children who were enjoying the lifelike exhibits. Behind the archives' doors was a vast library of maritime books as well as a repository for archival records that one could request in advance of an in-person visit. It was like TNA but on a smaller scale. There were visitor lockers near the information desk, and one then walked through security to access the research materials. We took chairs at a desk in the middle of the waist-tall bookshelves. At the end of these tables was the records retrieval desk.

We were all excited to see what the Major had found for us to view. He went over to the desk and retrieved one single box. It was heavy, slightly larger than a legal-sized box. As he brought it back to the table, we all wondered if it would solve the mystery of Sylvie's hidden past. We were here to research her brother, and I really wasn't quite sure what to expect.

The box didn't fail to deliver.

It yielded one sketchbook, about eighteen inches long and ten inches tall. There were about fifty pages inside. We flipped through the first few pages.

Sylvie's brother Franklyn was a talented painter.

"Now, just to double check," the Major murmured, as he flipped to the inside front cover. There, in bold ink, was 'Franklyn Carmine, Mediterranean Tour, 1939-1942'.

"It's amazing this survived all these years," Pamela whispered.

"It's amazing it survived the war. The British Navy was brought in to prevent the enemy from gaining needed access to the Mediterranean. It was a vital move that cut supply lines, essentially starving the enemy and preventing armament reinforcement for its offensive desert campaign," the Major said.

"It can't be normal for navy personnel to work with sand under their feet," I said, also in a low voice.

The Major chuckled. "Those navy boys did a grand job under heavy fire. We wouldn't have won in Egypt without them."

"I'm so glad the sketchbook survived. I feel so much closer to my ancestor now that I can hold this in my hands," Pamela said.

"It looks like your Franklyn was quite a prolific artist," I said. "Look at these beautiful sunsets and camels that he painted." I flipped through the pages slowly, admiring the warm apricots, mauves, and yellows that Franklyn had mixed together in an expert manner, showing the big ball of fire in the sky slowly slipping behind the horizon, a couple of shadowed camels in front giving it atmosphere. "He's got a great eye for distance and perspective. That takes either natural talent or many years of training."

"Is it all sunsets and Egyptian desert?" Pamela asked.

There were quite a few similar paintings, all watercolors, and all cleverly assembled from what I assumed was a pretty rudimentary box of colors he'd been able to squirrel away in his seaman's chest. Sailors weren't allowed to take a huge volume of personal belongings with them on board ship.

I inhaled a deep breath. "This is different." I showed her a new page.

"My oh my," Pamela said.

We were looking at a series of Cairo street-life scenes, 1940s paintings depicting open-air vegetable, bread, and meat markets, donkeys hauling rundown carts, and a few vendor stalls hawking souvenirs and spices. It was a hot, arid, and exotic world, one I had never visited.

"He obviously enjoyed his time there," I said. "Look at the care he's taken to detail the lines on this man's face, the water dripping off the donkey's whiskers at the water trough." Being a painter myself, I knew that only those truly enamored of their subjects would bother with such great detail.

Franklyn was a kindred spirit.

The wonderful insights into Franklyn's time in Africa continued. More street scenes, scenes inside an Egyptian home, a table laden with all sorts of local dishes, including brightly stuffed peppers, lentil soup, rice with noodles, and much more. It was a glimpse into a different culture, one that was very special indeed.

Pamela turned to the next page.

We all gasped.

The page contained three images, all showing different perspectives of a small silver sphinx. "It's exactly like the one I have in my heirloom box," she said, reaching for her phone and scrolling through her photo gallery until she found the image.

"Here we are. Look at that," she whispered, showing us the picture. "It's a perfect match to what Franklyn painted."

"Excellent," I said. "That means they probably were together when the sphinx was given to Richard. The men had quite a bit in common."

Luckily we were alone in the library, so very low voices were passable for now, so long as we were mindful of other researchers who might arrive expecting utter quiet.

"Did you have any luck looking up Major Donoughan?" I asked the Major.

"He was a leader in Cairo in the 1940s, during World War Two. The only other reference I could find was his attendance at a meeting with some upper military brass in 1941. I took down their names and was able to link two of them with Special Operations Branch."

"Spy handlers?" I asked.

The Major nodded. "Or saboteurs. But you won't be able to prove it."

"I imagine all of that work was super hush hush, even today, it seems," Pamela said.

"It helped save our nation," the Major said in a focused voice.

"So, we have grateful thanks from a man known to be linked with spy operations. That would help confirm why we can't find any other information about Richard. He was almost like a phantom, according to the archives we have access to," I said.

"Exactly how I feel," Pamela said.

"You might find something else by looking a little closer at those paintings of the sphinx," the Major said. He pointed to an area underneath the sphinx's chin, at the start of the top of its neck. It was a tiny circle in the metal.

"What is that?" Pamela asked, looking closer as she enlarged the photo.

"It looks like a button of some kind," I said.

"Like a secret compartment?"

"Quite possibly," the Major said. "There were a lot of fancy gadgets and acts of sabotage used against the enemy in World War Two."

"Now I want to race home and see what that button actually does," Pamela said.

"Exciting, yes. But what's this over here?" I pointed at a small bit of writing on the spine of Franklyn's wonderful sketchbook.

It was faint, and it was hidden, but it was there: 'Jesmyne Lane Boarding House'.

"I think we've just found our next clue in the Sylvie and Richard mystery," Pamela said.

"A boarding house from the 1940s. I really doubt it still exists. There were so many people bombed out of their homes, multiple families sharing one house, the likelihood is very small," the Major warned.

"We can certainly look it up in old London directories. There can't be that many 'Jesmyne Lane Boarding Houses' on the rosters."

"Is that something we can do here, or do we need to go back to the computers at Greymore?" Pamela asked.

"I can use my phone to access the website we need." I checked and saw the time was already 3:30 p.m., and we still had to get back home. I had hoped to avoid rush hour because standing up for an entire train journey wasn't exactly a pleasant experience, no matter one's age.

"It's going to be for another day, isn't it?" Pamela said.

I checked my screen again. "I didn't budget enough time for the second extracurricular activity. But don't worry, we can slip it in and eat a late dinner at the train station instead if you both agree."

"Altogether fine by me," the Major said. "I'm rather enjoying our adventure."

"I'm not keeping either of you from anything?" Pamela asked, looking a bit panicked.

"Only some paperwork I'm avoiding. Believe me, this is far more intriguing," I said.

"Well, ladies, are we finished with the sketchbook?" The Major flipped through the next few pages and we were back to street scenes. "In all honesty, I think we have found the secret that Franklyn was trying to tell the world without being censored by his commanding officer."

＊＊＊

Greenwich Train Station. Later That Day.

The good news was that the online City of London business archives site I located did have a 'Jesmyne Lane Boarding House' listed. The bad news was we had no idea if it was the correct one. It would be easy to assume that because there was only one listed in London it was the correct one. It was even more easy to assume that navy men being deployed would start from the same place after basic training, all shipping out from a main London station and onto their overseas assignments. This was all dangerous thinking. The first rule of genealogy was to question everything and assume nothing. Assumptions led to branches on the family tree that were glued on as opposed to those that had naturally sprouted. This type of ancestral silviculture resulted in incorrect ancestry linkages and had to be avoided at all costs.

Jesmyne Lane Boarding House was once a business consisting of a group of four houses owned by an Arnold Higgenton, a nineteenth century businessman who made his fortune by selling animal feedstuffs. The archive page that I'd accessed on my phone said that he was an enterprising young man who ran a clean operation, genuinely caring for his lodgers.

"Here we are," I said, as the train slowed to the station in the East End of London, a place that was known for its terrible poverty in both the nineteenth and twentieth centuries. "According to the map, it's supposed to be about a four-minute walk from the station."

"I'm excited to see this, because I have no idea what to expect," Pamela said.

We walked the four minutes and soon found out. Jesmyne Lane Boarding House was now a pothole-ridden car park. The online business archive directory hadn't told us that. None of us had been with it enough to pull up a map showing the current neighborhood buildings; now we were stuck with acres of asphalt and a few sketchy-looking young hooligans eyeing our purses.

"I wonder if there's another boarding house with this name somewhere else," I said after looking at our sketchy surroundings.

"Ladies, I think it is best if we depart before we outstay this neighborhood's ever-so-brief welcome," the Major said. He stood a bit straighter, knowing that we needed to leave for the station before we made any more mistakes.

Pamela looked at me, an apologetic expression on her face. "I'm sorry to have wasted your time on this, both of you," she said.

"Never mind. It's all part of family history research. We expect lots of dead ends and wrong turns," I said.

She looked at us with a somewhat guilty expression. "I'm very grateful you're so understanding. I wouldn't have dragged you out here had I known–"

"These things happen," the Major said. "Let's now focus on getting home."

Waterloo Station. Night.

We stayed in London to wait out the peak commuter rush home. Waterloo Station was an amazing transport hub and one of my favorites in London. I was always quick to visit one of the well-known grocery stores that had a retail outlet in the station and pick up some treats for the journey home. Lunch had been a rather hurried, somewhat soggy sandwich from a tiny little shop somewhere near the Greenwich station. A late supper at a Waterloo Station restaurant and we were off to catch the 9:17 p.m. service home. Waterloo was one of the larger stations that had both train and Tube connections. Following our meal, we'd use a less-frequent train service that would take us as far out as Plumsden, where we would pick up the vehicle.

Whenever I rode a train or the Tube, I found the side-to-side rocking motion very conducive to lulling me to sleep. I got into the motion of the carriage, as did most others on the journey; it was a calming sensation. As the train lurched to a stop in the middle of a stretch of track that had no station anywhere near, I heard a collective groan permeate the carriage. The train waited, engines running but going nowhere.

An announcement came over the public intercom:

> *"Ladies and Gentlemen, please be advised that due to theft of copper wire from railway infrastructure, repairs must be made before this train can continue. We apologize for the inconvenience."*

It was repeated a couple of times, much to the frustration of the passengers looking to get home today rather than next week.

The Major shook his head. "I can understand works on the lines, but outright vandalism and theft? I have zero patience for that. Those vandals have no idea how many people's lives they're disrupting."

"It's pretty sad," I added.

We waited ten more minutes. We waited another twenty minutes. I noted a lot of checking time on phones, as well as frantic texts as people rescheduled dinner, dates, and childcare arrangements. The seasoned commuters took it all in stride, used to transportation hiccups. It was the tourists who looked a bit panicked, trying to hide their worry about whether they would make their connection at the station further down the line.

The public announcement system crackled to life again:

> "Ladies and Gentlemen, the buffet counter carriage is now closed."

With true British wit, a young man two rows ahead of us in the carriage quickly yelled out, "Thank you!" much to the amusement of his fellow passengers.

We were actually lucky to have a buffet; this was a long-distance train that had come down from northern England, one that was supposed to terminate in Carlingheath later tonight.

This was a time for goodwill towards others. I opened up my shopping bag and started to distribute out my snacks, not only to the Major and Pamela, but also to those sitting nearby. I supposed today's train ride was akin to genealogy research. There were a lot of ups and downs, starts and stops, and brick walls. The best advice was to always come prepared, with supplies as well as an understanding attitude.

***

Two Hours Later.

Additional long and uncomfortable hours passed. Economy seats were fine for a commute, but not for hours on end going nowhere, bored stiff. I was now out of food, just like everyone else. I'd read all the overhead advertising, twice, as well as memorized all the stops along the line.

Another announcement:

> "Ladies and Gentlemen, we apologize for the additional inconvenience, but this service is now terminated. Please disembark the train following the instructions of crew members for a transfer of all passengers to busses for the next leg of your journeys. Thank you."

I checked my watch. Bussing us from here would likely take another hour. The looks on all passengers' faces were grim.

The Major leaned over. "I hope the station they're taking us to is still open when we arrive."

It was now 11:57 p.m.

Chapter 29

Somewhere En Route Home. 1:00 a.m.

The three of us were on a double-decker bus, Pamela and I together in one row and the Major right across the aisle from us. To his right was a businessman who hadn't said a word the entire journey, choosing instead to read never-ending news on his tablet. Outside, the streets were deserted and the night was dark. We'd actually backtracked to the station we had passed through before the train broke down.

"The driver said just up ahead," the Major said.

We all craned our necks to see what was in the offing. Through the murky blackness we saw the little town's train station emerge. By now it was just us, the businessman, and a couple of other late-night commuters on the bus. We'd done the milk route and dropped off nearly everyone else before us. The bus driver stopped outside the station and we disembarked. The three other people on the bus hurried down side streets, obviously not needing a train because this happened to be their hometown.

Lucky them.

We could enter the station, yet all the services, ticket windows, and personnel wickets were closed. We faced two long, dark, and spooky tunnels leading to platforms. At the end of one, we could just make out a night janitor sweeping the floor. The Major signaled for both of us to come with him, and we entered the dark tunnel.

Our footsteps echoed against the curved tile walls that held small posters hawking anything from chocolate bars to a West End play. The janitor was a huge, burly man, head down, earbuds in, busy focusing on the task at hand.

The Major had to yell to get his attention. "Pardon me! When is the next train to Plumsden?"

The janitor looked up, took off his earbuds, and said in a calm voice, "You're out of luck, mate. Station doesn't open for another three hours. All you can do is go wait on the platform. Number two, it is."

"Right you are," the Major said. He turned to look at both of us. "Ladies, rather than warming a bench for three hours, I think I will call for assistance."

"A taxi? Are they even working this late?" Pamela asked.

"It'll be hard to find one in a smaller town like this," I said. "This place is well-known for rolling up its pavements at midnight. Even the pubs close by then."

The Major gave us a reassuring grin. "Ladies, have no fear. I will get us out of this forthwith." He pulled out his phone and looked up one of his contacts. He tapped 'dial'.

"You think you can get a taxi for us at this time of night, or should I say morning?" I corrected myself. I looked at my own phone and saw that it was way too early in the morning for anyone to even consider getting out of bed, unless they were insomniacs or used to working the graveyard shift.

The Major got a funny little smirk on his face and held up his index finger, implying for us to cool our heels as he waited for his call to be answered. "Hello? Harvey?"

***

We sat like three ants on a log, plonked down on the bench outside the train-station entrance, in its designated 'kiss and ride' zone. The dampness of the night air had set in, and I was about ready to pull my shopping bag over my head as a poncho for another layer of heat. Pamela was examining the fabric of her umbrella, likely wondering how she could disassemble it and wrap it around her body like a cape.

At that very moment I made a vow; if there ever was a court case involving these switching-station copper-wire vandals, I would be the prosecution's star witness.

Fifteen additional minutes passed. On the sixteenth minute, we heard a faint rumble. The rumble grew closer, as did the sound of multiple tires slapping against damp pavement. We all looked up and saw a gigantic, camouflaged army troop transport truck making its way towards us.

"You have got to be joking," I said, turning to the Major. "That's our ride?"

"Don't knock it 'til you try it," the Major said with a grin.

"Does it have seatbelts?" Pamela asked. "I don't like to travel on the roads without a seatbelt."

When Harvey brought the large truck to a shuddering halt, air hissing out of the brakes, the truck looked absolutely superimposing. It reminded me of those gigantic oilsands trucks that they used in Canada. Well, perhaps it wasn't really that gigantic, but at o'dark thirty in the morning everything was out of proportion, including my judgement.

"Seatbelts? Seatbelts?" Pamela said. "Major, we do sincerely appreciate your help but–"

Just like when he drove his tank into my field, Harvey popped his head out of the window, giving us a wave. He looked perfectly content sitting way up high in his driver's seat.

"Good morning, ladies!" Harvey said with a big grin on his face. "Oh, hello to you too, Major."

"Hi, Harvey. Do you possibly have anything larger to drive us home with?" I asked. The truck was gigantic. It surely could have transported a brontosaurus. I was surprised it was even street legal. But I supposed it had a steering wheel, solid tires, and what looked like all the proper running lights and headlamps. At this point, we had no other choice. I wondered if we'd all be sitting on the front bench seat, replicating our ants-on-a-log position on the bench.

No such luck.

Harvey jumped down from his perch and went around to the back. He opened the tailgate, and it made the tiniest of squeaks.

I turned to Pamela, panic-stricken. "He's going to make us ride in the back?"

"Oh, don't worry about that. It's quite comfortable, I assure you," the Major said.

"Comfortable? I've seen these vehicles in the movies. There's about forty troops lined up on benches, all densely packed together. Does the man not own a normal car?" I asked.

I might as well have been babbling to a brick wall. The Major and Harvey were busy undoing the back doors. A ramp came down, and after all this excitement, it wouldn't have surprised me if an ice cream truck rolled out.

Harvey poked his head around the doors. "Ladies, welcome aboard," he said.

We walked around with incredible trepidation and then we stopped in our tracks, shocked. The big smiles on the Major's and Harvey's faces were now fully understandable. For we weren't looking at any ordinary army troop transport truck. No, this was a modified one, one that had been completely remodeled inside, turning it into a deluxe recreational vehicle. This was luxury at its finest, completely unexpected inside the shell of a military truck.

"She has two double beds, kitchen, toilet and shower unit, two tables plus a pop-up, flatscreen TV." Harvey rocked back on his heels, waiting for both our reactions.

Pamela turned to him. "One question. Why?"

Harvey shrugged. "I bought it at a surplus auction and couldn't see a lovely vehicle like this go to the scrapyard. Over the last three years it's been a labor of love. At first, I just wanted to have a place to sleep and cook a few meals on the road. But then the project just expanded. I suppose I went a little bit overboard."

"You think?" I said.

We got in, and that's when I noticed that there was no barrier between the driver's bench to the back of the vehicle. When it first opened up, it was so dark outside I hadn't noticed. Pamela and I each took a comfortable seat near a side table, and yes, each one of them had a seatbelt. The Major rode with Harvey up front. As one of our Scandinavian researchers liked to say, "All is in order."

Chapter 30

GGRS. 8:15 a.m.

The man with the cast on his arm couldn't stop laughing.

"I'm glad you find our travel perils so amusing, Ewan," I said to him, frowning. It was a frown that I couldn't keep on very long, however, because I also saw the humor in our experience.

"So, in the end, Pamela and I decided to camp out in the back of the truck for the rest of the evening. That's why when you all arrived here it was parked out front, looking like we'd been invaded." I peered out the window. "The Major must have already picked up Pamela. He's taking her back to Plumsden so she can rescue her car and hopefully have a somewhat decent day."

Ewan was taking all of this in with great interest. "I'd say that the Major and Harvey have gotten themselves back into your good graces after the tank turf incident."

"Yes, two out of the three men have redeemed themselves." I gave him a pointed look.

"I am at a slight disadvantage right now," Ewan said, lifting up his injured arm.

"I know. However, we can set you up with a headset and you can use your other hand to dial," I said. A brilliant idea just crossed my mind.

"And call whom?" he asked.

"Find the correct Jesmyne Lane Boarding House associated with Sylvie and Richard. We know it exists, we just don't know what city or town."

"And how am I supposed to find that?" he asked in an incredulous voice.

"Operator assistance?" I replied with a very sweet smile on my face. There was no way I was going to easily forgive him for his part in the tank versus meadow turf incident.

"Maude?" Ewan called out, searching frantically around for the research guru who managed our site.

Luckily Maude wasn't too busy at the moment. She came over and took him in hand. "Now, Ewan, it's not as hard as it seems. There are numerous online databases and records in archives one can check. What is the name of the business again? You could even consider starting to look through census indexes with the family name and the approximate date they lived there and see if there's anything available."

"But it was the 1930s to 40s," he said. "The census records are only released when they're over a hundred years old, so that won't work."

"Ah yes, but the business may have been in existence long before the lodgers we're seeking stayed there," Maude said. "Find that, then call up the local council offices or archives for more information."

"Hence the phone call," I said, a sweet smile on my face again.

"And does that wipe the slate clean?" Ewan asked.

"I think you owe her a nice dinner after all the trouble you've caused," Maude said without a second thought.

I felt my cheeks burn and went back to my paperwork. It was getting hard to deny, this attraction between Ewan and I.

There was a thud and a grinding of gears outside. I went over to the window and saw Fred Todling arrive in what could only be described as a farm truck. It was certainly not a vehicle that any self-respecting solicitor would drive, especially when clients might see him. But this wasn't Fred's truck. I recognized it from the earlier crows and bin bags incident. This was none other than Ozzie Boggs's pickup truck, with a new canopy over the truck bed.

Fred got out and unfortunately stepped right into a puddle. He was dressed in country tweeds, right down to his plus-four trousers fastened with a brass button just below the knees, sporting jacket and matching cap. Ozzie disembarked from the driver's side, and the hinges on his door squeaked so loudly they could be heard through our windows.

Maude took one look and put both hands on her hips. "If those two think they're coming in here to do some research right now, they are sadly mistaken."

The cause of her acid comment hit my nostrils one second later. A faint stench of pig manure wafted into the research site, making Maude rush around to shut nearby windows. I saw Fred converse with Ozzie out in the parking lot. Barnaby was usually a very clean animal; my guess was that he got the runs when he was being transported.

Better Ozzie's farm truck than Fred's nice sedan. How handy for them.

"Oh, this is going to be good," Ewan said, sidling up to the window. "Isn't it Barnaby's day at the vet's?"

I groaned. "Now it makes sense. Doctor Grierly is coming to vaccinate the miniature goat herd today. I'll bet Fred had Ozzie pick up Barnaby and drive him here to save on the house-call fee."

"We need those manure-scented men and Barnaby kept out of our pristine research site." I looked around and saw the faces of trepidation from multiple researchers and staff. "Ewan, I'm putting you in charge of this. No potbellied pigs are to enter this research site. And–"

I took a deep breath when I saw the truck's tailgate open. Holly bounded out of the canopied pickup bed. "And no English Sheepdogs in here, either."

"And then my debt is considered repaid?" Ewan bargained.

"Let's see you accomplish this first, and then we'll talk about tearing up the debt papers."

Ewan was outside in the parking lot, talking to both Fred and Ozzie, faster than I could say 'boo.'"

We all clustered around the window, watching with great interest as Fred brought out an old chicken-coop ramp and affixed it to the open tailgate on Ozzie's truck. He'd obviously done this before, because he even had little clamps to make sure that the ramp stayed in place. Next, Fred opened a large crate in the back and out snuffled Barnaby the potbellied pig, on a leash. He was a force to be reckoned with, with all his rolls of fat and tiny little eyes. But everyone knew he was no evil monster. He was always friendly and wouldn't hurt a fly. The only person truly terrified of Barnaby was Gertie, and she was on the road right now doing her youth ministry activities.

Or at least that's what we all thought.

The back door to the hall slammed, likely louder than she'd planned. "Julie, I'm back! And you'll never guess what I've just done," Gertie announced in a loud voice as she breezed into the research site.

I went over to give her a hug, and before I could explain what was going on in the parking lot, she babbled, "I filmed a very sedate, orderly youth choir video. It follows all rules and is utterly, amazingly confident."

"So, in other words you made something that is going to get zero views from your online youth audience?" Ewan observed, now back inside the building.

"You just wait. My followers will love it," she said.

"I have an idea they'll want to see something much different," Ewan said, gesturing for her to come outside with him. I knew Gertie's preference was to text back her youth choir members as soon as she parked and could safely use her phone, so Gertie likely didn't know Barnaby was out front. She'd probably driven around behind the building just before Fred and Ozzie arrived.

When I saw the gleam in Ewan's eye, I knew something was up. I smiled back at him and grabbed my phone. This was going to be excellent online entertainment.

Ewan showed a contented Gertie outside. I filmed through a newly opened window and captured a perfectly clear angle of Fred walking Barnaby on his leash around the corner of the truck. It would be an unexpected parking lot meeting for Fred, Gertie and Barnaby. Gertie's reaction was absolutely expected, mirroring when she found Barnaby rooting around in a holiday home kitchen.

Gertie's high-pitched wail started off an octave below where it ended. It didn't help that there was a puddle in the midst of where she was about to escape. One of her leather-soled shoes caught the muddy bottom of the puddle and she slipped, going right down on her backside, Barnaby immediately tore the leash out of Fred's hand to go over and investigate. I could see things were going very sideways and got a bit worried; I wasn't one to choose a joke over someone's suffering. As Gertie's wailing grew louder, the pig snorted louder and ended up doing a small little circle around her as he prodded her with his friendly yet inquisitive nose. Apparently, Gertie was more attractive-smelling than a truffle. It was just one of those flukes when someone with a phone happens to be in the right place at the right time.

Gertie curled up into a little ball beside the puddle and yelled for assistance. I went over to help and saw her start to laugh at the ridiculousness of it all. Once I determined she was alright, wounded pride being her only injury, I leaned down and whispered, "This has to be worth ten million views or more."

Luckily Gertie saw the funny side of it. "I'd wager fifteen million, on the low side. At least it was over in a few seconds." I helped her stand up. She was splattered in mud, head to toe, and left to go clean up.

Doctor Grierly, the area's clean cut and long-serving veterinarian, arrived in the midst of all this chaos. The wise man seized the opportunity while Barnaby was distracted to give him his booster shots. Holly got hers a few moments later, during a millisecond where she paused from chasing Barnaby and galumphing around the parking lot. If there were awards given out for the most leaping, bounding, and tongue-lolling dog in the world, Holly was certainly the top contender.

Ewan did his best and stood at the front doors, preventing either animal from getting inside the front hallway and therefore into the research site. I couldn't hold the tank turf incident against him much longer, especially as he protected us while suffering a broken arm. But I'd at least made him earn his way back up into my good graces; I'd made my point.

As the fervent group of three outside finally rounded up Barnaby and Holly to put them back inside their crates, I saw Fred and Ozzie both lean against the closed tailgate. I decided the jig was up and went outside to speak with the instigators of this muddy mess.

"Good morning, Fred. I didn't know Greymore had turned into a veterinary patient drop-off and treatment zone."

Ozzie piped up to take this one. "I'm sorry, I suppose that was my fault. I merely offered to drive to meet the vet after Fred's vehicle broke down. You see, we have a bit of a barter exchange going." Ozzie puffed himself up a bit, looking awfully important and pleased with himself.

"Oh?" I didn't dare wonder what on earth these two had concocted this time.

Ozzie put one hand through each of his suspenders. "Yes, indeed. I have decided to sue my cousin, and Fred is representing me on a contingency fee basis. He only gets paid when I do."

Not if, but when.

I looked surprised and Ewan's eyebrows went up. With a nod and brief wave, Doctor Grierly made himself scarce, heading for the miniature goat herd at the back.

"What, exactly, are you suing him for ... chocolate?" Ewan asked.

"In a manner of sorts. They won't hand over the ownership easily, so I've had to resort to legal means."

The thought of Ozzie charging into the confectionery company's boardroom, demanding keys to the front door and unlimited free samples, created quite the image in one's mind.

"That's a pretty big company to take on, you both know that, right?" Ewan asked.

This time it was Fred's turn to get indignant. "My good man, of course we are very familiar with the vast, corporate expansiveness of Zerruston's Fine Confectionery. However, what the firm's misguided leadership fails to recognize is that a solid, well-researched legal strategy will certainly out do, out step, and out argue any type of wimpish, feeble lawyerly response that their own solicitor wishes to send, via postal, courier, or electronic mail, in our direction. This is a case that we will win. And, interestingly, we have proven it using genealogical research."

We all just stood there, some even with mouths agape.

Fred felt really good about himself, so confident that as he strutted back towards the pickup truck, his foot caught the muddy edge of the puddle, and he went down in the exact same spot as Gertie. We were now faced with a soggy, tweed-attired solicitor who had the largest eyes for courtroom victories and oversized potbellied pigs.

I nudged Ewan. "Too bad I left my phone inside during Puddlegate Part Two."

Chapter 31

Pamela arrived on site an hour later. Her eyes shone with excitement.

"Back again so soon for more punishment?" I asked.

"A herd of wild miniature goats couldn't keep me away," she said. "I'm still so frightfully ashamed about the travel fiasco I put you and the Major through this week."

I patted the top of her hand. "It happens. Just be glad you're not tracking down a potbellied pig."

She gave me a very confused look in return. "I'm sorry?"

I sighed. "Long story. How can we help you today?"

Pamela brought the silver sphinx out of her purse. "I followed up on the artwork we found in Franklyn's sketchbook at the Maritime Museum."

"And?" I leaned over with anticipation.

"I've done it already. You do it." She pushed the sphinx across the smooth counter towards me.

I picked up the precious object, holding my breath. It was moments like this that made one think of all the hands touching this object in the past. It went back to the very miners who extracted the silver from the depths of the earth. Then one had to consider who melted the silver into a mold and then who tooled the silver into its fine sphinx design. The craftsmen also had to create the requested secret compartment inside this model. Beyond that, someone had engraved the sphinx with its inscription at the request of a senior military officer. The gift had then been duly passed along to Richard Palmer, who obviously considered it a treasured keepsake. It wasn't just a silver trinket that was worth its meltdown weight on the open market. Love, care, and talent were poured into this marvelous object. After Cairo, it came halfway around the world to be here in my hands here today. It was like that for so many different types of family history items, whether they were heirlooms, family bibles, or personal diaries. It was fascinating to ponder how they were actually created and what sentiments were poured into them so they could exist the way they did over time. The details took one's breath away.

The sphinx was cool in my hands, like one would expect a heavy metal object to be. It was only four inches long and about three inches high. I used a fingernail to depress the tiny button underneath its chin and, with a satisfying click, it responded. But it didn't open.

I looked up at Pamela, questioning what I was witnessing.

"I had the same problem." She dug into her purse and pulled out a knitting needle. "Try this, it opens it fully. Trust me."

I depressed the pointed end of the knitting needle on top of the button, carefully, ever so carefully, and with a full, satisfying click, the sphinx split fully open like a sandwich, top layer from its bottom. Tiny hinges inside kept it closed and unnoticed by the untrained eye.

"The craftsmanship on this is exquisite," I said, sensing we'd attracted a crowd around the information desk. Maude and

Ewan looked over our shoulders, as did Gertie, now changed into a clean café uniform and sans most of the mud splatters on her face.

"And what's this?" I pulled out a tiny roll of paper tucked inside a rectangular hollow on the base of the sphinx. When it was unfurled, I saw three addresses listed: a boarding house in Plymouth, a Cairo cabaret, and a 'Delzinnia Cottage' in Carlingheath.

"I think we found the boarding house. We were looking in the wrong city," Pamela said.

"It appears so. The Cairo cabaret is where Sylvie was on stage. But what is 'Delzinnia Cottage' in Carlingheath? We've never, ever run across that name in any of our research, have we?"

"It's a mystery to me," Pamela said.

Maude picked up the scrap of paper and looked at it closely. "Delzinnia Cottage. Isn't that the long line of retiree cottages on the outskirts of Carlingheath? It's just beyond that large group of retail shops, you know the one that has the supermarket, the drugstore, and medical office?"

I started entering an online search at the information desk computer. Delzinnia Cottage did indeed still exist, and Maude was right. "There's a whole bunch of cottages named after flowers and fruits. It's a group of seniors' houses overseen by the local council."

"So this note was written back in the 1940s. Why would there be a distinct reference to a retirement cottage out in Carlingheath? What on earth does that have to do with Cairo?"

Maude smiled. "It's not the cottage. It's who used to live there. That's where you'll find the connection."

"Where do I look for that?" Pamela asked.

I wanted to hear this answer because I'd never researched previous owners of a house in the quest for genealogy clues and answers.

Maude continued. "The fun thing about England is that house ownership records can go back for centuries. They are potential gold mines of information."

"Where do we look?" I asked.

"The local archives may have deed records on file. The local council offices may also have some older tax rolls you can look at. Even current neighbors can provide valuable information about previous tenants or owners."

"If they're willing to talk," I said. "And I'm not walking up the garden path that has a huge great dog with big teeth lunging at me."

"Of course. One must choose battles carefully," Pamela said.

It didn't take us long to find what we were looking for. And no, it certainly didn't require an in-person visit. We found a picture of Delzinnia Cottage online, currently for sale. Through some local archives' tax-roll records, we found that in the 1940s the cottage was owned by none other than Francine Winloame of Francine's Matrimonial Bureau. The current owner put it on the market eight months ago.

"That's funny. Considering the shortage of seniors' housing, I wonder why the cottage didn't sell right away. It looks in very fine condition," I said.

Ewan looked over my shoulder at the screen. "Who knows with real estate these days. A deal could have fallen through. The place could have some wiring issues, foundation cracks, a leaky thatch roof. Not that thatch roofing is bad, it just needs to be maintained properly over time."

Maude was busy on the computer beside me. She was a lightning-fast typist, and the screens in front of her face were flashing by so fast nobody could keep up. She settled on a newspaper obituary.

"And here's our answer," she said. "Listen to this. Francine Winloame passed away at the grand old age of ninety-eight. Survived by a sole daughter, also named Francine, of the lovely Carlingheath, England. I would bet you a piece of date loaf that Francine Junior is the one who's selling the cottage. I can't find an obituary for her, so perhaps she's moved into assisted living."

"Could we contact the estate agent and ask for more details?" Pamela questioned.

Maude shrugged. "Certainly can't hurt. Julie should make that call. Drop Aunt Edwina's name. That might help open the door a bit wider."

A jolly little man in a tidy suit and polka-dot bowtie approached the information desk. "I'm sorry, I couldn't help but overhearing. Are you looking for a seniors' care home in Carlingheath?"

I nodded. "Yes, and you are?"

"Rich Burrell. I'm actually a saddler by trade and came here to meet with Jacques about a tool that somebody had found in an heirloom box. When I overheard you discussing the care home in Carlingheath, I thought of my Aunt Lisette. She's lived in a wonderful building there for the past five years and just loves it."

Pamela turned around to greet him. "Pamela Fulham. So pleased to meet you. That tool was actually in my heirloom box.

Anything you can do to help us figure out the mystery of my ancestors would be gratefully appreciated."

"Well, I'm no expert genealogist, but I'd be glad to share what I can," Rich said.

The two of them went off to the chat room, leaving Maude, Ewan, and I to figure out the rest.

"Well, Maude, please continue your wizardry on the computer. You're faster than Ewan and I combined, probably," I said.

"Especially now," Ewan said, pointing to the cast on his arm.

Maude pretended to crack her knuckles and gave me a wise grin. "You'd be amazed at the skullduggery I've had to do behind the scenes over the course of my thirty years of genealogical research. Now let me see ..." Her fingers flew across the keys, clackety clack.

Half an hour later we were looking at a picture of a tidy, middle-class townhome in the city of Portsmouth, southern England. It had three levels, a bright, sunshine-yellow door as well as horizontal cream-colored siding on the ground floor and a wrought-iron fence with a bit of greenery at the entrance. This was topped by two more floors clad in brown brick. On the top floor one could see rock band posters concealing part of the open window. In the middle-floor windows were a living room and television. To the left and right were matching townhomes extending for ten more units on either side. In typical British fashion, each owner had painted their front door a different color. I suppose that was to give each residence uniqueness and ease of being located.

"Jesmyne Lane Boarding House," Ewan said. "It looks like a regular family home today."

"It's not that far from the naval base, so it is plausible that it was a boarding house Richard frequented back in the day," Maude said.

"It's the exact address on the piece of paper inside the sphinx. That's got to be it," I said.

We all looked at each other, a now-familiar expression on our faces. We spoke in unison: "Do I hear field trip?"

***

Waterloo Station, London. Next Day. 11:00 a.m.

The only promise I needed from Pamela was that on the way home I could stop off for more treats at my favorite shop in Waterloo Station. I had a particular fondness for that store's scones, chocolates, blackcurrant drink, and individually packaged salads. I knew it wasn't fine dining, yet it was fresh, portable, and tasty, so I was in. Once we got to Waterloo coming from the outskirts of Plumsden Station, it was a long yet straight ride down to Portsmouth.

Fully stocked with good snacks and e-magazines, the next hour-and-a-half journey practically flew by. I loved riding trains and experiencing the various topographical changes England had to offer en route. One always felt a bit removed from reality when whizzing along the rails, completely insulated from the outside. It was a privilege to travel in such a fast, convenient manner. I thought back to our copper-wire incident from a few days ago and had to smile. I suppose it was akin to the feeling New Yorkers got when their city was snowed in beyond belief by a nor'easter;

it made one tougher. Resilient. And I was glad of it, because it was how I was getting over my failed marriage.

I looked across the aisle at Ewan; he'd bravely volunteered to come along with Pamela and I, despite his broken arm. The deal was that he'd promised not to carry anything and risk reinjuring himself.

We ate lunch on the train, and by 12:30 p.m. we arrived at our destination. Once we'd sorted a taxi, it only took us fifteen minutes to find the townhome. It was exactly as we found it online, right down to the bright, sunshine-yellow door. A surly teenager of about sixteen, wearing over-the-ear, wireless gaming headphones, answered the door.

"Yeah?" he grunted in a monotone. He wore a 1970s heavy-metal band T-shirt and ripped jeans. His socks had holes, but he gave the impression that he preferred them that way. A mop of brown, wavy hair cut in layers partly covered his eyes. He wore a couple of heavy silver rings on his fingers, which looked calloused, likely from playing an instrument of some sort. Whatever instrument it was, my guess was that he played it very loudly indeed.

"Hello, we're from the GGRS. We called yesterday—I believe I spoke with your mother—to arrange a visit?"

No welcome. No greeting. All the teenager did was turn around and bellow, "Muuuuuuum!" He turned back to us and stared, holding the fort until he heard his mother behind him.

We heard rapid footsteps behind him. "Good grief, Rex. You're not trying to raise the dead. Well, perhaps in this case ... Well, hello!"

The disgruntled teenager disappeared.

Deirdre Lamerin came into view, wiping her hands on a tea towel covered in prints of lemons. "Julie? Which one of you is Julie?" she asked, her bright eyes dancing. "Don't take any notice of Rex, he's his usual grumpy self. Hormones and all that fun teenage angst stuff."

This was a nice change from our initial welcome. Deirdre was a pert, attractive woman in her forties with frizzy hair and a perfect complexion. Her enthusiasm spilled over way beyond the doorway and seemed to hit both Ewan and Pamela at the same time.

I smiled and extended my hand. "I'm Julie. And this is Ewan and Pamela. Thank you for agreeing to meet with us."

"Of course, of course, please come in," Deirdre said. "Sorry about the mess, my husband's away on business over in Brighton selling plumbing components, and I've got two teenagers who simply do not understand the concept of coat hooks."

We all had a good laugh as we trooped inside the narrow front hallway. She stationed us in the front living room on comfortable leather couches. She already had lemonade and biscuits out on a tray, perfect because the day was humid and still warm outside. And, of course, snacks were always important.

Deirdre perched up on a leather recliner, crossing her legs underneath her lithe body. "As I said to Julie on the phone, we've only lived here for about seven years. A mere blip on London's history. The woman who lived here before us was kind of a packrat, and she left a great stack of paperwork in the attic. I'm sorry I haven't had a chance to go through everything, but you know how it is. I'm an event promoter, and it takes most everything out of me being a mum with two busy teenagers plus running a home-based business. Somehow in the middle of all that I've got to find time for my husband too."

We all nodded.

"Anything you can help us with would be of great assistance," I said.

"I made copies of the most relevant papers I could find," she said. She got up and went over to the credenza at the side of the room. She picked up a fat file folder and handed it to me. "These are copies of the documents I found with the family name Palmer or Winloame on them."

"They were both here? Both families?" Pamela asked.

"It appears so. Arnold Higgenton was the owner, Richard Palmer and Francine Winloame were both lodgers. It looked like this place was associated with military personnel coming and going for training and then shipping out. I knew I was dealing with the military based on a couple of brass buttons we found in the attic as well."

"We're trying to trace the Francine Winloame who used to run a matrimonial bureau in London," I said.

"Like a wartime dating service?" Deirdre asked. "That's such fun!" She was a real live wire.

"Did you happen to find any information about the business itself or a gentleman named Franklyn, Franklyn spelled with a Y?" Ewan asked.

"Spelled with a Y. No, I don't recall anything like that. I found records going back to the 1920s of who owned the house. I found a business license for the Jesmyne Lane Boarding House but no Franklyn." Deirdre thought on it for a minute. "Maybe

Richard met Franklyn here and Franklyn introduced him to his sister Sylvie."

"Scant or incomplete records are frustrating," I said.

Deirdre nodded. "The lodgers' register book has a few pages missing, right around the dates you're seeking." She looked at all of us as we tried to process this data. She tilted her head to the side, curious. "I take it one of you is related to the people you're searching for?"

Pamela gave a rapid-fire explanation of how all the players were connected. "I'm Sylvie's great-granddaughter, and I would dearly love to understand a bit more about my family history, along with her work in Cairo."

"It all sounds pretty fascinating to me," Deirdre said. A phone in her back office rang. "Excuse me. I need to get that." She jumped up and left us alone with the papers, lemonade, and some rather delectable chocolate biscuits.

"Well, gang–" I started.

"Wait. Look at this," Ewan said, leafing through the photocopies after he'd finished his snack. He pulled out a will. "Francine's last will and testament. She's buried in her husband's family mausoleum up near Oxford."

"So why leave her will in this stack of papers?" Pamela asked.

"Maybe she helped Arnold Higgenton find a wife."

"Maybe he offered to help her daughter. Who knows," Ewan said. "I once found a will for a baron in an auction lot of brewery orders from an eighteenth century pub. It still intrigues me to this day."

Our hostess returned to the room, looking a little frazzled. "Sorry, my florist just filched out on me, and I've got a very upset marketing coordinator over at the bank. I'm afraid I'm going to have to love you and leave you."

We gathered up our belongings, taking last swigs of lemonade after filing paper copies away into handbags and satchels.

"Thank you so much for your time," Pamela gushed.

"I hope you found something of use?"

"We found a clue to what cemetery Francine's buried in, which may indeed be the answer to everything we're needing to find."

"Well, best of luck to you." Deirdre did look as though she'd prefer to join us on our family history quest instead of dealing with her wayward florist.

Chapter 32

**Limeknobble, Fourteen Miles North of Oxford.
Next Day.**

The churchyard wasn't anything like we'd expected. Set on a small rise overlooking a town of exactly 2,346 residents, the place was horrifically overgrown. Brambles and bindweed had taken over, and as the breeze blew underneath the crawling plants, the lighter ones rose and fell like sleeping giants. This was definitely a spooky place at night.

In a way, we were looking for ghosts. We knew that somewhere in amongst this tangled jungle rested a woman who was at the core of our genealogy research mission. Tombstones often provided clues to a person's past life, sometimes even key dates that perhaps were smudged or missing from parish records. In this case, we were hoping for something more about Francine's personality and the people that she cared for either on or off the job. It made sense that she was a caring person, because she was a matchmaker. She had to be able to read people's personalities and figure out good matches. She obviously had great intuition, enough to make a living from it. Essentially, we were just there to gather up the details.

"Careful where you step, I found a couple of soggy patches," Ewan called out. He was a few feet ahead of us already, clambering through tall grass that had gone to seed, avoiding brambles as best he could.

"Please be careful," I called after him. "You don't need to break the other one."

He held up his good hand and waved, still walking forward as men typically would when flagrantly ignoring the need for caution or a map.

We'd come into Reading by train from Plumsden, then switched to a fast train to Oxford. I suppose we all assumed that being close to a university, the village would be a well-kept, modern place. There would likely be a lot of do-gooder parishioners bustling around each day, tidying up the graves, even those belonging to people who'd lain here for centuries. Instead, we faced toppled tombstones, their inscriptions nearly worn away by weather's erosion over time. The tombstones were sandy brown or light grey in color, many covered in lichens and moss. It was sad, really, seeing how the people who were lovingly memorialized were now practically forgotten.

"Why is no one taking care of this churchyard?" Pamela asked.

"I think it's become redundant. It's happened to more than one church in England. Frankly, it's exactly what Gertie is trying to reverse," I said.

We walked up to the church entrance. It was unlocked, so we pushed open the heavy oak door, curved at the top to meet the arch in the opening. Inside it appeared to be abandoned, covered in cobwebs and dust. It didn't look like anyone had been here for at least ten to twenty years. The font was dry, and there was no silverplate anywhere. On the wall were dusty etched-brass and carved-marble plaques, tributes to notable citizens who had donated towards the church's upkeep over the centuries.

"I feel like an intruder," Ewan said. "I have such reverence for these places, but without the vicar here, it feels like we don't belong."

"Everybody is welcome in our church," we heard behind us. We turned to set eyes upon a wizened little elderly woman, no taller than five feet, dressed in a headscarf and long beige overcoat. She moved with a shuffling gait, likely hampered by severe arthritis. "I saw the door was ajar. My name's Agatha Bremridge," the elderly lady said.

"Ewan, Pamela, and Julie from the Greymore Genealogy Research Site in Oakhurst, Kent. We're looking for the Winloame family's mausoleum," Ewan said.

"Oh, that's on the north side of the churchyard. Would you like me to show you?" Agatha asked.

"If you don't mind," Pamela said. "Do you live nearby?"

"Three cottages down the lane. My husband used to be the vicar here before he passed. So sad how our little village church ended up in such decay. We recently even heard talk of it being converted into a residence with all the mod-cons."

Ewan looked up, and just at that moment the sun came out from behind a cloud. It illuminated a wonderful scene of parishioners taking in the harvest way up high on a stained-glass panel. It truly was a lovely assortment of deep, rich colors that spoke to the power of working together as well as the bountiful local soil.

"You just didn't have enough parishioners anymore?" I asked.

Agatha shook her head. "A lot of the young people left a few years ago when the house prices went up so dramatically. Many of our really dedicated parishioners moved into retirement homes in other cities to be closer to their children. I stayed, along with a few others, but we're all in our eighties now and the maintenance is just too overwhelming. Besides, I can hardly bend down to tie my shoes, let alone scrub a tombstone."

This didn't seem quite fair to those who had stepped across the well-worn church floors before us. It was sad that a church commissioned in 1699 was now an empty shell, devoid of worshippers, slated for a new purpose. But, on the other hand, it was the environmentally sound thing to do: help a family with much-needed housing. The only question was what would happen to the graves outside? It made for a rather unusual backyard, one exceedingly popular around October 31 each year.

"Follow me, please," Agatha said, already halfway out the church door.

We trailed after her, still in awe of this centuries-old place. She led us underneath several trellises of wisteria, the vines three to four inches thick in places. This was an old-timer plant for sure, and in spring was sure to cover the trellis in a vertical carpet of horticultural happiness.

"This must be the entrance to where the fancy people rest," Pamela observed.

Ewan gave her a funny look. "You mean the lesser people don't get past the wisteria?"

"Don't knock it," I said. "It wasn't uncommon for a pauper's grave to be dug up and the remains disposed of in order to make room for more burials in the future. It was done once the original corpse had decomposed just to bones."

We all shuddered.

"I hope when I'm laid to rest, everyone truly lets me rest. I don't want to be disturbed," Ewan said.

"I'll put a do-not-disturb sign on your tombstone," I said.

"Gee, thanks," he replied with a grin.

"Where did she go?" Pamela asked.

We all looked up ahead and saw that Agatha had completely disappeared. We were standing in the middle of a cobblestoned pathway, lined with bricks on either side, grass peeking through every fathomable crack. The walkway was dark, shaded by numerous ten-foot-tall mausoleums on either side. This was where the wealthy dead were laid to rest, locked away for eternity inside cool marble structures. Inside they'd have slabs made up like multitiered bunkbeds for each family member's coffin.

"Do you think they're all the same?" Pamela asked. "I've never been inside a mausoleum before."

Ewan raised his eyebrows. "I don't think most people visit the inside of a tomb until they are actually dead."

"That's not what I meant. I was asking if someone could personalize it for family members."

"I would imagine money would buy you anything you want," I said. "From my reading, I've heard that some of them even have little altars and tiled floors, complete with belongings from their homes."

"Kind of like an Egyptian pharaoh's tomb. Neat." Ewan was impressed.

"It wouldn't necessarily have to be gold. People get attached to the most peculiar things over time. I knew of one woman who was buried with the nightgown and crushed velvet slippers she wore in hospital after giving birth to a stillborn child thirty-nine years prior. She apparently never got over the tragedy, and quite frankly, I don't know if one ever could," I said.

"Sad, isn't it?" Pamela added in a soft voice.

"Agatha?" Ewan called out.

Still nothing.

I looked at the other two. "This isn't one of those weird times when all of a sudden we discover that Agatha is a ghost, right? Because that would be both really fascinating but also really disappointing because we are no further ahead with finding Francine Winloame's family mausoleum than when we first started."

As if on cue, Agatha popped her head around a corner of a tree. "Oh, there you are. Sorry."

"Any idea where the Winloame mausoleum is?" Ewan asked.

"It's right here. The one with all the weeds covering the marble." She pointed behind her at a little path that led us onto a red-gravel paved lane. It, too, was vastly overgrown, but we could see it led to somewhere special.

At the end of the short path was a white marble mausoleum, the family name 'Winloame' clearly etched in stone over the front entrance. There was an extremely heavy padlock on the front, and apart from a little bit of rust, it looked in very good order. This family had taken great pains to protect its dead from grave robbers. Thankfully today we were beyond the centuries where people needed to rob graveyards for corpses for medical students to study. I remembered seeing drawings of the metal grid cages that they used to bury people inside to protect them from an unauthorized scientific dissection fate.

"And here we are. We found her," Pamela said. She went up to the door and laid her hand against the dusty surface, leaving a firm palm print on the marble.

"You don't want to go inside, do you?" Ewan asked. He looked skeptical.

"Just trying to get closer to the woman who introduced my ancestors to each other," Pamela said. "So far it's all been papers, pictures, and trinkets. None of it's like having a living, breathing person in front of you."

I smiled. "You're far from being alone. Most adults never get to meet their great-grandparents. The generational time gap is just too great."

"Give it a hundred years, and if our fragile planet has resisted global warming, they'll probably have invented a way for us to live a hundred and fifty years or more," Ewan said.

"Aren't you a ray of sunshine," I said. "Don't spoil Pamela's fun."

"Apologies. Just feeling sorry for myself with this bum arm."

"What happened?" Agatha asked him.

"Rugby accident. And I'm not even on the permanent team roster," he explained.

She gave him a reassuring smile. "Doctors know how to heal people pretty quickly these days, young man. You'll be right as rain in no time." She took a closer look at who had signed the cast and saw all the researchers' names from the GGRS along with the charity's logo stamped in blue. "At least you have friends to see you through."

And maybe that's what this was all about. All the brick walls, all the stops and starts, all the wrong directions that one took while conducting family history research. What it came down to, when all was said and done, was sharing the highs and lows of this journey with other people. It was both intriguing and entertaining to have a wayward and mysterious ancestor. I thought back to Ozzie Boggs and remembered his initial dismay when he realized that most of his ancestors were of a criminal mind. Our experts Maude and Gertie had encouraged him, though, because criminals left a trail of paper and court records in their devious wake. So, from lemons he made yummy lemon meringue pie.

Pamela turned to Agatha. "Do the church records list who is buried inside each mausoleum?"

"They may. They'll at least show who is buried in the churchyard. I remember my husband having to enter one of these structures a few years before he died. What he found inside didn't match the record at all."

"How's that?" I asked.

Agatha got a gleam in her eye. "The lids of both coffins were off, and inside one of them he found three gold coins."

"No bodies?"

"Not a one. Turns out they'd robbed a bank ten years prior, created their own fictional deaths, and lived on the proceeds in dribs and drabs so as not to draw attention to themselves."

"Clever ruse."

Agatha emitted a polite snort. "Hooligans." She gave us a firm stare. "Well, I've done my duty and shown you where the mausoleum is located. Now I'll leave you to it."

We offered our profuse thanks and looked around a little bit longer after she'd left.

"So, team, are we at the end of the road with this location?" I asked.

"Not yet. Look at this," Pamela said, tracing something on the outside wall with her index finger. Ewan and I crowded around Pamela and looked up. There, under the eaves of the steep slate roof, was something quite unexpected. Etched into the marble were the unmistakable figures of a sphinx, an ostrich feather, and a Tudor rose.

Chapter 33

We stared at each other.

"What do you think it means?" I asked. It seemed oddly appropriate to search for meaning in the middle of all this quiet. It was a place where tall trees dropped their needles and cones into the crevices of the stones beneath them. The mausoleums here were quiet, majestic, their slate roofs covered in moss. It was a place of contemplation, yet the one we were looking at raised more questions than answers.

"I think Francine's sending us back to Portsmouth," I said.

"Why do you say that?" Ewan asked. "Oh wait. The Tudor rose?"

Pamela nodded. "That's where King Henry the Eighth's ill-fated battleship the *Mary Rose* sank in the harbor."

"The sphinx and the ostrich feather are obviously Sylvie and Richard. Their ties to Francine were deeper than we originally thought," I said.

"Maybe Francine was part of their espionage work?" Ewan said.

"That's not a bad hypothesis. I mean, Sylvie and Richard were indeed married, based on the marriage certificate we found, but what if the matrimonial bureau was just a wartime front for some other work?" I asked.

Pamela shook her head. "I don't buy that. Remember all the records we found at The National Archives at Kew? There is no way a hundred and twenty people would be willing to get married just to pad files at a sham marriage agency."

"You're probably right," I said. "So, if Francine's not a spy, then why is she so tied into Sylvie and Richard, so much so that she wants to guide her descendants back to Portsmouth?"

"What did the death certificates say about where they died?" Ewan asked.

"You mean Richard and Sylvie?" Pamela asked.

"Yes. What locations did they give?"

"London. And we all know how conveniently vague that is."

"Bingo. There's your answer. Just like these family mausoleums are protecting the dead, somebody wanted to protect Sylvie and Richard from being disturbed forever. They likely rattled a few cages when they were alive working overseas in Cairo," Ewan said.

"It's an awful lot of work to do just to protect a couple of bodies," I said.

"Perhaps. But we'll never know, just like the Major suggested, about the true size of their achievement for king and country. They likely earned the right to eternal, safe rest."

"And yet Francine wanted her good friends to be found by their descendants. This is Francine speaking beyond the grave, giving people like us guidance. Francine probably thought that those who take the trouble to track her down would already know how close she was to Sylvie and Richard and wished them no harm."

Pamela's eyes sparkled and she grew very excited putting these clues together. "That's why she left more than obvious clues. They're obvious to us because nobody else has the research to understand what all of it means. Most people seeing these etchings on the marble wall would just assume that they were some odd form of hieroglyphics, perhaps an odd hobby of the Winloame family when the tomb's occupants were alive."

Ewan leaned up against a tree, taking all this in with great interest. "I must admit, I am quite chagrined to tell you that your minds are working much faster than mine today. Regardless, I think both of you are exactly right."

***

GGRS. Next Morning.

I sat at my desk, a very serious Ozzie Boggs and Fred Todling in front of me. "What can I do for you today, gentlemen?"

"I was wondering if personnel from GGRS would be willing to stand as plaintiff witnesses in my court case," Ozzie said. He gave me what he probably thought was an inviting, friendly grin. Despite the full set of teeth he had on display, his smile actually reminded me of an evil wizard's sneer just before he boiled some fluorescent concoction in an iron cauldron.

"I'm not sure I understand. What does Greymore have to do with a confectionery company?" I said.

Fred inhaled. Exhaled. Then he started to explain in a slow, measured tone. "As I am sure, you, Julie Fincher, as the esteemed founder of this fantastic and fabulous research facility–"

I held up a hand. "Fred. Enough. When I have a client and his solicitor sitting here trying to get me involved in a court case, my radar goes into high alert. All I'm trying to do is run a charity that helps people with their genealogy and family history. I don't like the sound of where this is going." My last sentence was given in short, staccato words that left no room for interpretation.

Ozzie and Fred exchanged a furtive glance. Ozzie pulled out a photo from his files and showed it to Fred, who then nodded. Apparently I was about to be shown something from their inner privileged-and-confidential client-solicitor working relationship. I didn't know whether to feel special or frustrated; it was akin to being ten minutes into a blind date and frantically wishing that the previously arranged emergency call from a friend would happen any millisecond. I just didn't trust these two. They were up to something.

"I was hoping you'd act as a character witness for me," Ozzie said plaintively. "I need the court to understand that I'd be a good person to serve as new owner of the company."

I took the picture he handed me. It showed the confectionery company's head office with a fancy sign out front.

"You intend to take them on and win?" I asked.

"Yes," Fred said, giving me the luxury of an exceedingly short sentence for what was either the very first time or what seemed like it.

"Ozzie, I hardly know you. You've only been coming to Greymore for a short time. Aren't you supposed to call on people you've known for years?"

Fred cleared his throat. "Unfortunately, my client finds himself, how do I put it, somewhat lacking in the friends department."

I bit my tongue, refusing to even think of a snide remark. Instead, I chose to smile perfunctorily, thinking back to Ozzie's missing false teeth, the crows in the back of his truck, the potbellied pig transport incident, and the smoked-mackerel sandwiches. Oh, and let's not forget the day-old scones he was selling without permission at a markup in my lunchroom. No, I couldn't honestly say I was surprised that Ozzie found himself in this unfortunate situation.

Then again, I hated seeing anybody without friends.

"I don't think you quite understand, Julie," Ozzie said. He turned to Fred. "Can I show her?"

Fred gave me a very serious, long-faced look. "I think you must in order to convince her to be your witness."

"Witness? All I witness is family history research. Don't involve me in any of your court case shenanigans. Please."

"Just take a look at this video," Ozzie said.

I took his mobile phone with great trepidation. I wasn't really sure what to expect from the man who didn't think twice about skimming a few pounds off unsuspecting people in order to bolster his own wallet. So, with all that in mind, I pressed 'play' and the screen came to life. It was rather jerky and fuzzy at first but then I saw the video operator focus in on what looked like a moving production line. I could see little brown blobs covering the belt as it moved past a worker on either side.

Ozzie leaned over and explained. "You're looking at Zerruston's Fine Confectionery's production line, specifically the one that produced the soft, chewy caramel squares comprising one of the twenty types inside its most popular chocolate assortment box."

"How did you get the video?" I asked. It just didn't seem plausible that they let Ozzie stroll right into a clean food preparation facility, stand right up close, and take video.

"I have an insider mole," Ozzie said, beaming.

"Moles are by definition insiders, Ozzie. I think you're a little out of your league on this one," I said. I looked over at Fred.

"Please hear him out, Julie," Fred asked in a syrupy voice.

"All right. What is it I'm supposed to observe in this sea of chocolates?" I was getting exasperated by this point.

"Look at the man standing opposite us at the production line."

I did. I peered very closely and watched the video again. "Yes? What's the matter?"

Ozzie glanced again at Fred and they both shook their heads in a very somber, serious manner.

"He's not wearing a hairnet," Ozzie said.

"I can see that."

Fred straightened up and launched directly into solicitor mode. "That is a direct violation of quality control as well as health and hygiene regulations in both the county and the nation. One simply cannot manufacture food of this kind, in such close proximity to humans, without being fully hairnetted."

"I didn't know that," I said.

"How would you like to buy a box of twenty assorted chocolates for your dear granny, and then as she bites into the fluffy, sugared orange cream, watch her pull back to chew with a long, brown hair caught in her teeth?"

"That would be rather disgusting," I admitted.

Ozzie smashed his palms together. "Aha! She agrees!"

Nothing about Ozzie Boggs surprised me at this moment. But roping me into a lawsuit? That's not something I wanted to ever be involved in.

"They're not producing food to standard!" Ozzie yelped. "We've got 'em there!"

"And what does that have to do with Greymore and family history research?" I demanded.

"Everything," Fred said. He pulled out a sheaf of papers from his briefcase. It was about ten pages long, double-sided, and stapled in the upper left-hand corner. He flipped it open to a page already flagged with a sticky note. "If you'll focus on line item number three please, Julie?" He handed me the papers.

I took a look at what he'd highlighted and sighed. There, right in front of me, was a list of the GGRS's £10,000-£20,000 sapphire-level sponsors. And right after 'Sanderfuggins Spa Services' was none other than 'Zerruston's Fine Confectionery'.

Fred and Ozzie waited for me take all of this in. I looked at the list, looked at them, then looked back at the list. This time the wheels were turning in my head, and I didn't like where they lurched to a stop. I looked back up at them again. "You're blackmailing me?"

"Far from it," Fred announced. "We are merely hoping that such an esteemed patron of the arts and genealogical wonders of the world will see the utmost sense in accompanying us to said confectionery factory and assisting in the convincing of the ownership that my client, a solid citizen of his abode, shall be bestowed his rightful ownership in said confectionery corporation with all the rights and issues he is due with immediate and past posthaste."

I needed a dictionary and three hours to unpack that last sentence Fred let loose. He'd expelled so much hot air I thought I might pass out.

Focus, Julie. Focus.

Ozzie added some extra convincing. "We're hoping that the Duke of Conroy will accompany us as well. Two powerful names will help our case immensely." Fred looked at me, satisfied they had presented their ask in its full glory.

"Has Bertie agreed?" I asked.

Fred shifted in his chair, nervous. "Er, we thought we'd ask you first."

I shook my head. "I doubt Bertie's going to be available on such short notice. He's always tied up in some charity event or another these days. Or he could be on another one of his chutney sales runs."

"Well, then, perhaps it'll just be us three," Fred said, giving me an expectant look.

"Fine."

Both men yelped with glee.

"Gentlemen. I'll come along to keep the peace. Also, I'm going to suggest that we bring along Gertie. She's in this afternoon and is a lot more expert with this genealogy research than I am. Maude can stay and watch the shop with the researchers."

"Any objections?" Fred asked Ozzie.

"None whatsoever," Ozzie said. "The more the merrier. We'll collect both of you from here later today. Their headquarters is located an hour's drive from here, attached to the manufacturing plant outside of London."

"What exactly is the dress code?" I asked. I needed to know for not just one, but two people.

"Let the suit wear the suit. We'll just go business casual, there's no pretense about us. My family tree says it all," Ozzie said.

I didn't know how Fred felt about being called 'the suit', but he took it all in stride as he snapped his briefcase shut and got up to hold the door for his client. I did know one thing for certain: Fred Todling, Esquire, was making his unerasable, unforgettable mark on the world.

Chapter 34

Zerruston's Fine Confectionery, Outside London. 1:37 p.m.

Thank goodness Fred's four-door, well-appointed sedan was repaired. I couldn't see us making a very convincing case by pulling up in a dilapidated farm truck. Fred and Ozzie hadn't filed the lawsuit paperwork yet; they told Gertie and I they wanted to try the polite approach first. Polite hopefully would translate into a voluntary handing over of the reins.

Good luck with that.

The sweets factory was absolutely enormous. My eyeballs called it two football fields in length, accommodating its multitude of confectionery products sold online, in retail stores, and by bulk wholesalers. Suppliers' trucks were lined up in various delivery bays unloading things like sugar, binding ingredients, and colorants. It all moved like a well-oiled machine, I supposed, until one got to the manufacturing lines where the purported hairnet violation had occurred. Ozzie had been very quiet about his mole's identity, and perhaps that was the best thing. This was already odd enough. We were family historians, not accredited bonbon inspectors.

Fred handed his business card to the security guard manning the booth outside the chain-link fence surrounding the private wing of the building. "Fred Todling, solicitor. I'm here with my client and genealogy research experts to speak with Owner and Chief Executive Officer Dan Zerruly."

"Do you have an appointment?"

"I did phone and let him know we were coming," Fred said, elegantly avoiding the direct question.

The guard had a typed daily visitor roster he was quick to consult. "Sorry, sir. No appointment, no access. You're welcome to visit the retail store down the road and through the public entrance."

"But we must speak with Dan. It's of the utmost importance, and his secretary wouldn't even return our calls," Fred pleaded. "I know he's in the building because that's his car parked right out front. I recognize it from Club 18th in London." The solicitor realized he was now starting to look very foolish in front of me, his client, and Gertie.

"Sorry, sir. No appointment, no access. You're welcome to visit–"

Ozzie leaned over the front seat. "Now look here, I'm an owner of this company and demand to be let inside."

The guard looked at the family tree Ozzie held in his outstretched hand. He sized up the rest of the people in the car and I felt his eyes briskly cover me and then Gertie, deciding we were harmless. Then he went back to Gertie. His eyes narrowed. "Wait a minute, don't I know you from somewhere?"

Gertie groaned.

"I know. You're that singing priest, aren't you?" The guard grinned. "Why didn't you say so? The boss is a huge fan of yours. Convinced his kid to join the youth choir. Well done, you." The guard chortled then radioed somebody. All of a sudden the red-and-white-striped horizontal pole barrier went up and the gates to the kingdom opened. "Drive straight ahead. Mr. Zerruly will be down in a jiffy to see you."

※※※

The executive office's reception area was reminiscent of Bertie's club in London. Dark wood paneling, polished brass, expensive club chairs, and low, burnished wood tables. An assortment of extravagant lifestyle magazines were fanned out on the coffee table, casually announcing where to buy one's next yacht, vineyard, or private island.

The secretary, a well-groomed man in his mid-twenties, looked up from his keyboard. "Miss Porringer!" He leapt up like he was meeting a rock star. I suppose that's how it was with social media influencers. "I'm Mitchell Tumborne. It's so good to meet you!"

"Gertie, please." She looked a bit taken aback as Mitchell pumped her hand with vigorous abandon. She often confided in me that she didn't understand what all the fuss was about. We surmised that millions of people couldn't be wrong, and she was just an entertaining person to watch on screen. Today's experience was no different. Gertie's new role was to cash in on her fame, in a church membership way, of course, and this receptionist was another potential recruit.

"I'll get Mr. Zerruly down here at once. He said to let him know the second you walked in the building." Mitchell picked up his desk phone and called his boss, lightning fast.

No less than a minute passed when we heard the ding of the elevator to the right of us. None other than Dan Zerruly emerged, dressed in a bespoke pinstripe suit, turquoise-blue tie, and white shirt with pinwheel lollipop cufflinks. He matched the gilt-framed, eight-foot portrait on the wall to a tee. Dan advanced, holding out his hand in welcome.

Ozzie was a bit miffed that he didn't get offered Dan's hand first. Instead, it went to the singing priest and her cousin Julie, the two people consuming the spotlight.

Fred decided to do something about it and jostled his way in between Gertie and Dan. "Allow me to introduce myself. Fred Todling, solicitor, and my client, Oswald Boggs."

"Ah yes, the duo who claim to own my company," Dan said with a gracious smile. It was clear he thought their pending case had zero merit.

"I'm sure you'll agree, if you look at the family tree I brought. There is no question," Ozzie said, finally coming face to face with his newfound rival.

"I've got an idea that may resolve this once and for all. How about we leave the family tree for Mitchell to share with my expert, and in the meantime, I'll give you a tour of the factory?" Dan offered.

Dan looked for any objections and saw none. He gestured for Ozzie to give the family tree to Mitchell and then proceeded to take us up in the elevator. Even the elevator looked executive. Dark-blue carpet, brass and mirrors everywhere. If I ever got stuck in an elevator, this would be the one I would choose. It probably even had a secret compartment that stashed cold drinks and sandwiches in case of an emergency. I was so very tempted to press the little red alarm button, but a cooler head prevailed. Luckily the door sprang open right after my fleeting thought.

"We're going to enter the factory on the catwalk level. You'll have to put on protective gear, of course, to comply with health and safety regs," Dan explained.

Ozzie exchanged a glance with Fred, who merely raised his eyebrows in response. We were shown into a set of private, individual change rooms, each one stocked with a new hairnet, freshly pressed white coat and trousers plus white clogs for us to don. After we left the change rooms, they locked behind us, and we kept the keys so we could safely leave our personal belongings inside.

Once changed, Dan led us up to a large white door marked 'Authorized Personnel Only: Clean Whites Required'. He turned to us. "When we're inside, please note that some of the vats are filled with hot liquid sugar or melted chocolate. Please be careful where you step and hold onto the handrails at all times. You'll get an eagle eye view of what we do here, particularly helpful if you want to understand the workings of our company." He winked at Ozzie.

We walked in on absolute confectionery heaven. The whole place smelled like chocolate and gumdrops, something that the nostrils belonging to anyone under the age of eight fancied to the extreme. The only things that weren't white included stainless-steel delivery pipes, vats, and mixing equipment. One got a sense that the employees working on the factory floor were well-trained and efficient. Every single one of them was attired properly, including hairnets on every single head. I was beginning to wonder if what Ozzie had filmed was a complete aberration. I tried to see the finished production line but we were located too early in the factory process. I needed to look further towards the end of the line where the sorting, quality control, and packaging took place.

Half an hour later, we'd finished the first phase of our tour and headed into phases two and three. It was only an hour later that we found ourselves at the end of the line, looking at twenty different moving belts, each laden with multiple chocolates of the same kind. This was where they were checked, sorted, and assembled into the popular variety boxes that each held twenty assorted chocolates.

"None of us here can stomach chocolate anymore, but you're welcome to take as much as you would like," Dan said, pointing to an open bin of seconds that had either missed their full chocolate coverage or were grossly misshapen. It looked like a barrel full of rude rabbit droppings. He watched our faces fall. Then he let out a huge guffaw. "Just kidding! We donate or compost any seconds, nothing goes to waste. I'll give you each a couple of boxes of the brand-name stuff when we're done in here." He turned to me. "Do you see much of dear old Bertie these days?"

As soon as the question passed his lips, I saw Fred jab Ozzie. They thought that I had the upper hand just because of my handy friendship with an aristocrat.

Dan continued, "We used to play football together at our boys' school. We go back a long ways."

I nodded. "We do see each other a bit, recently at his London club and when he delivers his estate farm shop goods to Greymore. Bertie is super busy with his shop and Scotford Castle renovations, though. It seems to be a never-ending process."

"Isn't that the truth," he said. "I live in an eighteenth century listed building and commiserate. Lovely place but it's like a black hole with all the renovations that have to be done to maintain the authentic historical appearance. Still, I wouldn't have it any other way. We need to preserve the past for future generations. Hopefully one day my children will appreciate it."

I liked Dan. I really liked Dan. He was one of those solid types who had his head screwed on correctly. That would be opposed to Ozzie Boggs, a man who was trying to enact a corporate takeover based on a few weeks of genealogical research. I still wasn't fully convinced.

***

Later.

Apparently, the corporate family historian wasn't convinced by Ozzie's research either. We sat in a small meeting room at the end of our factory tour, one that was obviously used for regular tours given to the public. An efficient, gray-haired man knocked and then came in, Ozzie's rolled family tree in his hand. "Mr. Zerruly?"

"Yes, come in please, Wesley." Dan turned to us. "Wesley Zottles. My own family's genealogist who also happens to be a solicitor by trade."

So, now the big guns were launched. We'd been lulled into a false sense of friendliness by Dan while his obvious henchman was behind the scenes debunking Ozzie's research. At first I was really miffed, but then I put myself in Dan's shoes and told myself I'd likely have the same reaction. Clever. Offer them kindness then swoop in with hard evidence. Brilliant.

It was about to be parish register against parish register, database against database, certificate against certificate.

Wesley wasn't pulling any punches. He sat beside Dan and unrolled the family tree with one quick snap of his wrist. He looked up at us, a grave expression on his face. "You've done some very impressive research but I'm afraid you've gone up the wrong ancestral line. You see, Samuel the First had two sons, Samuel the Second and David. Samuel the Second had a son Samuel the Third and a daughter Margaret who married Adam Zerruly."

"I know that," Ozzie said.

"Well, unfortunately there's another Samuel in the mix. Samuel the First's other son, David, also had a son named Samuel. That's the Samuel you're descended from."

Ozzie took a big gulp of air.

"It is, decisively, a fatal blow to your claim as David never had a part in the confectionery business. The Wormston fifty percent co-ownership went to Samuel the Third." Wesley paused for a moment. "Perhaps your ancestor had fallen out of favor with his family."

Ozzie's face went bright red and he scowled. "That's impossible. I checked all the records three times over."

Wesley kept his cool. "The two later Samuels were first cousins because they shared the same grandfather. Both married Mary Smiths. That's why this research caused all this confusion."

Ozzie had his arms firmly crossed over his chest.

Wesley moved in for closure and put two printouts of parish register documents on the table. It was obvious he'd been researching this for far longer than the time we were on our factory tour. There, in black and white, were documents showing full names and dates as well as the ancestors' occupations.

"You see, Ozzie, your Samuel was a pawnbroker. The other line, the one we rely upon here at this company, shows the occupation of Samuel the Third as a confectionery business owner."

"But if the duel was illegal in the first place," Ozzie started.

Wesley shook his head. "The will that Samuel the Third wrote, the one where he left all his assets to charity since his wife was already deceased and they had no children, including his fifty percent ownership of the confectionery company? His sister challenged the will on grounds that it wasn't properly witnessed. She won her case, thus securing her brother's assets for herself and henceforth the Zerruly family."

Fred looked at Ozzie and shrugged. Gertie looked at me and shrugged. I had nothing to add; it wasn't my research, and I had certainly told Ozzie umpteen times to make sure he triple checked his sources. Unfortunately, to us it looked like he'd cooked himself a real kettle of fish.

Ozzie narrowed his eyes. "Your workers here don't all comply with health and safety regulations, and I can prove it. What do you say about that?"

"I'd be happy to bring in our quality-control inspector as well as our health and safety regulations officer to speak with you," Dan said. "They will need evidence, however, as well as the source of the video plus the date and time it was taken."

"How do you know it's a video?" Ozzie snapped back.

"I assume you were the sender of the anonymous email threat?" Dan said, pulling a folded piece of paper from his pocket. "And I quote: 'You have a severe hairnet problem at the factory. I can prove it on video.'"

There was silence in the room. Both solicitors were turning this verbiage over in their minds, one deciding how serious the threat was, and the other deciding how serious his client was.

Dan decided to deal with it head on. "Mr. Boggs. If you'd like your cousin Elridge Bacon to lose his job here, that can be arranged."

"He has a wife and four kids," Ozzie muttered.

"He was working without a hairnet on purpose and was paid by someone to film him doing so," Dan said. "You know how seriously we take these issues. It goes right to the heart of our products' quality."

Ozzie said nothing.

"I'm willing to let this go. I've already had the entire hour's worth of production destroyed and composted, the length of time that your cousin Elridge admitted he wasn't wearing a hairnet. I won't press any charges so long as you sign this release," Dan said.

"And what exactly does this release say?" Fred asked, shifting into client protection mode. He took the document from Wesley and read it over. "Ozzie, you'd be signing away your rights to the firm in exchange for them not suing you for making threats and ruining £78,000 worth of sweets ... May I have a moment to confer with my client?" Fred asked.

"Of course," Wesley said.

Fred and Ozzie left the room and hovered outside the window. We actually saw them miming, gesticulating, and arguing with each other. It was like watching a reality TV show with the sound turned off. After about a minute and a half of this, they came back inside.

"My client has one question," Fred said.

"Yes?" Wesley said.

"How did you get Elridge to talk?"

"We didn't do anything. His conscience gnawed at him that night. He came forward of his own volition."

"I don't believe you," Ozzie said. "Blood is thicker than water."

"But apparently not thicker than chocolate," Gertie added. She and I had kept pretty quiet during this odd exchange, a smart move indeed.

Chapter 35

"Can I get a picture with Gertie before you leave?" Dan asked, letting down his guard now that the serious stuff was over. Ozzie had signed the release and was trying to slink out of the factory with as little additional injury to his dignity as possible.

"Sure." Gertie posed with him.

"My kids will be pleased as punch," Dan said with a broad smile. "Everyone in our family eagerly awaits your next creation. That recent one with muddy sheepdog? Classic, absolute classic."

Fred gulped, knowing he'd been somewhere in the background of that video. Luckily Dan didn't appear to have noticed, remembered, or cared.

Dan escorted us out through the retail shop, a key finishing element on any well-planned factory tour. The smell of chocolate and sugar was overwhelming, sweet satisfaction, and very tempting after being on a tiring tour. One's skin felt instantly coated with invisible sugar floating through the air. Faint factory sounds could be heard, but it was largely muffled by the tall cases of pristine wrapped boxes and formal confectionery displays covering every available surface. As we walked through the shop, Dan handed each of us three boxes of chocolates. "Peace offering, Ozzie."

"Hmmph," Ozzie grunted back. His face was sad and twisted, his candy-mogul dreams completely shattered. He'd ridden quite a roller coaster today, and his adrenaline ride was now finished. To put it plainly, Ozzie Boggs looked absolutely miserable.

I was disappointed that all this genealogical research had led us to a dead end, however, that's how it went with family history. Take the good with the bad. Expect a brick wall and be grateful when daylight appeared.

There really wasn't much else for us to say, because all of us were simply in awe of the sweets world that surrounded us on all walls, ceiling, and floor. The shop was two levels, a circular ramp going from the first floor up to the second. On every wall, on every surface, were plastic cylinders of sweets, such a bright cornucopia of colors, textures, and designs that one's eyes couldn't take it all in at once. The largest pinwheel lollipop they had was three feet in diameter, certainly a showstopper and perhaps even one for the record books. The first floor had a vast counter where individual chocolates were sold behind glass, surely a hundred different kinds. Stacks of chocolate boxes were in every corner, and they also stocked an immense collection of pale pastel boxes intended as wedding favors. As visitors walked the ramp going up to the second floor, they read about the firm's history on the various milestone graphics. From humble beginnings centuries ago, one could watch the development of the firm up to today's modern, technology-based corporate enterprise. The company held no less than thirty confectionery machinery patents and forty sweets' names trademarks. The second-floor trophy case held oodles of confectionery competition silver cups, ribbons, and plaques, giving an awesome display of the company's achievements and recognition of its products' top quality.

"I did enjoy meeting all of you, sincerely," Dan said, after he'd given us a minute or so to internalize this bright impact on the senses.

Overall, it had been cordial, even though Ozzie hadn't gotten what he wanted. His dreams of being a millionaire confectionery mogul were now completely out the window. Yet as he caught a glance of someone walking by the front of the shop, his attitude changed. It was his cousin, the one in the video without the hairnet. Ozzie frowned, and I knew this wasn't good. Elridge saw him, nervously smiled, then came into the shop.

"Hiya, Ozzie, no hard feelings, hey? I've got a family to support," Elridge said. He was a gangly, thin man, the kind of person who would blend into a crowd faster than drizzling rain on a cheap poncho.

Ozzie approached. I knew we were in trouble when I saw him quietly rip the cellophane off the top of his first freebie box of chocolates. For a moment I thought Ozzie would start pelting his cousin with candied cherry, mint bits, sticky caramel, and moist strawberry. Yet, he did not. Instead, Ozzie offered his cousin the first pick of the box. "I don't want to be the lone wolf at the next family gathering."

Elridge backed away. "Oh, no, thank you. None of us who work here can stand eating chocolate anymore."

Ozzie frowned, contemplated, and then had me worried.

I recalled that Fred stayed behind a bit longer in the meeting room to speak with Wesley. Fred now entered the shop the very second an upset Ozzie discovered the jiggly candied jelly display.

Ozzie took aim at his cousin but his throw wasn't accurate. Fred stood frozen in place as a large jelly in the shape of an octopus with eight fat tentacles landed squarely in the middle of his face. The octopus stuck there as soon as the sticky, sugary mass hit warm skin. After that, it slowly slipped down Fred's face, like an ocean-going squid slithering down his chin with stealthy intent. The rest of the candied jelly display sagged left, wobbled right, then collapsed, taking down a few other towers of confectionery with it. There was now a large, likely irreversible stain on the custom carpet at Fred's feet.

Oops.

I looked over at Gertie and just shook my head. She was video recording the whole thing.

Fred scraped the octopus jelly from his face and yelled out across the shop, amazing everyone present. "Ozzie Boggs! I cannot, no, I will not, represent you as a client of my esteemed firm if you persist with this escapade!" Even when riled or under duress, Fred still used many more and much larger words than were needed. I no longer questioned it. I just accepted it. But the solicitor actually had a backbone and now we'd seen it.

"That's it!" everybody heard Dan Zerruly roar from the side door. "Ozzie, I've been patient. I've had documents carbon dated. I've turned a blind eye to your destructiveness here at the factory. But now you've gone too far. I'm calling the police."

***

GGRS. Next day.

Gertie sat in my office across from me. We were alone, watching the video of the confectionery-shop incident.

"You have to admit, Ozzie's got pretty good aim," she said.

"Fred wore his octopus well," I added.

We grinned.

"So?" she asked.

"Bail was set at £10,000, approximately the amount of retail damage Ozzie did to the sweets store when he threw the jelly that stained the custom carpet plus damaged those premium displays."

"It's unbelievable. A grown man lobbing a candied jelly. When's Ozzie getting out?"

I shrugged. "Don't know. He has to raise the bail money first, and that's between him and Fred right now."

"Well, how about I cheer you up a little bit? I've got a surprise for you." Gertie said it with a lot of gumption in her voice.

"If this involves anything to do with chocolate, lollipops, marshmallows, or anything else sweet, even the teensiest hint of sweet–"

"The church youth group cleaned up Agatha's churchyard."

"You're kidding. What a lovely thing to do." This made me happy. This made me smile. This made me believe in humankind once more.

"We had about thirty youth volunteer. One boy even brought his farm's pet goat to help with the lawn. They worked together with the local seniors' club as well as the gardening club. Now all of the graves are tidied, every single one with fresh flowers on them. Not a single one is overgrown nor forgotten anymore."

"What a touching gesture. You just elevated the word kindness to a new meaning," I said.

"I'm so proud of them and super glad it makes you smile. This will do it even more." She handed me a file and gestured for me to open it. Inside was a photo of the village of Limeknobble, the one where the overgrown churchyard was located. Of course, now it was a much larger town, but this was a photo from 1890. It showed twelve picnic tables all lined up together down the high street, tables laden with cakes, fancy pastries, and tea.

"Do you remember seeing a 'Doctor Toffmerle' listed on one of the church's indoor plaques?" Gertie asked.

"I believe so. In all honesty, so much has happened in the last couple of days that everything's becoming a bit of a blur," I said.

"No problem. Just trust me on this one. Doctor Toffmerle was a wealthy man who would sponsor an annual tea for the undernourished. He kept it going for forty-three years until he passed."

"And to think that that's all been forgotten. What a tragedy," I said.

"Exactly. Family history means more than just shining up a plaque on the wall or making sure it's there in the first place. It means appreciating what people have done in the past, respecting those who came before you. Seeing this photo is what spurred the youth choir to take action. You see, I posted it online along with a photo of the overgrown churchyard."

"Was Agatha there?"

"Apparently she directed the gardening, making sure that the youth planted things like they had forty years ago when Doctor Toffmerle was alive. She can remember the right plants, just needed lots of help bending down to get them into the soil. I've got loads of pictures from the cleanup day to show you." She handed me her phone, and I scrolled through fifty-two pictures showing the youths and Agatha working together with the seniors and gardening clubs' volunteers.

"This is wonderful, Gertie. I hope someone videoed it too because it would make a wonderful thing to post online."

She grinned. "Oh, don't you worry about that. When the goat got loose and started to rampage down a bed of newly planted begonias–"

"Ten million views?" I asked her.

She shook her head. "Try twenty-one million."

"No." I was stunned.

"Never underestimate the power of a farm animal."

My telephone rang. "Just a minute, please," I said to her, answering the phone. I held a hand over the receiver and mouthed, "Pamela."

Gertie nodded.

"Can I put you on speaker phone?" I asked.

Two seconds later I did.

"Hi, Pamela. I'm here with Gertie," I said into the phone.

"Ladies, guess what?" Pamela asked, excited.

"What did you discover this time?" Gertie asked.

"Francine's daughter. Remember Rich Burrell, the saddler who was in the other day to help with the heirloom tool that Jacques posted online?"

"Yes," I said.

"Well, he heard back from his Aunt Lisette who knows Francine Junior. Can you call a girl Junior or is that just for boys? Any-hoooo, Aunt Lisette spoke with Francine the younger and she'd love to meet us. She's asked to see my heirloom box and, well, I'm pretty excited."

"I would not have guessed," I said, grinning back at Gertie.

"Can I possibly, I mean, I know it's a lot to ask but ..."

"Can we leave in an hour?"

"Done."

Chapter 36

**Francine Junior Philmond's Home, Carlingheath.
Two Hours Later.**

Francine Junior's two-bedroom flat was cozy, one-level living. She greeted Gertie, Pamela, and I in a wheelchair. Her blue eyes were incredibly bright and sparkly, enhanced by the gorgeous purple blouse and matching trousers that she wore. She had snow-white hair filled with wavy curls that reached to the back of her neck.

Our hostess was sharp as a tack. She greeted us with a welcoming smile. "Come in, come in. Don't mind me being a little bit behind you, I've got an extra set of wheels to worry about in here." She maneuvered her wheelchair like a race car driver. Not bad for someone who was supposed to be in her dotage.

She settled us in her living room, filled to the brim with comfortable sofas, porcelain lady figurines, and a grandfather clock that emitted a reassuring 'tick tock'. Her home was warm and inviting, captioning a life well-lived and with kindness. Tea and biscuits were already waiting on the coffee table in front of us.

"Please, help yourselves," Francine Junior said. "I find that teapot a little heavy to lift now. Tracy from food services was just in to help me get ready for your arrival."

"You have a lovely living arrangement here," I said, meeting our hostess's eyes.

"I stayed in Delzinnia Cottage as long as I could. But the stairs and narrow hallways finally defeated me. The people here are really nice, and they actually care. I don't feel abandoned like some poor people stuck in places that are all about the money instead of helping seniors."

"We're thrilled to find you," Gertie said.

Pamela nodded. "We're hoping you can help us understand more about your mother's work at the matrimonial bureau and how she helped Sylvie and Richard."

"Of course. But first, tea and biscuits. Please."

Francine's helper Tracy was obviously a keeper. She'd stocked a plate high with shortbread and chocolate biscuits. There were also slices of lemon and cherry loaf, moist and freshly baked. I was salivating at the thought of biting into a warm piece of cake, enjoying the sweet mixed with the tartness of lemon.

We dug into the snacks.

Francine Junior noticed my eyes roaming over her family photos of her husband and grandchildren. She also had a massive collection of Christmas cards.

It was a bit early for those.

She saw what I was looking at. "Please, don't mind last year's Christmas card collection. When my mother ran the matrimonial bureau, she used to get over two hundred cards a year. They would cover our mantle and bookcase, sent from all over the world. When she closed down the business and later passed away, my Christmas cards dwindled down to about twenty-two per year. I really miss them. It's just not the same Christmas celebration without cards."

"I understand. My father's the same way. Nostalgic," I said.

"Everyone seems to do email greetings these days," Gertie said.

Francine Junior shook her head. "It's not the same as receiving an envelope in the mail that someone's taken the time to handwrite. And I'm not talking the cards that just say 'Merry Christmas and Happy New Year' and then sign their name. No, I long for the nice, newsy letters from relatives and friends."

Pamela was taking all this in, slightly overwhelmed by this living link to her ancestor's past. "Was your mother close to Sylvie and Richard Palmer?" she asked.

Francine Junior nodded. "Oh yes, they were her favorite couple. But I'm sure you know that by now."

"The symbols on your family's mausoleum?" It was a delicate subject because I didn't want to let Francine Junior know that her family's resting place was in such disrepair until Gertie's youth group and local clubs had combined efforts.

"Deflection. My mother was buried in Limeknobble because that's where her husband's family was laid to rest."

"Can you tell us more about the symbols on the mausoleum wall? The sphinx, an ostrich feather, and a Tudor rose?" I asked. I reached for another slice of lemon cherry loaf; it was absolutely delicious, and I made a mental note to speak with Jacques about adding it to the café's menu.

The delightful senior nodded. "My mother had them inscribed before she passed, as a talisman, a signal to Sylvie and Richard's descendants. She always told me that if someone really wanted to find them they could, so long as they had their wits and a few heirlooms to help them along the way. Did you bring the box of treasures?"

Pamela handed it to her. "I brought everything, just in case you wanted to see them."

"I remember this box. It was a gift from my mother to your great-grandmother Sylvie," Francine Junior said. She opened the lid and parsed through the contents, lingering on the pretty ring. She held it up to the light and looked directly at Pamela. "Do you know what this means?"

"I assumed it was a gift or an engagement ring," Pamela said.

"Oh my dear, it means far more than that. Richard was quietly speaking in jewels to his sweetheart. It was very common in the Victorian age, and he just carried that tradition forward. Notice how it's a ruby and sapphire?"

"Yes, I noticed that," Pamela said.

"The initials. Think of the initials, dear girl. 'R', ruby, is for Richard. 'S', sapphire, is for Sylvie."

Pamela smiled. "I had no idea. I think I was just captivated by the sweet inscription 'I will return to you' on the inner band."

Francine Junior nodded. "Richard did come back from his secret espionage work in Cairo to be with the woman he loved for the rest of his life. Tragically, as you know, he died here in England. My mother always said it was so sad, him surviving all he did in World War Two yet being killed in a tram accident back here at home."

"Sylvie must've been devastated," Gertie said.

"My mother told me she was filled with deep sorrow. But Sylvie carried on and raised their daughter Isabel. She told her all about Richard and how brave he was."

I had to ask. "Do you know specifically what Richard did in Cairo during the war?"

Francine Junior put a finger over her lips. "We don't talk about that. He took his secrets to the grave, and we respect that."

We all contemplated Richard's extreme sacrifice for the nation.

"Mark my words, that man is a true English hero." Francine Junior looked in the box some more and then steadied it on her lap. She looked directly at Pamela. "Your mother never told you, did she?"

"Tell me?" Pamela said.

"About this," Francine Junior said, as her gnarled fingers traced the underneath of the lid until they found a little depressed area. She pushed it in gently and we heard a click, wood separating from wood. A two-inch-square trapdoor fell down, revealing a folded piece of yellowed paper inside the lid. She gingerly pulled it out and then handed it to Pamela without reading it.

"You want me to be the first to read this?" Pamela asked, astonished.

Francine Junior nodded. "You've earned it, dear."

Slowly, ever so slowly and carefully, Pamela unfolded the delicate paper. We could see something handwritten but waited until she read it aloud.

Cairo, Egypt
March 23, 1945

Dear Sylvie,
If I do not come back from Cairo, please know that you are the love of my life and I shall always treasure the time we had together. My love for you has no boundary. Know that my fondest desire is to be with you in England, near our special rose, once again. I wish to grow old with you.
Love always, Richard.

Our hostess continued, "They first met in Portsmouth. My mother arranged a train connection where they could meet at the *Mary Rose* site—their special rose—and have tea for a couple of hours before Richard had to ship out again. Of course, that was long before the shipwreck was brought up from the ocean depths in the 1980s."

We were stunned into quiet appreciation. It was a tale of a different time, different challenges, yet their love endured.

"It's so poignant," Pamela said, her eyes brimming with tears. "Did Richard know Sylvie was carrying his child?"

Francine Junior nodded. "My mother said that Sylvie told him before she came home to England. She knew she had to leave cabaret work with a child on the way, so they put baby Isabel first and separated. My mother was glad that they could reunite because she said they had a love like no other. She had many happy couples, but none as devoted as Sylvie and Richard."

"And true love conquers all," I said.

Pamela's box of heirloom surprises just kept on giving.

Chapter 37

Portsmouth. Next Day.

Within a day, Francine Junior had become a fast friend of our genealogy research group. She eagerly snapped up our invitation to come with us to Portsmouth and pay her respects to Sylvie and Richard.

We had a wonderful lunch at 'The Octopus Reach', fitting considering the confectionery escapade we'd recently undergone. The pub was one in Pamela's chain of restaurants, and my seafood salad was fabulous. Pamela had clam chowder with crusty white bread, and Gertie and Francine Junior both had a cheese and pickle sandwich. With chips. No sense in living too tame when on the road with one's friends.

Thankfully there was ample parking at the cemetery. Francine Junior told us to look for a pair of tombstones in alabaster marble, a sphinx and ostrich feather etched into each. There was no map. There was no guidebook. So we walked, Pamela pushing Francine Junior's wheelchair as we traversed the paved path.

Gertie was the smartest of us all. She pulled out her phone. "I don't know if this is any help or not, but the longitude and latitude of Cairo is about thirty and thirty-one. Are the graves labeled that way?"

"Not individually, but we're in row twenty-seven right now," I said.

"Bingo."

We walked over to row thirty.

Nothing.

Row thirty-one.

We found them.

It was a tidy, well-kept pair of graves, and neither one bore a deceased's name. Richard's was inscribed, 'He gave his all for King and Country' and his tombstone bore a sphinx. Sylvie's stone read, 'She gave her all for King and Country', and her tombstone bore an ostrich feather.

"No names on their graves. They really wanted to disappear."

Francine Junior looked up at us. "Remember, it was different times back then. One only thought of winning the war and saving one's loved ones. Revealing secrets as part of gossip just wasn't in anyone's mindset. We have to respect their choice."

Pamela bent down and laid a bouquet of red and yellow roses on each grave. "Someone's taking care of them, and I know it wasn't my mother."

"It's the local ladies auxiliary and Legion groups. Your mother didn't approve of Sylvie working in a cabaret. Truth be told, Sylvie explained to my mother that she wore a fancy but modest dress and sang to entertain weary, wounded men. They never got near her on stage, so it was all respectable. She gave them reason to carry on because some days the horrors of war became far too much."

"I suppose one had to live it to understand it," I said.

"Exactly, dear. Exactly correct," Francine Junior said, taking my hand in hers and giving it a squeeze.

Pamela went over to Francine Junior and gave her a hug. "You've helped me find my family, and I'll always be grateful."

***

GGRS. Next Day.

A sheepish Ozzie Boggs trudged into the research site. At first he didn't make eye contact with anyone, so I decided to show him that he was still welcome. "Ozzie, you're back. Are you here to do more research?" I gave him what I hoped was a bright, happy smile.

"You're still talking to me?" He stopped and didn't really know where to put his feet next.

"Of course. Everybody makes mistakes. You just happened to be more vocal—and, um, enthusiastic—about yours than others."

The entire research site had fallen silent. Ozzie felt about thirty pairs of eyes on him. The clicking of computer mice and printing of paper had all stopped. He was like a slow-moving glacier permeating the room and freezing everything. That was until our fixer, none other than my favorite aristocrat Bertie, the Duke of Conroy, glided in behind Ozzie.

"Bertie? You just delivered chutney yesterday," I said, quite surprised to see him.

He grinned. "I'm here to bridge the gap between Ozzie and Greymore. One of my staff showed me the confectionery store video, and that made me jump in my vehicle and go rescue Ozzie from jail."

"Why?" Ozzie finished for me.

We all looked to Bertie for an explanation.

"Twenty-three and a half years ago, Dan Zerruly cheated me in a yacht race. I simply reminded him of that fact, including a rereading of our London club's motto."

"'Be kind to others and expect less in return'?" I asked.

"Yes, but not that formal one. We have an unwritten rule between members that we shall not cheat each other. I've always taken the high road and never told Dan that I knew he cheated me in the yacht race. Until yesterday. Dan's agreed to drop the charges and provide GGRS with free sweets for life, delivered once a week." Bertie gestured at a staff member who was standing beside him, clad in a Scotford Castle golf shirt and carrying a large cardboard box.

Bertie peered inside the box and murmured, "What do we have here this week? Candied octopus jelly. Can I interest anyone? Please follow me to the lunchroom."

"I don't think I could look at another candied jelly for the rest of my life," I said.

Ten others stampeded into the lunchroom, tempted by sugary treats. That left Ozzie with Gertie, Ewan, Maude and I.

"So, Ozzie, are you still researching your family tree?" Gertie asked him.

"I'd like to," he mumbled, staring at his feet. "Because this place, what you have here ..." He stopped and looked up, meeting each of our eyes with a shy glance. He cleared his throat, confident. "I suffer from bouts of depression, and you've always been so welcoming to me, making this a safe place. It's become quite special to me." He was humbled in front of us.

One never took advantage of a humbled man.

I went over and shook his hand. "Ozzie, you are most welcome here. We'll help you as much as we can."

He looked up at me with shy eyes and then suddenly threw his arms around me in a big bear hug. I think my eyes nearly popped out of my head, but I just went with the moment. Ozzie Boggs was now a friend. I looked around the room and knew that everyone felt the same way. We all had our individual little quirks, fascinations, and peculiar habits, but that's what made us unique. What bound us together was a love of family history. No matter where or when, the GGRS would deliver … even if the project involved jellied octopus, spies, ostrich feathers, saddler's tools, cryptic jewelry, or snooty clubs. We were far too tenacious to give up or take no for an answer. Family history demanded an extraordinary amount of patience and determination.

I looked at my friends; these were the stalwarts who adored looking at a variety of online research websites, parish registers, historical newspapers, and maps. I got a warm sense of belonging and knew that Aunt Edwina would be proud of everything we'd accomplished together. I looked at her photo hanging on the wall behind the information desk and for a split second was sure I saw her wink at me.

THE END

Acknowledgements

I owe a world of thanks to the dedicated archivists, family historians, and genealogists who ensure our valuable records are preserved, transcribed, and available for future generations. You are unsung heroes and make the world a better place. Thank you for all that you do.

As always, to Penny, Brenda and Val: you are my dream team of fact checkers and beta readers … all simply marvelous. Aunt Edwina is glad for your help.

Huge thanks to Olivia McCoy at Smith Publicity for your enthusiasm and guidance – Aunt Edwina is impressed.

Thanks also to the publishing team at FriesenPress, especially Jess Feser and James Stewart. Sincere appreciation to Rebecca Hendry for both her editorial insights plus being a willing participant in super serious punctuation discussions. Aunt Edwina is grateful.

Special thanks to Wolf Wenzel for drawing such a fun cover for this novel. Admirably, you never once questioned the need for mango chutney and miniature goats artwork. Aunt Edwina is amazed.

About the Author

Lynne Christensen is a world traveler who enjoys visiting museums and archives. She grew up roaming around graveyards in Europe with her genealogy-loving parents in search of elusive ancestors. A lifelong learner, she earned both Master of Business Administration and Bachelor of Commerce degrees plus has multiple years of experience in marketing and corporate communications. Her writing is published in numerous magazine articles, case studies, advertisements, and technical manuals. She lives on the West Coast of Canada in a house full of fascinating books.

www.auntedwina.com

CPSIA information can be obtained
at www.ICGtesting.com
Printed in the USA
BVHW040725161122
651046BV00001B/1